"A good old-fashioned murder mystery."
—ReviewingTheEvidence.com

"Jes Battis takes the readers on a tension-filled journey of murder, mystery, and temptation . . . An intriguing story line; easy, flowing dialogue; and fascinating characters all combine to keep readers engaged, but it's the never knowing what's around the corner that will have readers coming back for more." —*Darque Reviews*

"Battis manages to make the world come alive as a workable universe with infinite complexity." —*SFRevu*

"[An] absorbing paranormal detective tale . . . The combo of cutting-edge technology and magic highlights a procedural thriller filled with ominous twists. Telling the tale from the point of view of a stubborn, rule-breaking heroine keeps the tension high and the risk palpable." —*Romantic Times*

"Compelling new urban fantasy [that] mixes equal parts forensic investigation, modern science, and down-and-dirty magic to create something new and different . . . a great start to a new series." —*The Green Man Review*

"Unique." —*Night Owl Romance*

Ace Books by Jes Battis

NIGHT CHILD
A FLASH OF HEX

A Flash of Hex

Jes Battis

ACE BOOKS, NEW YORK

THE BERKLEY PUBLISHING GROUP
Published by the Penguin Group
Penguin Group (USA) Inc.
375 Hudson Street, New York, New York 10014, USA

Penguin Group (Canada), 90 Eglinton Avenue East, Suite 700, Toronto, Ontario M4P 2Y3, Canada
(a division of Pearson Penguin Canada Inc.)
Penguin Books Ltd., 80 Strand, London WC2R 0RL, England
Penguin Group Ireland, 25 St. Stephen's Green, Dublin 2, Ireland (a division of Penguin Books Ltd.)
Penguin Group (Australia), 250 Camberwell Road, Camberwell, Victoria 3124, Australia
(a division of Pearson Australia Group Pty. Ltd.)
Penguin Books India Pvt. Ltd., 11 Community Centre, Panchsheel Park, New Delhi—110 017, India
Penguin Group (NZ), 67 Apollo Drive, Rosedale, North Shore 0632, New Zealand
(a division of Pearson New Zealand Ltd.)
Penguin Books (South Africa) (Pty.) Ltd., 24 Sturdee Avenue, Rosebank, Johannesburg 2196,
South Africa

Penguin Books Ltd., Registered Offices: 80 Strand, London WC2R 0RL, England

This is a work of fiction. Names, characters, places, and incidents either are the product of the author's imagination or are used fictitiously, and any resemblance to actual persons, living or dead, business establishments, events, or locales is entirely coincidental. The publisher does not have any control over and does not assume any responsibility for author or third-party websites or their content.

A FLASH OF HEX

An Ace Book / published by arrangement with the author

PRINTING HISTORY
Ace mass-market edition / June 2009

Copyright © 2009 by Jes Battis.
Cover art by Timothy Lantz.
Cover design by Lesley Worrell.
Interior text design by Laura K. Corless.

ISBN: 978-0-441-01723-2

ACE
Ace Books are published by The Berkley Publishing Group,
a division of Penguin Group (USA) Inc.,
375 Hudson Street, New York, New York 10014.
ACE and the "A" design are trademarks of Penguin Group (USA) Inc.

PRINTED IN THE UNITED STATES OF AMERICA

10 9 8 7 6 5 4 3 2 1

For Seba and Brianne,
who deal with me.

And for Vancouver.

Acknowledgments

I wrote this book while living in New York, Vancouver, and Montreal. So it's been a busy year for me. Thanks to Lauren Abramo and Ginjer Buchanan for continuing to have faith in the series. Thanks as well to the entire staff at Ace Books for their hard work. And to Ella and Connie, my two first and best readers.

I drew upon the usual suspects while doing forensics research: Vincent di Maio, Tom Bevel, Dorothy Gennard, Bill Bass, and Kathy Reichs. Someday I'll be able to afford a subscription to the *Journal of Forensic Sciences*.

I feel very uneasy writing about such a contested neighborhood as Vancouver's Downtown Eastside, even though *A Flash of Hex* is set mostly around Commercial Drive and the downtown core. All I can really do is acknowledge that uneasiness and thank the many overlapping communities within the DTES for their indulgence.

A final thanks to the Harvey Milk High School in New York and the Triangle Program in Toronto. Just for existing.

1

"Somebody's dead—and I can't decide between Boston cream or jelly."

Derrick was fiddling with his messenger bag. Something pricey with useless metal straps that he'd bought from Holts. He pulled out a yellow form, glared at it, pulled out a green form, then muttered something under his breath and shoved both of them back into the bag. Paperwork at mystical crime scenes could be a real bitch.

"I *want* the jelly." I stared intently at the pastry case while the exhausted Tim Hortons employee—Francis, his name tag said—drummed bitten-down nails on the plastic countertop.

"So get the jelly." Derrick adjusted the shoulder strap. "We've got to go, Tess. Selena's waiting for us, and the scene is a good six blocks from here."

"I want the jelly," I murmured, as if this were something existential, "but the powdered sugar is going to get all over my coat."

"You could wear gloves."

I beamed at him. "That's brilliant." I rummaged through my purse for a moment, then drew out a pair of latex gloves.

My full kit—with tape lifters, dusting powders, forceps, and other scene paraphernalia—was in the trunk of the car, but I always carried extra materials in my purse. I slipped on the gloves.

"Francis, I'd like two jellies, please."

He stared at me.

"And two coffees," Derrick added. "It's almost three thirty in the morning."

"Of course." I smiled at Francis. "Two double-doubles, please, and could you put sleeves on those? I'd rather not get a third-degree burn."

Francis took my handful of change wordlessly, and returned with our order. The fluorescent bulbs overhead cast odd, unnatural shadows across his face. He was one of those guys who could be eighteen or forty-eight—pinpointing his age would be impossible. Like trying to pinpoint time of death. I almost smiled at the thought.

The door to the restroom opened, and I saw a momentary glimmer of harsh, purple light. Most cafés this close to the Downtown Eastside had installed black lights in their restrooms to keep IV-drug users from shooting up. The dim lighting made it too hard for them to find a vein. A woman wearing a bright red kerchief and a black leather jacket emerged shakily from the restroom, blinking as her eyes adjusted to the drastic change in lighting. I saw her fiddling with a fanny pack, shoving something that looked like a piece of elastic tubing back into it. Her pupils were pinned, eyes rolling, head nodding slightly. Obviously, the black light hadn't stopped her.

Nobody reacted. At the corner of Hastings and Heatley, only a few blocks from the heart of the Downtown Eastside, everyone was used to watching neighborhood residents fixing in bathrooms, on corners, in alleys, or in whatever space they could find. We were on the edge right now, the uneasy intersection between Chinatown, the club district, and the recently trendy Strathcona neighborhood, where yuppies and hipsters now mingled with longtime residents, battling for affordable housing.

We weren't headed there, though.

Instead, we'd be going into the heart of the yuppie urban core—the trendiest downtown real estate—flanked by the Pacific Ocean and nestled in between stately banks, rambling used bookstores, and the finest, most overpriced pub food in Gastown just a few blocks away.

I handed Derrick his coffee. "Okay. Let's get walking."

Francis didn't wave good-bye.

It was a relief when the cold air outside smacked me in the face. Derrick sipped his coffee silently, chewing delicately on his doughnut, while I slurped mine, spilled some on my sleeve, cursed, then almost dropped the cup. This was a pretty accurate tableau of our different personalities, I thought. Two odd shadows walking down Hastings Street. What bound us together when we were so obviously different?

Only we knew.

"Where are we going again?"

"A residence at the corner of Hastings and Richards. Very posh. Building's called the Crescendo. One of those up-in-an-instant places with marble countertops and gleaming new fixtures."

"Yeah, until two weeks after you buy it, when you realize that the cupboards are crooked, and your bathroom's the size of a postage stamp, and your upstairs neighbor wears heels all day long."

We walked past the gleaming concrete towers, past Harbor Center and the Wosk Centre for Dialogue. (Did dialogue actually occur there?) The pavement was a dark ribbon, backlit by lights from the buses that roared by.

"Selena said they might be bringing in a profiler," Derrick said. "Some expert from Toronto."

I frowned. "Why? This isn't a serial case."

"Apparently, there've been two other murders that are similar—one in Hamilton, the other in Scarborough. So they want to bring in an expert."

"I suppose people are still thinking about William Pickton—anything that looks close to a serial murder is going to need special attention," I said. "And the Downtown Eastside is just six blocks away from this neighborhood. The overlap is unavoidable. These kids may come from rich families, but no matter how connected they are, they're still dying uncomfortably close to the DTES—and that's a place that's been the target of a serial killer in the recent past."

"Does Selena think this killer might be a copycat?" Derrick wondered. "Someone using magic to kill in the same manner?"

"In my experience, Selena almost never assumes anything. But after Marcus . . ." I shivered involuntarily, remembering against my will how our former boss, Marcus Tremblay, had turned out to be a killer as well. It had barely been six months since Marcus had me tied to a chair with a gun pointed at my head.

Derrick looked at me. "Bad memories?"

"Just a little spooked. I don't say his name very often."

He rubbed my shoulder. "You don't have to. He's gone, Tess. He's buried, and we're safe. As safe as we can be in our line of work, at any rate."

I could still see Marcus's cold eyes staring at me, totally devoid of feeling, like the gray, impassive eyes of a shark. I could feel Sabine's hand gripping my throat, her fangs exposed as she fantasized about tearing into my subclavian artery like fresh meat. And Mia's lost expression. Mia's pain, the light draining from her eyes as she realized that her parents were dead, that nothing would ever be the same again.

"Safe as anyone in this neighborhood," I muttered. "Anyways, with Marcus gone, Selena's basically working two jobs until she can find and train a replacement."

"Yeah, she's been extra-prickly about it."

"I would be, too. I don't think she's slept in six months. And the big bosses are breathing down her neck, watching her every move. She can't afford to be sloppy. If there's even a hint of serial murder with this case, she'll have to make arrangements for a larger investigation."

"All while keeping it quiet," Derrick said. "The last thing Vancouver needs to know is that someone is killing sex workers again. Someone who isn't human."

"Was Pickton human?" I stared at the pavement, which was

littered with food wrappers, Styrofoam fragments, and the occasional needle. "He may have killed over forty sex trade workers. What about Gary Ridgeway, the Green River Killer? Were they actually *human*? Or something else."

"You know what I mean. Magically inclined."

"Fuck. It would take magic to survive anywhere in this city."

The Crescendo loomed like a steel-and-glass space station before us, or some futuristic Mayan stele, gleaming and dark with the white-on-black checkering of windows with their lights on, off, on, off.

"It's the second floor," Derrick said behind me. "Number 208."

We walked past the perimeter team, pushing aside the yellow scene tape marked MYSTICAL CRIME SCENE—DO NOT CROSS. The lobby was floored in marble, like the surface of the moon, a sinuous tongue of black basalt. No one was at the concierge's desk.

A temporary station had been set up by the fire exit—a plastic tray table with spare kits, gloves, and neatly folded Tyvek suits. I pulled a pair of plastic booties over my Fluevogs (you don't mess with thigh-high boots), and Derrick did the same, managing a little hop from side to side as he tried not to lean against the wall. I pulled my hair back in a motion that had become ingrained over the years and slipped on a worn blue Canucks hat. Go team. I wasn't sure how they'd feel about their product being used at a mystical crime scene.

We climbed to the second floor, hugging the walls as we advanced down the freezing hallway to 208. The air-conditioning was turned up uncomfortably high, and I shivered in the almost holy silence of the brand-new hallway, with its Berber carpeting and light sconces on every wall. Even though it was now 4 a.m., I could hear various sounds from the other apartments: muffled televisions, applause, laughing, yelling, cursing, thumping, and—most eerily of all—total silence. A door to my right opened abruptly, and an elderly woman scowled at me. Her skin was jaundiced, and one of her hands kept clenching and unclenching involuntarily, scratching against the fabric of her red polyester slacks. The skin on her face was splotchy and peeling, covered in what looked like psoriasis.

I attempted to smile at her. "Everything's fine, ma'am."

"Fuck you," she hissed. Before I could react, she vanished behind the door.

"Nice," Derrick said. "We should come downtown more often."

Room 208 was covered in OSI tape, gleaming faintly in the dark. Derrick and I signed in, and I was just about to lift the tape when Selena Ward appeared. She was wearing a sleek gray trench coat, dark gabardine slacks, and boots twice as expensive as mine. I strained to figure out what brand they were, realizing that it was childish but unable to resist. It was like the woman had access to a twenty-four-hour sample sale that nobody else knew about. Her hair was braided tightly, and she looked exhausted. Being the lead detective and acting director of the Mystical Crimes Division will do that to you.

"Selena. How are you?"

"Shit." Her eyes scanned the hallway. "Everything is shit."

"That's really descriptive," Derrick said. "Should I write that in the log?"

"Siegel, I've done eight night shifts, back to back, with no break. Earlier today I fell asleep, collapsed on the copier, and Rebecca had to spray water in my face to wake me up." My eyes widened at Becka's courage. "My husband thinks that I'm losing my mind, and we haven't had decent sex in months. That's *months*, not weeks. Do you know what that does to a person?"

Derrick swallowed. "It must be—really traumatic . . ."

"It puts me on edge," she continued. "Not just the lack of sex, or the lack of sleep, but the total lack of *help* from anyone in this shitty department. Do you know what I mean by 'on edge'?"

"I'm beginning to get the picture," he murmured.

"It means that my days are bad, and my nights are worse. I get dragged to inhuman places like this, and I have to sift through and stare at inhuman acts, committed by deviant sociopaths. And then *I* start to feel like that. Like I could do something really nasty and homicidal—maybe without even being provoked. Maybe just because someone looked at me the wrong way." Her eyes were dark. "Get it?"

He nodded rapidly.

"Good, I'm glad we understand each other." She handed something in a paper bindle to one of the evidence techs, then looked at me. "Here's the situation. We've got a young male DB, maybe eighteen, nineteen tops. Blunt force trauma, restraint marks, throat slashed. And there's a twist."

I frowned. "What does that mean?"

"You'll see. There's been some interference with the body, and we won't be able to say anything for certain until the autopsy."

"Interference?"

"Just step inside." She lifted the tape. "And keep it together. This is as bad as it gets around here."

I swallowed around a lump in my throat. If Selena was spooked, then something incredibly horrifying had gone down in this room. I could sense it myself even as I stood in the doorway—the hairs on my arms and neck stood on end, and I felt a coldness in my lungs that had nothing to do with the air-conditioning. In our line of work, there were demons and necromancers, and then there were . . . other things. Older things without names, things you didn't ever want to meet. And I knew, without even having to confirm the feeling with Derrick, that I was in the presence of evil.

I ducked under the tape. A quick examination of the door revealed that it was intact, without any sign of forced entry. The room was dark, save for a lamp on the bedside table, and the glowing lights of the street. The sliding glass door was open, and the air in the living room had the tang of cold. We walked through it into the bedroom. The bed was undisturbed. The plush duvet was neatly folded down, and the sheets were so tight that I almost expected to see hospital corners. Nothing but straight, precise edges.

"Bed hasn't been used," I said. "Or the killer cleaned up."

The coppery smell of blood was stuck in my throat. I examined the wall adjacent to the bed, which was streaked with rising and falling lines of red, like sine waves.

"Arterial spray," I said. "Selena said that the victim's throat was slashed, but the arc isn't very high."

"Maybe the victim was prone? On the bed?"

"Or the cut was shallow." I glanced at the intersecting arcs. The blood was so vivid that it looked like spray paint, and I could see a smattering of tiny white dots mixed among the crusting edges. "Vacuoles in the blood," I said. "Air bubbles. Consistent with a throat wound—the victim was gasping for air."

Derrick was looking at the floor. "There's no blood pool. If the killer slashed through the carotid or the jugular here"—he pointed to the wall—"then the victim should have fallen to the floor. There should be blood on the bedspread and on the carpet, but there's none."

I nodded, frowning. "The edges of the blood on the wall are skeletonized—partially dried. But there's no swipes, no disturbance. The directionality is wrong. As if the blood *only* hit the wall at high velocity, but didn't drip or pool anywhere else."

"So where's the rest of it?"

I could hear something dripping. I made my way carefully around the bed, to the far side of the room, and my eyes widened.

Someone had placed a vessel on the floor. It was a cauldron—cast iron, incredibly heavy. Like something you'd expect to see the witches from *Macbeth* stirring on a barren heath. The surface of the cauldron was smooth and black, unmarked. It had four clawed feet that sank slightly into the sodden carpeting. I watched, transfixed, as a drop of blood shimmered in the air for a moment, as if hovering, and then fell into the cauldron with an audible sound. A leaking pipe, or a clogged sink.

Derrick's face went ashen as he looked up. "Oh my God."

I followed the drop of blood in reverse. I followed Derrick's eyes, and at first, I didn't even register what I was seeing. It didn't seem possible, even when I see the impossible just about every night. But this was different. This was—unspeakable. And I understood, grimly, what Selena had meant by "a twist."

The boy's body was on the ceiling.

He was suspended there, completely still, by a series of complex materia flows that I could now feel itching underneath my skin, like a trapped sneeze. He floated. His skin was milk white, since all or at least most of the blood had drained out, slowly but steadily, into the cauldron on the floor. It took precision to arrange that kind of placement. It took trigonometry, and an incredibly warped mind. The cut to his throat, as I'd suspected, was shallow—a dark red comma that traced the edge of his left carotid artery, while the right side of his neck was clean, untouched. The killer had given him a wound that would take a while to bleed out. Not too long, probably less than ten minutes given the pressure in that particular artery, but it would have seemed like a million years if you were dying.

"He couldn't have screamed," I said, swallowing. "Not with that wound. All he could do was—*wait*."

Derrick shook his head. "Jesus."

The energy holding him in place, fueled by magic, was similar to the capillary force that pushed blood upward through the veins. The same force that made a drop of blood pause, perfectly still, on the surface of your skin, bending into the concave shape called "meniscus," before it fell to the ground, splashing with scalloped edges.

"We'll have to wait for the materia to wear off." Selena had appeared behind me. I had to consciously will myself not to jump out of my skin. "If we try to neutralize it, we'll eliminate any useful traces that might linger."

"You think we can run it through a biometric database?"

Selena shrugged. "I doubt anything will come up, but it's worth a shot. Unless he's been aura-printed from a previous crime, or he works for us, the pattern won't be on file. Or it might be too degraded for a match."

I let my eyes move over the surface of the boy's body, trying to stay impassive. He was thin—gaunt, really. The planes of his shoulders were clearly visible, and his belly was slightly distended, probably from lack of food. There were old track marks on his arms, and one new mark, a puckered red hole on his tricep, just above his brachial artery. I pointed to it. "You got a picture of this?"

Selena nodded. "It's obviously fresh. The veins in the arms and wrists are usually the first to collapse from shooting up. His veins don't look so bad."

"He couldn't have been using for long, then."

She shook her head. "Just a baby."

Ugly bruises were starting to show on his wrists, and a purple band was slowly appearing across his chest.

"Huh." I traced the long bruise with my fingertip. "Check this out. Almost looks like a seat belt mark. The kind of thing you'd see in a high-speed collision."

"Could materia do that?" Derrick asked. "I mean, if the killer used magic to restrain the kid, might it appear like that on his body?"

"Hard to say." Selena shrugged. "But with enough pounds per square inch, a burst of energy could probably leave a mark like that."

"So he was alive when he was restrained." I followed the path of the bruise, which started at his left clavicle and ended at his waist, just above the pubis. "The bruising tells us that much. And look at the rest of his body."

Derrick leaned forward. He didn't usually get this involved in the forensic aspects of cases, since his skill was in psychic profiling. But the past six months had changed him as well. Getting attacked by a Vailoid demon, watching me self-destruct, having to protect Mia and then seeing Marcus die right in front of him—I didn't know how deeply he'd been changed, but I could certainly feel it. Even his powers seemed different. Almost sharper. I couldn't describe it.

"Some minor bruising on the wrists and feet," he said, "again, something indicative of restraints. But no other marks. And his face is untouched." He looked at me with a kind of sick realization. "The killer didn't want to damage his face. He wanted us to see it, or wanted someone else to see it—

maybe a loved one. He wanted him to die but stay completely recognizable."

"Someone's been doing extra credit reading." Selena gave him an approving look. "Maybe we should make you a forensic tech, Siegel."

He blushed slightly, then looked away.

"Why the cauldron?" I asked. "What's the significance?"

Derrick shrugged. "Sadism? The victim has to watch himself die, drop by drop. He can't look away."

"It's a *coire*," Selena replied grimly. "A traditional witch's cauldron. Centuries ago, some of them were rumored to be so powerful that they granted immortality."

"Wasn't the hero Taliesen born out of a cauldron?" Derrick said.

Their conversation faded away as I stared at the boy's face. Dark lines under his eyes from lack of sleep. Sunken cheekbones, cracked and bloodless lips. He didn't have the sores that suggested heavy crystal meth use, but he definitely got high. A faint trace of stubble that ended, abruptly, with the incised wound to his throat. Like a slashed photograph. His eyes were open. I'd seen dead eyes that were still wide with fear, and eyes that didn't see anything at all, but these eyes were different. They were just—tired. Glassy and dark. No thin black line— *tache noir*, caused by the sclerotic tissue drying out—had appeared yet. The boy's eyes still radiated feeling, but also a terrifying numbness. A sadness that was larger than my ability to witness it, too vast to contain through notation, photography, videography.

"The killer's a traditionalist," Selena continued. "He's telling us that he knows us, that he knows our past and our mythology. He's mocking us. This is a reverse baptism, an aborted birth. A desecration."

Most dead bodies create a black hole, sucking up everything in the room. This boy's body seemed to glow with a crushing sadness, an indescribable and softly haptic sense of grief, that made my hands shake.

"Tess?" Derrick gave me a funny look. "You all right?"

I nodded, dropping my hands to my sides, but not before

Selena noticed the tremor. "Fine. Just tired. And confused. I mean, why him? What did this kid do? He must weigh ninety pounds soaking wet, he's not a hardcore user. And look at his hands. His cuticles aren't bitten down, and his nails are healthy. Even if he cruised the street, it must have been a recent thing. This kid has a home, a family."

"He should be playing *Guitar Hero* in the basement," Derrick said.

"The apartment's registered to some overseas landlord—I doubt they've been here in the past six months, but they're not renting out the unit either. It's been empty and unlisted for quite some time."

"You think this kid was a rent boy?"

"It's possible," Selena said. "There's no pattern, though. The two other victims from Hamilton and Scarborough were both girls. Their parents are mages—high-society types. Powerful and rich. Well connected to the CORE division in Ontario."

"Both white?"

She shook her head. "The first, Tamara Davies, was First Nations. *Métis*. Parents involved in occult research and theory. The second"—she glanced at her notebook—"Andrea Simms, was white. Her mother, Lyrae Simms, was the senior advisory for practically the whole East Coast, until she died of breast cancer last year. Andrea had a full scholarship to York. All of them had dark hair, but other than that, the killer doesn't seem to discriminate. We've got two trust fund teenagers, and now possibly a street kid. All killed in the same way. Until now, we didn't think the first two were connected."

"What about the *coire*? Were there cauldrons at the other sites?"

"No. This is the first time this element has appeared. The killer's perfecting some kind of new ritual. Testing out a new game."

"But why would he kill in three different cities?" Derrick asked. "And then cross over into a totally different province? That doesn't make sense."

"No, it doesn't. But we've got a ridiculously large sample

pool to draw from. In our world, half of the population—hell, two thirds—could be considered killers. Vampires, demons, necromancers . . . all of them kill without discrimination or remorse. All of them fit the classic profile of a psychopath. But this killer is different. He, or she, is using materia to aid in the killing."

"But it's not necroid materia. There's no trace of necromancy here, or at least none that I can detect."

Saying the word "necromancy" made me think of Lucian Agrado, which was something I'd been doing a lot of lately. Even though he scared the hell out of me, I still wanted to see him. Possibly *because* he scared the hell out of me. Possibly because I never got to finish what we started that night, six months ago. Before the gates of hell opened up and sucked my whole life into them.

Lucian also knew the dark side of this city like nobody else. He didn't frequent the Downtown Eastside, but he must have known people who did. People, creatures, and things without names. I was going to have to talk to him eventually.

I could still hear Selena's last words to me on the subject:

Stay away from him. The CORE would never tolerate anything more than a friendship between the two of you. If they get wind of a developing relationship, they'll absolutely destroy both your lives. They won't hesitate.

"So this wasn't done by a necromancer," Derrick was saying.

I looked once more at the boy, still floating before me, like some foul and twisted parody of the Lady of Shallot. His sad eyes were the blue of lapis lazuli, the blue of a single vein thrown into relief. Flashbulbs lit up his body, silvering the edges of his skin until he drifted, molten, like clustered lightning or a shimmering piece of quartz.

I had to look away.

2

Security at the lab was pretty relaxed at 7 a.m. I swiped in at the first checkpoint, submitted my palm print, and within moments I was wandering through the glass-partitioned world of the Mystical Crimes Division. It looked like any other well-funded crime lab, but if you peered closer, you might see a few unusual pieces of evidence. Like a cursed amulet, or an enchanted shotgun capable of firing itself. There was a secure evidence locker for items like that, placed alongside the regular archive and drying room for more terrestrial samples. I passed the firearms lab to my right, where an intern was awkwardly trying to carry a lump of yellow ballistics gel as it wobbled on a plastic tray. By the end of the day, it would be obliterated by all sorts of different ammunition—blossoming Hydra-Shok bullets, Glazer Rounds that mushroomed on impact, Black Talons that could shred through human tissue at incredible speed, and even tracer bullets loaded with mandrake that reacted to mage's blood.

People waved to me as I walked, and I smiled back, but my heart wasn't in it. I felt drained, both physically and mentally. My arms and legs were moving, I wasn't tripping over things or running into walls, but for the most part I was on automatic pilot. I didn't want to talk about what had happened six months ago. Derrick tried, but I always evaded. Selena was too busy to ask about my health, and I was too busy to really think about it. So I showed up for work, I did my job, and at night I stared at the ceiling.

I got into the oversized service elevator and pushed the button—it only went down, so there wasn't much of a choice involved. The hydraulics groaned, and within a few seconds I was in my favorite place: the morgue.

Tasha Lieu, our medical examiner, was leaning over the autopsy table, dressed in green scrubs with a full apron. Blood spatter on the apron made her look like a curious parody of a Christmas tree. Happy Holidays.

I could hear music: the faint strains of hip-hop, Tasha's obsession. This time it was Aesop Rock, and his manic lyrics tumbled over each other, sharp and powerful, as they filled the air:

> *Must not sleep.*
> *Must warn others.*
> *Trust blocks creep where the dust storm hovers;*
> *I milk my habitat for almost everything I want,*
> *Sometimes I take it all and still can't fill*
> *This pitfall in my gut.*

It was a fitting anthem, especially for a pathologist who rarely seemed to sleep herself. I thought of the Latin plaque on Tasha's desk: *Hic locus est ubi mors gaudet succurrere vitae.* "This is the place where death rejoices to teach those who live."

I started to push the door open, then paused. I suddenly found myself breathing hard. Autopsies freaked me out on a regular basis, but this one was worse than usual. I inched forward, peering through the glass. The boy was laid out on the stainless steel table, looking even smaller than before. His eyes were closed, but I could still feel them on me, looking through me. I shuddered.

Tasha had only partially finished stitching him up, and the top half of his chest cavity was still open, as if a zipper had been pulled down and then stopped at the line of his breastbone. I was always amazed by the vivid coloration of organs, the pale yellow of fat tissue lining the walls of the chest, like foam insulation spilling out. It mingled with the rust-colored red of the muscle, purple in spots, yielding to the prosector's scalpel with such shocking ease. It takes only eight pounds of pressure for a knife to cut skin. Barely a touch. I'd felt the pressure of fangs sinking into my neck before—the betrayal of my skin as it was torn and macerated. Not such a tough exterior after all. If only I could have Kevlar instead.

In order to get to the heart and lungs, you first have to break through the ribcage—I'd seen Tasha do it before with a pair of large pruning shears. The *snap* always made me shudder. Not a careful sound, like tearing fabric, but the awkward *crack-snap* of bone as it was sheared through and broken up. She'd replaced the chest plate, but even though I couldn't see the fractures, I knew they were there. We broke up his insides and then put them back, barely held together, leaving our mark. It always seemed like a desecration. I couldn't stomach the thought of someone reaching into my body, prodding and weighing and breaking things, only to replace them all lopsided, like when your suitcase spills over at the airport, and you have to just shove everything back in—shirts, shoes, socks, toothpaste, keepsakes—until it's all mixed up.

Tasha's foot tapped the pedal that activated the digital recorder, and she began giving her post report. I strained to listen.

"Subject is a young white male, height five feet nine inches, weight one-hundred-twenty pounds, age indeterminate—judging from molar eruption and fusion of the pubic symphisus bone, I would place him between nineteen and twenty-one years old. Signs of malnutrition and possible eating disorder, including stomach swelling, acid damage to the teeth, and severely receding gum line. Stomach contents are largely liquid, suggesting that the subject hadn't eaten for a day, possibly two. Blood in the stomach suggests a peptic ulcer, with black, 'coffee ground emesis' consistency, but no abscess was found during the post examination."

Tasha glanced at her notes and continued. "Samples of hair, cardiac blood, and vitreous fluid have been sent for toxicology screening. Given the possible context of death, I recommend that thin-layer chromatography be used in order to determine potential drug interactions."

All I wanted to do was run back home, crawl into bed, and medicate myself into a deep, dreamless sleep. Instead, I opened the door.

"Hey, Tash."

"Tess!" She smiled. "Just in time. I'm closing him up now."

"Yeah, I saw."

She shook her head. "Don't be squeamish. If you can't get used to the sight of a little viscera in the morning, you won't be able to look past it and see what's really going on underneath the skin. Just treat it like another puzzle."

"I object to the phrase 'a little viscera in the morning.' "

She chuckled. "Very well. No more poetry. But do come take a look."

I leaned over the body. The patterned abrasion across his chest was darker and more visible now—it almost looked like a cross between a bruise and road rash. The bruising around his feet and wrists had stayed the same.

"I guess cause of death is easy," I said.

Tasha nodded. "Incised wound to the left side of the neck, just above the clavicle. The cut is roughly six inches long, and it transected the left common carotid artery. Very sharp and very precise." She pointed to the edges of the wound. "No tissue bridging, and no abraded borders. This was done with a sharp, double-edged blade, rather than a serrated knife."

"So not your average kitchen knife."

"It would have to be a dagger of some kind. No hilt mark, so it's more of a slice than a stab—the blade was drawn once cleanly across the flesh." She frowned. "In cases like this, you usually see that surrounding structures have been nicked or damaged, especially the subclavian artery which is nearby. But this cut is surgically precise."

"You think the killer's trained in anatomy?"

"Not necessarily, but you're dealing with someone who's incredibly detail-oriented, someone with a very steady hand. Not a rookie." She turned the boy's neck slightly, so that I could see the undamaged side, still traced with stubble. "The underlying musculature is untouched. Hyoid bone is intact, and there's no bruising on the rest of the neck. No trace of manual asphyxiation."

"It doesn't look like the killer touched him at all, except for that odd bruise across the sternum. And that could have been done with magic."

"I was thinking that as well." Tasha traced the edges of the bruise with her gloved fingertip. "It has all the characteristics of a restraint, but I didn't find any fibers that might indicate a rope or a belt. It's possible, I think, to manipulate certain kinds of materia flows to such a degree that you can apply gravitational force to something—an object, or a body."

"Well, he was floating when we found him."

"Yeah, I saw him before you did. I had to release the scene." Tasha shook her head. "A real gruesome tableau. Whoever the killer is, he likes to show off."

"Yeah," I muttered, "he's a real impresario."

"Usually," she continued, "in cases like these, you'd see a clean incision across the neck, transecting both common carotid arteries. The standard position is to grab the victim from behind, usually by the hair, elevating their neck and slicing horizontally. But in this case the killer was very careful to only cut one side of the neck. And even that cut is shallow."

"We think that he wanted the kid to die more slowly. A shallow wound like that would take a while to bleed out."

"God." Tasha sighed. "You know, animals, I get. They make sense to me. Even insects. But people are beyond me sometimes. What we do to each other, on a daily basis, is so much worse than science fiction."

"I know exactly what you mean." I forced myself to stare at a space just above the body, not actually seeing it. "You—ah—mentioned some potential drug interactions?"

"We won't know for sure until the tox screen comes back,

but I imagine that he was on something. His liver temp was higher than normal." She lifted up his right arm, revealing the track marks. "These are old. I noticed some damage to the alveoli and bronchioles as well—the kind of trauma to the lungs you might see in someone who smoked crystal meth. It turns your lungs to hamburger eventually."

"And what about that fresh puncture mark?"

"I sent a sample to histology. Could be any IV drug, really. And there's also the hybrid drugs out there, the kind that mix heroin with processed materia. You might as well freebase with napalm. It's a real one-way ticket."

"If this is a serial killer, he may be using drugs to subdue his victims. Especially if they're already users."

"This kid definitely used. He may have been just starting out, but he obviously smoked and injected drugs. And there was some dried blood in his nasal passageways."

"So he was snorting, too."

"The story doesn't get any happier."

The door to the morgue swung open, and Selena walked in, carrying a file. It would have been more accurate to say that she stormed in, if people actually could "storm" in real life. Her expression was something between chronic fatigue and complete mental breakdown. I unconsciously braced myself against the nearby steel counter, as if I were standing on a subway train that was about to lurch forward.

"Close him up," she called, her long legs rapidly bringing her across the room. "Cover up the wound on his neck. Do anything you can to make him look presentable—I don't care if you have to use mortician's makeup. Just do it now."

Tasha frowned. "What's up? You located next of kin?"

"Did we ever." Selena looked at me, and I could actually feel her vibrating from a few feet away. "Tess, it's been nice knowing you."

"Are you quitting?"

"I just might be." She closed her eyes momentarily. "We ran the ten-card of the boy's prints that we got last night. There was a hit in AFIS."

"So who is he?" I rolled my eyes. "Some celebrity's kid?"

Selena's look was grim. "His name is Jacob Kynan."

"Kynan?" I felt the color drain from my face. "As in, the *Kynan* family?"

"His mother is Devorah Kynan."

"Oh fuck." I gripped the edge of the counter. "Oh holy— *fuck*. Is she coming here? Is she on her way?"

"She's a bigwig, right?" Tasha asked. "I mean, I don't exactly read the community tabloids, but she's a big deal as a mage, if I remember."

"The Kynan family is one of the oldest empowered clans in North America," Selena said. "They settled in Vancouver at the turn of the century, and half of the Mystical Crimes Division was built with their money. Technically, Devorah Kynan owns this morgue—and this building."

"Well, if she wants a viewing, she's going to have to look through the closed-circuit camera like everyone else. She's not allowed in the autopsy suite."

"Tasha, we're talking about a woman who could level this whole building if she wanted to. If Devorah Kynan wants to see her son's body, we don't have much of a choice. Hell, she could drag him out of here on a gurney, and we wouldn't be able to do anything about it."

Tasha folded her arms across her chest. "That boy's body is not leaving here. This is still my morgue, Selena. I'm chief medical examiner. She'd be breaking at least three laws by removing him from this facility."

Selena raised a hand. "I know, I know. No offense implied, Tash. I'm just trying to prepare you for the inevitable. This woman is used to getting what she wants, and she's got friends in powerful places. Other dimensions. Things that you don't want crawling through your window at night."

"Does she know about the other two girls who were killed?" I asked.

Selena shook her head. "She only cares about Jacob. And the less she knows right now, the better. I don't want her going to the media. Politics, Tess. We have to be careful." She looked around, as if making sure that nobody else was listening. "We just got funding to bring in a profiler, but you can't tell anyone. *Especially* not Devorah Kynan."

"The guy from Toronto?" I said.

Her eyes narrowed. "I see that Siegel has been shooting his mouth off. That's the last time I let him eavesdrop on a departmental meeting."

"But this is good, right? If the department is willing to bring in outside talent, then they're taking the case seriously."

"I get it." Tasha smiled. "We deny that we're hiring a profiler at first, so that it looks like we've got everything under control in-house. But if anything goes to trial, we whip out the documents proving that we *did* outsource, and that we had outside talent on the case all along."

"You should be on the selection committee," Selena told her blandly.

Tasha's smile widened. "I'm very active at my kid's PTA meetings."

I momentarily pictured Tasha, fresh from an autopsy, showing up at a middle school classroom to discuss bake sale strategies. It was a mind-bending thought.

"What about the drugs?" I asked.

"We'll have to wait a day for the tox panel to come back." Tasha was bent over Jacob's body now, stitching up the Y-incision with coarse thread. I felt my stomach flip, and looked away.

"No talk about drugs until we know something definitive," Selena said. "I'm not about to tell Devorah Kynan that her only son was a junkie."

"But the evidence is all over his arms. She's going to see it."

"She's a mother." Selena's eyes were dark. "All she's going to see is her little boy lying on a cold autopsy table."

"How much time do we have before she gets here?"

Selena shrugged. "She lives in Shaughnessy, but if traffic is good on South Granville, she could be here in ten minutes."

"If it was my kid," Tasha said, "I'd speed the whole way."

Shaughnessy was one of Vancouver's oldest and richest

neighborhoods, with massive, three-story estates guarded by high hedges. A land of gated communities and tree-lined streets, with Mercedeses and Jaguars parked on every curb. The only time I ever saw it was when I was speeding down South Granville on the 98 B-Line Bus, which went all the way to the airport. I wondered if Devorah lived in a mansion, or if she was one of those wealthy landowners who leased out a number of properties, graciously allowing students to live in converted basement suites for nine hundred bucks a month.

"What about this profiler?" I asked. "Is he good?"

"His name is Miles Sedgwick." Selena shuffled through some papers, squinting as she tried to read her own notes in pencil. "Bachelor's in psychology from Dalhousie, and master's from the University of Toronto. With honors. He works on contract with our Toronto office, and he worked at both the Hamilton and Scarborough scenes."

"Can't we find a profiler from Vancouver?"

She made a face. "You picked a fine time to show civic pride. From what I've been told, Sedgwick is the best. And he's working for very little compensation."

"What—out of the goodness of his heart?"

"Who knows? He gets a living wage and a hotel room, but that's about it. You and Siegel can make sure that he gets settled in."

Great. The last thing I wanted to do was play errand girl to some uppity academic from Toronto. Secretly, I was afraid that he'd ask me to use the photocopier, since I still hadn't figured out how to change the toner.

"You can't even give him an apartment?"

She spread her hands. "We're not made of money, and besides, he didn't ask for anything like that. Just a space for his computer and files."

"Is he single?" Tasha asked, still holding the scissors and thread.

Selena glared at her. "You're married."

"I wasn't asking for me." She smirked in my general direction.

I shook my head. "Oh no. I'm off the market."

"Oh, please." Selena sighed. "This isn't *The View*. I don't give a shit if he's single, married, gay, straight, or into animals. All I care about is whether he knows how to profile a killer."

"Profilers are always straight and single," I said. "It's hard to maintain a relationship when you're constantly making flow charts about dismemberment and ritual killings. Not that it would bother me."

"No, you'd probably like it," Tasha said.

"This discussion is over," Selena said. "Right now, all we have to worry about is what Devorah Kynan's going to do——"

At that moment, the door to the morgue opened. It was like we'd called her into existence by saying her name. I felt a chill go down my spine.

Devorah Kynan was short. Almost petite. She had close-cropped black hair with a hint of silver, and dark, almost blue-black eyes. Her features were angular and severe, as if they'd been sewn into a tapestry. She had high cheekbones, and her mouth was compressed to a thin, expressionless line. No wrinkles, but I doubted that it was due to Botox or some other form of creative botulism. Maybe she just didn't age. And with the level of power that I could feel emanating from her, that seemed like a distinct possibility. The air all around her body was crackling like a frying pan. Flows of materia coiled along her arms, coursing between her fingertips, invisible but no less deadly. I'd felt the like of it only once, and that was when I'd met Caitlin, the former vampire magnate of the city.

She had a kind of beauty. It was cold and forbidding, almost metallic, but I could see it, in the same way that you might feel drawn to a soaring, modular sculpture made of glass and steel. She wore a men's blazer—probably Armani—that had been tailored to fit her small frame, thrown over a bloodred shirt with a high collar. The top button was undone, revealing an amber pendant with delicate golden tracery that lay against her olive skin. The soles of her flats clicked against the tiled floor of the autopsy suite. *Click-click-click.* And then silence.

Even though she was standing still, it seemed as if the room itself had stopped instead, completely frozen. All eyes were drawn to her. Even Tasha was motionless, still holding the scissors that she'd been using, only a moment ago, to stitch up the chest cavity of Jacob Kynan. Selena looked ready for battle.

Nobody said anything. I felt dizzy from the black-edged power that was coming off Devorah in waves. I'm not sure if she was even aware of it. I forced myself to meet her eyes. They were small and without feeling. I remembered that night, months ago, when I'd looked into Lucian's eyes and seen nothing but two black orbs, revolving in a killing dance against some eternal winter. The banality of evil, or maybe something else entirely. All I could see in Devorah Kynan's eyes was a plane of perfect steel, flawless in its consistency. A stream of codes and mystical binaries that threatened to overwhelm me.

Try to know me, those eyes said, *and you will lose.*

Finally, she spoke. Her voice was low and rich, without a tremor.

"Where is my boy?"

3

Devorah Kynan stood a few feet from the autopsy table. None of us moved. We were like some eerie tableau. Words died in my mouth. The emptiness in Devorah's eyes would have swallowed anything that I might say, any easy platitude or gesture of condolence.

"Ms. Kynan," Selena said finally. "You should come with me."

"I need to see my son," she replied.

"Of course you do. But there are some things we need to talk about first. It won't take very long, and then our chief medical examiner, Dr. Tasha Lieu"—she gestured to Tasha, who was doing her best to look professional—"can arrange a viewing for you. I know this is a difficult time—"

"My son," Devorah repeated. She looked at Selena, confused, as if seeing her for the first time. "I need to be with him."

"I understand that, of course I do," Selena began. "But there are matters—"

"You can leave now." Devorah approached the autopsy table. Her eyes swept over the length of Jacob's body. She didn't even flinch. "I need to be alone with him. I'll answer your questions later."

"Ms. Kynan . . ."

She met Selena's gaze. Nothing was said, but I felt a flare of power, like an electrical current passing between them. Selena took a small step backward. It wasn't a threat, precisely. More like a reminder of who was in charge.

Selena let out a breath. "All right. We'll be waiting outside."

Tasha looked angry, but Selena raised a hand before she could say anything. Slowly and awkwardly, like students who had just been dismissed, we filed out of the autopsy suite and gathered in the hallway outside. The door closed, and I could smell industrial-grade antiseptic. We were silent except for the hum of the elevator.

"Well, that was really professional," Tasha said.

"Give her what she wants," Selena replied. "That way, she'll give us something. Hopefully, answers. It's just a minor infraction—"

"She's alone in the morgue, in *my* morgue, with the body of her dead son!" I'd never seen Tasha livid before. "She could be contaminating evidence! If this gets out, we could be looking at a violation from OSHA—"

"It won't get out." Selena's voice was even. "Give her the time that she needs, and she'll be cooperative. I understand how people like Devorah Kynan work. She's from a different time."

"And we're supposed to just adapt to her?" Tasha shook her head. "Excuse me for saying it, Selena, but this is bullshit."

"It's politics."

"Same thing."

I looked through the window of the autopsy suite. Devorah hadn't moved an inch. She was standing there, an intimate distance from her son's body, looking at him, the way you'd look at an unfamiliar painting that was beautiful but also strange.

Slowly, she reached for the white sheet and drew it down, revealing the Y-incision across his chest. She held on to the sheet with one hand, and I saw that her knuckles were pale from clutching it so tightly. Then she let it drop.

"What's she doing?" Tasha leaned forward. "Is she touching him?"

"Just let her be," Selena breathed.

I watched, transfixed, as Devorah walked over to the large steel sink. She picked up a washcloth and turned the water on, letting it soak. Her fingers were small and white as they gripped the detachable spigot. She turned the water off, then carefully removed her jacket, folded it, and placed it on Tasha's chair. She rolled up the sleeves of her shirt, and I saw a braided silver band on her left wrist.

She walked back to the autopsy table, washcloth in hand. I watched her remove the sheet, fold it neatly, and place it on the counter. Jacob's body was completely exposed now, bruised, white, and still. He had small feet. Size eight or nine. We didn't find any clothes or shoes with his body, but I imagined him wearing sneakers with gray socks, for some reason. He'd want a pair of comfortable shoes if he was standing at the corner of Main and Hastings all night. "Pain and Wastings," as a journalist had called it once, years ago. The name stuck.

Devorah reached out and touched Jacob's foot. I felt, rather than saw, her body begin to tremble. She stroked the pad of his foot with her thumb and forefinger. Then she ran the washcloth over the sole, letting it twine between his toes. She washed the other foot, letting the washcloth move slowly up his ankles. The water dampened the black hair on his legs, spreading it in soft whorls. Devorah smoothed it down with her fingertips, drawing the washcloth up his shins and toward his thighs. She was matter-of-fact as she reached his groin, gently scrubbing the coarse pubic hair and brushing his genitals to one side. Even at nineteen or twenty-one or however old Jacob was now, he was still her baby, and the memory of bathing and cleaning him would have flared in her mind as if it were yesterday. He was part of her body; he'd never really left her.

Her fingers danced across the pattered abrasion on his chest. She frowned at it, as if to say, *How dare you, this isn't your place, you don't belong here.* Then she continued, washing his hips, lifting him ever so gently. She lingered around his navel, her expression entirely unreadable. She touched it once. That was the site of his umbilical cord, the place where he'd been severed from her. I could almost see a pathway of light that connected the two of them, a thread still shining that linked them, something that death had degraded but not cut.

Tasha suddenly frowned. "Do you hear that?"

I realized, then, that Devorah was singing. We shouldn't have been able to hear it, yet we could. Gradually, the song got louder, although her voice never seemed to rise above a whisper. It was clear, sylvan and powerful, almost unbearable against the silence of the autopsy suite. Her lips parted as she continued to wash Jacob's body, and syllables that were like flakes of brilliance and pure life rose into the air, hovering around her. It wasn't a trick of materia—there was nothing patently magical about her singing. But it had its power. It was old and it was subtle, but I felt it cleave me all the same, like the kiss of an athame.

> *Yis'ga'dal v'yis'kadash sh'may ra'bbo,*
> *b'olmo dee'vro chir'usay*
> *v'yamlich malchu'say,*
> *b'chayaychon uv'yomay'chon*
> *uv'chayay d'chol bais Yisroel,*
> *ba'agolo u'viz'man koriv;*
> *v'imru, Omein.*

I'd heard this song before. It was the *kaddish*, the Jewish prayer of mourning. I remembered, then, that washing the body was a Jewish tradition. It was part of watching over the dead— *shemira*, I think it was called. I'd dated a Jewish boy, years ago, and when his grandmother died, I had to attend the funeral with him. Everyone had loved *Bobbe* Rachel. The rabbis tore black shreds of cloth, and I could still hear those words, dark and inviolate, swirling before me as they rose up to the vaulted ceiling of the *shul*. He didn't cry, but I wanted to, even though I'd barely known her. Isn't that strange?

I did remember, as well, that you were only supposed to recite that prayer at a particular place and time, in the company of a rabbi. Devorah didn't care. I imagined that exceptions must have been made for a mother's grief.

"V'al kol Yisroel," she sang, rubbing the washcloth against Jacob's neck. She touched the edges of the wound, closing her eyes. *"Vimru Omein. Jacob. Jacob."*

She stroked his neck. Her fingertip almost entered the track of the wound, and I thought of Caravaggio's painting of Saint Thomas putting his finger in Christ's wound. Tasha tensed up, but didn't move. All of Devorah's grief seemed to congeal and concentrate in her fingertip as it hovered over the laceration. It was her mother's right, her entitlement, to plunge it deep inside, to be joined with her son again as she touched the deepest and most interior part of him.

But she didn't. She placed her hand on his face instead. "Jacob. *Ahavi. Levi.* You bastard. You fucking bastard."

And she wept. I didn't know if she was talking to her son, his killer, or someone else entirely. She slumped across his body, her fingers curling in his hair. I could see her lips moving, but couldn't hear what she was saying anymore.

Tasha had turned away, and I did the same.

I wasn't allowed to smoke in the lab, which seemed like a crime.

Instead, I had to settle on stirring the contents of my Styrofoam coffee cup rapidly, as if I could make the day-old Sanka breathe like a fine Cab Franc. Selena was in the interrogation room with Devorah Kynan. I could hear what they were saying on the other side of the two-way glass partition—so far, it wasn't going well. Devorah had unequivocally denied any involvement in Jacob's death, as we'd expected, but now she was refusing to answer questions about his drug use. Maybe she didn't know anything, but I doubted that. Someone with her connections would have easily been able to keep tabs on a nineteen-year-old runaway.

I understood that junkies often didn't want to enter rehab

programs, or felt that halfway houses weren't going to help them in the end. It made sense, given that, in all of the Downtown Eastside, there were less than a dozen available beds for women who were detoxing, and only a few more for men. But people like Devorah Kynan didn't have to rely on shelters and underfunded social programming. She had access to the best rehab facilities, the most costly surveillance, and all the methadone that someone like Jacob would ever need. So what had kept her from forcing him to come home?

"I bear gifts from afar." Derrick came walking down the hallway with two red cups. "Well, from Café Artigiano across the street. But they like to think of themselves as European, so it's almost like a continental gift."

"Oh, gimme." I snatched the cup out of his hand. "Dear God, real coffee. Thank you. This crap from the break room is like drinking sawdust. I've almost considered buying a bulk pack of Pepcid AC."

Derrick frowned as I inhaled the mocha. "You know, it had a little swan that the barista drew in milk foam. I was going to show you."

"I don't care if it had the fucking Queen on it, Derrick."

He rolled his eyes. "This is why we always get kicked out of Starbucks. Remember that time the barista was slow making your macchiato, and you tried to use the espresso machine yourself? Remember that? When they had to call security?"

"Yes, yes, and we all learned something about fire safety that day." I scowled at him. "What's your point?"

"I guess I don't have one."

I let the hot, sickly sweet mocha linger on my tongue. I could already feel my hands getting clammy as the caffeine did its work, forcibly wrenching open that sleep-deprived corner of my brain that really just wanted to stay deactivated.

"Has Devorah said anything probative yet?"

I shook my head. "She's a locked strongbox. I don't know if Selena's going to get anything out of her."

"What do we do then? We've got no leads, and no physical evidence that ties this kid to the other murders."

"We'll have to pound the pavement, I guess. Ask around and see if anyone knew Jacob, if anyone else is missing him."

"People in this neighborhood aren't exactly big on talking, though. And we'll stick out like a couple of tourists."

I let the coffee settle in my stomach like dead weight. "We'll be persistent."

"You could always talk to"—he made a gesture—"you know who."

I sighed. "You can say his name, Derrick. He's not Voldemort."

"Fine. You can talk to Lucian Agrado, our favorite necromancer."

"I'd rather avoid that for now."

"Oh, I seriously doubt it."

My eyes narrowed. "Don't rib me about this. Lucian isn't some random guy that I picked up at Crush—"

"Like we'd ever go there."

"*Listen* to me." I glared at him. "Lucian is scary. I've seen what he's capable of. I don't want any part of it. Besides—it's against regulation. If they caught us sleeping together, our lives would turn to shit. Everything we've worked for during the past year could go straight down the drain, and for what? Casual sex?"

Derrick shrugged. "He may swing with the dark side, but he's got arms like Todd Bertuzzi. I'd tap that in a second if I had the chance. When did you suddenly become into CORE rules and regulations?"

"I'm into staying alive. It's kind of my motto."

"I feel the need to remind you that, about six months ago, your motto was more like 'I'm into rocking the sheets with a hot Latin death-dealer.' "

"Don't make me kick every square inch of your ass."

He sighed. "It always comes down to violence, doesn't it?"

"Just shut up and watch the interrogation with me."

Derrick stepped closer to the window. "I asked if I could be present, but Selena didn't think it would be a good idea."

"Someone like Devorah Kynan would feel your telepathy

coming a mile away. She could stir-fry your brain just by looking at you."

"I don't know about that." He had an odd expression on his
face. Was it pride? "I've been getting better, you know. Prac-
ticing."

"Of course." I rubbed his arm. "I didn't mean to sound
dismissive. I've noticed that your talents have been developing.
I'm sure Selena's noticed, too."

He smiled. "Really? You think she has?"

There was the insecure Derrick that I knew. "Obviously."

"Huh." His eyes sparkled. At least I could still make somebody happy.

I watched Selena shuffle through some papers. Devorah
was sitting across from her, absolutely still, hands folded. It
wasn't a contemplative gesture. I got the impression that, despite her calm exterior, she was using every inch of willpower
to keep from tearing apart the entire building. She didn't want
to be here. She wanted to be on the streets, looking for whoever killed her son. That's how I would have felt if someone
tried to kill Mia. Again.

My eyes narrowed. If that happened, there wouldn't be an
interrogation. There'd just be an unmarked demon grave.

"We need to go over this one more time," Selena was saying. "Approximately how long ago did Jacob run away from
home?"

"Last March," Devorah replied. Her voice was atonal—flat
and dead. "Almost a year ago. He'd been staying out before
that, visiting the neighborhood. I knew about it."

"But you didn't do anything."

"There wasn't anything to do. He's a teenager. Even if I
locked him in the basement, he'd find a way to wiggle out and
escape through a window. Jacob's smart. There was no way to
keep him from exploring—that life."

"Surely, you could have used your considerable resources
to keep him safe."

Her fingers twitched. Bad sign. "Are you suggesting that I
should have imprisoned my own child, Detective Ward?"

"You wouldn't be the first mother to try."

She shook her head. "I wasn't dealing with a dangerous criminal. Jacob has an IQ well over 180. He's been on every honor roll, won every conceivable award, and gone to the best private schools all his life. I couldn't just throw him in a cell and lock the door."

Selena folded her arms across her chest.

Oh shit. She was going in for the kill.

"In our experience, Ms. Kynan," she said—almost conversationally—"kids run away because of trauma at home. Violence, emotional abuse, molestation, neglect. It doesn't matter what school you send them to, or how well they appear to be doing to the outside world. They always bolt. And there's no shortage of people interested in using them and discarding them."

Devorah actually laughed. "That's a bold insinuation. Did they teach you that at CSI school, Detective? Try to shake up the grieving mother with allegations of abuse?"

"I'm just citing statistics, ma'am."

"Right." She leaned back. "Jacob never knew his father. He was a parasite, and I made sure to excise him from our lives."

"'Excise.'" Selena wrote down the word, as if hearing it for the first time. "Is that like having someone killed?"

"Don't play games." Devorah met her eyes. "We're both very smart women, Detective Ward. We had to sacrifice a lot to get where we are today. And the stigma never vanishes. We'll always be the ball-busting devils or the promiscuous whores, no matter what we do."

"I prefer ball-busting whore," Selena replied wryly.

"It's always something." Devorah was smiling, but it was a cold, almost frightening sort of smile. Could a person smile from despair? "We know who we are, and we know what we've done, what we have to keep doing, to hold on to these lives. So let's not play dumb. Obviously, I didn't have Jacob's father killed. He's a lowlife. I know where he's living and what he's doing—or not doing, to be more exact—and I can give you his contact information. But it won't be of any use. He's never seen Jacob."

"Never?"

"Not once." Her smile faded. "I made sure of that."

"See, here's what I don't get." Selena shook her head. "If you're so good at keeping tabs on Jacob's deadbeat father, why couldn't you do the same thing for your own son? Why didn't you pull him off the streets once he got in over his head?"

"You don't think I tried?" She looked disgusted. "I hired investigators. I put him in halfway houses, got him into programs. The paperwork's all there. But it didn't work. He kept going back, because he found something on the street." Her eyes darkened. "Something I couldn't give him. Something nobody could give him."

"Did you know what drugs he was doing? How much?"

To her credit, she didn't look away. "I knew everything. Some of it he told me, and other things I had to find out for myself. All I could do was beg him to stay safe. Whenever he was in a facility, I had him tested—HIV, Hep C, and everything else. He stayed clean."

"His blood results came back negative for both HIV and Hep C," Selena confirmed, glancing at her notes. "Who did he spend time with?"

Devorah grimaced. "The cast was diverse."

"But you never saw Jacob spending time with anyone older? Someone who may have been a supplier?"

"No. When I visited, he was almost always alone."

"Visited him where?"

She shrugged. "Squats. Shelters. Friends' places and little rooms and dark warrens that made me half-sick to visit."

"But you came anyway."

"I did."

"To take care of him. Make sure he was set up."

"Of course." Anger flashed. "He's my son. I had to make sure that he had clothes, food, the proper supplies."

"You mean gear."

Devorah's expression was pragmatic. "We do all that we can, Detective. And when that fails, we don't just stop being a parent. I made sure that he was using safely. Sometimes I gave him money, but he usually just gave it away. That was Jacob." She laughed softly. "You know, he used to give his presents

away to other kids when he was little. Once, I caught him trying to saw a Transformer in half! He wanted the boy across the
street to have something to play with. There were bits and
pieces of that thing all over his bedspread, and who knew
where he found the goddamn hacksaw—"

Her eyes went distant. For a moment, I saw a cascade of
anguish, utterly vast and devouring, like a black wave. Then
she shut the door. Her composure returned.

"I gave him what he needed," she continued. "Fresh needles, sterile cotton pads and gauze wipes, clean ties, caps for
mixing. Try explaining to your housekeeper why you have to
boil a pot full of bottle caps, so that your son has something
sterile to shoot his heroin."

"So you aided his drug habit."

"I kept him alive. A chronic drug user doesn't shoot up to
get high, Detective. He needed the drug to function. And
watching him go through detox, again and again"—she shook
her head—"it was more than I could stand."

"There was more than heroin in his system, actually." Selena glanced at a computer printout from the toxicology lab.
"One of our tests came back positive for a hybrid drug. I
believe they call it Hextacy on the street."

I looked at Derrick. His expression was surprised as well.
Selena must have threatened the toxicology lab with certain
death to get those results back so fast. And if she was sharing
them with Devorah, it meant that we had even less to go on
than I'd thought. We needed the Kynan family's help.

"Hex." The word seemed to stick in Devorah's throat. "It's
organic materia, extracted from blood and then processed with
heroin. Sometimes they add meth, just to make it even more
potent. There's no drug that's worse, especially for someone
with Jacob's genetic heritage."

"He'd be particularly susceptible, given his bloodline," Selena agreed.

Devorah nodded. "Hex was engineered with mages in
mind. It boosts your latent power to an incredible level, gives
you a mystical high, but it's also ten times more destructive
than cocaine or heroin."

"And you knew Jacob was using it?"

"I suspected. It was impossible to confirm, though. Drugs like heroin metabolize into morphine, but Hex nearly vanishes into airborne materia. It's difficult to trace."

"Are you a pharmacist, Ms. Kynan?"

She smiled darkly. "When your only son is an addict, you become quite well versed in these matters. I could probably write a book by now."

"If I ever wrote a book about this place," Selena dead-panned, "it would make millions."

"She's winding down," Derrick said. "She's going to let her off easy."

"Selena never lets anyone off easy. She just switches tactics."

"All right." Selena looked carefully at Devorah, who maintained flawless eye contact. She was undoubtedly accustomed to being interviewed. "I'm going to be honest with you. There have been two other cases similar to this one in the past four weeks. They were also the children of people from our world. People like you, Ms. Kynan. They were murdered in Ontario, and we think all three deaths are related."

"The same killer." Her voice was velvety soft. "Who are the parents?"

"Lyrae and Baxter Simms. Tobias and Patricia Davies. Lyrae passed away in February of last year."

"I know. Her cancer metastasized." Devorah rubbed her temples for a moment, wincing, looking tired. She could have been any middle-aged professional. Only the scent of her power gave her away. "Baxter moved to Quebec after Lyrae died, but Andrea stayed in Vancouver with a paternal uncle. Tobias and Patricia recently took a leave of absence from their posts in Manitoba. Now it makes sense."

Selena nodded.

"Aside from the Hextacy, was there any other magic involved?"

"The first two cases were normate. Aside from the victims' connections to our world, nothing marked their deaths as being particularly noteworthy. But Jacob's murder was different.

The killer used magic to subdue him, and there was a ritualistic element."

"Show me," Devorah said simply.

"Are you certain about that, Ms. Kynan? These images are graphic."

"I've already seen my son's dead body." Her face seemed to collapse for a moment, but then the mask returned. "I know that his death was violent. I know that his throat was slashed. Nothing that you can show me will make a difference now."

With genuine reluctance, Selena withdrew the crime scene photos from a nearby folder. She slid them across the table. I saw the bloody cauldron, Jacob's body splayed across the ceiling, and the arc of arterial spray on the hotel room wall. I shivered.

Devorah scanned the pictures as if they were a museum exhibit. Her eyes betrayed no feeling. Her shields were up for good now.

"A *coire*," she said. "How odd."

"The killer obviously has some knowledge of magical history," Selena said. "And he—or she—didn't use necroid materia. So we're dealing with a mage."

"One of our own," Devorah breathed.

"Exactly."

"And this cauldron—it was filled with my son's blood?"

I swallowed. How do you ask a question like that? How do you answer it?

"Yes," Selena replied levelly.

"Sometimes blood is used in rituals designed for longevity. But those are ancient. Forbidden by the Mage's Rede. And nobody knows if they even work anymore."

In the middle ages, the Rede was an informal code among witches, an oral tradition passed down through the generations. But this was the computer age, and the Rede had become a hefty online manual with footnotes and hyperlinks. Searching through it was like trying to read the guidelines for NAFTA.

"We think that the killer has been perfecting some kind of—performance," Selena said slowly. "The other two were designed as preparation, but Jacob was the first real test subject. We just don't know what the purpose is."

"It could be anything," Devorah said. "A plea for immortality, a shape-shifting, a curse. Blood has many uses. Were the other victims left on the ceiling?"

"No. Jacob was the first."

"But you don't think he'll be the last."

Selena's expression was grim. "No. I'm afraid not."

Devorah rose. "I understand." She handed Selena a card. "This has my cell number. I expect to be updated, day or night. Keep the information flowing, and I'll give you all the resources and contacts you need."

"Thank you, but we're perfectly capable of conducting this investigation without your help, Ms. Kynan."

The woman barely smiled. "We both know that's not true. Keep me informed, Detective, and things will run smoothly. If I feel that I'm being excluded, I'll have to contact my cadre of lawyers and explain to them how you coerced me, under duress, to give you an interview without legal counsel present. I'll also have to notify them about the OSHA infractions and code violations in your morgue—particularly how you let me view my son's body. Alone."

Derrick exhaled. "She's *good*," he whispered.

"Are we clear on this matter?"

Selena rose. "We are, Ms. Kynan."

"Thank you—Selena." Devorah extended her hand.

Selena took it. I felt the planets shift—two titans were clashing.

"I'm sorry" was all she said.

"Yes. I am, too."

The door opened, and Devorah emerged from the interrogation room. She didn't look at Derrick and me. She just walked away.

Selena leaned in the doorway with a sigh. I saw for the first time that she was sweating. Devorah had almost completely drained her.

"That could have gone worse," Derrick said.

Selena closed her eyes. "Yeah. She could have eaten my face off."

"But it sounds like she's going to cooperate."

"She'll cooperate as long as it's convenient for her. But if we piss her off, she's going to come at us with all the armies of hell."

"Not like we haven't faced them before," I offered.

Selena chuckled. "True that, kiddo."

"So where do we start?" Derrick asked.

"You start with Duessa."

"Who's that?"

Selena's look was incredulous. "You work in this city, and you don't know who Duessa is? Child, remind me why I promoted you to OSI-2!"

"Because of her good looks, of course." Derrick smiled, turning to me. "Duessa's kind of like a social worker for throwaway kids—the ones with power."

"The House of Duessa is a shelter for mage kids—almost like a co-op for addicts and runaways. They get food, beds, clean gear, and some medical care. She's seen all kinds of screwed-up kids coming through her place, including the sons and daughters of the most powerful mages in our community."

"She's not going to talk to us without some kind of referral," Derrick said.

"Of course not." Selena's eyes fell on me. "You know what that means, Tess."

Fuck. That meant talking to Lucian Agrado. It meant pouring salt on a wound that had been festering for six months.

"Just talking," Selena said. "Remember that."

4

Moonbase was still the hottest club for super-naturals—and various immortals—in Vancouver, although from the outside it resembled a warehouse or a paper company. Dunder Mifflin for vampires. It was within walking distance of Crush, the underage trolling ground, as well as the Roxy, which was just—gross. Plenty of snacks for those inclined to devour stupid teenagers. The last time I was here, I had to interview Sabine, the vampire who almost killed me. Good times. I don't know where she went after Caitlin banished her from the city, but I liked to imagine that she was Dumpster diving somewhere south of the border.

At 11:30 a.m. on a Tuesday, the building was understandably dark. All the vamps were still sleeping, warm in their Murphy beds, like Cindy Lou Who waiting for Christmas (i.e., dusk) to arrive. I sipped on the dregs of my Tim Hortons double-double, enjoying the crystallized sugar as it slid down my throat. No, it wasn't a beautifully pulled shot of espresso, but for a dollar fifty, their extra-large cup was the size of a bell jar, and it definitely made the morning pass smoothly.

I hadn't seen Lucian Agrado in quite some time, and despite the fact that this was strictly a business meeting, I didn't see any harm in looking good for the occasion. Hence, the vegan "leather" boots (Derrick made me buy them in a fit of social conscience, but they actually looked good), gray cardigan, patterned silk scarf, and jeans from Mavi that accomplished the impossible task of making my body look svelte. I have hips, and body fat, and breasts that don't always stand at attention. I'd rather tweak than hide, since it's not as if my genetic legacy was going to reverse itself anytime soon, but that didn't mean I couldn't weave an illusion here and there.

Besides—if I remembered correctly, Lucian hadn't complained the last time he saw me without my clothes on. And with that thought, I was slipping back into the dark and bad place.

Keep it together. This is CORE business. This is an official interview.

An interview with soft lips, and a tongue, and great skin, and spiky black hair that was baby soft to the touch, and Holy Mary, those arms—

—and necromancy. Evil. Powers of darkness.

I crossed Granville Street, which was quiet at the moment. A homeless couple dragged two carts full of junk behind them, followed closely by two dogs. Adrenaline Piercing was open, and I saw a preppy girl with caramel highlights, wincing in pain as the tattoo artist applied a vibrating needle to her stomach. Don't be a butterfly, I thought. God, not another butterfly. Stoners and drummers and their shady girlfriends gathered outside the Rock Shop, where you could still buy Skinny Puppy tees for twenty bucks. Tourists who had wandered too far north up the street were gazing in confusion at the grimy pizza joints and bars, wondering why they couldn't find Urban Outfitters. I could hear the rumbling of cars and buses on the Granville Street Bridge a few blocks up, the corridor to West Broadway and the land of boutique shops and hip cafés. Under the bridge, a very different economy was operating.

The entrance to Moonbase, with its wrought iron gate and creepy Doric pillars, was just as I remembered it. Undead Savannah chic. I smoothed down my sweater, took a breath, and knocked. My athame was in my back pocket. Not that I expected a scuffle, but it's always nice to have a ritual dagger close at hand. I'd left my Browning in the trunk of the car. It wasn't worth trying to sneak it in, and if I needed a gun in a building full of vampires, I was pretty much dead anyway.

I heard some shuffling, and then a heavy metal scraping. The door opened, and a guy in a tank top appeared. He was wearing sunglasses. I grinned as I recognized him—the same bouncer I'd spoken to the last time I was here.

"Tess Corday," I said. "Remember me?"

He kept to the shadowed area of the doorway.

"Huh," he said simply.

"I need to see Lucian."

The vampire scratched his head. "He doesn't work here anymore."

My stomach did a flip. "What?"

"He's—not—*here*." The bouncer sneered. "He turned over the keys last month. Said he wanted to get out of the club business."

"So what's he doing now?"

"What am I, fucking directory assistance?" He spread his hands. "Maybe he's working at a nonprofit. Maybe he's getting his fucking MBA. Who knows?"

I sighed. "Can you tell me where to find him?"

"Let's see your ID, *Detective*."

I rummaged through my purse and drew out my laminated CORE ID. The picture was not flattering. He scanned it and smiled.

"Level *two*. Somebody's moving up in the world, eh?"

I glared at him. "Do you need anything else? Some letterhead, or a reference or something? I've got a busy morning ahead of me."

"Don't get tetchy." His smile widened. "Give me your hand."

"Excuse me?"

"Your hand. I need to smell you."

I made a face. "Look, I've heard a lot of weird come-ons

before, but offering to smell me isn't exactly going to get you any trim, all right? That's not my thing."

"Just give me your hand. It'll only take a second, and I promise not to enjoy it." He crinkled his nose. "You're not my type anyhow. Too fragile."

"I guess that should make me feel better." Tentatively, I held out my hand, knowing that he could rip it off in a second if he wanted to. It was like sticking your fingers in a metal press and hoping that nobody pushed the button.

He turned my hand palm upward, and inhaled. His eyes closed. I resisted the urge to scream. His cold fingers encircled my wrist, and he brushed his nose against my flesh, raising goose bumps. I felt like a wine being tested, and briefly wondered how I would rate. Hopefully a sweet little Shiraz, something Chilean. More likely, a cheap Arbor Mist.

The bouncer let go of my hand. "Okay, you're good."

"It's creepy that you guys have my scent on file."

"Not your scent." He smirked. "His."

I felt my cheeks go red. "That's—I mean, I haven't seen Lucian in six months."

"Try three."

I blinked. Shit.

Okay, so I lied a bit. I may have met him for coffee a few months ago. It was awkward, and I didn't want to talk about it. He barely said anything, and I drank two mochas to compensate, until I was vibrating at an impossible frequency. When I got home, Derrick was confused by my sudden need to clean every inch of my bathroom, including the doorknobs.

"Fine—*three* months," I replied. "But even that's a long time for a scent to hang around. It's not like I haven't showered."

"I could tell you what you had for breakfast two weeks ago, if you like." He frowned. "Stay away from the chimichangas, by the way."

I filed that under GROSS. "Whatever. Do I have to sniff *you* now, or can you just tell me where he is?"

"Just doing my job. Only certain personal contacts"—he smirked a little at the pun—"get a copy of his home address."

The knowledge that I was on this list made me feel—well, kind of stupidly happy, I'll admit it. Happy and a little freaked out, since Lucian had made these creepy arrangements without telling me. He knew that I'd come looking for him eventually.

It was ridiculous to think, even for a minute, that I'd be the one in control this time. Lucian was always one step ahead. It drove me crazy.

The bouncer handed me a card with the address written on the back. I took it from him, and our fingertips brushed. Cold and dry. He could be an antiperspirant commercial. I smiled neutrally.

"Thanks for this."

He lowered his sunglasses a bit, and I saw his eyes. They were the color of ice.

"Any time."

I walked to my car without looking back. But I knew he was watching.

The last thing I'd expected to do this morning was visit a necromancer's apartment in the pathologically trendy Yaletown district, but here I was, trying to find parking on Davie Street as it became a steep incline before intersecting with Pacific Boulevard.

Yaletown butted against Vancouver's West End, where gay hipsters, artists, and designers shared space with urban retirees and two-dog families. Everyone wanted to live next to the beach, and at the corner of Davie and Denman streets, you could see muscle boys on rollerblades grinning as they passed Korean exchange students, huddled in a pod and clutching their ice cream cones, while bearish couples lounged on bright afghans with their Pomeranians yipping up a storm. Joggers in formfitting lululemon shorts huffed and puffed as they sped by, squirting arcs of filtered water from their Fiji bottles, and at night, the beach was filled with roaming kiosks, fire eaters, and occasionally a Tibetan monk with a cart on wheels who handed out paper fortunes. You could hear the sound of his gong echoing through the mist on chilly evenings, as tendrils of cream white fog drifted along the seawall, obscuring the distant tankers.

Unlike the urban sprawl of Toronto, or the old-meets-new, Victorian schizophrenia of Montreal (schizophrenic in a good way, like that crazy uncle who makes you feel oddly comfortable), Vancouver was a city of autonomous neighborhoods. The West End was a mixture of longtime residents, overtaxed students, and hopeful gay men competing for face time on the strip (from Burrard to Broughton, which roughly defined the borders of Vancouver's LGBT neighborhood). Commercial Drive, nestled eastward, was for activists, teachers, aging hippies, and lesbians who'd grown tired of the politics on Davie. Kitsilano, the realm of the eternal tan, was for UBC students, surfers, yoga instructors, and anyone daring enough to play shirtless volleyball at Jericho Beach. It shared space with Point Grey, the tree-lined haven of politicians and civil servants, and the Jericho Army Base, where army cadets got drunk and tried to sneak in strippers from the Copper Room.

Farther east, you had Nanaimo, an ethnic mix and settling point for families who couldn't afford rent on Commercial Drive. And then there was everything else—the suburbs, the in-between neighborhoods, the crisscrossing lengths of the Lougheed and Barnet highways, and the waterfront industries, where plastics were melted, sugar was refined, and more than occasionally, people disappeared.

Ask tourists, and they all say the same thing: "The city is so *beautiful*." But that beauty was surrounded by skyscrapers, glass condos, private marinas, and gated communities. You couldn't just plunk down a house next to Stanley Park and expect to enjoy its natural splendor—not unless you had about four million bucks to spare and healthy contacts among the real estate emperors who controlled property access within the city. New apartments, even in the suburbs, were like novelty items. Before the foundation was even laid, you could bet

that every unit was already snatched up and paid for by overseas millionaires and greedy developers.

While places like Shaughnessy and North Vancouver—
which was a separate municipality—served as bastions for old
money, Yaletown was the epicenter of yuppie wealth and
power. Hamilton Street practically shone with new blood, and
you couldn't enter a café or restaurant without experiencing
the invasion of the gorgeous twenty-somethings. Visiting this
neighborhood without an LV or Hermès bag was sacrilege:
instantly, all eyes would lock on your obvious fashion faux pas,
and the residents would converge on you like well-dressed children of the corn. Your best camouflage was a BlackBerry, a
decent scarf to draw attention away from the rest of your outfit, and a general aura of fierceness.

I had a Tim Hortons Big-Boy cup (favorite of truckers
across Canada), cigarettes, and a vintage shoulder bag. Not
good.

Hamilton Street was a minefield of concrete islands, slip-
pery stairs leading to narrow walkways, and shops on elevated
promenades that vaguely resembled Ewok houses. All of Yaletown used to be an old warehouse district, but imaginative
developers had transformed it over time into a kingdom of
high-priced loft apartments and fashion boutiques. Paternal
grandfathers like DKNY and Gucci competed with micro-
stores that were so fresh they'd practically just opened yesterday. French patisseries and Mayan hot chocolate cafés were
squeezed in between Bikram yoga studios, lounges-of-the-
moment, and upscale furniture stores that offered financing
plans if you wanted to buy an ivory stool or a cashmere pillowcase.

No dogs were without sweaters; some wore cargo pants.

The general vibe of zombification made it seem like a good
place for a necromancer.

In truth, I could guess why Lucian had settled here. It was
anonymous; slightly removed from the downtown core, but
still within walking distance; peaceful during the day but
packed with life at night; and it had the highest security in the

city. Apartments in Yaletown were like military structures, complete with their own police force.

Lucian was hiding from something. I wanted to find out what.

I stopped at the corner of Hamilton and Drake. I'd been expecting some kind of high-rise residence with mounted cameras and gun turrets. Necromancer's last stand. Instead, I found myself staring at the Drake Shipping Company. I blinked. There was a small office kitty-corner to the building, and the rest was taken up by storage. I looked at the address again. 212 Drake Street, Unit 3.

You've got to be kidding me.

The door farthest to the right was labeled STORAGE 3.

Lucian Agrado was living in a storage locker.

Each of the doors had a buzzer. Feeling vaguely like I was on a blind date that had gone terribly wrong, I pushed the button on Storage 3.

At first, nothing happened. Then I heard a *click*, followed by a buzz. Still a little uncertain, I reached for the door, and found that it was open. And heavy—like the door to a warehouse should be. Silently cursing Lucian, I set down my bag and Tim Hortons mug, grabbed the door with both hands, and tugged. I tried not to grunt. The last thing I wanted to do was sound like Monica Seles in the middle of Yaletown.

The door slid forward with an audible screech on its steel track, and a rush of cool air hit me in the face. Of course. Lucian had an air-conditioned storage locker.

"Hello?" I gingerly stepped forward, expecting to see a pile of boxes, and maybe a necromancer washing his clothes in a bucket. Instead, I found myself in a vast, echoing space with high ceilings and polished concrete floors. It wasn't a storage locker—it was a whole bloody warehouse.

I saw an office in the corner with windows on all sides, crammed with computer equipment, file folders, and two shiny laptops. A flight of stairs, draped in Noma miniature lights, led to a spacious mezzanine floor. Was that a couch? And a flatscreen? This place was a necro bachelor pad.

The ground floor had been lined with built-in bookshelves, and I spied a great deal of black, leather-bound spines, like the kind you'd see in a lawyer's office. A door in the far corner led to what I presumed was a bathroom.

"Tess?"

I looked up. Lucian was leaning over the balcony of the second floor. He was barefoot, and I could see his toes peeking through the slats of the ledge. He wore a ratty pair of blue jeans and a vintage Led Zeppelin tee, the one with the old guy carrying the lantern. That's right. I was disoriented, to say the least. I felt like I'd wandered into some unaired episode of *Felicity*.

"Nice digs," I said.

"Come upstairs. I'll fix you some coffee."

Sage Francis was playing on his stereo, and I could feel the bassline throbbing in the walls like a heartbeat:

Cuz there's a kink in the armor
A pothole I'm sinkin' in, sharing a drink with my father
It's a family affair, the vanity we share
The water line is rising and we do is stand there.

A family affair. Maybe that's what we were—Derrick and me, Mia and Selena, and now even Lucian. Some crazy, fucked-up, paranormal family. *Square Pegs* with an exclusive all-demon cast.

I started to climb the stairs, expecting them to be rickety, but they felt solid. Had Lucian built them? When did he find the time to build a fucking set of stairs? I suddenly wanted to be on the dark side's time clock. I'll bet he had great medical, too. His teeth were perfect.

"You seem pretty nonchalant about me showing up at your pad."

He shrugged, pouring himself a mug of coffee. "I knew you'd be around eventually."

"Yeah, all I had to do was get sniffed in broad daylight."

The corners of his mouth cracked into a smile. "Vampires

do have a unique security system. Much better than Alarm-Force."

I reached the landing and felt a sharp pang of—envy. This place was amazing. The couch was Pottery Barn, chocolate brown leather and draped with a soft white throw. Beneath the flatscreen was a professional sound system, including a turntable, and sliding drawers filled with CDs and DVDs. Refinished wooden crates in the corner held neat stacks of vinyl, which I instantly wanted to paw through. If he had Earth, Wind, and Fire, I would have to marry him.

Floating shelves displayed pictures and bric-a-brac. It was weird to think that Lucian had this warm and cluttered life outside of his . . . unlife. The right wall was taken up by a gorgeous reproduction of Chagall's *Paris Through the Window*. The golden cat with the human face stared curiously at the parachuting man as he drifted past the Eiffel Tower, barely a white shadow on the canvas. Squares of red, blue, and green dotted the sky, and the borders of the window bled rainbows, its glass invisible. The man with the blue face held a secret heart in the palm of his hand, as the *flaneur* with his cane met the woman in her wide-brimmed hat, floating horizontally across the *rue*. I grinned.

"That's my favorite Chagall."

"They say he drew the parachutist from memory," Lucian replied, "since the first successful jump was in 1912. Can you imagine what Chagall must have thought when he saw some idiot floating in the sky with a giant pillowcase?"

"It must have seemed like magic."

"Yeah. I remember when magic felt like that." He started to reach for a second mug. I handed him the Big-Boy.

"Fill 'er up."

"Jesus. You're not kidding with that thing." He filled the oversized cup and handed it to me, steam curling off the rim.

It suddenly occurred to me that I was standing in a converted warehouse owned by a necromancer, talking about Chagall. And I was kind of happy. It certainly didn't feel like a professional interview. In fact, it felt more like—

"Something to eat?" Lucian offered. "I could warm up some Thai."

"No. Thanks." I tried to clear my head. This whole situation was spinning me around, and he knew it. Always the one in control. Smarmy bastard. "I'm here on business, actually. I need to ask you a few questions."

"Oh?" He took a seat on the couch, gesturing for me to do the same.

Remembering what happened the last time I sat next to him, I chose the nearby chair instead. It was an old rocking chair, stripped and newly stained, and the dark wood felt warm and smooth under my hands. I could feel him in the oak, in the floor, like a subtle vibration. He was everywhere, all over this place. It was driving me crazy.

He smirked slightly at our seating arrangement. "What sorts of questions? Will this need to be recorded for a pending trial?"

"No. It's off the record."

"Then it's not really business, is it, Tess?"

I frowned at him. "It's about the murder of Jacob Kynan."

His eyes immediately darkened. The flirtation was gone. "I'd heard about that, yes. Devorah is ready to burn down the city."

"It's understandable." I reached into my bag and pulled out a manila envelope. "Would you mind looking at some photos for me?"

" 'Off the record' doesn't usually involve scene photos, does it?"

I sighed. "It's complicated. I'm here because Selena sent me. We need your help with this investigation, but we can't be seen"—I almost said "consorting"—"consulting with an outsider. So we have to keep this under wraps."

"And that's the only reason you stopped by? Because Selena sent you?"

I stared at him.

No. I came here because I want to kiss you, even with the golden cat watching us. I came here because I miss your lips, your spit, the smell of your hair, the curve of your thighs. I

*came here because I want to trace every one of your tattoos
with my tongue, like Braille, until they lead me to the dark,
warm center of your power.*

*If you so much as brush against him—your life is over. You
can't touch. Ever. Not even by accident.*

"That's the only reason," I said firmly.

He took the envelope wordlessly. His eyes scanned the pictures, moving over the blood and gore, but he didn't seem to
react.

"How's Mia?"

I was taken aback by the question. "She—ah . . ." I swallowed. "She's fine. She's starting the ninth grade at Lord Byron Middle."

He handed the pictures back to me. "A ritual kill."

"We know. But what kind of ritual?"

"Hard to say. Probably something to do with immortality.
The *coire* is for show, but the boy was probably chosen for
some specific reason." He stared at the photo of Jacob's track
marks. "Was he a runaway?"

I nodded. "We think he might have stayed at the House of
Duessa."

Lucian smiled slightly. "That makes sense. She's a real den
mother. Collects strays and kids with fucked-up lives, like butterflies."

"So you know her?"

He looked up finally. "Is that what this is about? You need
me to get you an interview with Duessa?" His expression
verged on disappointment. "You could have just asked."

"It isn't just that," I said. "We also need access to your
expertise."

"I don't understand."

"Lucian—whoever did this is plugged into the dark side.
He's working with seriously dangerous magic, and he's probably going to do it again. Soon."

A light seemed to switch itself off in his eyes. "And you
think—what—the two of us are related? That we're all part of
some big murder-happy family?"

"That's not what I meant."

"It's written all over your face. You think I can sniff this guy out like a bloodhound. It doesn't work that way, Tess."

"Of course it doesn't." I closed my eyes. "I'm sorry. I didn't mean to be such an asshole, okay? I'm not suggesting that you know who this guy is. But you *do* have a lot more contacts than us. People we can't get to."

"People who won't talk to you," he clarified.

"Basically, yes."

He seemed to mull this over. "What are you going to ask Duessa?"

"We think she must have known Jacob. We want to see if she also knew the other kids that he hung out with."

"His street family, you mean?"

"Sure."

Lucian rolled his eyes. "You can't just walk into Duessa's place and start asking questions like that. She'll throw you out on your asses."

"Then what questions should I ask? Give me some help here, Lucian."

His eyes seemed to flicker when I said his name. It was obvious that he took a subtle pleasure in hearing me ask for help. It kind of made me want to hit him.

"The only thing she values," he said slowly, "is trust. She has to trust that the kids who live in her place won't fuck up and bring the cops—or worse. She has to trust that when she hands out food, condoms, and clean gear, the kids are actually going to stay safe. And she has to make sure the dealers, the punters, and the kiddie trolls don't get too close. It's a delicate balance, and there's really nobody to help her."

"What about the other shelters?"

"They share resources, yes, but they're controlled by the government. Duessa's House is invisible—only a few normates have any idea that it exists at all."

"So how can I earn her trust?"

"The only way I can vouch for you is if I show up in person."

I shook my head. "Selena's not going to like that."

"Selena Ward is a good cop, and a pragmatist. She'll see

reason. Besides, it's not like you're putting me on the pay-roll."

Hearing a death-dealer call my boss a "good cop" was more than a little disorienting. What was his basis for comparison? I felt my stomach churning. I'd spent all morning trying to decide if I should tell Lucian the truth. Now felt like the right time. He was willing to help without anything in return, and I couldn't let him walk into something this complicated without knowing the whole score.

"We might be looking at a serial investigation here," I said. "There've been two previous murders in the past four weeks. They were both young girls, from—magical—families."

He frowned. "In the city?"

"No, in Ontario. But we think the killer is jumping borders."

"That's an awfully big jump, don't you think? And why skip the prairies? He'd have an easier time killing there."

"Something about Vancouver is attracting him. We don't know what."

Lucian stared at his hands. "Duessa must know about this by now. She'll be even more suspicious of you."

"We're not the enemy."

"But you'll only draw attention. If someone in our community lets the story slip to a normate journalist—she'll have reporters and news vans crawling all over. That would be enough to destroy the House completely."

"So we'll be careful. We'll let her control the interview."

"It's not that easy. You'll have to prove to her what your reasons are for mounting this investigation in the first place."

I blinked. "What do you mean? We want to catch a serial killer."

"Yes. But where do the kids fit in? Sure, they're the victims, but are they going to have a voice here? Are you going to treat them like human beings? If she thinks for a second that you plan to use one of these kids for bait—"

"Jesus, we'd never do that! You know we wouldn't."

"But she doesn't. And that's where the trust comes in."

I sighed. "Well, it's going to get complicated. Selena's got a profiler coming in—some academic dude from Ontario—and he's supposed to come with us."

"Another outsider?" He shook his head. "That's not going to look good."

"Derrick's coming, too. So that makes four, including you."

"Who's the profiler?"

"Miles Sedgwick."

Lucian's eyes widened. "He's good. I've heard about him."

I made a face. "Apparently, I'm the only one who hasn't."

"Well, Sedgwick's presence might actually work in your favor. If Duessa's also heard of him, she might feel more comfortable."

"It seems like we're doing an awful lot to put this chick at ease."

Lucian smiled. "You'll understand when you meet her. Duessa is someone—that you don't want to piss off."

"Is she a demon?"

"Possibly."

"Great. I'm starting to feel like my whole social circle is composed of demons."

"That's life, isn't it?"

I looked at the golden cat by the window. He was smiling at me.

"Yeah. That's life."

5

In the months since Selena had taken over Marcus Tremblay's old office, the stacks of paper and colored file folders had only increased, slowly breeding and multiplying until they threatened to overwhelm every inch of free space. Aside from a framed portrait of Selena and her husband, Gary—who was shorter, wore glasses, and smiled with surprising normalcy at the camera—nothing else had changed. The room's sole window, which had once overlooked a small square of park outside, was now completely obscured by books, binders, and legal broadsheets. Selena's desk managed to hold two bulging in-trays, a printer, a laptop, and various islands of paperwork that had been tagged to death with adhesive notes. I saw that she'd unplugged the phone and shoved it into a corner, where it sat lifelessly, unable to blink or buzz. It was only a matter of time until the receptionist figured out why her extension wasn't picking up.

Selena herself seemed to have grown organically out of the chaos, like a piece of chiseled marble, a glorious secret released by some Renaissance expertise from the insensate debris around her. Leather jacket folded over the back of a chair, fingertips clicking as she mechanically filled out another online report, her face reflected the sallow light of the computer screen.

"Tess. Derrick." She didn't bother looking up. "Have a seat—somewhere."

I took the chair across from the desk; Derrick, looking around in confusion without seeing anywhere to sit, finally just stood behind me. I felt his knuckles against the hard plastic behind my shoulders.

"Miles should be here in a few minutes," Selena said. "His flight was late—something to do with a lightning storm in Toronto."

"He didn't have a private jet?" Derrick rolled his eyes.

Selena kept glaring at the computer screen. "Experiencing a little Torontophobia, Siegel? I'd keep that under your hat. We don't want to piss off the expert consultant who's kindly agreed to work with us for back-alley wages. Right?"

"Right. Of course." He managed to look embarrassed.

"*There.*" Selena clicked a button and finally looked up. "You have no idea how many subpoenas and requisition forms that psycho Tremblay left behind. You'd think a killer would be more anal-retentive about doing paperwork, but as it turns out, he was the disorganized schizophrenic variety. Just our luck."

"Are they at least sending you some help?" I asked. "An intern, even?"

"What do you think?" Her eyes were surprisingly mellow. I found myself scanning the surface of the desk for an empty bottle of Jagermeister. "I just get e-mails about budget constraints and cutbacks. The entire city is in a slump—they've cut funding to every social program imaginable, and the CORE thinks that we have to fall in line. We can't 'appear' to have too much money, since at the end of the day we still have to pay taxes like any other facility, and it could look suspicious."

"The last thing you need is an audit," Derrick said. "I've heard that most of the people who work for H&R Block are vampires."

"Vampires I could deal with. *Netfile?* Don't talk to me about it." She sighed. "Anyways, don't worry about it. We always manage to get by. Your concern is figuring out what links these three victims."

"I spoke with—my contact." To Selena's credit, she didn't say anything wry about my dealings with Lucian. Maybe she was just too tired. "He can get us a meeting with Duessa, but he'll have to be present. She won't see us otherwise."

"If Duessa trusts your boy, then it's fine—he'll have to be there. The lady isn't easy to see."

"How come everyone seems to know about this Duessa woman but me?"

"Because we're all trained professionals," Derrick replied blandly.

"Because Siegel likes to hang around the break room and soak up gossip is more like it," Selena said, giving him a look.

"So—a little of both columns." Derrick flashed her a smile. "Either way, I do know what I'm talking about—sometimes."

There was a knock at the door. I looked up and saw a trim guy, about Derrick's age, standing in the doorway. He was shorter, five-nine maybe, but solidly built, and his blue button-up shirt clung to his shoulders in a way that made me notice. He had dirty blond hair and brown eyes, which seemed to dart quickly over each and every object in the room. Maybe he had a photographic memory.

"Miles Sedgwick." Selena stood up. He crossed the room and shook her hand. "Selena Ward. Nice to meet you." Her voice seemed to ring more clearly as she spoke to him, and I noticed that she maintained eye contact. I guess big shots from Toronto don't get the standard Selena mutter-and-ignore-you treatment. It made me bristle slightly.

He nodded and smiled at her, and she made a gesture with her hand, encompassing both of us. "This is Tess Corday and Derrick Siegel, the primary investigators on this case."

She kept looking at Miles as she introduced us, like we didn't even exist. Great—this was getting off to a wonderful start. I'd be photocopying and running errands for this guy in no time.

I was about to say "Nice to meet you" when Miles turned to

me and started moving his hands. The motions were quick, but from what little I knew of ASL, I recognized them as sign. He fingerspelled M-I-L-E-S with an oblique gesture to himself, then brought the middle and index fingers of both hands together, like two people meeting for the first time. He ended by tracing a slight circle in front of his chest with the palm of his right hand, and pointed to me. *Nice to meet you.*

Great. So I was an asshole. I was the biggest asshole in all of assholedom. Miles wasn't self-important. He was hard of hearing.

I clumsily mimed the gesture back to him—probably screwing it up—and fingerspelled T-E-S-S. It was hard to get my stiff and unpracticed fingers to distinguish between the E and the S handshapes, which both looked like closed fists.

Miles raised an eyebrow. Derrick began to snicker.

I glared at him. "What?"

Miles made a stylized L shape with his right hand, the thumb barely brushing his chin, and then smiled approvingly.

"You just told him that your name is LEZZ," Derrick clarified. "He fully supports your gay pride."

"Oh Jesus . . ." I forgot to look at Miles. "Tell him that—"

"It's all right." I was startled to hear his voice, which was soft and slightly nasal—but only slightly. "I'm severely deaf, but I can read lips. It helps if you keep eye contact with me when you're speaking."

I turned back to him. "Sorry." My hand hovered in front of me as I tried to remember the equivalent sign. "It's, um, been a while—I mean—my ASL . . ." I did remember that one, which I managed to execute slowly: fingers clasped netlike for "American," as if we were all one big happy family; then two index fingers rotating for "Sign," and finally, both hands in parting L shapes for "Language." I was rather pleased with myself. I could almost sign at a kindergarten level.

Miles made a slight face. "Please—don't use SimCom." When he saw my expression, which was probably blank with noncomprehension, he smiled and managed to look sympathetic. "Simultaneous Communication—when you sign and speak at the same time. It's very distracting, like watching a movie with foreign subtitles. They mostly just do that on television."

"Shit. Sorry."

"No, I appreciate the effort. But we can just talk like this"—he smiled—"until your ASL gets better."

"Derrick's fluent," I said. "If I suck, you can blame him, since he taught me."

Miles laughed and turned to Derrick. His hands moved quickly—both rose upward, palms facing him, fingers spread in front of his chest; then he put both of his fists together and had one travel in a half circle around the other, like the movement of a clock; finally, he brought the middle and index fingers of both hands together smoothly, facing perpendicular, fingers barely touching in the R position, and made a gesture that encompassed both Derrick and me. He raised his eyebrow. That meant it was a question. I think it was: *How long have you two been partners?* Or maybe, *Are you dating?* God, I hoped it was the former.

Derrick rolled his eyes. His hands moved almost as quickly, but Miles was still obviously faster and better at signing. Derrick held out his right hand at a slight angle, then traced the index finger of his left hand along the thumb of his right, lightly, as if outlining a vein; then he pointed to himself, tapping the crown of his head with a slight flourish. The movement shifted again, and he brought both hands with index fingers extended to his left shoulder, then out again, proffering something (or saying *ta-da*). Finally, he placed his left palm over his right, both thumbs up, then slid his right palm down and forward, as if on an invisible track.

Miles guffawed. The laugh was so warm, it actually qualified as a guffaw.

"What did you say?" I looked from Derrick to Miles. "What did he say?"

Miles grinned. "He said, 'Sometimes he thinks since birth.'"

"God, you're such a bitch."

"Okay, let's wrap this up," Selena said firmly. "Tess, you've represented your department proudly, as usual."

I glowered at her, but said nothing.

"Miles," she continued, facing him, "why don't you tell Derrick and Tess exactly why you're here, and how they can help you with this investigation."

Wasn't he supposed to be helping us? Obviously, Selena still thought that Derrick and I needed supervision.

Miles nodded and turned to us. His hands started to move—almost, it seemed, of their own volition—but then he obviously remembered my ASL deficiency and thought the better of it. He spoke instead, his voice soft: "I do contract work as a profiler for the Mystical Crimes Division in Toronto. My specialty is analyzing degraded materia flows and linking them to organic and man-made substances—in particular, narcotics."

"I thought you profiled serial murders," Derrick interrupted.

"Yes. I do. But I'm not a psychological profiler—I'm a *biometric* profiler. Sometimes we're called haptics."

"He profiles spaces," Selena clarified. "He can read materia flows like Siegel here can read minds." Her eyes narrowed. "Well, on a good day."

Miles looked at Derrick and smiled, almost shyly. Then his hands flickered through shapes, so fast they were almost indistinct. He brought both fists downward with the knuckles facing out, index fingers half extended in the X position. He gestured at Derrick, then mimed the act of reading a book with both hands open. He touched his right hand to his chest, and ended the sentence by tapping his head, eyebrow raised. Even though the movements were almost too fast for me to pick up, I still had a good idea of what he'd asked Derrick.

Can you read my mind?

Derrick looked embarrassed. He started to sign something back, then cleared his throat and shook his head.

"No. I wouldn't do that."

The ghost of a grin lasted for a minute on the profiler's face. Then he shrugged and turned back to addressing all three of us.

"Selena asked if I could do some profiling at the original

crime scene. I'd also like to be present for any interviews that you conduct. I'm trained and I know how to handle myself in a fight, so you don't have to worry about that."

"Maybe you can teach Derrick how to shoot properly." The words were out of my mouth before I could stop them.

Derrick flushed. Miles just grinned.

"Well, I could give you a tutorial, if Detective Ward is willing to let us book some time at the MCD shooting gallery."

"That's *not* going down as overtime," Selena replied, giving Derrick a firm look, "so don't even try to submit it."

"I'd also like to speak with the head of your toxicology lab," Miles continued gamely, "once the narcotic samples have been properly analyzed."

"That'll be our next stop, probably," Derrick said. "Right, Selena?"

"Yeah, you should all go bug Carla King. She rushed the prelim results for my interview with Devorah, but she'll have something more substantial now. After that, you can go pick up Agrado. Unless he'd rather materialize out of the shadows."

"I think he'd prefer the car ride," I said, flashing her a look.

Jesus. A telepath, a necromancer, and a profiler, all sharing the backseat of Derrick's rusted-out Festiva. It was going to be a colorful ride. I hoped that Miles wasn't too necrophobic. Or at least no more so than I was.

"I actually still have my luggage," Miles said sheepishly, gesturing outside, "so if we could stop at the hotel, that would be great. It's—um . . ." He reached into his pocket and unfolded a worn piece of paper. "The Holiday Inn at Broadway and Cambie."

"The *Holiday Inn*." I looked at Selena pointedly. "Wow. The CORE spared no expense this time."

"Budget cuts." Selena smiled apologetically. "You know how it is. I'm sorry, Miles, but it's all we can afford at the moment."

"Oh no, it's fine. Just as long as they allow pets."

Selena nodded. "We checked beforehand, and they're fine with it."

"Pets?" Derrick frowned. "Did you bring a cat or something?"

"My dog, actually. Baron."

"Is someone bringing him to the hotel?"

"No, he's waiting outside in the hallway."

Selena's eyes widened. "You got a dog past the security desk?"

Miles gave her a reassuring look. "Baron is quite charming when he wants to be."

Derrick's smile was almost childlike. "Can—we meet him?"

God, I forgot about his sweet, wholesome love for dogs. I was a cat person all the way—screw the unconditional love. I wanted something that withheld, like a real human.

Miles shrugged and looked at Selena. "He's trained to stay. But I guess I could call him if you want. He likes meeting new people."

Selena rolled her eyes. "If it gets you all out of my office faster—go right ahead. Call the pooch in. Then all four of you can go down to the tox lab. Just make sure he doesn't poke his nose into a DNA sample."

Miles turned to the doorway and shouted: "Baron!" With his slight lisp, it sounded more like *Ba-won*, and I wondered which name the dog actually answered to. Probably just his master's voice. I used to have a cat who only answered to "Get off the damn table."

I heard a *thump*, and then a gorgeous brown and white spotted dog loped into Selena's office. He was much bigger than I expected—probably a good ninety pounds of solid muscle—but he balanced on slim forepaws as he stood quizzically in the doorway. His eyes were the color of a Mayan hot chocolate. His tail was tipped with gray.

"Hey, handsome." Miles gestured, and Baron walked calmly over to him, completely unfazed by meeting three new people in a strange place. Miles tapped his chest, and Baron put his paws up, mouth open, obviously excited—but still an exercise in control. He gave Miles a tentative lick to the chin, as if to say, "Everything good?"

"That dog is better trained than my husband," Selena observed.

Miles grinned. "Yeah, he's just being good for strangers. As soon as we get to the hotel room, he'll start running in circles like a hellion."

Derrick got down on his hands and knees, and as if this gesture was more than he could possibly endure, Baron jumped up and began licking him fiercely. Derrick giggled and wrapped his arms around the dog's neck, scratching behind his ears and saying something that resembled *"whooz-a-guuud-boi-ohyesheisohmygoodness-whooz the best boi ever in the whole world, yes, mister-puppy-sir—"*

"Oh Jesus, I think we've lost him," I said apologetically to Miles.

"It's Baron's fault. He's totally unfaithful." He watched Derrick playing with the dog, and his eyes seemed to soften.

"Sorry." Derrick rose, trying to reclaim some of his dignity.

"Too late now. He's yours for life." Miles pointed at Baron, who was staring open-mouthed at Derrick as if he'd hung the moon. "What did I tell you? Faithless."

"In my experience," I said, "most men are."

"Don't drag your love life into this," Derrick warned.

"Yes. Please—no more dragging anything into this office." Selena gave us all a pointed look. "You can drag whatever you want into the tox lab, and then Carla can have fun dealing with it. But your director has paperwork to do."

"Of course." Miles patted his thigh, and Baron was at his side instantly, waiting for further instructions. "I can put him on a leash if you'd like."

Selena waved her hand in an air of general defeat. "It's fine. It was a pleasure meeting you, Miles."

"You, too." He looked at Derrick and me. "Are we ready?"

I doubted it.

"Sure." I put on my best, most expert smile. "Let's go."

The toxicology lab used to be part of one big Se-rology unit—a happy DNA family—until the division got too massive and entangled to control. Apparently, the old director got so tired of staining histopath samples from demons and analyzing short tandem relay patterns from warlock DNA that he just walked out one day, never to return. So it was split into DNA, controlled by the lovely and acerbic Ben Foster (don't forget the PhD at the end of his name), and tox, which was run a bit more loosely by Carla King. Ben made me crazy, but Carla was like an oasis of wry sanity in the midst of the MCD. She hated three things: gossip, bullshit posturing, and incompetence. And if she was in a good mood, she could run a sample through the GCMS in less than two hours for you, provided that you asked nicely and didn't look over her shoulder.

Carla was looking through a scanning electron microscope, which delivered pictures with colors and shapes so weird they might have been taken on Mars. This was her baby: the Hitachi Field Emission scope, which could look into your red blood cells and observe the tiniest bit of fibrinogen, or clotting material, as it was born within the platelets and thrombocytes. It took voyeurism to a new level. I thought most blood smears looked like a bunch of purple fish eggs under the HFE, but that's just me.

"Hey, Carla. Selena sent us for Jacob Kynan's tox panel."

"Oh, sure." Her eyes stayed glued to the lens. "Welcome to the histology drive-thru, folks. Just pull up to that window over there, and we'll get your order with a side of fries as soon as it's ready."

"I want Biggie Fries, then," Derrick said. "If this is Wendy's. Is it Wendy's?"

Miles gave Derrick an odd look. I realized that he couldn't read Carla's lips, since she wasn't looking at him. I cleared my throat.

"Pretty please, Dr. King? We have a guest."

Carla looked up, saw Miles, and smiled apologetically. "Crap. Sorry . . ." She extended her hand. "Carla King."

"Miles Sedgwick." He shook her hand. "I'm consulting on this case."

Carla made a gesture so quick I almost didn't catch it: She touched her index finger to her right ear, then to her mouth, and raised an eyebrow. The more polite way of asking: *Are you deaf?*

Miles nodded. "I read lips."

"That's good, because my ASL really stinks." Carla shrugged. "I'm learning for my niece, but all I can really do is ask her if she wants cookies."

"Well, that's an important question." Miles grinned. He held out his right hand palm upward, then made a motion with his left, fingers scrunched up, as if he were cutting out dough. "I think *cookie* might have been my first sign."

Derrick chuckled. "It sure wasn't the first one I learned."

Miles turned to him with a smile that was almost devilish, and his hands flickered through shapes: He raised both hands parallel, palms facing together, then reversed the motion and brought them down, as if laying cards down on a table. Then he shook his head, smiled, and wiggled his fingers under his chin, ending with a quick C shape against his forehead. It was a funny kind of slang, but I got it: *Bet not, you dirty boy.*

"Detective Sedgwick!" Derrick's eyes widened. "I'm surprised—how could you impute such dirty thoughts to me!"

Miles rolled his eyes. He touched his right index finger to his left palm, then arced it away, to suggest a spatial relation. Then he held out his right hand palm upward and placed his left hand over it, fingers clenched, as if picking something up. He drew his closed fingers up to his forehead, then spun both index fingers around each other and pointed to Derrick with a raised eyebrow.

Where did you learn to sign?

Derrick replied with a sign that I'd never seen before: a quick C shape next to his eye, then closed fingers, thumb and index touching. There was no mistaking the expression on his face: pride. A rare thing to see with Derrick.

Miles looked startled—then impressed. "Gallaudet! How?"

"Exchange program. I did an ASL certificate there."

This was news to me. I hadn't seen Derrick this enthusiastic about something in a long time. Guess it didn't hurt that Miles was a cool glass of water with sparkling eyes and a cute dog. I couldn't compete with that.

"Did they—ah . . ." He struggled for the words, then abandoned them and made three quick handshapes instead. He brought two fists together and mimed breaking them apart, like you might snap a twig; he swept his right palm in Derrick's direction, and then, with a grin, brought his fingertips together twice in a sign that I didn't recognize.

Derrick giggled.

I frowned. "Break your—*balloons*?" I asked.

Derrick broke into laugher, and was joined by Miles.

"I think it was *bust your balls*," Carla said, also smiling. "But I could be wrong."

Miles gave her a thumbs-up.

Great. I could already envision the rest of the day—Miles and Derrick in their secret ASL club, laughing at remedial girl.

"Yeah," Derrick said. "They really did *break my balloons*." He dared a glance at me, and was met with permafrost. He cleared his throat. "Anyways—um—it was a great experience. But we should probably get back to the tox panel."

Carla shrugged. "Doesn't bother me. I'm sick of looking at cell cultures."

"Selena's a bit testy, though. We don't want to incur the wrath of *la diva*."

Carla nodded. "Got it. Well, I already gave her the prelim. Jacob Kynan had traces of morphine and another degraded substance, rhGH, in his blood."

"Human growth hormone," Miles clarified. "The body produces it naturally as a somatoform chemical, but it's also the only known trace left behind by Hex once it's been fully metabolized."

"That's right. Drugs like Hextacy don't metabolize the same way as heroin and cocaine, but they still leave something behind. We call it 'protein 191,' which is the building block of human growth hormone. Generally, the only clue of Hex use we can find in a victim is a perimortem spike in HGH just before time of death."

"What about the morphine?" I asked.

Miles, who'd been looking at me, answered: "Morphine is

a metabolite of heroin. So the Hex was probably cut with heroin. Dealers use a wide variety of cutting agents: starch, acetaminophen, procaine, benzocaine, or quinine. None of it's particularly good for you, even in low doses."

"We didn't find any of those substances," Carla told him. "Which means that whatever he consumed was damn near pure."

Derrick shook his head. "The poor kid must have been out of his mind! Are we sure that he didn't die of an overdose before exsanguination?"

Carla sighed. "I doubt it. Hex also stimulates rapid-fire production of fibrinogen and other clotting substances in the blood, like albumins. Normally when you get cut, your bone marrow kicks out some cells—called megakaryocytes—which produce fibrin. The fibrin causes your blood vessels to constrict, which clots the blood."

"When you're on Hex," Miles added, "the vasoconstriction factor is about three times as potent. It almost mimics a vampire's ability to heal damaged tissue."

Carla gestured to the SEM. "See for yourself."

I sat down in her chair and looked through the lens. Jacob Kynan's blood was like a thriving metropolis on the glass stage. His erythrocytes swam by like scarlet, ovoid creatures, following the pull of some ancient tide. I could see the platelets gathering—they looked like crystalline jellyfish—and something in the corner, a spreading green stain, which I assumed was the Hex. When the green touched the platelets, they went absolutely crazy, multiplying in a frenzy until they became a knotted mass of white fibrin, pulsing beneath the scope.

I stood up. "So the Hex kept him alive instead of killing him." I could taste something awful in the back of my throat. "The killer knew that. He wanted Jacob alive as long as possible. Wanted him to feel his own life ebbing away."

Carla looked grim. "You'd have to confirm with Tasha, but from the shallow arterial wound that you described, I guess it would have taken nearly ten minutes for the boy to bleed out."

I nodded. "That's exactly what Tash said."

"But that still doesn't make sense," Derrick added. "I mean, there are lots of ways to keep someone alive with a wound like that. Why give him Hextacy? Unless that was part of the ritual."

Miles frowned in concentration, trying to track all of our conversations simultaneously. It was probably exhausting.

"Do you think he gave Jacob the Hex to make him more manageable?" I asked Miles directly. "Would it slow down his nervous system, or speed it up?"

"Hextacy stimulates the GHB that our brains already produce naturally," he replied, looking a bit relieved that he didn't have to follow me with his eyes. "Gamma hydroxybutyrate is a depressant, so it would slow everything down for him—relatively speaking. But when the GHB reacts with the organic materia in the Hex, it produces a massive power spike. Hallucinations, tachycardia, erratic respiration—"

"The last acid trip you'll ever have," Carla said.

Miles nodded. "Some mages claim that they can focus the high. It's what allows them to do complex spellwork—like a speed freak who can only paint or write when he's flying on meth. But the way you've described this kid, and from what I've read, I doubt he had that kind of focus. So he'd just be tripping. Probably terrified."

"I think that was the point," I said. "This killer's a real prize. Likes to find himself victims who can't fight back, then gives them the trip of their lives."

"Is there any way to trace the drug back to a dealer, or a specific batch?" I asked Carla. "Sometimes LSD gets printed in a distinctive way, right? Microdots with rainbow colors and pictures of unicorns, or 'windowpanes' made of gelatin—anything recognizable that could lead us somewhere?"

She shook her head. "Like Miles said, Hex barely even metabolizes. It's colored green sometimes to distinguish it from other liquids, but there's nothing traceable. And Hex dealers aren't your average soldiers pounding the street. They're hidden."

"But there's always a chain of command," Miles added.

"We just have to follow the product. First we find ourselves a crack dealer, a normate—"

"And he'll lead us to a supplier, who might know a name." I smiled. "They always give themselves up eventually."

"But first we have to go through Duessa," Derrick said. "If anyone's going to know the dealers operating at street level, it's her."

"Good luck," Carla said, returning to the SEM. "I'm ordering a flow-cytometry test for the Kynan kid—it'll analyze any degraded DNA in his splenic tissue. Might give us a more precise time of death."

"Thanks, Carla. You're the best."

"You know it." She waved at Miles. "Nice meeting you."

He smiled. "You, too."

Derrick gestured toward the door. "Are we ready to pick up the necromancer?"

Miles stared at us in horror. "What necromancer?"

I exhaled. "God. I'm never ready."

6

Hamilton Street was packed with cars and flush with reflected street-light when we parked outside Lucian's warehouse. Derrick swore as he maneuvered around the fragments of cobblestone and pockmarked scars in the pavement, all remnants of a time when Yaletown used to be the warehouse district. I stared at the puddles and the silvery lux of the street and all the expensive shoes as they hurried by. Umbrellas sprung open in harmony like black and checkered butterfly wings as hipsters and businesswomen and students all hurried to protect themselves from the weather. Umbrellas in Vancouver were more of an accessory than a tool. I could hear faint strains of mellow blue jazz circulating from Aqua Bar across the street, where the next generation of urban pros mingled with visiting actors and other glitterati who'd come to "Hollywood North" for lush scenery and cheap production costs. You'd be amazed at how many action scenes shot on the gritty streets of New York were actually filmed in downtown Vancouver with only a minimum of creative editing.

That's what my life could use right about now. Some creative editing. The role of Tess will now be played by Lauren

Ambrose from *Six Feet Under*, a much kickier version of me with better, natural red hair.

"So this is where necromancers are living these days," Derrick observed. "Nice shoe shopping, but does it afford easy access to body parts?"

"Shut up. Just wait here and I'll get him."

"No need. Looks like he's coming out."

Lucian was just sliding the door closed behind him. The outfit was vintage: black Defiance, Ohio T-shirt with a chocolate brown velvet blazer thrown over it. Blue jeans (painter, not skinny), black boots, most likely Caterpillars judging from the thick soles. *Hi, I'm a necromancer, and I'll be fixing your furnace today as well.*

"He looks like an extra from *Gossip Girl*."

I glared at Derrick. "Be nice."

Miles was quiet in the backseat. After we dropped off his luggage (and Baron) at the hotel, I thought for a moment that he might opt out of this trip entirely. But he climbed back into the car like a trooper, saying very little on the ride over. I didn't blame him. Trying to explain why we were employing—and I used that word loosely—the services of a necromancer was more than a little tricky. As a biometric profiler, he'd doubtlessly surveyed more than a few gruesome deaths engineered by that particular community, and working with one probably didn't sit well with him.

I turned around and gave him my most reassuring smile. "Lucian is good people. Don't worry. You can trust him."

"Debatable" was all he said. But he seemed to relax a little.

I got out of the car. Lucian's aura was on the down-low, but I could still feel his power curled and waiting, like a sated cat. He grinned at me.

"Thanks for coming," I said. "I really appreciate it."

He kissed me on the cheek before I could stop him. "Any time."

Fuckity-fuck.

I quickly opened the door to the backseat and all but shoved him inside. "Meet Miles Sedgwick. He's a profiler from Toronto."

Lucian buckled up and then extended his hand to Miles. "Lucian Agrado."

"I know who you are," Miles replied. He didn't take Lucian's hand.

"Huh. I see my reputation precedes me."

Derrick quickly signed something to Miles in the rearview mirror: both hands sweeping over each other palm downward, then waving in a quick circle in front of his face, like buzzing bees. *Don't worry.* If only it were that easy! But Lucian caught the motion. He turned to Miles, and I watched his hands flicker: a gesture toward Miles, then both hands pointing down with knuckles extended in the X position; both hands raised with fingers spread, then down and to the right, one closing over the other, as if pulling and tying a secure knot; finally, a hand to his own chest.

"He's right," Derrick said, although there was a definite note of annoyance in his voice. "You *can* trust him, for the most part."

Miles looked Lucian squarely in the eyes. "It's not trust that you deal in," he said, "or am I wrong?"

Lucian didn't look hurt. He just nodded. "All right. Hopefully you'll change your mind, but if not, I understand."

He was playing the likability card. Still, a part of me wanted to side with Miles. I'd seen what Lucian could do.

"Where did you learn to sign, anyways?" I asked, mostly to change the topic.

"My brother was deaf."

I stared at him. Somehow, I hadn't thought of him having siblings. It didn't fit with the whole nightwalker stereotype. Suddenly I imagined Lucian attending Thanksgiving dinner with a dozen aunts and uncles, grinning as he carved the turkey and passed the cranberries. Thanksgiving at my house was mostly a combat sport.

"Was?" Derrick asked curiously. "What happened?"

"He died." Lucian's face was expressionless. He leaned one arm against the window, looking away from me.

"Shit. Sorry." Derrick started the car. "I mean—"

"It was a long time ago," Lucian said. "Don't worry about it."

I looked at Miles, and saw that his expression had softened somewhat. But he still didn't say anything.

Driving from Yaletown to the Downtown Eastside was always a serious culture shock, even though the two neighborhoods were really less than twenty minutes apart. We made our way up Nelson to Granville, where the club district was just starting to shake itself awake. Punks strolled past the pizza joints and used CD shops, walking their dogs and sharing a smoke, while homeless residents dragged heavy carts, often stopping to chat with each other or commiserate about the city. A guy with a keyboard had set himself up on the corner, and with the window rolled down a crack, I could just barely hear strains of Rick Astley.

Hipsters and UBC students poured in and out of the Urban Outfitters like a tide of cynical coolness, all wearing graphic tees and studded white belts. Probably listening to Taking Back Sunday on their iPods, or maybe Hot Chip.

Shit, actually I kind of liked Hot Chip.

We turned right on Hastings, and the port shimmered in the distance, packed with luxury cruisers delivering rich couples from Texas into the welcoming, liberal embrace of Vancouver. The Centre for Dialogue, a multimillion-dollar kitten project of the University of British Columbia, sat with austere certainty at the corner of Hastings and Richards, and every nearby café was lined wall-to-wall with students tapping frantically at their laptops. But things changed as we drove farther east. We passed the new Spartacus Books—rebuilt after the old place burned down—and then several very different cafés that offered dark, secluded spaces for sparking up a pipe (or even a hookah), if one was so inclined.

Scattered people milled around the War Memorial as Hastings split into Cordova, which led to Gastown. Tourists always thought that Gastown's cobblestone streets and Victorian lamps were some authentic piece of Vancouver's history, but the whole neighborhood had actually sprung up as an attraction in the mid-1970s. Now it was bustling with upscale clubs, expensive bars, and seedy apartment buildings crammed close to million-dollar lofts.

As we got close to Hastings and Gore, on the border of Chinatown, the neighborhood took on a perceptible shift. There were more people on the streets, hanging around the entrances to bars and restaurants, and the convenience stores had iron grilles on their front windows. Cars slowed to adapt to the congestion, and people would often weave their way through oncoming traffic, forgoing the need for a crosswalk. The police presence was strong here, and even though their sirens weren't on, they were still cruising back and forth or just sitting on the corners, waiting for a disruption. No matter what time of day you passed through, you'd see a wagon or a squad car picking someone up. Alleys unfolded like strange chutes or tunnels leading into semidarkness, choked with Dumpsters and fire escapes gleaming like rusted-out iron skeletons against the fading light of dusk. People moved in the shadows, talking and sharing food and shooting up as furtively as possible. Old crack pipes, broken and dirty, seemed like strange coral reefs or silver dollars against the wet pavement.

We passed Hastings and Heatley, where a mix of people were gathering outside the entrance to the Pivot Legal Society. Last year, they'd launched a constitutional challenge on behalf of sex workers. Now they were one of the last legal bastions left in the neighborhood.

"Park anywhere along here," Lucian said.

Derrick squeezed the car into a minuscule space—thank goodness it was a compact—and we all climbed out.

"So, where is this place?" he asked Lucian.

"Hidden."

"Right. And you're going to sniff it out for us?"

Lucian made a face, but before he could say something, I stepped between them. "Let's just get there before it's too dark out, shall we?"

We crossed the street and walked down Princess to the corner of Cordova, about a block away from Oppenheimer

Park. Lucian led us past a chain-link fence and down a narrow walkway, not quite an alley but not actually a street. Miles was visibly nervous, but I didn't have anything reassuring to say. We came to a squat, three-story walk-up that looked like it had been falling apart for the last eighty years or so. The door was locked, but there was no security of any kind. I let myself go unfocused for a moment, and saw a few white threads of materia floating around the door. An early warning system?

Lucian pressed a buzzer. An indistinct voice answered, and he mumbled something into the speaker. A few seconds later, the door popped open. He smiled.

"Showtime. You ready?"

I shrugged. "As I'll ever be, I guess."

We stepped into a foyer, and I saw with surprise that the inside of the building had been gutted and completely redesigned. There were security cameras placed at key angles, and the hardwood floors, despite their age, looked recently scrubbed. Lucian led us down a hallway that terminated in a heavy steel door, warehouse-style. He knocked.

The door slid open, and a vampire greeted us.

I knew he was a vampire immediately. Sure, he looked about twenty-eight or so, with a neat little faux-hawk and horn-rimmed glasses, but he had immortal written all over his genetic signature. He looked bored, slouching in a pair of old Carhartts and a rumpled sweater.

"Please surrender all weapons at the front gate."

To my surprise, Miles opened up his jacket and I saw that he was wearing a Black Eagle fitted shoulder holster. He drew out a Sig Sauer pistol and handed it, grip forward, to Hipster Vampire. It disappeared behind the door.

"Thanks. You'll get it back when you leave."

"I'd better," Miles said.

The vampire looked at me. "Your knife, ma'am?"

My eyes hardened. "It's an athame, not a knife. And don't call me ma'am."

He rolled his eyes. "You'll still have to leave it with me."

"You'll have to tear my arm off first, Belle and Sebastian. Got it?"

Lucian sighed. "Just let her keep it. She can't do any damage in here."

Hipster Vampire shrugged. "Whatev. Just keep it in plain sight." He slid the door open and gestured for us to walk past him. "Go all the way to the end of the next hallway, then turn right, and you'll find the assembly room. She'll meet you there."

Assembly room? Miles mouthed in confusion.

I shrugged. Maybe there was going to be a PowerPoint presentation.

We followed Hipster Vampire's directions, keeping close behind Lucian, since he seemed to know his way around the place. There were doors evenly spaced along the hallway, and I wondered how many people lived here. One door was slightly ajar, and I caught a glimpse of two girls looking bored, watching television. Plastic bins were stacked up against the far wall, labeled SPARE CLOTHES and TOILETRIES. A boy was sitting cross-legged on the floor and eating something that smelled surprisingly good from a Tupperware container. It wasn't a frozen burrito, so there must have been a kitchen somewhere. He caught sight of me and half smiled, fork raised to his lips, noodles twined around it. He had a black eye.

We turned right at the end of the corridor, and were met by an open doorway. The room beyond was obviously the result of knocking down walls and joining old suites together, with its high, vaulted ceilings and exposed brickwork. Pipes and radiators had been painted—green, purple, and electric nail-polish red—and festooned with miniature lights and garlands. The nearest wall was painted with a mural: the ancient Greek hermaphrodites. Not slender androgynes, but the terrifying and beautiful giants, joined face to face, that Aristophanes recalled in *The Symposium*. They looked eminently capable of taking over the world, which was why the Olympian gods banished them.

The farthest wall had been painted entirely black—even the window was blackened—and a glowing pink triangle blazed against it like the face of God itself, with the words SILENCE = DEATH painted in white below it. As I stared at the words, I realized that they were glowing with a very subtle materia flow. I wasn't sure precisely what it was designed to do, but it definitely had a protective vibe to it. I could smell earth and air flows woven in. Maybe something to do with concealing the building? There were bookshelves on either side of the wall, sagging beneath the weight of binders, papers, and DVDs. Most of them looked like AIDS and STD educational stuff, but I also spied law and medical textbooks in the mix.

There were about twenty or so people in the room, but it didn't seem at all crowded. Tables and chairs were set up in one corner, and three girls were playing a board game—laughing and smoking as they rolled the dice. A boy was sleeping on a couch behind them, his fingers just barely curled around a magazine. He looked about eighteen or so, hair bleached the color of margarine, cigarette smoke giving him a sort of uncanny halo like something Donatello would have sculpted. An older woman sat on the floor next to him, tapping a message on her cell phone. A flatiron was plugged into the wall next to her, surrounded by power strips with multiple cords, wires, and extensions snaking across each other and plastered in duct tape. Pillows dotted the floors, along with discarded books, comics, and CD cases. I noticed a young girl in capris and a tight black sweater, shaking her head as she attempted to pick up the debris, her arms already full of random objects that threatened to tumble loose at any moment.

"Dukwan!" she called. "*Dukwan!* Ursa Minor's fucking burnt out again!"

The boy on the couch shook himself awake and groaned. "I fixed it last time. Why you waking me up just for that?"

"'Cuz you're lazy, and I can't pick up after everyone!"

He sighed. "Where'd you put the ladder?"

"Where it always is!"

Puzzled, I looked up—and froze in amazement.

The last time I'd forced myself to stare at a ceiling, what I saw was pure evil: a dead boy hovering in the air, all the blood drained from his body. What I saw this time was the exact opposite. The ceiling had been painted and covered in tiny winking lights—an exact replica of the cosmic mural in Grand

Central Station. Pisces glowed like a scattering of embers against the blue-black sky, while the lines that divided the heavenly spheres shone with crystalline fire. Like Grand Central, the constellations were depicted backward—in homage to the obscure medieval manuscript that the artist had copied them from—but there was also another unique touch. At the center of the stars, rainbow-colored lights had been arranged into a message: WE ALL FAIL.

Dukwan mumbled to himself as he clambered atop a rickety ladder. "At least *hold* it for me, Kim!"

She rolled her eyes, but steadied the ladder for him as he climbed.

"This place is crazy wonderful," Derrick breathed behind me.

I stared at the vermillion curtains, winking with beads and cast-off plastic gemstones, that framed a gorgeous old fireplace whose mantle was cluttered with pictures; two girls asleep on an air mattress, holding each other, fingers linked as they snored quietly; a boy lying on his back with an open book, frowning, his head propped against a sleeping bulldog whose pink tongue lolled against the floor in simple satiety. The dog shifted suddenly, moaning in his dreams—chasing rabbits across a sky dotted with high-rises and pigeons streaking like golden arrows—and the boy paused to scratch behind his ears. One of the pillows next to us moved, and I realized that it was a tortoiseshell cat with eyes the color of spearmint. She untangled herself from the scenery and wandered over, curious, her tail a question mark. Miles sank to one knee, hand extended, and she accepted his touch, beginning to purr.

"Well? Is it what you expected?"

The voice was smooth and masculine, but it wasn't Lucian speaking. I turned around, and standing in the doorway, her smile a mystery, was Duessa.

I'm not sure what I expected. A Hollywood madam, or royalty maybe? Duessa was understated, but beautiful. Tall—at least six feet, probably more—with toned, muscular arms and hands that looked far from delicate. She wore a vintage sleeveless blouse, orange with a golden fleur-de-lis pattern, and black low-rise jeans that showed off a tribal tattoo on her left hip. A few gold charms hung from her narrow belt, and her cream-colored, open-toed sandals were unmistakably Manolos. They made her feet look a bit smaller, but not quite enough to avoid notice. Her long black hair was draped neatly across one shoulder, and she wore almost no makeup. She was carrying—of all things—a can of paint, which she put on the ground. Her smile widened.

"Lucian, *papi*, is that you?"

"Duessa!" Lucian grinned, spreading his arms. *"Luces tan hermosa como siempre—como Helena de Troya, la cara que lanzo mil lanchas."*

She laughed warmly, embracing him and kissing his cheek. *"Seria mas como mil pollas papito—paraditos en atencion."*

Lucian snorted. Duessa made a *tsk* sound.

"Lucian! Donde estabas escondido guapito?"

"Es un secreto."

She shook her head. *"Yo puedo guardar un secreto papito. Mi vida es guardar secretos."*

Miles frowned in confusion.

Derrick signed quickly: both hands with thumb and index fingers pinched together, roughly forming the OK symbol moving back and forth; then his left index finger, pointed like a gun, lightly tapping the air. *Explain later.*

Miles nodded. I hope he planned to explain it to me as well, although I suspected already that most of it was pretty dirty. Lucian's dimensions just kept expanding.

"So what brings you to the House of Duessa?"

Lucian gestured to us. "Some folks from the CORE were hoping for an audience. Tess Corday is the primary investigator, and this is her partner, Derrick Siegel. Miles Sedgwick is consulting from Toronto."

Her eyes widened. "My, my. And what does the lovely Central Occult Regulation Enterprise need from Duessa? Is that still the acronym y'all are using? I remember back when it was COMO, the Conservancy of Mages and Others."

I drew out a picture of Jacob—just a head shot—and showed it to her. "This is Jacob Kynan. Does he—ah—frequent this place?"

Her eyes darkened. "You think I need to see a goddamned picture of one of my own kids? I *know* my kids. I know what that fucking butcher did to Jake."

"I'm sorry—of course you do, Mrs. Duessa."

Her expression shifted like soft clay, and she laughed. "*Missus* Duessa? Lucian, where'd you find this Nancy Drew?"

I got the sneaking suspicion that this wasn't going well.

Lucian smiled reassuringly. "Tess is legit. I'll let her explain, but I can assure you, her priorities are in the right place. The CORE thinks that this guy may be targeting street kids, and they want to work with the community in order to catch him."

Duessa put her hands on her hips. "The *CORE* wants to help us? Baby, let me tell you about the CORE. They're a bunch of shit-eating bureaucrats who don't give a flying fuck about these kids here. If it were up to them, my whole place would be shut down. I don't trust a single one of those neoliberal, candy-assed motherfuckers as far as I can throw them. And I've got a *real* good pitching arm."

"Look"—I raised my hands—"I don't like the CORE any more than you do, I swear it. But they've got financial backing on this. Devorah Kynan has promised her full support, and—"

"*Devorah?*" Duessa shook her head. "You're seriously gonna drag that little tight-assed, holier-than-thou bitch's name into *my* house? Devorah's part of the problem! You know how many times Jake came to me, cryin' about how his mother didn't give two shits about him, how she left him to rot?"

I frowned. "Ms. Kynan said that she gave Jacob a great deal of support, that she helped him with his drug habit—"

"T'ain't a *habit*, sweetbread. Biting your nails is a habit. Shooting heroin ain't a *habit*; it's a way of life. Jake was in deep. Started doing two, three bags a day, when he could afford it. But *Ms.* Kynan wasn't anywhere to be seen. He got clean gear from InSite and the other safe-injection spots. His friends made sure that he used as safely as he could. I gave him a place to come down, somewhere he could sleep safely without getting his shit jacked. But Devorah? That bitch was nowhere."

"That's not what she told us."

Her eyes widened in mock horror. "Sweet Jesus on a stick—a rich white lady, all *lyin'* and shit? Well, Officer, I ain't never heard that one before."

I sighed. "Okay, I see what you mean. She might not be telling the truth."

She folded her arms. "Well, that's nothing new. You can buy anything in this neighborhood except the truth. The truth is what you can never find."

"We just want to make sure this doesn't happen again."

"No—you want to make sure this doesn't happen to Ms. Devorah Kynan again. If it wasn't her son—if Jake's skin was a different color, or if the CORE found him in a dress or some shit—you think there'd be money behind this? You think you'd be in my neighborhood, talking to me right now? All you care about is helping out the rich parents of cute little mages-to-be. The *Occult Riche*."

Lucian looked at me. His eyes said: *Tell the truth. Just always tell the truth.*

I turned back to Duessa. Her look was still, like the surface of a dark pond. There was something in her aura that I couldn't place. Something hard and slanted that smelled of damp earth, broken stone, ash, and the weight of immeasurable years. How old was she? What power was she hiding?

"You're right," I said. "The CORE speaks one language, and that's money. But do you really give a shit where the support is coming from, just as long as it's coming? They want to help. They've given us carte blanche to do whatever we can. And it's not the—what did you call them?—shit-eating bureaucrats. It's not them you have to deal with. It's just us. And we're good people. I swear."

Duessa looked from me, to Lucian, to Derrick, and finally her eyes settled on Miles. She raised an eyebrow. "What about you, sweetheart? You got kind eyes, and you ain't said nothing about this so far. She said you're 'consulting'—and usually, that means you don't know jack shit about what's going on here. Am I right?"

Miles shrugged and nodded. "Pretty much."

"So what do you think? Is she straight-up? Is the CORE gonna help me and mine, or are they just gonna fuck with us like they always do?"

Miles looked at Lucian. Oh fuck. He didn't like necromancers, and so far, our case wasn't exactly looking all that clean by Toronto standards.

"I think they're a bit crazy," he admitted with a smile. "But I trust them. I think you can, too. They want to help."

Duessa smiled. She glanced at Derrick for a moment, and her eyes sparkled. "What about you, mind reader? You wanna take a peek?"

Derrick frowned at her. I felt a slight stir of energy from him, and then his frown deepened. "You're blocked," he said. "It's like reading a brick wall."

"Of course."

"So why did you ask?"

She chuckled softly. "Because I wanted to see if you'd try. Apparently, kiddo, you got a real pair of low-hangers on you."

Derrick blushed and turned away.

"You know," Lucian added, "Duessa gave some telepath a lobotomy once, years ago, because he didn't like her shoes. Or so the legend says."

"They're still telling that story?" She shook her head. "Shit, I've heard all kinds. That I tore some pimp's throat out for looking at me funny. That I set fire to some warlock because he insulted my outfit. Those stories have always been plentiful."

"Are they true?" Derrick asked quietly.

Duessa smiled. "Take another look. I'll open the brick wall a crack."

Derrick looked at her closely. I felt the power stir in him again—I couldn't see it, since it was dendrite materia, psychic energy, as different from the elemental energy I manipulated as Lucian's necroid materia. But I could still feel it, like a ripple.

Duessa's expression didn't change.

Derrick went white. I'd never seen the color drain from his face so fast. He looked away sharply.

I put a hand on his shoulder. "You all right? What did you see?"

He shook his head. "Just . . ." He looked at Duessa, then away. "Just do whatever the hell she says."

"Be nice," Lucian scolded. "They're just *niños.*"

"Yeah. You're right, baby. They don't know about the old ways—the blood of it all, the shadow and the dust. And the call. Across all those fucking years." Her eyes went distant for a moment. Almost sad. Then she looked at us again. "They're above-grounders. Not like us."

I looked at Lucian. His expression was untranslatable.

"No," he said. "Not like us."

Duessa shrugged. "Well, we might as well get to business, then. You want to learn more about Jake, you'll have to talk to Wolfie." She gestured to the boy who was leaning against the bulldog, still reading. "They were friends. And Wolfie's kind of a jack-of-all trades around here. Into everyone's business, but in a good way."

"That sounds like a start," I said.

"Wolfie!" Duessa made a beckoning gesture. "Come join us, *precioso.* This nice lady from the CORE wants to ask you some questions."

Wolfie put down his book and loped over to us. He was a short kid, a bit stocky, wearing a black Buried Inside shirt with the sleeves ripped off, blue jeans, and army surplus boots— probably from one of the many consignment stores on Granville. He rubbed a hand over his shaved head, and I noticed that his beard was patchy, like it was just starting to grow in. I couldn't tell how old he was.

"What questions?" he grumbled.

The kid had power. Thermal materia swirled around him, like a deep red wine poured out in zero gravity. It coursed between his fingers and along his wrists. I could feel it because my specialty was earth materia, and earth and flame are complementary.

"You're a spark," I said.

Spark was "street" for someone who could channel thermal materia.

He shrugged. "And you're a miner." He pointed to Derrick. "And he's a reader—not a very good one, though."

"Hey!" Derrick scowled.

"And you . . ." His cool gray eyes surveyed Lucian. "Huh. Death-dealer. You guys don't fuck around."

"No." Lucian was impassive. "We don't."

He looked finally at Miles, and frowned. "Weird. You've got a flavor, but you're not like them. I can't quite place it."

"He's a haptic," Duessa said. "He reads spaces. Right?"

Miles nodded.

"So"—Wolfie turned back to me—"what do you want to know?"

"It's about Jake."

"Oh. You wanna know about Jake?"

I stepped forward. "Anything you can tell us would be—"

"You wanna know about Jake *now*? After he's been cut up?"

I blinked. "Wolfie, I know you're upset—"

"You don't know shit." He shook his head. "Fuck all of you."

"Wolfie . . ."

A tongue of flame curled around his fingers. His eyes went red.

"Fuck. You."

Wolfie turned and walked out of the room.

I looked at Duessa.

"Well"—she shrugged—"looks like you got your interview."

7

Duessa agreed to cooperate with our investigation, but I still felt like we were leaving empty-handed, since Wolfie was the one with the real knowledge and he wasn't about to tell us anything. It didn't seem like such a good idea to push a volatile kid with the power to set you on fire. Sparks were always dangerous. And Duessa was—something else. A part of me felt like we were lucky to have made it out of there alive. Even Lucian seemed relieved when we dropped him off at the warehouse.

Pausing with the door halfway open, he grinned at me, a Cheshire cat. "You want to come up for a beer?"

I shook my head. "Got the boys in tow. We still have to drop Miles at his hotel."

"Bring 'em up. I'll bet a few drinks will grease those wheels nicely."

I chuckled. "You're getting that vibe, too, huh?"

"Oh, definitely. They're both adorable, but you know the odds for people like us." His eyes darkened, like coffee spreading over the surface of a ceramic cup. "We don't often get the happy ending, do we? Not after seeing the shit that we see."

I wanted a happy ending. Right that second, I wanted to pin him against the metal door of the warehouse, bury my tongue in his neck, and let the rest of the night sort itself out. Derrick and Miles could drive home. I didn't need to wake up early, and I'm sure I could borrow—

I snapped back to reality. A reality where CORE spies could infiltrate my life and turn over every secret rock, open up every locked chest of memory and transgression. They were ruthless, and all they needed was an excuse.

Lucian was right. No happy endings for us.

"What did Duessa mean when she said that I was an 'above-grounder'?" I asked slowly. "Are you guys in some secret club or something?"

"She was just being maudlin."

"But what did she mean?"

His face did something funny. I thought for a moment that he was going to kiss me, and what surprised me was that I actually wanted him to. Standing in the middle of the Yale-town crowds, beneath the neon and the clouds threatening at any moment to unleash rain, I suddenly very much wanted to do something inappropriate.

But he just brushed my forehead with his lips, and smiled.

"'Night and never mind," he said.

Before I could reply, I found myself staring at a closed door. Huh.

I got back into the passenger's seat, and Derrick gave me a expectant look.

"Well?"

"Nothing. He invited us up for drinks, but it seemed like—"

"A colossally bad decision? Like a train wreck, or NKOTB getting back together maybe?"

I curled my lip. "It seemed like something for another time."

"Huh." Derrick started the car. "So you guys *are* going to see each other again."

"Well, in the capacity of the investigation—"

"Oh, in the capacity of the investigation, yeah, totally." He raised an eyebrow. "Hello, have we met? I'm Derrick, and I can read your mind. This guy is under your skin, Tess. You're letting him in, aren't you?"

"You of all people should know that I never let anyone in."

Miles leaned forward between the two seats. "You're dating Lucian?"

I rolled my eyes. "This isn't college. He's not taking me to a dance anytime soon, and we haven't even slept together." I blinked. "Well, not exactly—"

"Ha and *ha*!" Derrick punched the dashboard. "That night when I slept over! I *knew* I heard the two of you going at it."

"We were not *going at it*. I mean, we fooled around a bit, but then it got—weird. He left. That was it."

"That was it."

"Yes. Do I need to draw you a diagram? It remains unconsummated."

"Does Selena know?" Miles asked.

"Yes, Miles, I told my supervisor all about the sex romp I had with Lucian Agrado. Then we watched *Top Model* together."

"You know, you're a very sarcastic person, Tess."

Derrick laughed. "Irony is like her favorite outfit."

I sighed. "Sorry, Miles. I don't mean to be a dick about this. But my private life isn't really up for debate here. Yeah, I made some bad decisions involving Lucian. But I doubt that anything's going to come of it, and it has no bearing on the investigation."

He shrugged. "Fair enough. I just wouldn't want you to get hurt."

"Do you have a history with necromancers? You seemed uncomfortable—I mean, that's understandable, I was scared shitless the first time I met him. But you seemed kind of—"

"Ready to shoot him on sight," Derrick supplied.

Miles flushed a little. "Yeah. I guess I have some trust issues."

"Does that extend to the whole undead community?" I asked. "Or is it just necromancers you don't trust?"

"It's complicated."

"Man," Derrick said, "what did we ever do before Facebook gave us the 'it's complicated' option? It's saved so many awkward conversations."

"When I say it's complicated," Miles answered, "I mean more, like, maybe I'll tell you after we've gotten to know each other better. Or not. Is that cool?"

"Of course. We're CORE employees. We deal in secrets, remember?"

"Mi vida es guardar secretos," Derrick repeated, smiling.

"Are you ever going to translate that for us?"

"Why don't you just ask Lucian?"

"Why don't you fuck off?"

"You guys bicker like brother and sister," Miles said.

"Yeah. We're closer than most blood relations."

"It's nice. You're lucky."

I saw the moderately priced lights of the Holiday Inn approaching. It seemed like we were consigning Miles to a prison cell with plaid carpeting. At least he had Baron.

"Well, you know"—Derrick had an odd, stumbly tone—"hanging out is always cool. Like, for the case and everything, but also—I mean, if you need something . . ."

Miles gave him a look.

"Like, or if you're out of soap—you know those little hotel soaps—or a shower cap, or something, or if there's nothing on TV except for old reruns of *Law & Order* . . ."

Miles grinned. "I'll give you guys a call. You can come rescue me."

Derrick's whole face brightened. "Of course! Yeah, totally. Any time."

"Good night, then."

Miles got out of the backseat. He waved good-bye, and then Derrick executed a near-fatal left turn at Broadway and Cambie.

"Articulate" was all I said.

Derrick just shook his head. "I'm like a parody of myself sometimes."

I kissed him on the cheek. "You'll always be my hero."

"Well, that's comforting, at least."

We drove east down Broadway, passing the trendy box restaurants—Milestones, Cactus Club, Moxies—where I always seemed to end up on a Friday night sharing garlic mashed potatoes with my parents, since they were such nice, wholesome places. The glass and steel condos gradually gave way to older apartment buildings, flanked by resilient shops that hadn't changed so much as a fixture in twenty years. The technical college campus was a ghost town, and I watched the 99 B-Line driving up and down the bus lanes, diesel engine roaring as it dragged ambivalent undergrads to the UBC campus in Kitsilano. The Rio Theater at the corner of Commercial and Broadway was playing an Almodóvar retrospective. Tonight's film was *La ley del deseo. The Law of Desire.* If I understood how that particular law worked, maybe my life would be easier.

We turned onto Commercial Drive, whose name couldn't possibly be more ironic, since it was a haven for hippies, activists, lesbian parents, librarians, teachers, grad students, and anyone else willing to share a rambling old house with eight other roommates. Punk houses stood next to walk-ups, co-ops, fair trade coffee shops, art spaces, and Beckwoman's, which started out as a tent near Grandview Park and eventually became a sprawling shop filled with beads, scarves, and other beautiful ephemera. The drive was ethnically Italian, and definitely had the best coffee and cannoli in town, but it had become a melting pot over the years. It was where you ended up if you were either broke and discovering your politics, or if you had a bit of cash (but not a lot) and wanted to start a family.

I rented a place here when I was still an undergrad, a shitty old walk-up on East Fourth, close to the train. The front door was always broken, and the entryway smelled perpetually like baking fish. But I did kind of love the little Hobbit hole. I'd walk down the alley between Fourth and Third to buy produce from Norman's Fruit Salad, or a big, greasy paper bag full of chips from Belgian Fries. I remember having dinner with some artist dude once at Café Deux Soleils. I wanted to get in his pants, but he just kept talking about his craft and how awesome Marina Abramovic was.

I never really thought I'd come back here. So weird how things change.

"Traffic is pretty light," I said.

"Yeah, everyone must be at a protest."

I chuckled. "Wouldn't that be funny if, like, there was a protest so far-reaching that everyone in the whole neighborhood showed up?"

"All the houses would empty out. There'd be no one left to give you dreads or fix your henna tats."

"Or replace the screen on your pipe."

We drove past Grandview Park, where a small group had gathered to watch some fire dancers; Havana was bustling across the street, serving up huge pitchers of *mojitos* that swam with fresh mint leaves. The street got quieter as we turned down Middlesex, a tree-lined way that bordered Victoria but was still removed enough from the thoroughfare to seem almost like another world. The apartments turned into three-story houses with towers and turrets, windows thrown open and breathing out various types of music, laughter, and other noises.

Derrick parked on the street, and sighed. "Home."

"Yeah. Always feels good."

We both got out. The house facing us was a ramshackle Victorian, a real money pit that would probably require some form of renovation for as long as we both lived. But it also seemed to have endless possibilities. Narrow staircases, original parquet floors, bay windows that opened onto a shared courtyard with a communal garden that was just starting to offer up beans, carrots, and giant cabbages. A patio where you could actually sit with lemonade—well, lemonade and vodka, let's be serious—and watch the hipsters on bikes as they made their way to WISE Hall for some concert or community buffet.

The cherry trees were exploding like crazy fireworks, and as I looked up, I could see a light in the kitchen window.

"You know," Derrick said as we made our way up the front steps, "I still remember the look on your face when Selena called you that night."

"You mean when she told me about Cassandra's will? And the house?"

He nodded. "You must've shit a brick when you heard."

How else are you supposed to respond when you find out that a demon left you an entire house in her will?

Well, not *this* house. After I met Cassandra, she must have realized something. Maybe she foresaw her own death, which I wouldn't put past her. Whatever the case, she had papers drawn up supporting my legal guardianship of Mia, who wasn't technically her niece, but no terrestrial court in the world was going to be able to prove that. Cassandra had left a very convincing paper trail.

When the lawyers told me how much her old house in Elder was worth, I almost passed out. I mean, it wasn't a princely sum by any means, but to someone like me, it was a hell of a lot of money. So I sat down and discussed it with Mia—did she want to keep the house, or sell it? I wasn't about to screw with all of her memories.

Her answer was firm. Get rid of it. Start over. Sometimes a teenager's clarity could be downright scary.

"Remember when we closed escrow on the place?" I asked. "You and Mia did the chicken dance—"

Derrick smiled. "And then we ate so much naan at Tandoori Palace, I thought I was going to throw up all over the front steps."

"Well, the beers didn't help. Since we're such awesome parents."

"Mia had a soda! And you barely drank any."

"Still . . ." I stared at him. "God, Derrick, what do we know about being parents? You're gay, and you don't even have pets! I set fire to my Jem doll because I wanted to see what her hair looked like when it was melted!"

"We're doing fine so far. I mean, she's still alive, right? No broken bones. No piercings that we know of."

"Except for the part where she's a protomage waiting to explode. You feel ready to deal with that when it happens?"

He shrugged. "I was kind of hoping she'd just go off like a nuclear device and take all of us with her. Then we wouldn't have to sort it out later."

I shoved him. "That's not funny."

"No. It's not." Derrick shook his head. "But I don't know what else to say. We're a fucked-up family. And the kiddo's got a lot more than magic to deal with."

"Those injections are expensive—lucky the CORE is covering it."

"I doubt they want to deal with the alternative."

"A fourteen-year-old vampire on the loose? No, probably not."

Mia seemed to take her VR+ diagnosis well, although with her it was always hard to tell stoicism from numbness. She was a cipher most of the time. And when I tried to remember what it was like to be fourteen, all I saw were vague images, flashes of parties and bad boyfriends and tragic outfits. Imagine being fourteen and living with Derrick and me, since your parents were dead and your aunt—who'd never really been your aunt to begin with—was gone. It blew my mind.

"We're going to have to rent the downstairs out soon, if we want to afford what's left of the mortgage," Derrick said.

"Yeah, but you'd be surprised how many communications or gender studies majors are willing to rent a bedroom next to the furnace."

I fumbled with the keys for a moment, but then the front door opened by itself. Mia stood in a square of lamplight, holding a bottle of cream soda. She'd recently graduated from softpunk clothing to full-on androgynous grunge, and was wearing old khakis from Value Village, a knit brown sweater, and wrist cuffs.

"Sorry we're late," I said. "We had to go downtown for a while."

"I'm fourteen, Tess. I don't mind being a latchkey kid."

"Did you break anything?" Derrick asked.

"Just your laptop. I spilled a Slurpee on it, and then I decorated the whole house in silly string, 'cuz that's how we crazy teens are rolling nowadays."

I slid my shoes off, sighing in relief, and went barefoot up the stairs to the living room. The nonworking fireplace had become an unofficial archive for pictures, bric-a-brac, and anything else that seemed to belong, including Mia's "top student in French Immersion" medal from grade six, and one of Derrick's old bowling trophies. He used to be king (or queen) of the Grandview Lanes. The wood floors gave off a rich, dusty smell, with the memory of years coiled in their blond, uneven lines. We'd painted the living room a light purple with just the hint of gray—well, Derrick and Mia mostly just got paint all over each other while I worked—and two salvaged brass lamps threw their shadows against the far wall, outlining the succulents and other plants growing quietly on the windowsill. My toes sank into the checkered carpet at the foot of the couch.

The TV was on—I think it was a documentary on meerkats. Mia's homework was spread across the couch.

"I made pasta," she said.

"What kind?"

She shrugged. "Whatever we had."

I walked into the kitchen and saw a pot simmering on the stove. Mia had opened up three different packages of noodles, and then added tomato sauce. She'd also raided the spice cabinet, and I saw a mess of chopped herbs on the cutting board. What other teenager felt the need to use fresh basil? Light from the courtyard was ghosting through the kitchen window. Our neighbor was smoking in one of the patio chairs. She was middle-aged, her brown hair tipped with silver, but the way she held her cigarette made her look like a beautiful young film star. Her eyes were distant, untraceable, as she delicately blew smoke through her nostrils. I often wanted to join her, but there was something about her silence, her aloneness, that seemed inviolable.

I grabbed a piece of fusilli and chewed on it thoughtfully.

The alphabet magnets on the fridge had been arranged to spell "caryatid."

"Not bad," I said, returning to the living room.

"Next time leave me the credit card so I can order Thai."

"Like that's going to happen." Derrick collapsed in the overstuffed chair by the couch, which we'd bought from some punk kids across the street. "Although ordering Thai sounds like a capital idea."

"So, did you find out more about who murdered that boy?" Mia sipped on her cream soda, totally unaffected, as if she'd just asked us if we picked up the laundry.

I winced. "You know we're not supposed to talk about cases."

"Come on. Remember when *I* was a case? That wasn't so long ago."

"You were never just a case."

"But you know what I mean. I've seen . . ." She faltered for a moment. It was so rare when Mia let herself actually show some emotion. I saw it flicker for a moment on her face, and then she pushed it down. "Whatever. I can deal."

"Yeah." Derrick smiled. "You're a real gladiator. But this shit—er, stuff . . ."

"You can say shit, Derrick. I think I've heard those bad kids across the railroad tracks using that word a few times."

He rolled his eyes. "Fine. This shit is bad. You don't want any part of it."

"But I'm always part of bad shit."

"Not this kind," I said firmly. "If I could lock you in your bedroom, I would. As it stands, I want to get away from this case, not delve further into it. Talking about it will just ruin the rest of my night."

"I'd totally escape if you chained me to the bed."

I immediately thought of what Devorah said to Selena. *Even if I locked him in the basement, he'd find a way to wiggle out and escape through a window.* Suddenly I wanted to bolt the doors and keep Mia from leaving the house until she was twenty. Or maybe never. But I knew better. The kind of shit we were trying to protect her from didn't find locked doors to be a problem. It could get in if it wanted to. It could always get in. That was why I'd stopped sleeping at night.

"How was school?" I asked her.

"Oh my God, it was *amazing.* In social studies we learned all about the Mesopotamian empire, and it was like—mmmm—the knowledge just *poured* into my brain like a magical rainbow."

I gave her a level look.

"Same as always. I argued with my fascist English teacher, who's forcing us to read *Catcher in the Rye* but won't let me talk about how, like, ridiculously gay it is. And apparently the boys in class are allowed to say 'bros before hos' all the time, but when I mention Emma Goldman, it's like I said a bad word."

"Can't you just watch *Family Guy* like other kids?"

"Seriously? Would it make you feel better if I was normal?"

"We wouldn't recognize normal if we saw it," Derrick observed.

"Sometimes, it's like"—Mia shook her head—"*gaaahhh,* all I want to do is burn the whole stupid school to the ground. And it's like, I *could*, and nobody knows that, and it just drives me crazy!"

Derrick and I both stared at her.

"I wouldn't *do* it."

"You couldn't," I corrected. "You don't have that kind of focus yet."

"It doesn't take a lot of focus to burn down a building," Derrick said.

"Okay, responsible parenting tip number one: When I tell Mia *not* to burn down the school, you're supposed to back me up. We need an undivided stance on arson."

"*No* to arson," Derrick said. "Unequivocally."

"Want a beer?" Mia asked.

"*No* to underage drinking!"

"Geez, it's not like *I* want one. Besides, you buy PBR. That's just gross."

Derrick turned to me. "What's the policy on sending our teenage ward to the kitchen to bring me a beer?"

"I think you should get your own."

"Yeah." He rose. "Fair enough."

I looked hard at Mia.

"What?"

"You're not drinking, are you?"

"No, I really prefer the powder, Tess."

"Be serious."

She laughed in exasperation. "No, I'm not drinking! I'm not smoking pot, or doing any other drugs. I don't have time— I'm trying to get ready for my AP exams."

"I thought those weren't for, like, three years."

"Hello? I'd like to *not* go to some state school, thanks. I'm preparing."

"What about Douglas College?"

"Eww, Dougie Day-Care? Please!" She shook her head. "And UBC is for surfers and burnouts who, like, want to learn creative writing and bang their drums or whatever. I'm thinking Berkeley, maybe Penn State."

Derrick returned to the living room, handing me a beer. "Those schools are pretty far away," he said.

"That's kind of the point."

"Why must you wound your guardians like this?" Derrick sighed. "After we provide you with the finest in discount clothing and Costco products?"

"You guys have powers. I'm sure you'll find a way to visit me."

"It'll take some magic to afford that tuition," I said.

"Yeah, but I'm sure the CORE will cough up something. I mean, they're, like, totally afraid of me, right?"

Derrick and I exchanged a look.

"So," Derrick said, "have you decided what department you'll be terrorizing yet?"

She shrugged. "They're pretty much all the same."

We were silent for a while after that. I watched the meerkats on television. Derrick sipped his beer, and I stared at mine, still unopened.

"Is *Idol* on?" Derrick asked.

"In twenty minutes," Mia replied.

I popped the top off the beer. It was bitter, but nice. Like it should be.

8

I woke up to a message from Lucian Agrado on my voice mail, which was odd, since normally I just got calls from BC Hydro or my mother:

> *Tess. Duessa wants to meet with you tonight, 11 p.m. at the Sawbones. She may have gotten Wolfie to come around. Don't be late, and go alone.* [A pause.] *But don't worry. I think she likes you.*

That was supposed to put me at ease? The Sawbones was an infamous pub in the Downtown Eastside that made the Cambie look elegant. It was a known locus for the mystical sex trade in particular, and folks of all persuasions could be seen nursing a beer there, waiting for their fetish to walk by. Mages often had kinks that only a certain type of professional could satisfy, and even less savory demons could get a little touch, if the price was right and the particulars were agreed to in advance. Vampire pimps often facilitated the deals, although some pros still managed to work alone. The sections of the Canadian Criminal Code designed to punish sex workers for "communicating" and pimps for "living off the avails" of prostitution didn't really extend to places like the Sawbones. There was a police presence nearby, sure, but most cops were afraid to make a bust there. Over the years, it had become—like the Downtown Eastside itself—a gray area.

The next message was from Ben Foster, the head of our DNA lab. Ben was supercilious to a fault, but he knew his job inside and out, and was regularly published in normate forensic journals. He sounded almost—rattled.

> *Tess, it's Ben from DNA. I've found something on the—ah—*coire, *or cauldron, left behind at your crime scene. It's—well, it's a bit odd. Beyond my purview, I think. You should come down and have a look as soon as you can.*

Ben spent most of his time manipulating gel probes of warlock and gargoyle DNA; once, he'd seen a Hydra blood sample spontaneously regenerate and attack one of the interns. If he was describing something to do with Jacob Kynan's case as "a bit odd," I needed to get my ass in gear.

I headed to the bathroom for a shower, and found Derrick standing outside in his pajamas, looking defeated.

"Colonized?" I asked him.

"She's been in there for at least twenty minutes. Can I pee out the window?"

"Just aim away from the garden." I banged on the door. "Mia! You may have forgotten, but there are other humans living in this house. Humans with biological functions. Derrick is about to embrace public urination."

"*God!* Go use the bathroom downstairs!"

"The plumbing still needs to be fixed, and I'm not in the mood to wield a plunger. Just hurry it up, emo."

"I'll be done when I'm *done.*"

"You'll be done when I come in there and axe-murder you!" Derrick yelled. "And don't think I can't read your mind through this door!"

"*Ooh*, so scared, Jean Grey! What am I thinking *right now*?"

Derrick concentrated for a moment. Then he scowled. "We really need to stop buying her thesauri. She has a frightening vocabulary."

"Maybe we should buy a parenting manual," I suggested. "They might caution against threatening to axe-murder your adopted kid."

"I was only kidding."

"No you weren't!" Mia called back. "I'm dialing social services!"

"Jesus, why did we get her that cell?"

"Because it had lots of weekend and evening minutes." I sighed. "Okay, I'm using the downstairs bathroom. Wish me luck."

Derrick made the sign of the cross. "Go with God."

After fifteen minutes and some creative moves with a plumber's snake—thanks for the tutorial, Dad—I was off and running for the train. Derrick needed the car, since he was driving Mia to school, and I didn't relish the thought of waiting for both of those drama queens to get dressed and ready. It's like, you have three matching pairs of jeans and a million T-shirts that look exactly the same, except for a cool button here and a pocket there—*why* must it take forty minutes to choose an outfit?

That's why I woke up early. This ensemble didn't arrange itself.

Ten minutes later, I'd already spilled coffee on the new brown leather jacket from Zara (luckily it was a coffee-colored shade). The goal was to protect the blouse, at least, since I could always throw the jacket over my shoulder. The train downtown was packed like Shinjuku Station in Tokyo, except that everyone on this train had sideburns and was reading McSweeney's. Well, not everyone. There was one pissed-off redhead, furiously scrubbing at a corner of her jacket while balancing a coffee cup on her knees.

Guess who that was?

By the time I got to the lab, residual caffeine had made me jittery, and I was afraid that my pupils might be dilated to scary Amy Winehouse levels. Ben Foster greeted me with a curt nod, which was about all you'd ever get from him. I wondered if his PhD in genetics from Duke had required some sort of complete personality erasure, or the forcible injection of academic bitchiness.

"Tess. Thanks for coming."

"You used the word 'odd,' " I said, removing my sunglasses. "That's very bad. It made me move twice as fast."

"Well, it's the only descriptor I could think of, to be honest." He gestured to the nearby computer. "Come take a look."

There was a copy of D-AFIS running, our more extensive version of the FBI's Automated Fingerprint Indexing System. The print displayed on the screen was slightly fuzzy, and its tented arches and loops seemed to fluoresce with green light, like underwater lichen. Fingerprints are hard to read. The lines and contours of each print form a delicate, dermal calligraphy—loop, whorl, arch, tented arch—and even the prints of identical twins can be different, since minute genetic or stochastic changes occur in the womb. But *seeing* those differences requires a great deal of expertise, and even our computers get fooled sometimes.

Some demons don't produce visible prints, since a friction ridge on your fingertip or palm needs oil and amino acids to leave something behind. Not everyone sweats. That's why we're often reduced to hunting for aura traces.

"This print looks old," I said.

"It is. The sample we found was quite degraded. There was also a trace of blood left behind with the print."

"Not surprising. There was a lot of blood in that hotel room."

"This blood didn't belong to Jacob Kynan."

I stared at him. "You think it's from the killer? Did you get a hit in D-CODIS?"

"Well—yes, and no."

"Spit it out, Ben."

He scratched his head. "The sample was old. Very old. We

had to use a Teichmann Test to analyze it." He smiled as his inner geek was activated. "It's sort of interesting, actually. You have to heat up the bloodstain, and then you put it next to a solution of glacial acetic acid and chloride. The fumes mix to form these hematin crystals, which look out of this world under the SEM. You know, a few years back I wrote this paper on crystal nucleation for the *Journal of Forensic Studies* . . ."

I stared at him levelly.

Ben blinked. "Right. Anyways, we did eventually get a hit on D-AFIS, as well as D-CODIS. But it's not what you think."

"So what is it?"

Ben tapped a key, and a new window opened on the screen. It was a woman's mugshot. Grainy and distorted, as if it had been transferred from old film, or maybe even microform. She was young and sporting a black eye, which her curling red hair couldn't quite obscure. Unlike most mugshots, her expression wasn't one of defeat, or lip-curling defiance. There was a silent strength in her eyes. A certainty.

"No," I whispered. "No way."

She'd obviously looked different when I saw her last. Older. Far more beautiful, with an aura that could burn you alive. But the resemblance was there all the same. Caitlin, the former vampire magnate, had once been this girl who was staring at me with sharp green eyes.

Staring at me, however impossibly, from an arrest record marked June 18, 1908.

"Back then, fingerprinting technology was brand new," Ben said. "But we started transferring the archival stuff to digital memory about fifteen years ago. Now we use the same WSQ storage system as the FBI, which compresses each image to 500 pixels. This old ten-card came up as soon as we ran it through D-AFIS. Back then, of course, we didn't have DNA, and ABO-typing had only just been invented by Karl Landsteiner. But the police sometimes took samples for what were called 'venal cases.' That's how we got a match through D-CODIS."

Height and weight measurements were all handwritten in faded script, as well as curious "trunk" and "middle" stats.

Under COMPLEXION was written: "sallow." I half expected to see "opium-eater" penciled somewhere. The charges included pimping, prostitution, and crimes of nature.

"This would have been only a few years after Faurot introduced fingerprinting in New York," I breathed. "Our records go back *that* far?"

"This is the CORE," Ben replied. "I'd be surprised if their records didn't go back to well before the Flood."

"Maybe Noah was one of the founding members." I peered at the faded image. "Caitlin Siobhan. So that's your real name."

"The Contagious Diseases Act was on the books in Canada by 1865," Ben said, "so the police took special care to detain any prostitutes who might be infected. Back then, a client could catch up to five years in jail. And sometimes a flogging."

I stared at him. "This is crazy. She gets arrested in 1908, and her print ends up at a crime scene literally *a century* later?"

Ben shrugged. "I don't know how it got there. But I can tell you this: There's no way a severely degraded print could survive for that long. With a nonporous surface like cast iron, a print could last fifty, maybe even sixty years. But not a hundred. And not in any condition for us to actually make a match."

I blinked. "So you're saying—what—someone got ahold of a hundred-year-old print and *stuck* it on the cauldron? Planted it? Is that even possible?"

"I guess there are some mediums that a print could survive on for that long. I mean, if the conditions were right—"

"Like, in a museum?"

He shrugged. "Maybe. On some kind of gelatin plate, kept away from the elements—I suppose it might be possible. Quite improbable, though."

"So, either this print was passed down like a family heirloom—"

"Or," he said simply.

"Or?"

Ben swallowed. "Or it was taken and kept by someone who knew Caitlin Siobhan when she was still a sex worker. Back in 1908."

I started to leave a frantic message on Derrick's cell—mostly just a mix of screaming, profanity, and creative adjectives—but then I thought the better of it and just texted him: *Heidi Klum*, our agreed-upon holy-shit page. I didn't want to risk bleeding any case details over the phone. And this was a world-class hemorrhage.

Caitlin Siobhan.

The vampire magnate, whom I hadn't seen in nearly a year. Not since she'd exiled Sabine, who'd tried to kill me several times. Caitlin, one of the most powerful immortals in the city, who'd vanished immediately afterward, leaving the vampire line of succession in absolute chaos. Leaving a poor seventeen-year-old boy named Patrick lying in a hospital room somewhere.

And there she was. A young, scared sex worker, or maybe even a madam, staring at me from a hundred-year-old arrest record. Not Caitlin the magnate, but just Caitlin, so young and far away. A century-old fingerprint. A tracery of shadow and silver that barely cohered on our monitors.

What happened to her? Did she get bitten after the photo was taken? Maybe she was working for some turn-of-the-century vampire pimp. Of course, back then, we wouldn't have been able to detect the vampiric viral plasmids in her blood. So she could have already been a vampire. Just patiently making her way through the ranks. But she must have pissed someone off. Someone with a very long memory.

I walked along Cordova, wishing I'd worn flats as the pockmarked street sloped down toward Gastown. The Sawbones was at the end of an alley, flanked by an expensive antiques dealer and a tacky tourist gift shop. Beavers and snow globes next to Georgian end tables and rugs that would cost a year's pay. Vancouver in a nutshell.

The normate crowd knew of this bar's existence, but anyone who went there was tied to the mystical underground in some way. Nobody was innocent.

There was no glowing sign at the end of the alley, just a door with a rune painted on it. Basically, *Welcome, warlocks, necros, liars, thieves, and anyone else looking to get their mystical freak on.* I touched the handle and felt an unpleasant tingle move across my body. Much better than a security camera. Materia flows hung like streamers around the door, without even an attempt to hide them. No funny business, and no normates allowed without express invitation.

The door clicked open, and as the air flows designed to conceal the noise inside parted for me to enter, I heard laughing, shouting, and demonic expletives. Some of the languages you might overhear in the Sawbones were mostly all consonants, so even when the demons weren't pissed off, they still sounded like it. Normally I brought Derrick to translate, but he was spending the night in, and he hated coming here. He claimed that some of the patrons didn't have "minds" to read, so much as big, gaping black holes of synaptic evil that sucked him in, giving him nightmares.

The décor was not what you'd expect from a paranormal bar. The floors were refinished hardwood mixed with tile, and the bar itself was a stainless steel L with vintage diner stools placed evenly. The space was a warehouse conversion, so tall pillars with their Doric capitals intact supported a bronze-paneled ceiling, and industrial fans moved lazily overhead, recirculating the stale and beer-soaked air. There was no chalkboard with specials—if you didn't know what you wanted, you shouldn't be here. And they pretty much had everything, from four-dollar bottles of Canadian to Henbane and Dragonroot on the rocks with a splash of Pepsi Lime.

The brown Naugehyde booths were mostly shadowed, since a lot of the patrons weren't especially partial to fluorescent lighting. But everyone looked human. If you somehow managed to wander in here by accident, you'd really have no idea how much immediate danger you were in. Until a dozen or so pairs of eyes locked on you—some of them without irises or pupils. Some black like the farthest reaches of space.

Duessa wasn't here yet, which was good. I imagined that she wasn't the type of person to suffer lateness well. I grabbed an empty booth near the back. Two necromancers were sitting across from me, and I could smell the necroid materia on their breath, pungent, like a split vanilla pod. They didn't even glance at me. Who knew what they were really interested in?

A very thin waitress approached me. She was probably early thirties, with crumbling blond hair and a mouth that twitched slightly. I noticed fresh track marks on the inside of her arms. No need to wear a long-sleeved shirt and hide it in this place. If anything, it was an advertisement.

"Yeah?" She sniffed.

"I'll have a whiskey sour."

"You CORE?"

"Not tonight." I looked at her evenly.

"Fine. Be right back." She wandered off.

It was a fair question. They didn't particularly like CORE employees poking around in their business. But this place generated a lot of money—money that trickled down to everyone, including members of the CORE. So nobody was about to issue a search and seizure warrant anytime soon. Mostly, it was live and let live. Everyone knew that the Sawbones was a hotbed for drugs, banned occult materials, sex work, and even human trafficking. But places like this had deep roots, and if we tore it down, another just like it would appear at the end of some other random, unmarked alley. We could remove the cause, but not the symptom.

The waitress returned with my whiskey sour. It was strong. Not the best way to make money, but something of a necessity when your customers are demons.

The front door swung open, and in walked Duessa. All conversation stopped. She was wearing a varsity letter jacket and sunglasses, with her long hair pulled into a ponytail. Everyone tried to stare without staring. She barely acknowledged them as she made her way over to me.

"Tess." She kissed my cheek.

I was a bit flustered, and awkwardly returned the gesture.

"Thanks for meeting with me," I said. "I know you must be busy."

She shrugged. "I'm always busy. But this shit's important."

The waitress ambled back over. When she saw Duessa, her eyes widened.

"Hey, Joanie." Duessa smiled. "How you doing?"

"Um . . ." She scratched her arms, then clumsily put them behind her back. "Okay, I guess. Tips are good."

"Mm-hmm." Duessa lowered her shades. "You ever need a place, you know where to find me."

Joanie nodded. "I know. I—um"—she shook her head—"I gotta go—the kitchen, you know, we're awfully busy—"

"Just bring me a club soda, will you, love?"

Joanie nodded and disappeared.

"She used to stay with us sometimes," Duessa said. "She's got mage potential, you know. Very subtle, but it's there."

"I didn't sense it."

"That's cuz it's pushed down way deep." She shook her head. "Baby got herself mixed up in the game. Real mixed up."

"You think she'll come back. To stay with you, I mean?"

"Can't say. If she needs a fix, she might come looking to score, or just for some clean gear. A safe place to sleep. But I doubt she'll be part of the House again."

"How does it work exactly—the House?" I asked. "I mean, is it only for kids with mage potential? Runaways and throwaways?"

Duessa folded her hands. "If I had the space, it would be for everyone. But as it stands, we only have so many beds. A lot of the kids sleep on blankets, foamies, sleeping bags, whatever they can find. People hear about us through the grapevine. We don't advertise through the regular channels, but I know people. They spread the word."

"Normates, you mean."

Duessa chuckled. "Never really understood what that term implied, sweetheart. Nobody's normal. Not really."

"Fair enough. So, you're funded independently?"

Duessa sighed. "I sank most of my own money into the

House. We pay overhead on the magic used to keep it hidden as well, and then there's the cost of supplies: blankets, spare clothes, food. A contact at the needle exchange gives us sterile gear, but the kids aren't allowed to fix inside. They know other spots in the neighborhood—places they won't be bothered. We don't supply any drugs or provide them with a space to shoot up. Just a space to come down afterwards, and information, if they want it."

"And you pay for all of it?"

Duessa gave me a sly look. "I'm not a social worker. Not a philanthropist either. I just try to help where I can. Some of the money comes from outside donors. And the kids give a little here and there, when they can spare it." Her eyes hardened. "I don't force them, and I don't ask. Whatever they give me gets put into an open account, and in the end it goes back to them in the form of supplies. But most of them can't spare anything, so they help with the upkeep."

I remembered the can of paint that she was carrying when I first met her, and Dukwan, the kid standing on the rickety ladder.

"Like a runaway co-op," I observed.

"You could call it that. I try to get them into programs, get them tested regularly—but a lot of these kids are lifers. They get pulled in by warlocks, necros, and other unsavory sons of bitches."

"You seem pretty comfortable with necromancers."

Her eyes sparkled. "There's a big dif between the average zombie rakers . . ." She motioned to the two guys talking across from us. "And people like Lucian Agrado. He and I go back a long time. *Long* time."

"I guess it would be inappropriate to ask your age." I gave her a hopeful smile.

"I've killed pretty girls for less."

I nodded. "Gotcha."

"Lucian"—she sighed—"he's a good boy. He's got a heart. But he's in as deep as I am, so you got to be careful around him."

"Into what, exactly?"

She spread her hands. "The game. The power. Whatever you want to call it. We've both got old debts, if you know what I mean. Lucian would never put you in danger on purpose, but—"

"I could get in the way of something."

"You're already in the way of something." She smiled. "Something with real big teeth. It's old, and it's hungry. And you're pissing it off."

"I'm not sure what we're talking about," I admitted. "Is this about the killer? Or something else?"

She shrugged. "I can't tell you much more. I've got contacts, and they tell me that something's on the move. Plus"—she leaned in closer—"I've seen killings like these before. The same mark."

My eyes widened. "Where?"

"Dig around, and you'll find them. It's had a long career."

"Why 'it'? The killer's not human?"

"What do you think?"

"Well, we know a mage did this, or something with mage training. But there was no aura signature left behind."

"No leftovers, huh?" Her look was calm, controlled.

She knew.

I bit my lip. Telling Lucian case details was one thing, but Duessa?

Still—could I really trust either of them more than the other? It was like choosing between the scorpion and the rattlesnake. The scorpion just had nicer shoes.

I breathed a silent apology to Selena.

"There was a fingerprint."

Duessa cocked her head. "Really."

"A very old fingerprint."

"Well, that fits."

I exhaled. "It belonged to Caitlin Siobhan."

Instantly, I felt something flare to life around Duessa. Flows of materia closed around us, like a network of silencing fabric. She leaned closer.

"That's a powerful name, doll. Be careful where you go tossing it."

"Did you know her?"

She sniffed. "We met a few times. I suppose we respected each other."

"Was she still a sex worker when you first met her?"

"She was a madam. But she turned the occasional trick." Duessa whistled. "That was a long time ago. Your people must have a great filing system."

I nodded. "We matched the print to an arrest record from 1908. Were you living in Vancouver back then?"

"You still trying to suss out how old I am?"

"It's just a question."

Duessa grinned. "No. I wasn't living here. But I was—living."

"Can you think of anyone else who would have known Caitlin back then? It was long before she became the magnate, so I'm not sure how powerful she was."

Duessa shrugged. "She was B-list, even back then. Someone to watch. Plenty of people—and things—knew her, or knew of her."

"Anyone obsessed enough to hold on to her fingerprint for a hundred years?"

"I couldn't say."

"No, of course not." I sighed. "But it would take something uncanny to preserve a print like that. Necroid materia, perhaps?"

Her mouth twitched. "Could be."

"And someone would have to hold a pretty stiff grudge. Or have a long memory."

"Or maybe it sees time different."

I blinked. "What do you mean?"

"Power does things to your perception, hon. Maybe it foresaw this ages ago. Maybe it always knew what it was going to do. That would make things easy."

"You're saying this thing can see into the future?"

"I'm saying everyone's got different eyes. And maybe it can part the veil more easily than most. But that's only a theory."

"So why is it going specifically after the children of

mages? And where does Caitlin fit in? She's a vampire, not a mage."

"That, I don't know."

"This—thing . . ." I stared at her. "Have you seen it? Do you *know* it?"

"I've seen a lot of fucked-up shit in my time, baby. And maybe I caught a glimpse of it once or twice. Maybe I walked into a room just as it was leaving, or I heard it somewhere in the distance. But no. We've never been officially introduced."

"So it's some kind of demon?"

"It's some kind of something." Duessa smirked. "That's for sure."

I massaged my temples. Now this was going in circles.

"And what about Wolfie?"

Duessa's expression shifted. I saw the fierce den mother appear again. "I met that boy when he was still a cub, working the docks. He's got power—you saw that—but a real short fuse. That's why I keep him close."

"But he knew Jacob Kynan."

"He and Jake were tight. Not out, though. The rest of the House didn't know."

"Why would they hide it?" I frowned. "I mean, a relationship between two guys doesn't seem out of the ordinary, especially among kids who see the type of stuff that we see on a daily basis. Most mages are pretty liberal when it comes to gay issues."

She chuckled. "It's a bit more complicated than that. Wolfie's got more than just the usual 'issues,' as you call them."

"Like what?"

"You'll have to ask him. I can nudge him towards you, but I can't push. He's like glass on the inside—you understand? Blow on him, and he'll break."

"Well, keep nudging. He knows something."

"So do you."

"Well . . ." I stared at her. "Wait, what do you mean? The fingerprint?"

"It's in there somewhere." She touched my head lightly. "Just keep digging."

"That's a big load of fuzzy."

"Ain't no oracle, sweetheart."

I closed my eyes in frustration. "Fine. What about the Hex? Did you know already that Jacob was using it?"

Duessa shook her head. "He was just moving up to heroin, last I heard. Wolfie would know more. But I don't think that child had much experience. He mostly followed the other hoppers around, did whatever they suggested."

"Hoppers?"

"The younger dealers. Slingers at street level."

I nodded. "So he wasn't into Hex, that you know of."

"No. And you're gonna have a hard time finding someone who'll admit to using that shit, let alone dealing it."

"We were hoping to make contact with a midlevel dealer and go from there."

"No guarantee he'll give up a name."

I sighed. "We don't have a lot of options at this point."

Duessa looked thoughtful for a moment. "Patches," she said finally.

"Excuse me?"

"Patches. He slings dope and tina mostly, some powder every once in a while. But a while back, one of the girls said she saw him with some Hex. It ain't much, but he might lead you to someone who knows more." Her mouth flattened. "You gotta know, this kid is dumb as a fucking sack of hammers. Once did a re-up in broad daylight. Couldn't hide a stash if his life depended on it. But somebody owes him a favor."

"What do you mean?"

"Someone's protecting him. And they might be supplying him with Hex, too. Push him the right way, he could pop out a name."

"Wouldn't he be a lot more frightened of you?"

She laughed softly. "He would. And that's why his little hoppers can smell me coming a mile away. He gets a whiff of the Lady on his trail? He'll split. But for you"—she winked—"charming little protestant white girl like yourself, upstanding citizen and all that, he might take you for a mark. And then he'll stick around."

"So, he'll deal with me if he thinks I'm stupider than he is."

Duessa laughed again. "Baby, you done almost got the hang of this game. Now thanks for the drink, but if you'll excuse me, I'm late for an appointment."

She rose.

"Thank you, Duessa," I said. "Your cooperation means a lot."

"You just be careful, girl." Her eyes bored into me. "When the shit starts to fly, don't you bring it anywhere near *my* House. Got it? And don't be trying to use Wolfie for some bullshit wiretap operation, neither—cuz *this* thing? It's not going to stand still long enough for your little microphones and computers to record it. This motherfucker's old and *smart*. You just remember that."

Before I could protest, she was already out the door.

She hadn't touched her club soda.

9

It was surprisingly warm as I made my way down Cordova to Waterfront Station, the transit hub for downtown Vancouver, which throbbed with students and businessfolk in the morning but would be almost deserted by midnight. I passed Steamworks, the trendy pub on the border of Gastown, where you could buy raspberry ale and mingle with the fit, upwardly mobile twentysomethings who ruled this neighborhood. The south harbor gleamed in the distance, a shifting surface of black with the outline of cranes and tankers wavering like metallic skeletons. Burrard Inlet was a barely distinguishable crescent of scattered lights and lapping waves, all the ships asleep for the night, dreaming of global commerce and the shouts of stevedores. The station itself, with its neoclassical elegance, was built by the Canadian Pacific Railroad in 1914 as a grand terminus for trains crossing the Rocky Mountains. It was actually designed by an architectural firm out of Montreal, which may have explained why it looked so much older and more irritably dignified than the surrounding buildings.

I walked under the purple awnings and through the heavy doors, and the deep, monastic silence of the empty terminal settled over me. Gothic lamps cast shadows against the polished marble floor, and I was suddenly aware of how loud my footsteps sounded, like some clumsy tourist bursting into a holy place. The vaulted ceilings and iconic pillars only reinforced the idea that this was not simply a terminus station, but rather the Church of Transit, where railway, skytrain, and ferry lines all intersected in a sacred calculus of globalization. God moving over the face of the helipad.

I walked beneath the brass clock, noting that it was twelve twenty, which meant that I still had an hour before the last train left the station. If I was lucky, there'd be one waiting for me downstairs. I hurried through the concourse, past the CPR walkway that led to the ferries and West Coast Express trains, and down the escalator to the subway platform. It was broken, as usual, and my boots clicked madly against the uneven metal steps as I made my way precariously down. I always had nightmares about the possibility of an escalator fatality. Bouncing face-first off all those sharp edges and angles. You'd end up at the bottom looking like a piece of ground hamburger.

The subway platform was empty, save for a punk couple with matching jean jackets making out in the corner. I shivered and stuck my hands in my pockets, doing the useless little walk-hop-glance that people always do when they're waiting for the train to come, as if enough perambulation will make it arrive faster.

I dialed home and got the answering machine:

You've reached Tess, Derrick, and Mia. If you're calling from the lab, you can reach us on our cell phones more easily at—

I waited for the beep. "Guys, it's me. Pick up. Mia, if you're on the other line, I'm going to kick your butt, since this is a school night and you should be in bed. Or studying something. Like trigonometry. I don't know, whatever they're doing in ninth grade now that you're probably way too smart for. Anyways, I'm just catching a train from Waterfront, so I'll be home soon. And I'm starving."

I clicked the phone closed and sighed. Maybe Derrick picked up something on his way home. Something that could be microwaved. I was craving coffee, but if I had some now, I'd never sleep. And it wasn't like I slept very much to begin with. The dreams wouldn't let me.

"Excuse me, miss—do you have the time?"

I was amazed that she'd managed to disengage her lips from her boyfriend long enough to ask me a question. I turned around, and in a split second I was able to register two very important facts—

The girl was a vampire.

And I was fucked.

Her hand closed around my throat, fingers pressing into both carotid arteries and cutting off the blood flow. Twelve seconds until I blacked out.

"Tess Corday." She smiled. Her fangs were in full view. "They didn't tell us that you were such a tiny little bitch. Snapping you into pieces will be like—"

Luckily, vampires always felt the need to make a bad simile, which gave you a very small but useful window for retaliation.

I dropped to my knees and yanked her down with me, the motion jarring her enough to loosen her grip. My elbow caught her in the face. Before she could tighten the vise again, I pressed my palm against the tile floor, reaching down for the vital flows of earth materia that were much stronger and nearer in a place like this. Green light flared between my fingertips, bringing with it the sweet smoker's rush of fire-kissed power that coursed through my lungs, dizzying. I flung the strand of materia outward, not even bothering to channel it through my athame, just letting it burn as it hissed pure and electric from the palm of my hand.

She flew backward and rolled, slamming against the far wall of the platform. A human might have broken something, but she'd only be a bit dazed.

Dammit. Why was it always *vampires*?

Her boyfriend leapt at me full-on. Amateur move. He couldn't have been more than a few decades old, and was still infatuated with his own strength. Good for me, since it meant he was less experienced. The downside was that he was also more willing to take risks, so I might end up dying in a more creative way. I heard crucifixion was back in vogue. That'd be different.

I sank to one knee and slashed my athame in a wide arc, hoping to slice deep into one of his calf muscles, or—if I was lucky—the popliteal artery. Sever it and you win a prize: blood spurting like a chocolate fountain at a wedding. He did a left sidestep to avoid me, and I reversed the motion, thrusting up hard with both my wrists around the handle. The skewering blow didn't connect, but it did force him to twist awkwardly in midair. He landed on his knees a few feet away.

I reached into my bag and unfastened the secret pocket where my Glock slept, waiting patiently. After realizing that even sweet and huggable Miles Sedgwick packed a firearm in order to visit Duessa, I'd decided to do the same for our second meeting at the Sawbones. Thank the holy powers above.

In case you're wondering, you cannot fit a sidearm in a Kate Spade bag. She's not big on providing space for ammo. I recommend something vintage, which is a nice way of saying old (my bag was vintage), or a chunky Hermès saddlebag, if you've got the cash. Just be sure that you don't care about the lining, since it'll be covered with GSR and blood in a few weeks.

I pumped my arm and threw the bag as hard as I could at the vampire. He grinned and caught it one-handed. As he was beaming at my stupidity, I chambered a round, aimed upward to offset my position, and fired. Even with my other hand trying to steady the grip, I still felt the recoil explode through my shoulder. That would hurt tomorrow.

I looked up. I'd been off by a few inches, and the bullet tore through the vampire's throat instead of his skull. He gurgled and screamed—it might have been profanity, I couldn't tell—and dark gobbets of thick, rotten-looking blood oozed from the keyhole wound in his neck. As a rule, unless they've just fed, vampire blood is dark and runny, like molasses. No plasma—just rotting heme. When it touched the floor, it instantly grew coils of furry mold. *Aspergillus*: the hairlike fungus that grows on decomposing blood. Usually it only appeared in cases of severe decomp, but with vampires it was standard. Their insides were like an expired milk carton.

Don't think. You've got seconds, Tess. Seconds.

I went for my athame again, but strong arms locked around me from behind. The girlfriend. I felt her small tits digging into my back.

"Hey, Tess." Her voice had a singsong quality to it—heavy on the crazy. "How many ribs do you think I can break before you pass out? It'll be super-fun to see!"

I grunted, spread my legs, and smashed the butt of my Glock into what I approximated was her kneecap. She swore, but didn't let go. I swung in the opposite direction, craning my neck to the left, and was rewarded by the sickening contact of my gun with her nose. The barrel crunched into her sinus and orbital ridge, and hot blood sprayed against the back of my neck. She screamed. Her grip loosened, and I launched myself forward, rolling and coming up on one knee.

The carnage was impressive so far. Sid was still bleeding from his ruined throat, and Nancy was clutching her broken nose. Vampires do heal from the neck up, but it takes longer, and if the damage is severe enough, it'll actually scar. That was the goal.

I took a second to aim at Nancy and fired again. The bullet should have blown through her left eye socket, but she regained her composure enough to leap away. Vampire speed was a pain in the ass. The round lodged into a sign above the tracks instead, proclaiming that litter was a punishable fine.

Nancy was getting her finesse back. She leapt off one of the walls, grabbed an exposed pipe, and swung at me with her legs. For a moment, I saw a flash of her boots, which had polished spikes attached to the soles. Very *Kill Bill*. I ducked and slashed with my athame. The edge struck one of the spikes, and it clattered to the ground, steaming at the point of contact. There isn't much that consecrated, blood-fed steel can't cleave through like polymer.

"I'll shove that thing right up your tight virgin ass, bitch!" Nancy had spittle at the corners of her mouth.

"That's more of a third date kind of thing," I told her. "But if you're really nice, I'll let you touch the twins."

"You mortal piece of shit! Everything Sabine told us was true!"

A cold wave passed through me.

"Sabine?"

Nancy laughed. "Who do you think sent us, brain trust?"

"What does Sabine think she's playing at? She can't get within ten miles—"

"That was before the magnate stepped down. Or hadn't you heard? There's no law anymore, biscuit. No rules."

"What about—"

"The successor? Nobody can find him. And as long as he stays hidden . . ." Her smile was wide. "School's out. We get to do whatever we want."

I kept my gun trained on her, holding the athame perpendicular to the grip, like a cop would normally hold his flashlight. I looked far more confident than I felt. If Sabine was somewhere close by—

"Where is she?" I demanded.

"Right. I'll give you her address, and you can grab a coffee. She wants to *kill* you! And she wants it to last!"

"If she really wanted me dead, she wouldn't send you two fuckwits. She'd come at me herself, to make sure the job got done."

"Too busy for that. She trusted us to put you in the ground. Or, you know—the bottom half of you, anyways. We might stick your head on a pike."

She's stalling. Why is she stalling?

Fingers locked around my arm from behind, and I remembered: Sid.

"I feel better," he said, drooling a bit of blood on my cheek.

Then he threw me onto the tracks.

A lot of things go through your mind as you're about to hit an electrified third rail. Official CORE training is not one of those things. Luckily, I kept a grip on my athame, and it reacted with a mind of is own as it brushed against the electrical field generated by the tracks. The blade shone like a piece of kryptonite, and a mesh of earth materia rose up to envelop my body, instantly grounding me.

This, however, did very little to ease the impact. I hit the edge of the rail with my left shoulder, and pain blossomed along my arm. I saw spots before my eyes. I tried to shift position to see what the vampires were doing, but the movement almost made me puke. My shoulder was dislocated.

Shaking, I tightened my right-handed grip on the athame, trying not to move my left arm at all. But every twitch sent a vein of white fire through the joint. My fingers were numb. I tasted bile.

"Did that hurt?" Sid was standing over me, grinning. "Sorry! I always forget how totally useless humans are. Like sacks of shit, really."

I got to my knees and stepped shakily over the third rail. Where did Nancy go? Fuck. If I turned around too quickly, I might pass out. She couldn't have been approaching from behind. There was nowhere to go, except for—

I felt a rumbling beneath my feet.

Oh Holy Hell.

There were two lights in the tunnel. My twelve thirty train was finally arriving.

"Should we let her fry?" Nancy appeared behind Sid. She'd recovered my Glock from the ground, and was now casually aiming it at me. "Or should I just blow her away? We could wait for the train, too—but that seems like cheating."

Sid peered over the edge. "How about it, kiddo? Unlike us, you only get to die once. So you'd better choose something—"

"Jesus. You know what your real problem is . . ."

I slammed the athame into his foot. The blade easily parted the leather of his boot, going straight through the arch of his foot and striking sparks against the tile below. I twisted the handle like a corkscrew, and he screamed. Blood welled up around the guard of the blade, soaking through his grimy white sock.

"You just can't stop *talking*."

I could feel the train coming. It was death on a screaming monorail, its lights burning through the shadows of the tunnel. Hot, industrial-strength lights, throwing off thermal materia like ribbons of casual energy. I pulled them into the athame, fixing all of my concentration into a starburst tip at the very point of the blade. It grew warm. Smoke curled from Sid's boot. I couldn't shut off the pain, so I let it fuel my anger. Nothing like fire and anger. It doesn't make for good focus, but sometimes it's fine to be sloppy.

His blood boiled. It looked like cherry filling, bubbling and seething out of the ruin of flesh, bone, and twisted leather. His scream went up a notch.

I smiled at him through my pain. "You be sure to give Sabine a real big 'fuck you' for me, Sid."

Then I closed my eyes, lowered my head, and let loose. The power tore through me, and my grunt turned to a startled cry. The fire always hurt.

But it hurt Sid a lot more.

There was a flash of orange-on-white light, and a tendril of flame snaked up Sid's boot, curling around his pant leg. He swore and tried to shake it off, but his foot was nailed to the ground. The flame tore greedily at his jacket, breathing in little bursts and pops as it spread to his shirt. Then his hair went up like Dark Phoenix.

I slid the athame out of his boot, and he stumbled backward, flailing his arms and screaming as his body turned to a column of fire. The smell of his rotten blood going molten was indescribable. I gagged.

"Andreas! Fuck!" Nancy stared at him in horror. "You— fuck!" Her eyes were all white, like a rabid animal. "I'm going to fucking tear your head off!"

Andreas fell to his knees. He kept smoldering, but his screams had lessened.

I gripped the handle of the athame with my teeth, hoisting myself onto the ledge with my good arm. Using my leg as leverage, I managed to roll onto the platform, just in time to see

Nancy bearing down on me. The Glock was aimed at my head this time.

"How's it feel to get fucked by your own useless weapon?" She laughed and squeezed the trigger.

Nothing happened.

She hadn't counted on the biometric trigger, which was keyed to my thumbprint.

Before she could retaliate, I lunged.

I grabbed the collar of her jacket firmly with my good hand. Her eyes narrowed in confusion. I wedged my athame into the space between two tiles, pressing my elbow against it. Then, with the last bit of strength I had left, I sat down hard and buried my knee in her stomach. It knocked the wind out of her.

I could hear the hiss of the train. Its glow moved across the platform, outlining Sid's crumpled body, which still smoldered like a pile of tires.

My shoulder twisted. I screamed from the pain. With the handle of the athame digging into the crook of my arm, I used it like a fulcrum. My boot buried itself crosswise between the vampire's legs, and in one motion, I lifted her off the ground. My ankle trembled, but it didn't snap.

She grabbed at the tiled floor, her nails scratching against it. I pushed, grunted, and used all of my body weight to flip her over.

The back of her head slammed into the ledge. Before she could twist away, I pushed her forward, so that her head was dangling like a doll's into empty space.

"I don't know, Nancy." I smiled grimly. "How's it feel to get fucked by a train?"

Light blossomed. She screamed. The skytrain tore past me in a streak of red and white, and then Nancy's head was gone.

Blood sprayed in a fan across my jacket. Her body went limp, and I fell backward, panting.

I smelled the reek of something truly disgusting as Nancy's very, very old body evacuated its contents for a split second. Then, what was left of her shuddered violently. Black veins marbled her arms and the macerated tissue of her neck. A foul vapor breathed from her desiccated pores. Bone, tendon, and muscle alike all turned to a dark jelly, which dried out in seconds, until she looked like a pile of leaves. Everything wilted in on itself. The leathery flesh turned to dust, and the dust became a spreading stain the color of parchment on the ground.

That was how a vampire died. No clean *poof.* More like a compost heap.

Also, unlike in the movies, her clothes remained more or less intact. She may have been a hundred or so years old, but denim was truly immortal.

Still sick from the pain, I managed to slide Nancy's leather jacket from the puddle of brown gel and ash. I crawled over to Sid and threw the dripping jacket over him. It smoldered and reeked. I kicked at the smoking lump, trying to wedge it into a corner.

I heard the *whoosh* of the train doors opening. Exhausted and ready to pass out, I rolled onto my stomach. I could see the clean, white interior of the car.

It was empty.

This is Waterfront, the automated voice said. *Terminus station.*

I closed my eyes and made a sound—halfway between a laugh and a sob.

I don't know how I got to Yaletown. Maybe I walked all the way down Richards, or maybe I even got on a bus without realizing it. My shoulder was electric. I'd dealt with broken bones, fractures, and dislocations before, but the pain was always a surprise. You never remember what it feels like until it happens again, and suddenly your whole body is on fire and all you want to do is curl into a ball and throw up. My face was bruised and banged up as well, and some people who saw me on the streets looked mildly alarmed. Most just walked by without even changing expression. Maybe they thought my boyfriend had beaten the shit out of me. Or my pimp.

There were lots of places I could have gone. The CORE clinic on Davie would have patched me up and even given me some Demerol. If I'd gone back to the lab, Selena would have taken care of me. But then I'd have to fill out a report. I couldn't go home—I didn't want to scare Mia. I suppose I could have gone to Saint Paul's, like a normate, and gotten fixed up by a regular doctor. Canada's health care system didn't discriminate against mages. Everyone got to wait three hours in an uncomfortable chair for shitty treatment, regardless of their occult persuasion.

But here I was, standing on Hamilton and staring at the door marked STORAGE 3. Lucian's warehouse. Tonight I was the queen of bad decisions, apparently.

I knocked on the door with my good arm. He was a necromancer—he must still be up, right? Casting bones or whatever they did. Or chilling. Did necromancers chill? He certainly had the apartment for it. I imagined him playing Nintendo Wii for a moment, and actually started laughing. Fire shot through my arm, but I kept laughing, more from hysteria than anything else. I felt tears roll down my cheeks.

Lucian slid the door open, and for a second, his composure vanished.

"Tess?"

I must have been a real sight—bruised, my face covered in dried blood, my left arm sagging, as tears stung my eyes. But I was giggling.

"I'm sorry," I said, half laughing and half sobbing. "Lucian, I'm sorry. I didn't know where else to go."

He wrapped an arm around me. "Come in. You must be in shock. What the hell happened to you?"

I let him lead me shakily inside. My boots echoed on the polished concrete floor. The air was so warm, and it smelled good. It smelled like him. If he propped me up against a wall, I would have fallen asleep that very second.

The small, rational part of my brain realized that he was right—I was in shock from the pain, and sleeping was the last thing I wanted to do. I might even have a concussion. I swallowed and tried to focus.

"Two vampires . . ." I mumbled. "Waterfront. They jumped me. They said . . ." Recognition suddenly tore through me. "Lucian, they were working for *Sabine*."

"Sabine's far away," he said, leading me into the bathroom. "Don't worry about her. For now, let's just get you taken care of."

"She's not far away." I tried to stand still for a moment, but his hand on my back was surprisingly firm. "The vampires said that everything's in chaos, there's no magnate, and everything's turned to shit! We need to find Patrick—"

"Right now, we need to fix you up. One thing at a time, Lois Lane."

He sat me down on the edge of the bathtub. God, it was so fucking *clean*. My bathroom looked like crap. Suddenly, I was convinced that I might give Lucian typhoid or some other toxic disease that you get from living in filth. I didn't fit into his perfectly ordered life. I needed to live in a commune somewhere.

He started to pull my jacket off, and I cried out when he moved my left arm.

Lucian sucked in his breath. "Dislocated?"

I nodded.

"Okay." Gently, as if he were dealing with a terrified animal, he slipped my jacket off inch by inch. My blouse was spotted with blood. "Looks like you gave as much as you got, eh?"

I smiled weakly. "Yeah. They thought I was going to be a pushover. The girl called me a skinny little bitch."

"You're anything but." He gently placed his hand on my shoulder. "You've done this before, right?"

I nodded.

"It hurts. But it's over fast. So I'm going to do it on the count of three."

"Okay, but, like, *really* on three. Don't count to two and then surprise me, like they always do at the clinic." My eyes narrowed. "I don't like surprises."

"No more surprises. Promise."

"Okay."

"Ready? Take a deep breath."

I inhaled.

"One. Two . . ."

He wrenched my arm upward. I screamed. It felt like hot fangs biting into my shoulder, tearing it apart. The bile rose in my throat, but I swallowed it down.

"Done," he said.

I gasped for air. "You lied—you didn't count all the way—"

"I promised not to surprise you. Were you surprised?"

I shook my head, laughing softly. "No."

"No." He smiled. "Now let's see your face." He gently probed my swollen cheek. "Man, they really belted you one."

"They threw me on the tracks."

"But your athame grounded you?"

"Yeah." I frowned. "How did you know that?"

"I do actually understand how materia works, Tess. Just because I don't channel the same kind as you doesn't mean that I don't get it theoretically."

"Huh."

"I'm going to do a little something here. Don't freak out."

His fingers moved along the surface of my face, just barely touching me. I felt something—like a tiny shock. My eyes widened, and I saw faint currents of light arcing from Lucian's fingertips. Like he was a living plasma globe.

"What are you—"

"Just debriding your wounds. Necroid materia can be used to kill dead skin and tissue. It strips away the first dermal layer and speeds the healing process."

"Wow. You should become a dermatologist. You'd make a fortune." I laughed and squirmed. "It tickles a bit."

"It'll help. Trust me."

He took his hands away, but the warmth remained. My face tingled. I looked at his tub and sighed.

"Damn. You've got a *Pretty Woman* tub."

"Yeah. I like taking baths."

"You don't hear a guy say that very often."

"Well, I'm not really normal. Not by any stretch of the term."

He dabbed a washcloth over my face. Always gentle. I didn't flinch. His eyes were very brown as he concentrated. I could smell something on his fingertips. Was it the residual necroid materia? It smelled almost like sage and burnt oil.

"Do you want to have a shower?"

I shook my head. "I don't think I have the energy. I'd pass out under the hot water, and then you'd have to drag me out of here like a drowned rat."

He laughed. "Yeah. Maybe we should just get you to bed."

"Oh God." I rubbed my forehead. "Mia's going to freak if I don't come home tonight. I'm such a shitty parent—*fuck*—"

"Shhh." He shook his head. "You live with Derrick, right? He'll handle things. And if I remember correctly, Mia's a pretty tough kid."

"How do you know so much about me?"

"I take good notes." He smiled. "Let me get you a painkiller."

He reached into the medicine cabinet and pulled out a bottle.

"Is it Valium?"

"No. I don't stock anything stronger than aspirin. But it'll keep the swelling down. Your body should take care of the rest."

He poured me a glass of water from the bathroom sink. I felt like I was six years old again, and almost expected him to feed me a spoonful of cough syrup. I swallowed the pills down.

"Thanks."

"All right. Follow me."

He led me up the stairs, one hand always on my back. It almost made me want to cry, but I bit my lip and didn't say anything.

"I can sleep on the couch—"

"Shut up. It's a big bed."

It was indeed. And very, very inviting. He pulled back the comforter. We undressed in silence. Not awkward, though. I watched him slip off his shirt and wrangle out of his jeans. He watched me kick off my boots and pants. It wasn't voyeuristic. There was something oddly comfortable about it.

"Wait," he said as I got to my blouse. "Let me."

Gently, he slipped the blouse over my head. His hand rested on my hip. I made a small noise when he touched my shoulder, and he sucked in his breath, like he might break me. His fingertips brushed my arm.

"Okay?"

Lucian was looking expectantly at me. He stood there in a tank top and fitted—very fitted—boxers, looking frozen, as if waiting for further orders. I noticed a new tattoo creeping out from under his thigh, partially obscured by the hem of the fabric. It was text. I couldn't read it, but I wanted to. Oh boy, did I want to.

"Okay," I said simply.

I crawled onto my side of the bed, and he crawled onto his.

He flipped the light off, and the room was blanketed in cool semidarkness. The Noma lights coiled around the stairs gleamed like snowflakes, casting a dotted brilliance over both of our faces.

We were silent for a while. There didn't seem to be anything else to talk about.

Finally, I shifted. "Lucian?"

"Yes?"

I hesitated. *Oh God.*

"Could you . . ." I swallowed. "I mean, I don't want to— you know—at least not right now. But it's been a long day. And I feel . . ." I sighed. "Could you just . . ."

Silently, he rolled over.

I felt his arms encircle me from behind. His legs curled into mine. The soles of his feet rubbed warmly against my ankles. I felt his breath on the back of my neck, sweet and even. His hands rested lightly beneath my breasts. I felt his chest expand against my back, breathing, in and out, in and out. He didn't pull me tight. But he held on.

I let my fingers curl around his. My hands were freezing;

his were warm and surprisingly soft. I drew his arm up to my chin.

I fell asleep a few seconds later.

I didn't dream.

10

Lucian was gone when I woke up. I'm not really sure why I'd expected him to stay, like we might go out for breakfast and chat. He left me a polite note telling me that I could stay as long as I liked. A spare key sat on top of the note. I wasn't quite sure what to do with the reality of that. I told myself that he was just being pragmatic, and left immediately without snooping around the warehouse. The key felt like a grenade in my pocket. I kept it separate from my house keys, as if there might be some form of cross-contamination otherwise.

Mia was still asleep when I got home. Derrick, however, was very awake. And pissed. But his anger dissolved as soon as he saw my face. I told him what happened, and then, at his gentle urging, I called Selena and repeated the whole story again. She'd just pulled a double shift, so she was still at the lab and slightly wired from coffee. Her voice sounded brittle with exhaustion when she told me to stay home. Normally I would have protested, but the thought of not going to work filled me with such a warm sense of relief that all I could do was thank her and collapse into bed. My own bed, this time.

I wasn't sure what Derrick had told Mia. Something practical. He was much better at defusing her anger than I'd ever been. I think our relations were always more volatile because we were both girls, and I was the closest thing to a mom that she had anymore. Derrick was the one who always got to be silly and make her laugh. I was the one who told her to clean up her room before the mold on the dinner plates started growing toxic fuzz. Sometimes it scared me how much I sounded like my own mother.

Now it was 1:30 p.m. on Tuesday—my impromptu day off—and so far I'd managed to put on an old pair of tear-away track pants and Derrick's Food Not Bombs T-shirt, which was about three sizes too big. Derrick was doing my paperwork like an angel, so all I had to do was pick up Mia from school. I couldn't wait to freak out all the soccer moms when I pulled up in the Festiva, my face looking like I'd gone a few rounds with Miguel Cotto.

My left cheek was a blotch of purple with greenish edges, my split lip stung like hell whenever I took a drink, and my shoulder still made popping noises when I moved my arm. A Demerol cocktail would have helped the situation, but stoicism seemed like the right way to go. So I dragged my ass around the house, grimacing and halfheartedly cleaning while I tried not to think about how many more vampires might knock on my door tonight.

The TV was on without sound. I caught sight of a tall, skinny blond girl, and for a moment my heart skipped. I thought it was Sabine.

Jesus, it's just some model. Or that annoying chick from The Hills. *Simmer down, Tess.*

I flipped the CD player on. Mia had obviously been using it, since she'd left her *Modern Life Is War* CD in there, and I wasn't in the mood for epic punk. I dug through a stack of jewel cases, pulled out *Night Flares* by Greg MacPherson, and popped it in. His sweet, gravelly voice was soothing, like a compress made of warm tea and whiskey.

I eased myself back onto the couch, trying to move my shoulder as little as possible. My eyes had trouble focusing on the silent TV, but it was also soothing in a way, so I left it on.

I reached behind the couch with my good arm, pulling out a small, intricately carved wooden box with Celtic knotwork on the lid. It was barely hidden, but I didn't think Mia would be rooting behind our sofa anytime soon. It would be a miracle of housecleaning if she did, and if her room was any indication, that miracle was about as far away as the Rapture.

I opened the box, withdrawing a small plastic screw-top container and a ceramic pipe, still chipped from the time Derrick accidentally dropped it on the counter. Gently, I tapped some of the contents of the bag into the pipe, making sure not to spill, and dabbing at the excess with my thumb and forefinger. I drew a lighter from the box and placed it on the table. Then I closed the curtains to satisfy my own paranoia.

I stared at the pipe.

My stance on drugs has always been complicated. I'd seen firsthand what heroin, crack, PCP, cocaine, crystal—and now Hex—could do to a person's body and soul. I'd seen addicts rotting from the inside, their lives complete shit, spending each day searching for the next hit. But then there were gray areas. I went to college with this amazing artist who built room-sized sculptures made of brass, steel, and fiber optics. He had an appalling coke habit, but still managed to work every day. I don't know where his money came from. He was definitely an addict, but his life seemed to work just fine.

Would I ever let Mia try ecstasy or LSD? You bet your ass I wouldn't. But how could I control her every second of the day? A small, persistent, maybe wrongheaded part of me thought, hell, maybe she *should* try them once. Maybe everyone should. But I might have been full of shit. What did I know about anything? What did I know about being a parent? I almost cried when I had to fill out her school paperwork for the first time, and my dad still did my taxes every year. Otherwise I'd never get a refund.

What would Miles say? He specializes in solving drug crimes. What would he say if he knew you were puffing on a pipe in the middle of the afternoon?

Luckily, Miles wasn't about to be installed as my new superego. For all I knew, he was mixing up a batch of crystal in his hotel room, whistling happily as he added the drain cleaner and the sodium. You never really know people, even when you know them, even when you see them every hour of every day. That's why houses have rooms with doors. To keep us all from killing each other.

It's not like you're some crazy smokehound. This bag is probably stale, it's been sitting underneath your bed for so long.

Derrick would be annoyed if he found out, since he enjoyed getting silly and watching cartoons with me in the middle of the day. He'd managed to get the eighth of an ounce from this guy called "Extreme Jeff" who knew his sister's roommate. It was all very classy, like debutantes getting stoned in *Brideshead Revisited*.

I lit the pipe and drew in a few breaths. It was a bit old, sure, but the stuff never really went bad. I started coughing immediately, since I hadn't smoked in so long, and had to reach for a glass of water on the end table. A part of me felt like I'd just regressed back to college.

It was always very different from smoking cigarettes. Nicotine is a stimulant. It burns all the way down, but there's a mellow honey to the burning, like a chili on your tongue. It wakes you up almost immediately, and the smoke itself seems eager as it escapes through your nose and mouth, curling above your head. If you're a former smoker, getting a whiff of nicotine is like smelling barbecue. You may not be hungry enough for a full meal, but just the scent of it makes your mouth water in anticipation.

This was the opposite. The smoke lingered in my mouth and lungs, heavy and floral. I stretched out on the couch and sighed. The shift was very gradual as I took another few puffs, then wisely set the pipe down. Very subtly, I felt my body loosen up. The cramps in my stomach eased off—a side effect of the coffee I'd guzzled earlier this morning. I closed my eyes. There was a light, pleasant tingling in my forehead, as if a very small orchestra had just set up their instruments and started playing in there.

Thinking about music, I grabbed the remote for the CD

player and turned the volume up. Greg McPherson's voice was so tactile and vivid as he sang about flying over Reno, I wanted to invite him into my living room and slow-dance with him. I'll bet he smelled good, like a proper Nova Scotia boy, fresh from the sea. I'll bet he could waltz.

The next few hours were a pleasing blur of activity, some of it practical but most of it completely disorganized. I hunted through my CD collection for an album whose name I couldn't precisely remember. I straightened and aligned everything on the coffee table, since its air of crookedness suddenly seemed insulting. I folded the newspaper and placed it in Derrick's chair, for when he came home. Then I laughed at the gesture for what seemed like twenty minutes, since I couldn't imagine myself being more like June Cleaver. June Cleaver if she was mildly baked in the middle of the day.

After that, everything got lost in a maelstrom of cleaning and creative design. I was just wiping streaks off the sliding glass door with Windex, wearing my orange kitchen gloves, when I heard the doorbell.

Shit.

I did a quick mental diagnostic. How bad was I? Could I answer the door? Could I be trusted to entertain a guest? I silently recited all the capital cities of Canada. I tried to recall the last e-mail I sent. It was to Derrick. Something about picking up spray cheese from the supermarket on his way home.

I walked over to the bookshelf and scanned the titles. Happily, I was able to read each one without getting distracted by the color, shape, or spatial positioning of each book. Okay. It'd been two hours, I think I was good to go.

As I passed the table, I spied the pipe sitting there, looking innocuous. I replaced it in the box for good measure, then slid the box under the couch. The doorbell rang again. It was either a very persistent Girl Scout, or someone who knew me. Actually, the thought of mint cookies didn't sound too bad right now. I jogged over to the foyer, rummaging in my pockets for stray money. How much did those cookies cost again? Maybe they took Visa now.

I opened the door, about to say "Sorry," but the apology died on my lips.

"Tess!"

It was my mother.

We were dressed almost exactly the same, except that she wore jeans instead of track pants, and an old T-shirt from the record store she used to work at years ago. Back when they were still called record stores, even if they sold CDs. She took off her prescription sunglasses and beamed at me. But the smile died when she saw my face.

"Jesus! What happened to you?" Her hands flew to my cheek. They were cool and soft, like always. "Did you get hit by a truck? Oh baby—"

"I'm fine, Mom." I beckoned for her to come in. "It was a work thing. It's really not as bad as it looks."

"You know I hate your job. I've told you that a million times. I *hate* it. You shouldn't be putting yourself in these kinds of situations. And now you've got a family!"

"It's not like I got knocked up and moved to Surrey, Mom. Derrick and I are like co-parents, and Mia's already fourteen."

She swept past me and up the stairs. "But she still needs you to take care of her, and how are you going to do that if you're stuck in some alley somewhere, getting kicked and punched by some crazy bastard who's high on PCP? Oh, Tess." She'd already disappeared into my kitchen. Not a good sign. "You don't know how much I worry about you. I worry every day. I barely sleep a wink at night, just thinking about you and Derrick. And Mia . . ."

Ah, I see we'd come back around to that again. My mother's arguments had a certain rhetorical circularity to them.

"Mia's fine, Mom. We're all fine."

She was digging around in my cupboards now. Probably reorganizing my soup tins and instant noodle packages. "Lord knows that child is resilient, after what she's been through. I'm not disputing that. But she doesn't need any more surprises. Oh—for goodness' sake, Tessa, where's your Earl Gray? Should I look in the basement?"

I closed my eyes and leaned against the wall.

It would be impossible to tell my mother what I actually do—what I actually *am*. And even if I could find the proper words, the CORE expressly forbids it. I signed papers that were notarized. Once you become a registered mage, psionic, or lab technician, you agree to absolute nondisclosure. Only people involved in our world can really know who we are and what we do.

When I was twelve, my life changed forever. Strange things started happening whenever I was around. Broken objects mysteriously fixed themselves. Dead plants came back to life. Dogs and cats followed me home from school, even when I cried and screamed at them to just go away. It's called materia overflow. Your body becomes an open receiver for all different kinds of energy flows, and you just sort of—*emit*. All the time, in all directions. It happens until the power settles down and becomes more structured, more stable. Until then, you're like a walking battery.

I thought I was going crazy. I wanted to die. My parents—ensconced in their warm, fuzzy, small-town world—just thought I was going through a difficult phase. My mother talked to me a lot about the wonders of menstruation. I didn't know how to say: *Mom, I got my period a year ago, and I hide Kotex under my bed. And yesterday I blew up the microwave at school.*

Then one day I got pulled out of class to see the guidance counselor. Nothing new. Only, she wasn't the normal guidance counselor. She was an older woman, tall and thin, with gorgeous white hair and a kind smile. Meredith Silver. Eventually, she'd become my mentor. At the time, like many CORE officials, she was "scouting" at my middle school, looking for mage potentials by posing as a counselor. She found one.

Meredith explained everything to me. Even at twelve years old, I understood the enormity of what I was getting myself into. I was scared. But she made me feel safe. She taught me that the power wasn't evil or destructive—it was a natural kind of resonance, a feedback loop from the physical universe that allowed me to shape and sculpt the forces that made Earth what it was.

Heat, electromagnetism, gravity, architectonics, condensation—all of it responded to my body. I could change anything as long as I preserved the equilibrium that made life on this planet possible. Change too much too fast, and you screw up the balance. A butterfly beats its wings in the Amazon Rain Forest, and thousands of kilometers away, there's a hurricane. The same principle holds true for human beings. Meredith taught me the old rule of three: Everything you send out comes back to you three times over and resonates across the fabric of the world, like a string drawn sharply across a cello. Nobody was cut off. Everything I did affected every other living thing. So I was never really alone. And I was responsible, at twelve, for the entire world.

Heavy stuff.

After that, I went deep into the mage's closet. Derrick always jokes about being out as a gay man but deeply closeted as a telepath, and I understand what he means. I came home and told my parents exactly what Meredith advised me to: that I'd been selected for a gifted after-school program, and would need to attend special classes in downtown Vancouver. My parents were over the moon. I was puking a lot.

The CORE grabs you early, when your powers are still malleable—not in some cultish way, but because they want to prevent you from falling in with the wrong crowd. How do you think vampires, necromancers, and warlocks are created? They were all kids, too, once, with the same limitless potential. But they veered left where I veered right. Or maybe I veered left—nobody's ever sure what the "right" choice is. Look at Lucian. He wasn't a monster. At least he didn't seem like one.

Training lasts for six years. After eighteen—if you manage to survive—you go active as a mage and enter the registry. Then you can choose to specialize as a detective, a field agent, an instructor, a technician, a policy writer, a litigator . . . the CORE has never been lacking in positions. You tend to learn pretty quickly where your strengths and weaknesses lie. A lot of potentials never really develop a taste for working in the field, but they might go on to become excellent lab jockeys or occult prosecutors. Some have borderline or weak proficiencies that wouldn't allow them ever to see a combat situation, but their determination makes them suited for other, equally important jobs. Some get lost in the system and never find their way out. The CORE has always had its own asylums and "long-term care" facilities for those poor souls whose power only ended up consuming them.

I had an early proficiency for manipulating earth materia, which made me a natural candidate for field agent. But I also loved the thrill of investigating occult crimes, especially murders. So I was groomed for the OSI program. But this isn't something that you can discuss with your parents over Sunday dinner. Which brings us back, to borrow a rhetorical move from my mother, to the very crowded occult closet.

As far as my parents knew, I'd developed an interest in specialized law enforcement when I was still in high school. Now I worked for an auxiliary branch of the RCMP dedicated to solving hate crimes. In a way, it wasn't entirely a lie. I did solve hate crimes within the occult community all the time. I just didn't mention that I was investigating the murders of vampires and goblins.

And then there was Mia. Explaining *her* to my mother was a lot more complicated than hiding my identity as a mage.

"I'm making you some tea. You look like you can use it."

There was no use going into the kitchen now. She'd colonized it.

"I drink coffee, Mom," I said, collapsing onto the couch.

"Coffee stunts your growth. And it gives you kidney stones."

I stared at the spot on the table where the pipe had been sitting. Guilt settled in the pit of my stomach.

She emerged with two steaming mugs and set one next to me. For twenty-five years of my life, the smell of my mother's favorite Earl Gray tea had been like a homing beacon, drawing me back to a world of comfort and familiarity. I knew exactly how she took her tea—a bit of 1 percent milk, no sugar, piping hot, with the mug only half-full. ("Otherwise, it's just like drinking hot dish water.") If I lost all five of my senses, I'd still be able to functionally prepare a cup of tea for her, I'd done it so many times. The memory sequence was altogether Proustian.

"Do you remember what I told you," she began, "when you first said you were going to take that child in? Do you remember?"

"I don't know, Mom. Was that the yelling part, or the crying part, or the part where you said I was a lunatic? There were several different reactions."

"Oh, I did no such thing."

I rolled my eyes. "Fine. You told me that I was too young, that Derrick was too young, that we were both too busy to raise a teenager."

"Don't make me sound so negative. All I said was that you'd need help. Remember? I said that you couldn't do it alone." She shook her head. "Poor little bobbin. First her parents, then her aunt. Imagine if you hadn't found her."

"She would have ended up in foster care."

My mother put a hand over her heart. "You know how bad that system is. She would have been in hell."

I'd been careful—with Derrick's help—to give my mother a mixture of lies and truth in order to explain Mia. She knew that we'd met during an investigation. She knew that we'd developed a bond, and that I'd filed to become her legal guardian to keep her from ending up in the system.

She didn't know that Mia had vampiric viral plasmids in her blood, that she was a mage potential, or that Derrick and I had saved her (or maybe she saved us) from getting murdered by Marcus Tremblay, my former supervisor. She didn't know that Cassandra had willed her house in Elder to me—how could I explain that? As far as she was concerned, the Crown had endowed Mia with a living stipend, and Derrick and I had combined our savings to mortgage our new home on Commercial Drive. If she ever caught a whiff of the fact that I might have lived in Elder—a few blocks away from her—I'd never hear the end of it for the rest of my life.

"I always told you that you were born grown-up," she continued, "that you took responsibility from such an early age. But you know, Tessa, when you said that you were buying this place and taking care of Mia—it was your first real adult decision. I felt it. My baby grew up in that moment." She smiled. "And I've never been more proud."

"Oh, Mom." I rolled my eyes.

Secretly, I was pleased. I'd always be a momma's girl.

"But obviously, you need help. I mean, look at this living room. And what are you feeding her? All I could find in your fridge was instant pudding. Do you want the poor girl to end up a midget, or get some kind of hormonal imbalance like poor Jamie Lee Curtis? She needs to eat vegetables!"

Ah. There it was. The double-edged Mom compliment.

"She eats fine, Mom. She cooks for herself when we're not home."

"What? Are you running some kind of Gypsy commune? A fourteen-year-old girl shouldn't be making dinner for herself, Tessa."

"I was making my own dinner when I was twelve. Remember when you worked double shifts at the record store and the nightclub?"

She sighed. "Of course."

"Well, Mia doesn't seem to mind. And Derrick's a great cook."

"Of course. He's gay. He provides a wonderful mothering influence. But it's up to you to provide the discipline."

"I don't really have the time to explain to you everything that's wrong with that observation, Mom." I leaned back in the couch. "But trust me—Derrick and I do just fine. And I do give her discipline."

"So, you're saying that her room is nice and clean? If I check it right now, it won't look like Chernobyl?"

"Come on—my room was never clean!"

"But Mia's different, honey. You know that. She's special."

"Oh, so I wasn't special," I mumbled. I was suddenly six years old again.

She rolled her eyes. "I have drawers and closets at home

filled with every drawing and macaroni ornament and poem you've ever written, baby—a living testament to your special-ness. You *know* what I mean."

Ah, the Corday pragmatism. Love dished up with a dose of shitty *vérité*.

"I know what you mean," I said grudgingly. "Mia's a ge-nius. With the right kind of attention, there's no limit to what she could accomplish. But that also leaves her open to a lot of scary stuff. Her emotions are volatile. The last thing she wants to feel like is a normal teenager, but it's happening to her, and she hates it."

"Just like you hated it." She smiled. "I know you and Der-rick are trying your hardest. That kid is never going to suffer for a lack of love. But she needs more than you can give her."

"What are you suggesting?"

She folded her arms. "Your father and I are thinking of selling the house."

My head started pounding.

"Absolutely not."

"Why?"

"Because—I . . ." I felt flushed. "Because—the market—it's bullish right now, or bearish, or a buyer's—something! It's not a good time to sell. You and Daddy would lose so much money. And prices here are skyrocketing."

"Breathe, honey." She stroked my arm. "We don't want to move in next door. We're thinking of Coquitlam, or Surrey. Somewhere close by. You'd still have your space, but we'd be able to visit much more often. And Mia would have somewhere to stay while you're both working. Your father's retired now, and honestly, I think she'd be a nice distraction for him. It would certainly keep him from driving *me* up the wall."

I shook my head. "Mia has a home. She lives here, with us—"

"Tessa. Honey . . ." Her smile was beatific. "Nobody's try-ing to steal her from you. We just want to help. It would be her choice to visit. We could drop off groceries every once in a while. Take her off your hands. That's what grandparents *do*."

The desire to hyperventilate slowly subsided. I realized that it wasn't just my connection to Mia that was making me freak out. I was still reeling from the fight yesterday. Everything in my life seemed fragile. I couldn't hold on to it all. I couldn't lock Mia in her room for the next four years.

Also, I had to stop smoking in the afternoon.

"I get it, Mom." I sighed. "And I appreciate it. I'm just still a bit shaken up from yesterday. My emotions are fucked . . ."

She frowned at me.

"*Messed* up. Everything's just a little intense right now."

"Of course it is. Did you catch them at least?"

I blinked. "Who?"

"The criminal. The one who did that to your poor face!"

"Oh, yeah." Lies mixed with truth. "Yeah, they've been dealt with."

"That's good, at least. One less crazy person on the streets."

I wished.

"Speaking of Mia—shouldn't she be getting out of school? It's three o'clock."

"Crap! Yes!" I bolted upright, then winced from the pain in my shoulder. "I have to pick her up."

"Let me drive." Her eyes narrowed. "I don't trust that car of Derrick's. It seems unreliable. You should really invest in a Prius. Your father adores his."

Normally, I would have howled in frustration at the thought of driving with my mother, who insisted that second gear was a perfectly reasonable place to stay while going sixty kph down a residential street. But I still didn't feel up for driving.

"Thanks. That would be great."

A few minutes later, I was ensconced in my mother's air-conditioned sedan, which would never be paid off as long as she lived. My graduation picture was still affixed to the dash-board with a suction cup, and the seats were eerily clean. The Festiva was more like a mobile Tim Hortons franchise. My mother hummed absently to herself as she turned down Charles Street, negotiating the narrow residential lane that was now crowded with kids wearing backpacks. Other sedans were circling hungrily for parking spots, but my mother was a pro. She wedged us between a jeep and an SUV, her wheel barely touching the curb. It was like watching a figure-skater in action. Everything she did was elegant; she even cut off other soccer moms with a smile and a wave.

As we pulled up to the school, I noticed Mia talking to an older boy. She was smiling—not in a flirty way, but genuinely smiling. Nothing like the sullen princess at home who hogged the bathroom and yelled at us because we didn't buy fair trade coffee beans. This was a very different Mia.

The boy turned around, and I got a good look at him. Tall, dark hair, brown eyes. A bit awkward looking, in the way that all male teenagers are, but still handsome. I'd seen those eyes before. In fact—

My heart froze. I must have gone white, because my mother gave me an odd look and put a hand on my forehead.

"Tessa? Everything all right? You look pale, sweetie."

"I'm . . ." I swallowed, unable to take my eyes off the boy. "I'm fine, Mom. Just tired. And my shoulder hurts."

"I've got some Motrin in my purse. Here, let me find it."

Mia got in the backseat and flashed me a smile, although nowhere near as bright as the one she'd reserved for the older boy. Then she kissed my mother on the cheek.

"Hi, Nana."

"Hi, kid. I stopped by to visit Tess, and she asked me to make supper for you."

"I did no such thing."

She swatted at me. "Oh, hush. You could use a nice meal."

"Sweet! Something with real protein." Mia sat back and fiddled with her knapsack. "Oh my God, math was, like, *insane*. The teacher didn't even know what he was talking about. He's so old, and he keeps using these, like, wooden props to demonstrate what a radius is. But they're *really* made of wood. And he dropped one of them on the floor, and Brad-the-douchebag-Connelly started laughing—"

"Mia, I don't approve of that term," my mother said from the front seat, smoothly merging into traffic.

"Sorry, Nana. Brad Connelly is a total philistine."

"That's much better."

"Who was that boy?" I demanded. I tried to make my voice sound less accusatory, but it must have been obvious, because Mia narrowed her eyes at me.

"Overreact much? Geez. His name's Patrick. He's just this guy I met in the library while I was studying for my presentation on the Organic Food Movement. I asked him if he'd read Vandana Shiva, and he *hadn't*. Like, ever. So I had to school him."

"How old is he?"

She shrugged. "Seventeen, maybe? I don't know, whatever it says on his fake ID." She laughed when I glared at her. "Don't go all McCarthy on me, Tess. He's just some boy. He seemed nice, so I talked to him."

"Well"—I struggled for some rationale—"you know, boys like that only have one thing on their mind. And it's not the Organic Food Movement."

"Tess!" My mother managed to scold me without looking up from the road. "That's a little puritanical, don't you think?"

"No kidding!" Mia folded her arms and scowled at me. "Besides, is it so crazy that some nice guy might actually like me? Am I so fugly and repulsive that he should have run away screaming from me, like my body was covered in scales?"

"I didn't say that."

"Whatever." She looked out the window. "He's nobody. Just some guy."

I knew that was far from the truth. The last time I'd seen Patrick, he was hooked up to an EKG monitor, waiting to become the next vampire magnate. I remembered the mark on his left hip. The sign of power.

I needed to install a dead bolt on Mia's bedroom door.

And I needed to find Caitlin Siobhan before someone else died.

11

I had to wait until Mia was asleep before calling in reinforcements.

The hours before consisted of watching my mom cook a fabulous meal of spareribs, garlic-braised roast potatoes, and acorn squash oozing with melted butter and brown sugar. Essentially, ten times better than anything I could ever whip up after pulling a double shift at the lab. Usually, I just got one of those rotisserie chickens from the grocery store. But Mom was on her A-game for sure tonight. Derrick ate so much I thought I was going to have to roll him into the living room, and Mia actually stayed at the table for more than five minutes. Afterward, we watched *The Tudors*, which I thought was a bit racy, but Mia insisted that she was purely interested in the show's historical veracity. Derrick was interested in the veracity of Jonathan Rhys Meyers's codpiece, which seemed to get larger with each episode.

After a full-on war between my mother and me over who would wash the dishes—guess who won?—Derrick and I were finally left alone in the house. I peeked my head into Mia's room, and saw that she'd fallen asleep listening to her iPod again. Gently, I disengaged the headphones, closed her bedroom door, and returned to the living room.

Now it was time to plan. Or panic. Whichever came first.

"So it was really Patrick? I mean—really?"

"Yes, really! Do you think I need bifocals?"

"I think you may have drunk too many iced Americanos, and you know how your vision gets fuzzy when that happens."

"Derrick, I saw what I saw. He goes to her *school*. I mean, Jesus . . ." I shook my head. "They're so close. They're practically friends. And this has been going on for almost a year!"

"There's no way we could have known. Obviously, Caitlin has kept his whereabouts a secret from everyone—"

"But she wanted us to find him. I mean, it can't be a coincidence, right? She's playing with us, Derrick. She's planning something. And after what Ben dug up at the lab, you know that she's involved in these killings somehow."

Derrick sat down cross-legged on the floor. "Let's try to come at this without being too reactionary. If Caitlin's trying to put Mia and Patrick together somehow—trying to keep them close—maybe it's because she thinks we can help. Like, we can keep an eye on both of them or something. Maybe she needs our help."

"She can bench-press a car, Derrick. Why would she need our help?"

He shrugged. "She obviously knows something that we don't."

"She's the only one who's been alive long enough to give us any real context on these killings. She *knew* him, or her, or *it*—that's the word Duessa used. Whatever 'it' is, Caitlin's one of the few people who ever caught the live show."

"Well, if we can find Patrick, it stands to reason we can find Caitlin."

"But we only found him because she wanted us to. He could be staying in a hotel for all we know."

"Only one way to find out." He grinned. "I'll go get my laptop. We can get remote access to the CORE databases here."

"You might want to call Miles, too. If we end up pulling an address, he could be useful when we visit the actual site."

"Oh." He looked flustery for a second. "Yeah, of course, he's got mad skills with the spatial profiling, right? I'll call him. I mean"—he blinked—"he gave us his number, right? It's probably in my cell."

"On speed dial?"

He stuck his tongue out. "Shut up."

"Your crush is seven shades of adorable, but for now, we've got to focus. Is that going to be a problem?"

His eyes narrowed. "I don't know, Tess. Maybe we should invite Lucian over. After all, there might be necromancy involved, right?"

I tried to keep my expression cool. "There might be."

"Maybe he'll wear that little tank top ensemble that he's so fond of. Will that be a problem for you?"

"Point taken, *betch*. Now grab the computer and call Sedgwick."

For someone who'd just eaten his weight in spareribs, he ran down the hallway with surprising speed.

Twenty minutes later, Miles arrived with Baron in tow. He'd opted to take a cab, reasoning that he could always bill the CORE later. I think he was secretly afraid of the Festiva, which made a lot of sense.

"The Scooby gang's all here," I said, smiling as he walked up the stairs with Baron, who looked sedate, as always.

Miles smirked at me. "How long have you been wanting to say that?"

"Since the end of *Buffy* season seven."

"That's what I thought."

Miles sat on the couch, and Baron collapsed beside him, tongue lolling.

"Does he need any food or water?" I asked, suddenly switching into some type of cross-species mother mode.

"No. He's my familiar, so he just feeds off my vital essence."

We both stared at him.

Miles laughed. "He's fine! We're both fine. Don't worry, he's not a weredog or anything like that." He made the sign for "dog," which was mimetic: two quick pats on his right thigh, as if he were saying, "C'mere." Baron perked up his ears.

"No, he's just the cutest pup in the whole world." Derrick was instantly down on all fours, rubbing Baron's ears. "Yessir, Mr. Puppy! Aren't you?"

"Miles, tell him to focus. Please."

Baron rolled onto his back, paws kicking the air like he was riding a bicycle. Derrick unceremoniously buried his head in the dog's belly. His comments after that became inaudible.

"Hey. Dog Whisperer." Miles tapped him on the shoulder. He looked up sheepishly, and Miles made a gesture: both hands gliding together, meeting at the fingertips. *Focus.* He raised an eyebrow.

"Gotcha." Derrick sat up. "I'm all ears."

Baron looked dissatisfied for a moment, but then lost interest and curled up into a comma shape, falling asleep at the foot of the couch.

"All right." I pushed the laptop in their direction. "Here's what we've got so far. I pulled Patrick's school records at Lord Byron, and he's listed as living at 418 Victoria Drive. That puts him in the right school district."

Patrick's smiling face was displayed on his school ID. He looked like anything but a vampire magnate potential. His brown hair was messy, and I wanted to smooth it down like my mother used to do for me.

"Tracing the address was simple. It comes up as a cute little rancher. Nothing flashy, just your standard late-seventies house in East Vancouver. The kind built just before the Expo boom that went up a million dollars in price only a few years later. But . . ."

I clicked on another window. A scanned PDF document appeared—it was a rental agreement.

"I called Becka and had her trace the rental papers. As you can see, they were signed by a Lindsey Cole"—I gestured to the digital signature—"which is a dummy name for Caitlin

Siobhan. I cross-checked it against Patrick's school records, and his emergency contact is none other than Lindsey Cole. But look at the landlord's signature on the bottom."

"Tamara Whitehall," Derrick read. "Who's she?"

"That's a good question. I searched through some real estate databases to see if she owned any other properties. And guess what?"

I clicked a third window, and another rental PDF appeared.

"Tamara Whitehall rented an apartment to someone named Katrina Glass. A two-bedroom on Nanaimo and Penticton streets. And look at the dates."

"They're within days of each other." Miles peered at the screen. "Do we have anything on this Tamara Whitehall?"

"Not on her, no. But her sister has a record." I pulled up a CORE datasheet. "Brynn Peterson. She was arrested four years ago under the Communicating Act. She used to work out of the Sawbones. And Tamara posted bail for her."

Brynn Peterson looked rough. Thinning blond hair, bleary eyes, a few scattered sores on her face. Her lips were cracked and slightly parted in the image. She looked ancient and far away, despite her recorded age of twenty-two.

"Meth-head," Derrick observed.

I nodded. "So, it seems that Tamara Whitehall has some skeletons in her closet. Maybe she owed Caitlin a few favors?"

"Maybe Caitlin helped her out with Brynn," Miles added. "Or she made sure that Tamara never ended up in a CORE holding cell."

"And Caitlin knows all about the mystical sex trade." Derrick leaned forward. "She'd know how to get Brynn out of the game. Maybe she even called in a favor with Duessa."

"Either way, this apartment has got to be where Patrick's living. A two-bedroom on Nanaimo, just out of the school district, but close enough for a bus ride?" I shook my head. "There's no way it could be a coincidence."

"So, what do you think? Should we call Selena?"

"Not yet. I want to drive by the place first."

Derrick gave me a level look. "Oh, so we're breaking policy again. And what will our story be this time?"

"There's nothing wrong with driving by someone's house. It's not against any CORE directives."

"Oh, and if Miles happens to pick up a vibe from the place—what—that's just icing on the cake? And we'll file it with Selena in the morning?"

"Don't get all Deputy Dog on me. It's a preliminary sweep. We'll talk to Selena once we find out more."

Miles shrugged. "I actually agree with Tess. Driving by a house doesn't really constitute a full-scale investigation. And wouldn't Detective Ward want us to gather as much information as possible before reporting back to her?"

"Tess has a history of neglecting to report back to *Detective* Ward," Derrick clarified. "In fact, we're both on her permanent shit list."

"Well then." Miles grinned. "If you're already in trouble, it can't hurt you much more, can it?"

"I love how you think, Miles." I smiled at him. "Did you bring your piece?"

He patted his jacket. "I've got a permit to carry concealed. I hope it's still valid in British Columbia."

"Nobody's going to be pulling us over tonight."

"Hey! Hold it!" Derrick spread his arms. "Not to rain on your SWAT parade, but let's just take a moment to consider this." His eyes were steely. "Caitlin signed the dummy rental for a reason. She's hiding, and she doesn't particularly want us coming by for a nightcap. Do we really want to piss her off?"

"She's hiding well enough from normates, but Caitlin's smart enough to know that we'd find her pretty quick if we tried. I think she wants to establish contact."

"The problem is, I don't want to establish contact with her fangs. She may not be magnate anymore, but she's still a centuries-old vampire. And from what you told me about Patrick, he's got a lot of power as well. Dangerous, unfocused power. So what happens if they catch us snooping around their apartment?"

"If Caitlin wanted to kick our ass, I think she'd have done it by now." I gave him a reassuring smile. "Derrick, we'll play it safe. I promise. If any of us gets a bad feeling, you have my permission to turn the car around. We'll drive straight to the lab."

He ground his teeth. "What about Mia? I'm not leaving her alone."

Miles shrugged. "I don't mind staying here and watching her."

"Well, she's fourteen, so it's not like you'd be baby-sitting. She'll probably be asleep the whole time. But just in case . . ."

"Totally. I don't mind at all."

"Mia's going to freak out if she wakes up," Derrick said. "What if she maces him, or gives him a head injury?"

"I can hold my own." Miles smiled. "And if something else comes knocking, I've got the Sig Sauer." He looked at Derrick. "My abilities wouldn't be much help unless I was practically on her doorstep anyway. You should be able to read the scene yourself. I've got complete confidence in you."

Derrick blushed a little. "Thanks. But you've got me whipped in that department. With your powers, I mean."

Miles grinned and signed something quickly: Both hands moved past each other in the O position; then he placed the knuckles of his right hand to his chin, pinkie and thumb extended, and shook his head lightly. He brought both hands together in a thumbs-up sign, and concluded with what was quite obviously a whipping motion. He stuck his tongue out mischeviously at Derrick, whose blush deepened. I didn't need a cerfificate in ASL to translate:

Nothing wrong with being whipped.

The drive to Nanaimo was short and tense, as Derrick fiddled with the radio and I watched the dark, serpentine expanse of Hastings Street gliding by like a river of asphalt. Vancouver's answer to the Nile. We passed the Native Community Center, along with scattered cafés and restaurants that were like outposts on some strange journey between pockets of the city proper. Traffic jammed up as we got closer to the intersection of Nanaimo and Hastings. Residents crowded into Donald's discount supermarket before it closed, and I spied a few couples sitting at the Sweet Tooth Café, sharing one of their epic cinnamon buns (they also served pretty decent Thai food, incidentally). The Roundel was packed with young hipster parents, spearing forkfuls of organic greens and braised tofu while their kids lounged in SUV-sized prams or shoulder Björns. The cook there yelled at me once because I didn't finish my tempeh steak. A few skater punks loitered outside the liquor store, rubbing their hands and smoking to keep warm, hoping that someone might buy them a six-pack of Coors. Music drifted indolently from a side street. It sounded like Eva Cassidy.

We turned down Penticton, just past the London Drugs, and everything went quiet. Magnolia trees flamed silently out the windows. A stray tricycle was parked against the curb, and the elementary school across the street was empty and still. Derrick pulled up to a small church on the corner of the block, which advertised Christian yoga. He cut the engine and shifted in his seat.

"Why park by the church?"

He shrugged. "Holy ground? Maybe she can't get us here."

"I think that's only true in *Highlander*."

"Oh. Shit." He sighed. "Well, the apartment's in plain sight, at least."

It was one of those disorganized multistory East Vancouver houses that had been partitioned into apartments years ago. Not the kind of place I'd expect Caitlin to live, but then again, I really didn't know anything about her. Maybe she appreciated old, idiosyncratic things. And bad plumbing. Maybe the place had been gutted and completely redone. I suddenly pictured her on an episode of *Trading Spaces*, explaining why she'd gone with eggplant walls for the living room. Come to think of it, with that brilliant red hair, she did look a bit like Laurie Hickson-Smith. Why did vampires and designers always have such great hair?

"What now?" Derrick asked. "Should we have stopped by a Tim's?"

"Ugh. No, I don't want any more coffee. Let's just wait."

"Can we listen to music?"

I glared at him. "Haven't you ever been on a stakeout before? We have to stay tense and keep our concentration razor-sharp."

"Goldfrapp helps me concentrate."

I rolled my eyes. "Fine. Put the radio back on."

Ten minutes passed. Not a single person walked by, and the house remained still. I tapped my fingers against the car window. Maybe we *should* have grabbed a coffee.

"I know what you're thinking," Derrick said.

"That's because you're a telepath."

"But it's no less true." He raised an eyebrow. "I saw a newspaper dispenser at the corner of Nanaimo."

"Crossword?"

"They had 24. The *good* crossword, not the pansy one."

"But we'll need coffee."

"Roundel's still open."

I sighed. "Derrick, we may be the worst cops ever."

"We're not cops. We're OSI investigators. Our pension is much better." He smiled. "Besides. I'll only be gone for a few minutes, and you can stay here. On *The Wire*, they always have coffee and newspapers."

"And Omar."

"I loves me some Omar, true."

I exhaled. "Fine. But hurry. And be careful."

"It's less than a block away. I'm not going to New Westminster."

"You know what I mean."

He nodded. "Got any money?"

"Oh, for . . ." I rummaged through my purse and pulled out a crumpled twenty. "Get me a Twix while you're at it."

"Then I have to go to the corner . . ." He blinked when he saw my look. "Right-o, chocolate on demand. See you in a bit."

I watched him lope down the street. Derrick had a certain kind of affable walk, as if his whole body exuded a kind of gentility. He was a good person. You *knew* he was a good person just by looking at him. I didn't have that. I didn't know how to get it. These days, I didn't know much of anything except for how to work the TiVo.

Who knew if Caitlin would ever come outside? In a few moments, Derrick would be back, and we'd tear into a crossword. That was my life. And it was a good life. Sometimes I felt stabbed with joy whenever I thought about my life, about how full it was and how confusing at the same time. But a small, persistent part of me wondered if I hadn't opted out of a very different dream. What if I'd really concentrated on dating and meeting new friends and all of that shit that's supposed to make you happy? What if I hadn't bailed on that nice, normate banker guy who lived in the West End? It wasn't his fault that his name was Lorne. Just because I couldn't picture myself yelling out "Lorne" in the bedroom—that was my bad, not his. And who yelled out stuff anyways? What had I been expecting?

I met Derrick when I was just starting college. Those were premium dating years, and during the course of our friendship, I'd barely been out on more than a dozen blind dates or setups. I'd slept with a few guys, nobody special, most of them forgettable, like those sentences in a manuscript that you cross out later once you're thinking more clearly. Nothing like that almost-night with Lucian. We hadn't even got to the good stuff. But I'd be lying if I said I didn't still think about it. Frequently.

Was Lucian Agrado the closest thing to a "normal" guy in my life? How sad was that? Why was it so hard to meet a nice bookstore clerk or barista or waiter? I was twenty-five years old, and I didn't have a single friend who wasn't paranormally inclined.

Maybe I just wasn't trying hard enough. The city was full of normal people, right? I mean, statistically, it had to be true. So why wasn't I meeting any of them? Did I have to stand in the street and wave my arms?

I thought about the possibility of Derrick and Miles. They could be really good for each other. So why did I feel the sharp edge of jealousy whenever I pictured them together, like something nibbling at the base of my spine? Derrick had given up a lot in his life. Unlike me, he'd actually been in a real, committed relationship. But he broke the rules. He said too much, and the guy bolted. It seemed like a shitty payback for one moment of honesty.

Derrick should be happy. Miles seemed genuinely interested in him, and Derrick was obviously into Miles, given how his brain dissolved like tapioca whenever the dude was nearby. I pictured them doing a crossword together. Miles laughing and pointing to a horizontal clue, the cap of the pen dangling from his mouth. Derrick nodding, leaning forward, pressing his lips to Miles's forehead as he spelled out VERNAL. Miles in blue jeans and a rumpled T-shirt, bare feet resting on Derrick's lap. Matching iced coffees sitting together on the end table by the couch.

Derrick looking up. His eyes sad. "Don't you want this? Tess?"

Miles grinned at me. He raised an eyebrow. His bare foot rubbed against Derrick's thigh, and I saw his hand snake around his waist.

"I . . ." My mouth was suddenly dry.

Derrick shook his head. "You fucking bitch."

I blinked and snapped out of it.

Suddenly, I felt like I was suffocating in the car. The windows were starting to fog up. I closed my eyes.

When I opened them, Caitlin was standing outside.

I hadn't heard her close the front door. She was wearing a long gray coat, and her hair was swept up. She didn't shiver against the cold. She was holding something, but I couldn't see it from here.

All of a sudden, I had no idea why I'd decided to come. Did I want to talk to her? What would I say? *So, Patrick's a senior, huh? He must eat a lot, and I'll bet he hogs the bathroom and steals all the hot water. Oh, and by the way, can we talk about that time at the turn of the century—you know, when you were still a pro?*

A part of me was thrilled that I'd been right. I'd followed the trail that Caitlin left for me, and now here we were. But what happened now? What did she need from me? What did she have planned for Patrick?

"Tell me something," I whispered. "Caitlin Siobhan. Tell me something about this killer. Tell me what it is."

Caitlin looked up.

I always forgot about vampire hearing.

Of course, she'd probably smelled me ages ago. Our eyes locked. I could still feel her power, even this far away, even locked inside the car. She may not have been magnate anymore, but she was still a walking nightmare.

Her eyes were still. Almost sad.

"What do you want?" I asked her through the window. "Caitlin, how can I help you? How can we help each other?"

She stared at me for another beat. I felt my heart constrict. Behind her, a single window on the top floor of the house gleamed with yellow light.

Was it Patrick's room? Was he doing his homework? Listening to music?

Maybe he was jerking off. The thought made me smile despite myself. He was seventeen, after all. Imagine if he missed his chance to take over the world because he was rubbing one off to Internet porn or a hot picture of Dita Von Teese. Pants and boxers around his ankles, toes curling in his pure white socks, quick and dirty with one arm thrown over his face. That's how my teenage boyfriend, Alex, used to jerk off. Watching him answered a lot of questions for me about the male mystique.

I used to think about Tim Curry when I masturbated as a teenager. What does that say about me?

Caitlin didn't say anything. She put something in her pocket. Then she turned and walked down the street, disappearing at the corner. I could have followed her, but it seemed pointless. Her look had said more than any awkward conversation could. She knew something, and she was into this deep. So was Patrick.

Now I had to keep them both away from Mia.

I leaned back in the seat and closed my eyes. A few seconds later, my cell rang. It was Selena.

"Stanley Park," she said simply. "Twenty minutes. You'll see us."

"Same deal?" I asked her.

Silence crackled on the phone. "Get down here as soon as you can. Bring Siegel and Sedgwick. We'll need all the help we can get."

I snapped the phone shut.

That eliminated one suspect. Not even Caitlin Siobhan could be in two places at once. I'll bet she knew something that could, though.

Derrick appeared, struggling to open the car door as he held a folded newspaper, two coffee cups, and a shopping bag.

"They didn't have Twix," he said, "so I got you a Big Turk."

12

We arrived home to find Mia and Miles watching an old VHS copy of *Uncle Buck*, with John Candy about to drill through the bedroom door.

"I don't get why the daughter is such a cow," Mia was saying.

"It's a difficult age for her," Miles replied.

"Yeah, but why is she so hella mean to everyone? And her hair is so *curly* and, like, so tight. Maybe that's why she's so pissed off."

"Because of the perm?"

"Yeah."

"It's possible."

"You were right, though. This movie rocks. Wait . . ." She laughed. "What's the sign for 'movie' again?"

Derrick touched the palm of his right hand to the index finger of his left. Then he waved the fingers of his left hand.

"Oh, like a movie projector. Cool."

"You're a natural at sign."

"That's so weird, because I suck at French. I can never remember the verb tenses. But talking with your hands is different. I like it."

"Something smells amazing," Derrick said as we walked up the stairs. Baron was sandwiched comfortably between Mia and Miles on the couch. He stared lazily at us, but didn't get up. Mia scratched behind his ears.

"Miles made curry popcorn," Mia said, gesturing to the green Tupperware bowl that they were passing between them. "It's *major.* That's what Posh is saying now. Everything's *major.*" She giggled. "We watched *The Beckhams* earlier."

"What happens if she has a major crisis?" Miles asked.

"She'd be like, 'Blimey, this is majorly *major*! David!' "

"Quick, David, put the kids in the bomb shelter!"

"No wait—doesn't she have, like, that insane closet—"

"With the MRI in it? To scan her outfits?"

"Yeah! They could totally hide in there!"

"Kids! Into Mommy's MRI, quickly!"

Mia laughed and took a handful of popcorn. "There's peanuts in it," she clarified, "and yellow curry. You should take notes."

"Right." I collapsed into the chair by the television. "Here's the thing. We have to go to Stanley Park tonight."

Miles looked at me sharply. "Did Selena call?"

I nodded.

"Is there another body?" Mia asked.

I glared at her. "We are not having this conversation."

"It's not like I haven't seen a body before. Remember?"

I winced. "I'd like to make sure you don't see any more. I think that's the lowest we can set the bar as your legal guardians—trying to keep you away from crime scenes."

"But our life is pretty much one big crime scene." She licked the curried butter from her fingertips. "Right?"

"I can stay longer . . ." Miles began.

"No, they need you at the scene."

"Then"—he glanced from me to Mia—"what should we—"

She sighed explosively. "I'm *fourteen*. I'm not a baby. Just go to your stupid crime scene and leave me here. I'll finish the movie and go to bed."

"We're not leaving you alone."

"Tess . . ."

"This has nothing to do with your independence, okay? Serious shit is about to go down, and we need to keep you close."

"God, why don't you just get me a leash?"

"There's always . . ." Derrick hesitated. He didn't look happy. "I mean, what about Lucian? Could we call him?"

"The necromancer?" Mia glared at me. "What, I can't be trusted to take care of myself, so you're going to leave me with some dude who raises the *dead*? Great, Tess. That's really great parenting. Why don't you find a vampire, or one of those Thyroid demons from last year—"

"Vailoid demons," I corrected, closing my eyes. "I guess we could call Lucian. It's not like he'll be asleep at this hour."

"Can we trust him?" Derrick blinked. "I mean, this is different from the investigation. This is our *home*."

"They're not different," I murmured. "They never will be. Not anymore. Everything's just so—screwed up."

"That's awesome!" Mia stood up. "Fine, call the creepy necromancer! I'll go call social services and tell them you're endangering a minor!"

"You'll do no such thing!"

She stormed down the hall. "I'm getting my phone!"

"You don't have any minutes left—and *we* pay the bill!" I called back after her.

She slammed the door.

Miles gave me a reassuring smile. "She's an amazing kid," he said. "You're doing a great job. Don't worry."

"Yeah. We're about to win parents of the year." I rubbed my eyes. "Next she'll be making out with a vampire. Or shoplifting."

"There isn't a room big enough to hold her," Miles said. "She's smart, and she's powerful. She's going to do great things someday. But for now, she's a regular teenager who hates everyone and everything."

"You can sense her power, too?"

He nodded, eyes wide. "Oh yeah. She's like one of those deluxe barbecues, throwing off heat."

"That's our kidlet." Derrick sighed. "So—you're making the call, right? I'm not talking to the dude."

I rolled my eyes. "Of course I'll make the call."

Honestly, I was as anxious about talking to Lucian as Derrick was. I still hadn't mentioned my sleepover to anyone, and Derrick just assumed that I'd gone to a CORE clinic and stayed until morning. I didn't feel like muddying up the waters any further. And the key to his warehouse still felt heavy in my pocket. It felt like a big, heavy cluster of secrets.

Lucian arrived twenty minutes later, wearing blue jeans and a vintage Canucks jersey—the black one with the crazy yellow skate on it. I stared at him critically.

"What?"

"Nothing—at least you look harmless, That's a good thing."

He rubbed his eyes. I noticed that his hair was uncharacteristically askew.

"Were you actually sleeping when I called?"

"Not yet, but I was looking forward to it."

"Sorry."

He shrugged. "Life happens. It's not a problem."

"Tonight, it's more like death happens."

"That's business as usual." He followed me up the stairs. "So—this is where you live. You know, you've never invited me over."

"I'm aware of that."

He took in the living room and nodded. "I like it."

"Your approval means the world to me." His expression fell. I sighed. "Sorry. I'm a crazy bitch tonight. I just want to go to sleep, but that's become an impossible luxury. I don't mean to take it out on you."

"I can handle it."

I decided not to unpack that statement. "There's coffee and doughnuts in the kitchen," I said, "and Mia's room is down the hall. She probably won't come out. If she does, try to be nice. Don't tell her anything about the investigation."

"Are you sure? I thought I'd debrief her, and then later we could raise some skeleton warriors—you know, just for kicks."

I stared at him levelly. "Sarcasm is too sophisticated for me at this hour. Please tell me that you're fine with this."

He laid both hands on my shoulders. "I'm fine with this."

Miles and Derrick emerged from the hallway. They were signing rapidly to each other, but I couldn't catch what they were saying. Derrick's smile evaporated when he saw Lucian, and he cleared his throat.

"Hey."

Lucian nodded. "Hey."

Miles looked at him. "Hey."

"Hey."

"Oh, for fuck's sake." I shook my head. "Let's all just bust them out and start measuring, shall we? Derrick, go warm up the car. Miles, can you make sure that both of our kits are in the trunk? And don't forget the extra flashlight batteries."

They wavered for a moment.

I blinked. "Was I unclear?"

Derrick mumbled something. Then they both headed down the stairs.

"You should have been in the army," Lucian said.

"My dad always says I should have gone into real estate." I chuckled. "He doesn't know how many Realtors are actually undead."

"That's a common mistake."

I looked at him squarely for a moment.

"What?" The corner of his mouth twitched.

"Just . . ." I smoothed my hair to keep my hands occupied. "Thanks for doing this. I appreciate it."

"It's not a problem, Tess."

"I need to know that she's safe."

He smiled. "I won't let anything happen."

"But you and I tend to be danger magnets. Or had you forgotten?"

"Go deal with the scene. I'll deal with the dishes."

I laughed. "God. Maybe you are the perfect guy." It escaped before I could stop it. I felt the blush creep up my face.

Shit.

Lucian looked satisfied, but made no reply.

I ran outside, barely remembering to throw my jacket on before the cold hit me. I was awake now. My nerves were on fire.

Stanley Park comprises over 1,000 acres. Bigger than Central Park, which is only 846 acres, give or take a tree. It isn't especially safe at night, but people go there anyway. Some trails are known to offer up anonymous sex, if that's what you're looking for. Not a tourist attraction that Vancouver likes to advertise, but it's there all the same. The seawall stretches almost nine kilometers around it, like a medieval barbican or some other strange fortification, patrolled by roller-blading teenagers rather than knights. The peninsula upon which the park sits—designed as a military reserve back in the 1860s—abuts the Pacific Ocean, now watching over everyone and no one, an empty fortress whose gears and cannons were long ago overgrown with rich dark moss and silent, cavernous roots.

The city was still trying to repair the damage wreaked by severe storms a few years back, which had destroyed centuries-old redwoods and torn a swath through Prospect Point like some mad giant on a rampage. But with 200 kilometers of trails and roads crisscrossing each other like joined arteries deep within the flesh of the park, it was still the perfect place to hide a body.

When I was little, my parents used to let me play in Cathedral Grove, where all the oldest trees were. I sat on the eight-hundred-year-old stump of the Hollow Tree, where wagons used to pause for photographs at the turn of the century. I stared at Siwash Rock with its statue of the beautiful girl in a wet suit—some glamorous secret lover of Jacques Cousteau in his youth, I imagined—and Deadman's Island, whose shadowed contours had become a mass burial site for Coast Salish peoples during the smallpox outbreak of the late 1880s. To me, the park had always been like something out of a fantasy novel, like Tolkien's Mirkwood or the home of the elves.

Now it was just another crime scene. And I felt betrayed, as if by nature itself.

We crossed the Lion's Gate Bridge, glowing steel-green like a floating emerald walkway in the night, some piece of Faerie that had come miraculously unstuck. It closed the distance between the first narrows of Burrard Inlet and the North Shore, giving way to the residential splendor of North Vancouver, as well as the south entrance to the park and just about the only place you could hope to find parking. The bridge's name was derived from the mountains that it faced, "the lions," which towered from the north and cast their shadow over us all. The lights atop the bridge gleamed like a strand of pearls—a gift from the Guinness family. My mother used to tell me they were fairies that had fallen in love with the city and stayed here.

Tonight they looked more like white blood cells, poised to attack something nameless and horrifying. Whatever was doing this. The thing that Duessa had called simply "it."

The lights of the bridge flickered as we drove. I felt like a strand of film in a movie projector, my life flashing forward. Planes of even darkness loomed on either side of us, waiting. Traffic was backed up due to construction, but Derrick was surprisingly adept at cutting people off and finding creative new lanes that only a compact could fit safely into. He ignored the sound of the horns blaring behind us. Miles in the backseat kept smoothing out an invisible wrinkle in his pants, looking a bit queasy.

We turned off at the set of orange lights, speeding down the parkway. The transition was gradual. The trees began to multiply, until suddenly the park was all around us, looking uncharacteristically sinister. Trails branched off and disappeared in all directions. Moonlight danced on the water to our right, and I could see the glowing neon sign for Monk's restaurant at the foot of the Cambie Street Bridge. There was also a floating Shell station with a glowing icon for boats, and I could remember standing in a nearby grove when I was barely eighteen, making out with my college boyfriend beneath the light of those same signs. He had nearly hairless wrists. Odd for a boy.

We saw the lights. Flares were placed approximately ten feet apart, burning green against the dark. The occlusion field was a lot stronger than normal, since it was difficult to mystically cordon off a quarter-mile stretch of Stanley Park. The materia flow, usually more like a spiderweb touch, hit me like a coffee spike to the chest. I glanced at Miles and Derrick, seeing that they felt it, too. The air around us was running hot.

We parked by a group of unmarked sedans in a gravel patch, as close as we could get to the scene. A portable site had been set up with extra kits, batteries, gloves, Tyvek suits, and a pile of gel cell generators for alternate light sources. I could see the flashbulbs of a dozen cameras in the distance, just past the line of trees.

"Guess we're hiking," Derrick said, grabbing supplies.

My kit felt reassuringly heavy. I pretended that it was full of knowledge and experience rather than just scene equipment. Miles looked oddly uncomfortable as he stood there, empty-handed. I gave him a PVC apron and some shoe covers. He smiled, as if grateful to carry something.

As we made our way past the tree line, I could hear competing voices, the hum of equipment, and the sound of portable generators. A scene photographer nearly bumped into me as she passed, her eyes on the monitor of her digital camera instead of the pathway. She apologized and kept going. I started to reach for my own camera with the ring flash—we used it for macrophotography of small bloodstains—but Derrick was already handing it to me. He smiled wanly. It was a "get ready" look. We knew each other too well.

The trees thinned and gave way to a small grove. I recognized this area as the site of the Japanese War Memorial, a secluded and peaceful spot that was usually shaded by flowering magnolias. Not a big draw for tourists. Yellow caution tape was wrapped around the entrance to the clearing, and I ducked underneath it. Derrick held the tape for Miles so that he could follow suit, and a camera flash lit his profile up momentarily. The yellow tape—emblazoned with the words MYSTICAL CRIME SCENE—DO NOT CROSS—seemed to glow like a strand of spun gold in Derrick's hand. As Miles paused underneath the fluorescent tape, he was backlit, as if by an arcing sunspot in the middle of the night.

The space around the monument was brilliant beneath a floodlight, almost unreal as it glowed in waves of heat. There was a concrete circle flanked by iron posts, each linked by rusting chains. A Y-shaped tree split the darkness behind us, and a manicured hedge to the right gave the impression that we might have wandered into some psychotic, fucked-up country club. Blue tarp and netting were hastily rigged up in the surrounding trees, in case of rain. But it was a clear night. Beautiful and warm.

Lines of cement radiated outward from the monument, like spokes from a wheel, and I found myself unconsciously stepping over them. *Step on a crack, break your momma's back.* Who knew what was possible at a mystical crime scene? I looked up, following the memorial tower as it soared upward, a graven pillar with a torch crowned by fangs of iron. It hadn't been lit since 1985, and I could only imagine how eerie that light must have seemed. The ghosts of all fifty-four Japanese soldiers—the counted ones, anyway—who died in the First World War.

At the base of the tower was a series of delicate panels made of granite, sloped and smooth, like the segments of an orange. Each post lined up with the diagonal grooves cut through the concrete slabs. My eyes followed the line of architectural symmetry, along the dark space between the panels and to the closest iron post—flecked with blood—where the boy was handcuffed.

He was naked. His arms were twisted behind his back, and he leaned forward, limply, on his knees. I couldn't see his face. A generous pool of blood had collected on the ground beneath him, some of it flowing along those carved spokes. The result was a bloody mandala, or a kind of shocking, vermilion wheel that coursed beneath my feet. I slipped on the shoe covers, suddenly wishing I could levitate.

"Where's Selena?" Derrick asked.

"I don't know. I'm not even sure if Tasha's been here yet to release the scene." I slipped on a pair of gloves. "I doubt anyone's leaving early tonight."

There was power in the air, and not just from the occlusion field. I could taste the footprint of something vast and hungry. I felt bile in my throat.

I approached the monument. No clothes or shoes in sight—what did it do with them? Burned, maybe? Or kept as a memento? The boy's hair was caked with blood, but I could tell that he was blond. I was sure that if I lifted his head, I'd see a perfect surgical scar running across his left common carotid artery. The handcuffs threw me a bit. If it had the power to suspend Jacob Kynan from the ceiling, why would it bother with handcuffs? Maybe it was just playing with us. *See, I can use your tools. I can look human if I want to. Just like you.*

"Just a baby."

I turned to see Tasha looking at me. She'd managed to creep up from somewhere, still holding her medical bag.

"Young, huh?" I swallowed. "This thing seems to like them young."

"Thing?" She gave me a curious look. "Is that the word we're using now?"

I shrugged. "Seems to fit."

"Well, the story's the same as last time. One cut to the neck with an incredibly sharp and precise instrument. It would have taken him eight, maybe ten minutes to bleed out, given his slight size. No other visible signs of trauma, except for a fading bruise under his left eye. I bet I'll find healed fractures during the post, though."

"Not a stretch if he's another runaway."

"His liver temp was thirty-eight point five. No signs of rigor yet."

"Huh." I edged closer to the iron post. "He was running hot. Drugs?"

"Could be. If he died less than two hours ago—which the

lack of rigor seems to support—then his liver temp should be closer to thirty-six degrees."

"But it's a warm night." I could see the purple of the blood settling in his hands and feet. The smaller blood vessels usually displayed lividity within thirty minutes of death, but I didn't see any fixed spots of discoloration, or *purpura*. Bodies that had been dead for more than eight hours usually looked like they'd been speckled with a paintbrush.

"Did you notice any insect activity?"

"Just blowflies, and they usually don't lay eggs at night. If we'd waited until sunrise"—she shook her head—"man, it would have been like an insect metropolis. But right now there's no oviposition that I can see. We'll show the scene photographs to Leigh Mussel. She's the entomologist, so she might catch something that I missed."

"What's that?" Derrick asked, pointing to the blood pool. I followed his gesture, and my eyes narrowed.

"A void. Looks like some weird tool mark."

Selena finally appeared over my left shoulder. "Look closer."

I held her glance for a second. I could see the barely coiled desperation in her eyes—the look of someone who'd slept maybe a handful of hours in a week. Now she was on the verge of total collapse.

I did as she said. Gradually, the white edges of the shape grew more distinct as I looked at it. A handle. A slim, tapered wedge. Someone had laid this tool down immediately after cutting the boy's throat, so that his blood had pooled around it, forming a perfect void. It was deliberate. But why? First the *coire*, and now this.

"It's a knife of some kind," I said. "No. A dagger. Double-edged from the look of the blade."

Selena gave me an expectant look.

Something clicked.

"You're kidding me" was all I could say.

She shook her head. "I wish I was."

Miles spoke for the first time: "It's like those daggers you carry."

"An athame." I reached unconsciously for my own, which was fastened safely in its leather sheath. "That's the weapon. It's killing them with a consecrated blade."

"And it's leaving us bits and pieces of some fucked-up history." Selena rubbed her eyes. "Icons of our own craft—the cauldron, the dagger. It knows us. It's killing with our most sacred tools."

"This is different from Jacob, though. The kid wasn't restrained with magic—just plain old handcuffs. And he's been bruised."

"That bruise is healing," Tasha clarified. "It's probably from a few days ago."

I reached over and gently cupped my gloved fingertips underneath the boy's chin, lifting his head. There was faint lividity in his face due to the position of the head, giving it a purplish cast. His left eye was still slightly swollen, and the bruise underneath it was fading. But his right eye was open.

I remembered him eating spaghetti from a Tupperware container. The secretive look on his face. The flash of his tongue.

It was the boy from Duessa's House.

"Shit." It came out as a whisper.

"Tess?" Derrick gave me a look. "Everything okay?"

I took a step backward. His blood was dark against my latex gloves. I could almost feel its texture, slick, like liquid shadow. I shook my head.

"Tess?"

"It's him, Derrick. It's the kid from Duessa's. The one with the black eye."

"What kid?" He stared quizzically at the body. "I didn't see anyone like that. Was he in one of the rooms?"

I nodded. "I saw him."

"Me, too," Miles added. "Just for a second. But I saw him."

We exchanged a look. I understood. Usually, you don't encounter bodies that you've seen in daylight hours. When I first saw the body of Mia's aunt, Cassandra, it was like something shifted inside me. The rules changed. Even though I hadn't known this boy, I felt the same thing now. Like some dark, invisible force were plucking the strings of my life. Fingering the frets and playing with me.

It had to stop.

I took off my gloves and wiped the sweat from my forehead. Suddenly the world was spinning. I felt myself lurch to the side.

"Whoa." Derrick grabbed my arm. "Tess—"

"I'm fine." I sucked in a breath. But I didn't push him away. "I'm just tired, and—and"—I stared at Derrick—"I *knew* him. I mean, not really. I never talked to the poor kid. But he *saw* me, you know? Just for a second, but it was this real moment, and now he's dead. And he's a little kid. He's just a fucking little *kid* . . ."

My voice broke. I looked away, swallowing hard.

"Do—ah . . ." Miles cleared his throat, looking at Selena. "Do we have a name? It doesn't look like he left any ID behind."

"Duessa's on her way. She'll know."

My eyes widened. "You called her?"

"Of course. He's obviously one of hers."

Somehow, I couldn't imagine Selena having Duessa's number on speed dial. It strained my mind a bit.

"There she is now," Selena said.

Two shadows emerged from the line of tress—one tall, the other short. It was Duessa, with Wolfie close behind. A passing technician said something inaudible to her, probably about contaminating the scene. She gave him a withering look, and he hurried away in the opposite direction.

Selena waved her over. Duessa approached the perimeter of the monument, her expression impossible to read. She was sedate in a wool skirt and short black coat, but her boots had a serious wedge heel. Wolfie remained by her side, but didn't touch her. Lucian was the only one who'd ever dared, at least to my knowledge. I remembered the faint press of her lips on my cheek. It still made me shiver.

"That's Henry," she said. Her voice sounded dead.

"Have you got a last name?"

She turned to Selena. Her eyes were almost mauve in the

light. "Lawter. He was a runaway. Parents died three years ago. Kristen and Araby Lawter."

"They were CORE," Selena said, eyes dark. "Consultants, not field agents. But Kristen was a specialist in materia interactions."

"So the pattern's still there," Derrick said. "Another child of mages."

Wolfie's arms were rigid. I could feel how tightly coiled his power was, like a golden spring ready to snap. The air next to him was much warmer than the ambient temperature in the clearing.

"How did he get the bruise?" I asked.

Duessa didn't look at me. Her gestures were economical—she made eye contact only when she had to. She moved along a different continuum from the rest of us. We were all just extras in her spatial narrative.

"Client," she said simply. "A real asshole, but his money was nice. Paid triple if Henry went bareback, and even more if he could breed."

I frowned at the term, which I hadn't heard before. "Breed?"

"That's the big show, darling," she said, her mouth crooked.

"He let the client ejaculate while they were having unprotected anal sex," Derrick said, his voice low. "About as high-risk as you can get."

"But lucrative," Duessa added. "And if you've got no ties and no self-esteem and no fucking shred of hope, well—you let people do that shit to you. No matter what anyone says. And Henry had the right body for it. Little, blond, and smooth. That's how they like 'em. He was never out of work."

"Where was the money going?" I asked. "Was he using?"

"Would you let someone do that to you without being high first?" Duessa shook her head. "Of course he was using. Coke, mostly."

"And Hex," Wolfie said.

I'd almost forgotten he was there. His voice was flat.

Duessa turned to him. "That so, love? When did it start?"

Wolfie shrugged. "About a month ago. He wanted to try

something different. The powders weren't working anymore, and he wanted to expand his client base."

"How old was he? Barely sixteen?" I felt a lump in my throat. "He shouldn't have a client base! He shouldn't be into Hex at all."

"That's how it works, baby." Duessa finally met my eyes. "Nothing's the way it should be. Everything's different. Like we're trapped on the wrong side of the mirror. But you can't always get them to see it. Mostly, they just live on the other side."

I heard what sounded like a helicopter. The tarp made snapping noises as a strong wind clawed at it. Then I could hear a throng of new voices coming from the other side of the clearing.

"Mother-*fuck*," Selena said. "She wouldn't!"

Devorah Kynan emerged from the trees.

A scattered group of people were running behind her. Lawyers, mostly, and reporters for CORE publications. We didn't have our own newspaper exactly, but we did have periodicals and print networks of a sort. H. L. Mencken wouldn't want to read them.

"Detective Ward!" Devorah strode evenly to the foot of the monument, taking the whole scene in with a single look. "Why didn't you call me?"

"Ms. Kynan . . ." Selena closed her eyes in frustration. "Really, we've only just gotten here ourselves. A lot of evidence needs to be processed, and I'd appreciate it if you could wait until morning—"

"The hell I will! Another kid ends up dead, and you think I'm going to go back to my office and do paperwork?"

"That wouldn't be anything new," Duessa said, "would it, Devorah?"

The two women locked eyes. I immediately felt the urge to run as fast I could. They were two wolves circling each other. Their collective power made the hairs on the back of my neck stand on end. Like those giant Sentinels from the *X-Men* comics. But scarier.

"What are you doing here, Duessa? Run out of children to exploit?"

"Fuck you."

Devorah laughed. "That's your response to everything. Well, how do you plan to deal with this? Another one of your precious 'kids' with a slit throat. Security must be pretty lax in that stinking warehouse of yours."

The air between them was a solid thing, salivating darkness. Duessa didn't move a muscle. Her eyes burned.

"Don't fucking talk to me about my kids. You didn't give two shits about Jake, so don't come around here talking about *my* family."

Devorah stepped forward. "I loved Jacob. I lost a *son*. What did you lose, Duessa? Another tax credit? Another reason to feel good about yourself?"

"You self-righteous bitch . . ." Duessa's entire face went a shade darker. "Don't you *ever* pretend to know how I feel about my family. All you see are throwaways and addicts—that's all you people ever fucking see. But I know them. I knew Jake better than you ever did, and deep down, that makes you feel sick, doesn't it?"

Devorah laughed coldly. "Jacob would never tell you anything. He knew you were trash. You and your whole twisted little family—"

"Lady . . ." Wolfie stepped between them. Fire arced in his palm. "Trust me when I say that you're one word away from—"

"Wolfie, don't . . ." Duessa began.

It was too late. I felt Devorah gathering a wave of power. The air between them went suddenly dark and heavy, as if someone had turned up the volume on the night. Duessa didn't move, but I felt her power rise up to meet Devorah's. The two didn't crash together—but they touched.

Time slowed down.

When two different types of materia intersect, they create a locus of energy, called a *halo*. Lightning is a good example. But not just anyone can produce electrical materia. It requires a tremendous amount of power and focus. Other physical forces, like gravity or electromagnetism, could be shaped and twisted in the same way, but it was like trying to stab God in the eye. You didn't do it unless you were prepared for the consequences. Fucking with the building blocks of the physical universe was not something to try for fun.

When those two fields of energy met, the space between them actually began to decompose. For just a moment, the night seemed to peel back, and I could see glowing strands of multicolored vapor moving beneath it. Curls of red, green, and gold energy slithered and crackled as they moved across each other. I was literally looking at the concrete wiring of the universe—the buried forces that made life on Earth possible.

A web of liquid silver seemed to hang over both of them. The darkness moved. I smelled something burning, and my stomach was in my throat. One of the glowing strands—a molten white curl of light with coruscations of blue—came unglued from the air. It began to move, ponderously, circling both Devorah and Duessa. I'd never seen it before, but I recognized it from descriptions.

Weak nuclear force. Radioactive materia.

"Shit" didn't really cover it.

"Devorah!" Selena's voice seemed to be coming from far away. "Devorah—stop this *now*! Get control of yourself!"

She was talking to a grieving mother. Control wasn't high on the woman's agenda.

Nobody could separate the two women. If I even brushed up against that deadly white tendril of force, every nucleated cell in my body would come unstuck. Not an especially pleasant death, even within the myriad of complex demises that we saw every day in our line of work.

Luckily, I didn't have to test out any theories. I felt Duessa draw back the curtain of her power. The night smoothed itself down, like a cat's ruffled fur, and those vaporous and hungry spirits faded back into discrete invisibility. Devorah pulled back a few seconds later. Her eyes were grim.

"Another time," she said.

Duessa simply nodded.

Devorah looked at Selena. "Don't try to cut me out of the loop," she warned, "and don't let *her* get in the way."

Duessa said nothing.

"We'll be in close contact," Selena assured her. Only I caught the slight tremor in her voice. She was more than a little shaken up.

"I expect to hear from you the second the autopsy is complete. As of tonight, your Mystical Crimes Division is only working one case. Make it your priority."

With that, Devorah left the clearing, taking her cadre of lawyers and assistants with her. I exhaled.

"That was awesome. Especially the part where we almost died."

Duessa shook her head. "She wouldn't have gone that far. Bitch is a little crazy, but she couldn't very well incinerate her whole investigative team." She smirked. "That'd be counterproductive."

"Let's just hope you didn't contaminate the scene with all that energy," Selena said. "If there was an aura trace left behind, you may have painted right over it with that little pissing contest of yours."

"Trust me," Duessa replied. "Whatever did this—it didn't leave anything behind that's—what do you call it?" She smiled, as if to herself. "*Probative.* Yes, that's it. There's nothing like that left behind."

Selena turned to Miles. "Do you sense anything?"

"I'll need more time," he said, "and access to the area around the body. I can't promise anything, though."

"Nobody expects a miracle. But if you recognize anything from those scenes back in Ontario, it might prove invaluable down the road."

"Don't tell *her*," Duessa said, biting her lip. "She'll subpoena your ass before you can blink. Hopefully, she doesn't know you've got a haptic working for you. She probably wasn't paying too close attention."

"Could you have stopped her?" Selena asked flatly. "Are you two equals?"

Duessa laughed softly. There wasn't a trace of humor in the sound. Then she touched Wolfie's arm.

"It's time to tell Miss Corday what you told me," she said gently. "Then come home. We're having a late supper. Bring some polenta."

13

Wolfie shifted in his chair, sliding the glass of Coke forward, then back, then forward again in a maddening way. He'd absolutely refused to come down to the lab, so I took him to the Ovaltine Café on Hastings. I couldn't think of any other place, and at least it was on his home turf. He knew that he could leave at any time. Pink and green light from the café's neon sign bathed him in an eerie glow. It reminded me of a psychic I'd seen once, sitting in the window of her small shop, backlit by a wild rose-quartz glow. Her dark eyes had seen straight through me as I walked by.

Now, Wolfie's dark eyes looked anywhere but into mine. I feared that he was ready to bolt. I kept ordering drinks, then a plate of fries, in the vain hope that it might keep him in one place. So far, he'd eaten half the fries and drained three glasses of soda, barely saying a word the whole time. His fingers glistened with crumbs and ketchup; my salad—which looked like someone had put it through a garbage disposal—lay untouched next to a squirt bottle of ranch dressing that the waitress had thoughtfully supplied.

"Wolfie," I said, "if you drink any more, you're going to rupture something."

He chuckled and slid the glass away. "Yeah. Probably."

"Feeling ready to talk yet? I can wait longer, if you like."

Actually, I couldn't. I had to pick up Mia from school in an hour. She required at least the semblance of normalcy in her life, even if she knew that both her guardians happened to be investigating an occult serial murder.

I wanted to seem friendly. Obviously, this kid had been shit-kicked and fucked over one too many times, and he didn't trust anyone. I figured a gentle touch might be best. Also, I'd be lying if I said I wasn't a bit afraid of him. I'd felt his power, raw and untried as it was. He could burn this place down by twitching his little finger, and I wasn't sure I had the resources to stop him.

"It's hard," he said after a beat. "All of this shit. It's hard to put into words, you know? Especially after what happened to Jake"—he swallowed—"and now to Henry." Anger flickered in his eyes. I felt the air between us raise a few degrees in temperature. "I mean, he was just a *puppy*. Never hurt anyone. We all protected him, right? Made sure he was safe. But he kept buying Hex from that sick *fuck*. That . . ."

He shook his head. His cheeks were flushed.

"Did you see this guy?" I asked, trying to keep my voice level. "Did you get a good look at him?"

"Only saw him from behind, if he was walking Henry to the car. He always wore a black hooded sweatshirt."

"What about his shoes? Or his pants?"

His mouth dipped in a sour expression. "Boots. Real fucking gaudy ones, too—black and polished, like ex-military. Steel on the bottom. And they were painted."

I perked up. "Painted how? Like, with an airbrush? Or acrylic paint?"

He shrugged. "Just painted. On the heels. Two hearts— one was whole, the other was broken and bleeding. One says HEAVEN, the other says HELL. Fucked, eh? I'll bet he thought they were real cool. Picked 'em up at Cheap Thrills or some shit."

I smiled. "That's good. That helps, Wolfie. Gives us somewhere to start."

"Yeah?" He nodded. Some of his anger had dissipated. "Okay. Cool."

"What about his pants? I know it's an odd question—it's not like you go around memorizing details about a dude's pants. But if something stands out, it could make him easier to find."

"They were black," he replied. "Everything was black. They looked expensive. Designer shit, like from Holt Renfrew. Sometimes Kim or Dukwan'll swipe clothes from there." He shook his head. "They think it makes them hot shit. But they never get as far as the change room, so the damn pants are always too big or too small. They look like idiots in them. But the guy's pants—they could have come from a store like that. Or, like—what's that really expensive place that sells jeans? In Yaletown?"

"Mavi," I said. "You think they might be from there?"

"Maybe. A lot of dealers actually work in the financial district, and they're dressed to the nines. This guy's clothes—even the hoodie, you know—they all looked pricey. All fitted and shit, like they came from some boutique."

"Kangaroo jacket," I murmured.

"Huh?"

"Oh—nothing." I smiled despite myself. "That's what my mom used to call them. Kangaroo jackets. People always look at me funny when I say it."

"Well, it is kind of funny." He cracked a smile. It was slight, but there.

Progress.

"This dealer—did he sell to anyone else? I mean, did he just go for boys, or was he after girls as well?"

I didn't want to say Jacob's name, especially knowing that the two of them had been "tight," as Duessa called it. I was hoping he'd volunteer the information. Wolfie, however, saw through me like a plate glass window. He scowled.

"Just come out and ask what you want to ask."

I nodded. "Fine. Did you see him with Jacob Kynan?"

"He went by Jake. No one called him Jacob, 'cept for his mother." His eyes narrowed in distaste. "And she's a fucking head case."

"I've had a few run-ins with her already," I told him, "not including tonight. And I'm inclined to agree with you. But there's also a lot of misinformation flying around. Everyone's saying something different—"

"What, about Jake?"

I felt him crank up the thermostat again.

"About a *lot* of things," I replied, placing both hands on the table. "That's why we're talking now. I'm hoping you can clear some of this up for me. For us."

"We're talking right now because the Lady asked me to," he replied flatly. "If she hadn't, this wouldn't be happening."

"I understand that."

He drummed his fingers on the tabletop for a second. Then he sighed. I felt something ease open inside him—a door swinging on rusty hinges that led somewhere dark and secret.

"I met Jake a year ago," he said at last. "Duessa told me that she'd seen this boy trying to score a fix by the old sugar refinery on Commissioner Avenue. I used to hang out there—a long time ago—so I knew it." His eyes went soft for a moment. "'Wolfie, he's real pretty,' she said to me. 'Too pretty.' I knew what she really meant. He was in over his head, and if he stayed out there too long, someone was going to slit his throat or smash his face in." He folded his hands together. "She was calling in the favor, you know? I was barely sixteen when she found me in the same place. Too young for that life. Too young for surgery without my parents' consent, and they fucked off a long time ago, so that wasn't going to happen. So I had to improvise."

At the mention of surgery, I felt something click.

I looked closely at Wolfie's face without appearing to stare. His soft jawline and delicate, almost petite chin. His narrow shoulders and slender hands, one folded atop the other in a surprisingly prim gesture, like he was sitting in a church pew. His smooth wrists and short goatee, a bit patchy in places. I couldn't ask him, but I was willing to bet that Wolfie hadn't been born biologically male, just as Duessa hadn't been born biologically female. My eyes snapped back to the table, but he'd caught me looking.

He smirked. "Curious now, eh?"

"I . . ." A flush slowly crept up my cheeks. "I'm sorry, Wolfie. I didn't really notice before."

"Isn't that a good thing? It means I can pass." He chuckled. "We're all passing, right? Everyone's passing for someone, or something. You can pass for human real well, but I smell the demon in you. It's my gift."

I wasn't quite sure what to say to that. "I guess I do try to hide it."

"Of course you do. Just like your pretty-boy partner, the telepath, tries to hide that he's queer. Just like the haptic tries to hide that he's deaf. It's habit. Evolution. We all try to pass for somebody who fits in better." He adjusted his trucker's cap, which read I ♥ SASKATOON. His sideburns were slightly damp from the heat of the café. "When I hung out at the docks, I had to tape my tits up. That hurts, you know. Ever ripped off a wad of duct tape? It'll make you scream if you're not careful."

"I—can only imagine," I said.

Wolfie laughed. "Is this making you uncomfortable, *Detective* Corday?"

I blinked. "Yes. A little. But that's my shit, not yours, right?"

A look of surprise crossed his face momentarily. "Yeah. That's a good answer. Better than most I hear."

"I don't really have a lot of trans friends," I admitted.

"You mean you don't have any."

To my credit, I kept myself from blushing this time. "No. You're right."

"Everyone moves in different crowds," he said, shrugging.

I nodded. "So, Duessa helped you, right? With surgical alternatives?"

"She helped me get my top done. Matched me dollar for dollar, and then gave me a safe place to heal. After that, I started working on the inside. Training the new kids, making sure they knew what was safe—handing out the disposable cell phones, dealing with the food and the clothes and the clean gear."

"So you owed her. She basically promoted you—got you off the street. When she told you to do the same thing for Jake . . ."

He nodded. "I had to. And she was right. He was pretty and smart, but not smart enough to make a living. He came from a different place. His whole life, everyone just handed him shit, and he thought this wouldn't be any different. But he hadn't realized how fucking hard it can be. The life. He didn't know."

"And you schooled him."

Wolfie shrugged. "I taught him what I could. Listened to him complain." He shook his head, smiling. "That boy could whine like a bitch, you know, but he had a silver tongue. You never got tired of hearing him piss and moan. He had this way of turning it into a story, and you'd just nod your head. And then he had you." His eyes fell. "Just like that. He had you."

"It sounds like you had each other," I said gently.

He scowled. "Don't go all PFLAG on me, Tess." It was actually the first time he'd addressed me by name. "Jake and I had times. It wasn't easy. He never knew what he wanted, and me—well, I guess I knew too well for my own good."

"You wanted Jake."

Wolfie rolled his eyes. "He was always going back and forth. I like boys, I like girls, I like trans-fags, I like straight fucking jocks." He sighed in disgust. "But near the end—I mean, before . . ."

He rubbed his thumb and forefinger together. His eyes scraped the table.

"We were in sync," He said. "We understood each other. And you can say what you want about that boy, but *damn*—even when he was a spoiled little rich kid who didn't know what side of the bed to piss on, he still knew how to make you hum. He was *good*. No matter what was on the menu, if you catch my drift."

"I'm sure he was a real Renaissance man in the sack," I supplied.

He snorted. "Aw, don't make it sound like that. It wasn't just, like, he gave great head, or whatever. Even if he *did*. He just knew what to do. He kissed like someone who understood a lot more. Does that make sense?"

I thought of Lucian, who kissed like he'd lived nine lives and counting.

"It does," I said ruefully.

"That fucker . . ." His eyes darkened, and I realized that he wasn't talking about his lover anymore. "The guy with the boots. Jake knew him. Before."

"Jake was buying Hex from him?"

He looked guilty. "They dealt more than once. I warned him—I told him that the dude was giving off some weird energy. He tasted like death. I *told* him. But Jake needed the drug. And he sold it cheap. Everyone knew that."

"So Jake kept buying from him."

Wolfie made a face. "Sometimes he went to the dude's place to fix. Whenever he came back, he seemed—different. Like he was bleeding from the inside, but he didn't want anyone to know. Like his spirit was broken. He even smelled different." Wolfie made a face. "Like burnt oil. Ashes."

I remembered, with a start, how Lucian's hands had smelled faintly when he used necroid materia. Ashes and burnt sage. Had we been wrong about the necromancy? There hadn't been any necroid trace left behind, but—if this thing really was using the same power as Lucian, there was a chance we'd be able to track it.

"Whenever I warned him to stop buying from the fucker," Wolfie continued, "he just raved about how pure the stuff was. And how cheap. And by that time, he was doing two, maybe three bags of heroin a day. On top of the Hex. So there was no stopping him."

"Did Jake introduce Henry to the same dealer?"

He nodded, his jaw clenched. "Fucking asshole. I told him—Henry's just a baby! He can't deal with that kind of heavy shit. But Henry idolized Jake. Always hanging around him, copying him, trying to get with his old clients. If Jake told him to do a shot of napalm, the little twat would have done it."

I remembered Henry's slight frame—his oddly empty eyes, and that ghost of a smile on his face. He'd seemed so fragile. Impressionable.

"Fucking Henry." Wolfie closed his eyes. "Never listened."

"It wasn't your fault," I said.

His eyes snapped up. "Oh, hey, thanks, CORE lady! That'll help me sleep at night, when I'm dreaming about my fucking boyfriend getting his throat slit by some *thing* that smells like ashes and death. And all that goddamn blood. You know what that's like? Seeing that shit whenever you close your eyes?"

I held his gaze.

"Huh." His mouth twitched. "Maybe you do after all."

My mom had lent me her car ("for safety's sake, dear"), and I felt weird sitting in the leather-upholstered driver's seat, like when I was six and used to walk around the house in her Mary Janes. She never had a problem with it until the day she caught me wearing her sunglasses with an unlit cigarette dangling out of my mouth, pretending to gossip about the neighbors. That was when the dress-up games ended. "I have similar stories," Derrick told me once, "although mine all end with me stealing my mother's eighty-dollar lip liner and trying to drink Vanilla Stoli."

I slid into a parking space close to the school's entrance and flicked the radio on. Thank God for The Police. Mia would complain, but I didn't feel like participating in her current post-punk phase. I liked my eighties rockers, with their big hair, tight jeans, and soaring synthesizers. They didn't age well, though. Look at Pete Burns. Sometimes I had nightmares about his radioactive lips chasing me around the house.

I scanned the common area outside the school, which had exploded with throngs of teenage girls who were all frantically texting each other. The boys loped around them like hungry coyotes, adjusting their wrist bands and smoothing down their Pete Wentz hair as they lit up cigarettes. Not much changed. Back when I was in high school, the boys all looked like Kurt Cobain, and the girls had only recently rediscovered baby doll tees and vintage skirts.

Mia appeared from nowhere, sliding into the passenger seat and dumping her knapsack on the floor. "Oh my *God*. Would it kill them to spring for an air conditioner in this cheap-ass school? At least the junior high in Elder had a real computer lab with central air. Now we just have cast-off Macs and, like, this broken-down fan that could explode at any minute and decapitate a student or something."

"What did we learn today?" I asked her, smiling as I pulled away from the curb. My mother's car was so smooth and quiet, it felt like I was driving a velvet slipper down Woodlawn Street. Mia leaned back and closed her eyes.

"Well, I learned that globalization is alive and well. Coca-Cola, like, controls our entire campus, and if you want to eat something without disgusting animal by-products, you have to almost get hit by a dozen cars crossing First to get to the world's crappiest convenience store. Oh, and our history teacher flunked out of Dalhousie."

"Nice." I tried to keep my tone neutral. "Did you hang out with that guy today—what's his name again? Patrick?"

She snorted. "Way to go, Inspector Gadget. I totally didn't see that one coming. And *no*, I didn't see Patrick today. We're not even friends. We just, like, run into each other sometimes. In the hallways, or out in the courtyard, or whatever."

"Just curious," I said.

"I mean, sure, we're sleeping together. But it's not like he's my first."

I glared at her.

"God, Tess! Unwind that crazy-ass nerve of yours. I'm not sleeping with anyone. I'm not going to raves or smoking crack. Every day, I eat a veggie wrap, do my homework, and take pictures for the photography club. Not exactly Paris Hilton."

"You joined a club?"

She rolled her eyes. "Don't have a heart attack. I *can* inter-act with other humans my age. When they're not completely lame."

"I didn't even know you liked photography." I took a hard left onto First, cutting off an SUV. "Do you need a digital camera? We can go shopping for one."

"Oh, can we *please* go to Best Buy? I love chatting with awkward, skinny dudes wearing yellow shirts."

"We could go somewhere else."

"They lend us cameras to use. Besides, you can't afford to spend four hundred bucks for a good SLR camera."

"Don't worry about our finances." She was absolutely right, though. "I could always sign out one of the super-cameras from the lab. They've got this sweet Nikon D200 with a CCD image sensor. Four-thousand-pixel resolution. I'm sure Becka wouldn't mind if I borrowed one."

Selena would flay me alive if I lost a two-thousand-dollar SLR camera. But seeing the gleam in Mia's eye was worth it.

"That is a sweet camera," she murmured. "Maybe—"

My cell started ringing. I glanced down. It was a CORE internal number. Great.

"Speaking of the lab," I said, flipping open the phone. "Tess."

"Hey, it's Tasha. Sorry to call you on your day off."

I felt a chill. Tasha didn't make casual phone calls from the morgue. "Hi, Tash. What's going on?"

"I just finished the post on the kid from the park. Henry, I think you said his name was. He's still listed as a John Doe."

"Nobody's come forward? No family?"

"I'm afraid not."

I sighed. "What did you find? Do you want me to swing by?"

"If you could—there are a few anomalies you might be able to clear up."

I didn't like the word "anomalies." "Okay. I'll be there in twenty minutes, if traffic cooperates. I'm in East Van now."

"I'll see you in forty-five," Tasha said dryly. Then she hung up.

"Are we going to the lab?" Mia asked.

"*I'm* going to the lab. You're going home."

"But Derrick's still at work." I saw a mischievous glint in

her eyes. "You can't leave me alone, right? I mean, someone could break down the door, or come through the window, or, like, materialize out of smoke in the kitchen or something. Like Gary Oldman in *Dracula*. Wouldn't it be safer if I stayed with you?"

She had a point. I exhaled.

Mia knew exactly what that meant.

"I wouldn't have to go anywhere near the morgue," she pressed. "I could just hang out with Derrick in the psi-tank. Or in Selena's office."

I was already making a U-turn on First.

"If I see you anywhere near the morgue," I told her, "something very, very bad will happen. Much worse than anything the forces of darkness could throw at you."

Mia only grinned.

Tasha had been right. Forty-five minutes, two traffic jams, and one accident (not related to us) later, we pulled into the lab's underground parking. I swiped us in. The security guard applied a stick-on visitor's pass to Mia's jacket, which she seemed quite proud of. I dutifully slung my CORE ID around my neck. It felt like an albatross.

Derrick managed to smile and look confused at the same time when he saw us. He was in the middle of filling out a work order for something called a cortical stimulator. It looked expensive.

"Hey! What are you two doing—"

I unceremoniously pushed Mia toward him. "This one's your responsibility for the next twenty minutes. Don't let her out of your sight. If she escapes, I want this entire place on lockdown."

"Geez, overreact much?" She rolled her eyes at me, then turned to Derrick. "Can I fire a gun? A Luger or a Glock, maybe?"

Derrick grabbed her firmly by the shoulders. "Operation Evil MiMi is in full effect. She's not going anywhere near live ammo."

"I hate when you call me that."

"But it's Mariah's nickname."

"That's why I hate it." She sighed. "Can I at least play with one of the telekinetics? It's fun to watch them break stuff."

"I have a great activity for you," Derrick said, already leading her down the hallway. "It's called learning to forge Selena's signature."

"Oh, that might be fun—"

"You're driving her home!" I called back.

Derrick made a thumbs-up sign. Mia walked two steps ahead, pretending that she didn't know him, but glancing back discreetly to make sure he was still there. I smiled once, then headed for the elevator.

The morgue was cold and smelled like steel. Among other things. Tasha was leaning over the autopsy table and wearing a Tyvek suit. She'd just put her tape recorder away and was scribbling a few notes when she looked up and saw me.

"Hey, Tess. Thanks for coming in. What's the weather like?"

I glanced at the table, which was slanted to allow for the drainage of various fluids into a copper basin on the floor. A detachable shower spigot lay on the counter, and pink water swirled into the drain like some gruesome version of a child's finger painting. I swallowed. Henry's body was half-covered by a white sheet. His head was propped up on a rubber block, and his arms lay still at his sides. They were so small and white, like the arms of a porcelain doll.

"It's sunny," I said. "Not too hot."

"I've heard about sunlight. The descriptions sound lovely."

I chuckled without much humor. "We should go out for a drink sometime. There's this pub that Derrick and I like in the West End. Great patio."

She smiled, obviously caught off guard. "I'd like that. Speaking of Derrick, there's someone I'd like to set him up with—"

"Oh God. Please not another cousin, Tash. The last one was a mortgage specialist. He tried to convince Derrick to open a mutual fund, and I had to hear about it for days afterward."

"It's not my fault that he has such high standards." She sniffed. "I mean, you can only date artists and creative types for so long, right? He's getting older. He needs to think about settling down and finding himself a nice, stable husband."

"He's twenty-five."

"Trust me—in this city, that's long in the tooth. His party days are behind him. And this guy's *so* nice . . ."

My eyes narrowed. "Is he a relation of yours?"

She could tell that I was cracking. "Not at all. He's a friend. Great job. And cute. I heard him talking the other day about how he's tired of going out to clubs, and how he wants to find a nice guy. And I said, I've got the *perfect* one for you." She winked. "And don't worry, I didn't mention all of that boy's neurotic tics, or the fact that he's living in a crazy alternative marriage with you. I figured that's more of a date-with-dinner revelation. Right? By that time, it'll be too late for George to back out."

"His name is George?"

"He's so cute, Tess—"

"You mentioned that already. And what does he do for a living?"

"Well, he's a computer programmer—"

"*Noooo . . .*"

"But not a loser type! He's hip! He has a Mac."

I shook my head. "No programmers. Besides, I think Derrick's got a crush on someone right now."

"Well, a crush is one thing, but this guy's actually serious. A crush isn't going to put a down payment on a house for you."

"We already have a house."

"But wouldn't you like an even nicer one?"

I sighed. "Just give me the guy's card. I'll pass it on." I had no intention of doing so, but I also knew that Tasha wouldn't give up.

She smiled triumphantly. "I'll put it in your mailbox."

"Awesome." I returned my attention to Henry. "Now what can you tell me about this poor kid? Did the tox panel come back yet?"

Her expression instantly shifted, and I was talking to the chief medical examiner again, a board-certified professional who'd completed a graduate medical degree in clinical pathology. A woman who took apart demons for a living. Part of working for the CORE involved becoming accustomed to gallows humor, as well as learning how to let a bit of light, a bit of boring old regular life, into the darkest of situations. It was how we held on to being human. Or maybe as close as we ever got to being human.

"This little one's body tells a horror story," she said. "Plenty of old breaks and fractures, some still healing." She pointed to his films on the light box. "You can see a focal fracture on his right ulna. Showed up as some deep bruising. Might have been caused by a pipe or a baseball bat."

I shook my head, staring at the spiderweb pattern on the clean white bone. "I heard he had a rough client or two."

"Well, that's just the beginning." She pointed to a frontal view of his skull. "Look at the jaw. This is what we call a Le-Fort fracture: a glancing blow to the mandible and zygomatic arch of the face. Theoretically, a fist could cause this. But I'd say there was some unnatural power behind the blow. You can see how the cracks extend to the maxilla and down the jawline. This would have incapacitated him."

"Isn't the bruising a bit light for a serious fracture like that? I saw him the day before he died, and he looked like he'd been in a scuffle. Nothing as bad as that."

"Just stay with me. I'll explain in a moment." She pointed to the next film. "Here you've got a spiral fracture to the fibula. That's caused by violent torsion, or twisting. We often see it in child abuse cases, when a parent grabs on to a child's arm with too much force. I took this X-ray about two hours ago." She took it down and replaced it with a new film. "But look at this."

I glanced at the same bone. The spiderweb fracture was much smaller. "Is this the same X-ray?"

Tasha nodded. "Taken fifteen minutes ago. Just before you got here."

"I don't understand."

She turned off the light box. "It does stretch the mind a bit. This kid's body is like an osteology textbook—he's got just about every kind of fracture that we have a name for. But they barely show up on the dermal layer. And they're fading."

"I can see that. So, what"—I blinked—"are you saying this kid's like Wolverine? He's got a healing factor?"

"This isn't a comic book," she replied. "It's very real. Every fracture in a human being—even someone who's a little more than human, like you—heals in the same way. It's just how your body works. First, there's a hemorrhage at the point of the fracture. Then the ruptured blood vessels produce a substance called fusiform, which joins the ends of the broken bone together, like a quick fix. Cells called fibroblasts accumulate at the point of contact, and they produce more cells— macrophages—that eat away at the dead tissue. It's the same principle as clotting, really, except on a larger scale."

"But it works differently with vampires and some demons, right? They produce more fibrin, or they produce it more quickly."

She nodded. "Vampire bone marrow produces osteoblasts and other cells almost immediately to facilitate the healing process. But this kid isn't a vampire—he tested negative for the viral plasmids. In fact, he heals faster than most vampires."

I stared at her. "Seriously?"

"You have no idea." She pointed to the cap of the bone— the epiphysis—which gleamed on the X-ray, like a perfect new golf ball. "In humans, something called a periosteal cap gets produced by the bone cells. Its job is to separate the necrotic bone from the new bone tissue. But this kid's healing factor bypasses that completely. When I took a sample of the bone, I could already see new capillaries beginning to grow out of the hematoma. His body produces new bone matrix at an incredible rate—*postmortem*. I'd say he heals twice as fast as a vampire. If it wasn't for the blood loss, he might have even survived, given the proper medical attention."

I looked down at Henry. He didn't look especially like a demon or a superhero.

"So he's a healer," I said. "That's rare. All I know is that it has something to do with organic materia and genetic mutation."

She nodded. "That's not the whole story, though. Like I said, many of these fractures were in various states of healing or regeneration. The oldest was probably sustained about three weeks ago."

I looked down at her gloved hand. It was hovering less than an inch above Henry's head, almost touching him. I'd never seen Tasha act this way before.

"So he was obviously abused," I said. "Repeatedly. Was he raped?"

She nodded slowly. "Hard. Many times over. There was scar tissue and heavy tunneling in the anus. There was even a pelvic fracture. You don't usually see that in males—not even hustlers."

"But this couldn't have all been from the same client. Or if it was . . ."

"Tess." I felt like she was trying gently to lead me somewhere, like a doctor who didn't want to say "cancer." "This boy suffered repeated trauma that should have killed someone his size. If it wasn't for the genetic anomaly that allows him to heal, I imagine he would have been dead several times over. And I can't help but wonder . . ."

Her eyes were dark. I swallowed. My stomach gave a great lurch as I finally understood what she was telling me. Or trying not to tell me.

"You think that was the attraction," I said numbly. "That clients picked him because they knew he could withstand—punishment."

She said nothing, but held my gaze.

"He was a human punching bag," I said. "Kicked, smashed, raped, again and again. And he let it happen, because he was desperate for the money. He was literally killing himself, over and over again. Until last night. When it finally stuck."

"The Hex may have had something to do with it," Tash added quietly. "As you know, it does speed up the clotting process. But with all that fibrin and platelet material rushing to his neck wound, there wouldn't be anything left to fuel his healing factor so that he could repair the broken bones. All of those fractures may very well have put him into cardiac arrest before he ever bled out. But we can't know for sure."

I closed my eyes. "I'm glad we can't find a relative."

"Why?"

"Because I don't know how to fucking tell some poor aunt that her nephew was beaten, broken, and raped to death. Or that it might have been worse if he'd survived."

I took one last look at Henry. I wasn't sure what I was going to tell Duessa, or Wolfie for that matter. Not this. I looked at his face. The bruise was almost completely gone, and the swelling had vanished. Even now, his body was slowly knitting itself back together, without any brain activity. He'd be brand new when we buried him. New and empty, like a building without any furniture.

I turned around and headed for the exit. "Thanks, Tash. I'll let Selena know."

"Where are you going?"

I pushed open the doors. "To find a drug dealer named Patches. You might be seeing him on your table in a few hours."

14

It was quiet on the corner of Hastings and Colum-
bia, where Duessa had told me I might be able to find a loose
community of hoppers, slingers, scammers, and other undesir-
ables who hung out with Patches the Hex dealer. You could get
anything on this corner from crystal meth to black tar heroin
and joints dipped in embalming fluid (not a smart choice, even
for vampires). Hex was still a bit tricky, though. As a hybrid
drug, it was a thorn in the CORE's side, and our vice division
patrolled the neighborhood ruthlessly looking for buyers and
dealers. I marked more than a few agents under cover, dressed
in grubby clothes and carrying bulging wallets with flash rolls:
wads of cash that seemed authentic at first glance, but were
actually fake once you got past the first couple hundreds on
the top. Sometimes, if the operation was particularly involved,
an agent would get authorization to carry scads of real money.
Enchanted, of course. We may deal in occult crime, but we're
still a business, and the CEOs like to make sure that their
money always comes back to them.

Duessa had coached me a bit on my story, reminding me

that Patches wasn't exactly a valedictorian, so it couldn't be too complicated. Obviously, if I managed to reach the supplier, the story would have to change. He (or it) was apt to be a lot smarter, and far more dangerous.

A diverse group was milling around the entrance to a run-down apartment building. Slingers, soldiers—the muscle—kids, sex workers, and various other hangers-on who didn't have anyplace else to go. I heard a variety of calls:

"Spider bags! Spider bags for twenty!"

"Cabello!"

"Mosquitoes! Got Mosquitoes!"

"Real tops!"

"Blue bags! Looking for Blue bags?"

"Bin Laden! Bin Laden hey!"

"DOA!"

"Elbows!"

"Christmas tree baby!"

"Scootie! Shabu!"

It was like eavesdropping on a kindergarten playground with its own bizarre slang, only these kids weren't talking about G.I. Joes and Transformers. The one thing I'd learned about drugs over the years was that people will eat, drink, smoke, snort, or inject just about anything if they think it's going to get them high. You can make crystal meth in a dirty bathtub with starch and Drano. You can grind up heroin with children's cough medicine, or mix it with ketamine (which makes you puke like Linda Blair in *The Exorcist*), or drink it with Strawberry Quik. People will do anything to get high, because when you're high, you don't have to think about how shit-caked and fucked up your life really is. At least for a little while.

Magic was about getting high, too, if you pared it down to the most basic level. Materia could get you high—it could release you from your body, make you feel like you were soaring across the universe on a trail of hot sparks. It also came with its own price, in the form of week-long hangovers, illness, and even death by overdose. The CORE was a dealer of sorts, and sometimes, I couldn't help but think that we recruited kids in the same way as these hoppers and slingers. Get them young, show them how to use their powers "responsibly"—that is, without getting killed—and teach them how to find and recruit others. The two worlds weren't all that different from each other. We just had fancier offices and better security.

I walked over to a girl wearing a grubby pullover, jeans, and a worn pair of Chuck Taylors. I couldn't tell if her outfit was brand new or actually drawn from a Goodwill bin. She didn't look quite as high as the rest of the group, which led me to believe that she might run with Duessa. Her hair was neatly combed, and she wore a minimum of makeup, along with cute brass-bell earrings.

"Hi," I said. "Got a second?"

She looked me up and down and smirked. "I don't score from cops."

Right. New plan: Change my outfit.

I tried to make my smile look bashful. "Is it that obvious?"

She shrugged. "To me it is."

"Well, I'm not a cop exactly."

"I know what you are." She lit a cigarette. "I see your type around here."

"I've got different reasons for being here, though."

"Oh, really?" She blew smoke over my head. "How about that."

"Duessa sent me."

Her eyes narrowed. "The Lady sent *you*."

I nodded.

"No offense, but—you don't seem the type she'd normally do business with."

"I'm not. But she's cooperating for the moment. We're both trying to figure out what's been going on around here lately."

Her expression darkened. "You mean the runaways getting slashed up? Like that poor little kid in the park? I heard they came from rich families."

I nodded. "We're trying to help."

She laughed. "Heard that one a million times. Heard it from

the government, from the mayor, from the cops, from the reporters, even from the fucking churches. Thing is, sweetheart—that helping hand? Never seems to come. At least not until some pretty white bitch like yourself gets strangled or cut up in pieces." She inhaled. "Pardon my language. I'm a bit cranky today."

I started to reach into my pocket for a twenty, and she grabbed my arm.

"*Jezuz*, you want to get us both locked up? We can't do this in the middle of the fucking street. Come over here."

I followed her to the entrance of an alleyway. My hand strayed to my athame, which was cool against my hip. Just in case.

"Now." She sighed. "What is it you want? I don't usually eat kitty, but if you're willing to throw in a little extra, that's fine."

I blushed. "It's not a date I'm after. It's information." I handed her two twenties. "Would this make you—um—less cranky?"

She raised an eyebrow. "It'd be a start. What are you looking to find out?"

"I need to connect with Patches."

She rolled her eyes. "That sloppy motherfucker? He's an idiot. Why are you looking for him?"

"I heard he's got some nuke." This was the current slang for Hextacy.

She frowned. "That shit's not for amateurs." Her eyes burned up and down my body. "And pardon me for saying, but you wouldn't know a crack spoon from a hair dryer. What are you doing looking for Hex?"

"The two kids that were murdered . . ." I began. "Both were high on Hex when they died. We think whoever killed them is connected to a supplier. Maybe it *is* the supplier, who knows? But I have to figure out where this stuff is coming from, and Patches is the only one around here who deals in it."

She absorbed this for a second. "Patches wouldn't know a supplier from his own candy red asshole in the dark. The only reason he pushes nuke is because he can charge twice as much for it, but it's hard as fuck to transport. The supplier would have to be close."

I blinked. "That's something we didn't know before. Thanks—"

She raised a hand to cut me off. "Listen. I'm telling you this because it's common knowledge. Any tweaker who'd ever tasted nuke could tell you the same thing. I'm not going to risk my own ass here. Got it?"

I nodded. "Totally. Understood."

"Patches stops by here twice a day to collect money. If he's stupid enough, he might do a re-up with all the cops watching. But that kid's blessed or some shit, because he never gets caught."

"I've heard that."

"Look . . ." She dug around in her purse for a second, then pulled out a slip of paper with a number written on it. "Text this number. Punch in 151 or 247. That means you're looking for something expensive, which'll make him show up faster. There's no code for nuke, but I doubt you'd want to buy any. If he thinks you know too much, he won't say a thing. And don't bother calling, because the cell's probably a burner, which means he'll toss it by the end of the week."

I smiled. "Thank you. This really helps."

She looked at me expectantly.

"Oh—sorry." I handed her two more twenties.

"There. Night's looking up now. Thanks, baby."

"Is there—I mean . . ." I hesitated. "Is there anything I can do for you? I mean, I could put you in touch with a shelter. Or Duessa's House—"

She laughed softly. "Don't take this the wrong way, sweetheart. But fuck off."

Then she turned and walked back down to the corner. I watched her go. I couldn't help but think what a fabulous agent she'd make for the CORE.

I pulled out my cell and texted 151. A few seconds later, I got a message back:

Ten.

When I emerged from the alley, the woman had vanished. I stood around uncertainly for a few minutes. What was I supposed to do now? Should I lean against a wall and act cool? I felt as if every movement was giving me away. But nobody seemed to care. Business went on as usual.

A few minutes later, a guy came loping down Hastings wearing a brown canvas jacket and dirty black jeans. He had a shaved head. A cop car drove by slowly, and he stared at the ground but kept walking.

"Five-oh!" someone yelled. "Five-oh creepin'!"

The cop car paused at the corner, then sped up and continued down Hastings. At least they weren't yelling things about me. Yet.

Patches walked straight up to me. So much for being undercover.

"Yeah?"

"Oh—um . . ." My nervousness probably looked adorable to him, but it wasn't an act. I'd never bought drugs off the street before. Once, I bought a joint in Stanley Park, but it took me almost an hour to work up the nerve. This was very different territory.

"Follow me," he said simply.

We walked a little to the side of the apartment complex, next to a shaded patch of tulips that was overgrown with weeds. I kept one hand on my athame. It's not like we were in some rat-infested basement, but I still felt exposed.

"So? What are you looking for?"

I didn't know if I should hedge around the subject or just come out and say it. I decided on a mixture of both.

"I work for someone," I said, mentally parsing through the details of Duessa's cover story. "He's got rank in the CORE."

"I don't fucking deal with them." He turned to go.

"No, wait! This guy's rich. But he's a nuke-hound. Loves the stuff. He's got the money, but not the connections."

His eyebrows narrowed. Well, it was really more of a unibrow, which gave him a distinctly ogreish appearance.

I kept going. "He's willing to pay in cash—or in favors."

He blinked. "What sorta favors?"

There. I had him.

"He's got a direct line to the ADA. Can get you out of just about anything, or finesse it to look better. Shave a few years off an existing sentence . . ."

This was the cherry on top of the sundae that Duessa gave me. Apparently, Patches had an older brother—a real douchebag—who was serving a three-year sentence in a CORE prison for beating up some warlock's girlfriend. Classy. But we certainly weren't above using it as leverage. My feeling was that Patches wanted his brother sprung less out of filial affection and more for much-needed backup.

He leaned in closer. "You can get someone's time shortened?"

I nodded. "How many years you need taken off?"

Patches smiled for the first time. "Maybe we can work something out."

"How much would you need up front?"

He scratched one of his arms, then winced. Apparently, Patches wasn't above sampling his own product. This could be useful.

"Two thousand."

Shit. I'd heard it was expensive to process the organic materia needed to make Hex, but two thousand as a down payment? That was ludicrous. But then again, so was injecting yourself with raw magic.

I pulled out my own flash roll. Selena had been kind enough to give me a pretty large discretionary fund, with the warning that I'd be flayed alive unless I returned every last earmarked bill. I slowly and deliberately counted out ten hundred-dollar bills, then another ten. Patches looked like he might start drooling right in front of me. Clearly, he'd overshot the price without expecting me to comply.

I held out the wad of cash. "This means I deal with the supplier."

"That's not—"

I snatched back the money. "I deal with the supplier, or I don't deal at all."

His face darkened. "Listen, little girl—"

"No, *you* listen, shitbird." I took a step toward him, letting my power flare a bit. Even someone as magically constipated as Patches would be able to feel it. "This guy does not fuck around. He's not going to deal with a midlevel soldier like you." "Low-level" would have been the more accurate term—and Patches was far from a soldier—but I thought the inadvertent compliment might soften him up. "He wants the real deal. And he's got more than enough money."

"It's not about the money." That was a lie. It was always about the money.

"Well, what is it, then?"

Patches looked around nervously. "The supplier doesn't normally talk to people. That's my job. He . . ." I saw his eyes widen at the fuck-up. Nice. "I mean, the boss—you know, the supplier doesn't *meet* with people. It just doesn't happen."

"A second ago, you said it doesn't *normally* happen."

He looked confused. "Well, no—"

"But two thousand in cash up front isn't usual. Dealing with the CORE isn't usual. This is an extraordinary situation. You follow me?"

He nodded. "But the supplier—"

I shook my head to cut him off. "No. Let's make this real easy." I counted out the bills again, then placed them in his warm, dirty hand. "Don't even call this a down payment. You take this to your supplier, and you call it a gift. A token of appreciation from my employer, who'd very much like to get in touch with him. You make sure he understands that there's a lot more coming, and that we want to deal in bulk. Understand? No individual vials or crystals or any of that shit, no eighths of an ounce or dime bags or papers. We want to buy something solid."

He looked uncertain. "So—I just give this to him?"

"That's exactly right. You give it to him as a token of our interest. A symbol. It represents our commitment to this business endeavor. And if he's interested, you give him this number . . ." I scrawled down the number of my disposable cell phone on a scrap of paper, handing it to him. "You tell him to send a message, and I'll meet him anywhere he likes. But make sure he understands that this offer isn't going to last forever. My employer isn't too keen on waiting for product. And there are other markets we can go to."

"What other markets? Shit—"

"Patches . . ." I smiled coyly. "I know you and your supplier aren't the only show in town. And we aren't above dealing with the scum of the earth—and below—if you know what I mean. We thought we'd take the high road first. You came recommended to us."

"Yeah?" He licked his lips.

"Oh yes. I was told that *you* were the man to deal with. And I do appreciate a man who knows how to deal."

"I got lots of skills," he said with a shit-eating grin.

"I'll just bet you do." I laughed. "You know, I'd be lying if I said I didn't possess a pretty wide skill set myself. That's why I hope you'll be in touch soon." I brushed his chest lightly. He smelled like bad cigars and Brut roll-on. "Real soon."

Before he could reply, I turned and walked away. It seemed like the properly filmic thing to do. And I thought I'd played it with exactly the right amount of panache, expertise, and sluttiness.

After filling out the appropriate expense forms (and promising Selena on pain of death that I'd get the money back), I found myself at Commonwealth, the old faithful pub that lay exactly between home and work. It was about as different from the Sawbones as you could get: refinished hardwood—still richly scarred in a few places, and dotted with pools of light that came through the screen door—mismatched folding chairs scattered around black oak booths and broken-down card tables, and a jukebox in the corner that played nothing but Peter Frampton. The bar was stainless steel with an old brick façade, and various trinkets and weird items poked out of the dusty corbels, including an ancient troll doll, a medal for perfect penmanship, and a stuffed armadillo. All we knew about the bartender was that her name was Tina, she loved to wear berets, and she'd probably been a pretty fierce lady killer in the mid-to-late-eighties.

Every Friday, Derrick and I allowed ourselves a two-drink minimum while Mia was out shopping with my mother. If shopping turned into a movie, we even had the possibility of coming home to an empty house. At twenty, this would have been depressing. At twenty-five, it had become the impossible dream.

Halfway through my second pint of Stella, I was starting to unwind. I'd never been a big drinker—at least not since college—but sometimes it was nice to have a few beers and pretend that my life wasn't chronically in danger. Inebriation didn't tend to mix well with mystical focus, but most mages had substance abuse problems, so . . . you figure that one out. Derrick was even more of a lightweight, so his cheeks were already rosy, and he grinned at me.

"What?"

I took another sip. "Just wondering what would happen if every mage in the world got, like, supertanked, all at once. Would there be an apocalypse?"

He chuckled. "More like a fuck-alypse. All that sexual tension? The miners and the sparks would be all over each other."

"You'd like that."

He shrugged. "Mama's been dry for a while. I wouldn't complain."

"What about Miles?"

His eyes narrowed. "What *about* Miles?"

"Well . . ." I made a vague motion with my hands. "You two seem into each other. He's nice. And cute. He smells good. And in the same business as us, so it's not like you'd have too much explaining to do."

"Is that our criteria now? Anyone who works with us?"

"He doesn't technically work with us. He's an outside contractor."

"He's also a colleague. A peer . . ."

I wiggled my little finger. "You *waaant* him, oooh, you want him to be your peer, don't you? Let's be *peers*—"

"You're trashed."

I gave him an indignant look. "This is my second beer. If I'm trashed, then my life has truly become depressing."

"So, what about Lucian? He's an outside contractor."

"Yeah. Way on the outside. Like, in another dimension."

Derrick shrugged. "He seems okay."

I stared at him. "Oh my God. Did you just admit that Lucian Agrado, the bane of your existence, is—*okay*? Did that really happen?"

He grimaced. "Don't spread it around. But lately, the guy hasn't seemed that bad. He's actually been kind of helpful."

I finished my beer with a guilty swallow.

"We're on a mission, I see."

I stared at the counter. "I may have gone to Lucian's that night—you know, when the vampires attacked me."

He rolled his eyes. "Of course you did. And he gave you a key."

My eyes must have looked like a cartoon character's, because Derrick laughed and rubbed my shoulder. "Remember how I'm not stupid, hon? I saw the look on your face when you showed up the next morning. And I emptied your pockets when I did the laundry. Ever since that time you stuck a jawbreaker in there, and I thought I heard gunfire when it was just the candy exploding—"

I sighed. "Yeah. I should have known that you knew."

"That's generally a safe assumption."

"What am I going to do about this, Derrick?"

"About Lucian?"

I stared into my empty glass. Tina wordlessly replaced it with a full mug. I gave Derrick a questioning look, and he nodded his assent. Guess who wouldn't be driving?

"Lucian Agrado is a black hole in my life." I wrapped both hands around the mug. "A very sweet, charming, and sexy black hole."

"He seems to care about you."

"Sure. He cares about the powers of darkness, too. You

didn't see what he did to Sabine last year. It was like raw evil pouring out of her eyes and mouth." I shivered. "What does it mean that I'm attracted to—that? To someone who can do that?"

"We can do some pretty fucked-up stuff with materia, too. Like setting people on fire, or causing earthquakes, or reversing gravity. Lucian doesn't exactly have the monopoly on destructive power."

"But necroid materia is different. You can feel it, right?"

He nodded slowly. "It does feel strange. Oily. Like something that's gone bad, or was never good to begin with."

"It feels wrong." I took a drink. "Everything about him is wrong. But he's *nice*. I don't get it. He's nice, and funny, and he has abs, Derrick. What am I supposed to do with that? Darkness isn't supposed to have abs!"

He shrugged. "We've never been good at choosing the right men."

"You especially!" It slipped out before I could stop it.

Fuck.

Derrick's expression fell. "Yeah. Me especially."

I hugged him. "I'm sorry. I didn't mean that, sweet thing. I'm just tired and a little drunk. You've done fine in that department."

"Yeah, my track record shows it."

"That wasn't your fault. Thomas . . ."

He winced a bit at the name, like he'd been burned. "Thomas was a long time ago. But that fuckup still reverberates, let me tell you."

"It wasn't a fuckup. You told him the truth. It's not your fault that he couldn't handle it, Derrick. A better man would have handled it."

"His leaving was the least of my problems."

That was true. Derrick broke the cardinal rule by telling his boyfriend—well, fiancé, really—about the CORE. The only reason he wasn't punished more severely was because he'd omitted a lot of sensitive details. But the damage was done. Thomas ran like the wind, and Derrick's career as a telepath went straight down the toilet.

"That was the reason I never got promoted," he was muttering now, "why I never got the proper training, why I always had to hear those assholes in the psi-tank snickering at me. Even when they weren't talking, I could still hear them. And all for what? Some beautiful fucking normate guy who didn't even bother to stick around."

I kissed his cheek. "He was a dummy."

"Really?" Derrick looked exhausted. "Maybe he was the smart one. Maybe we both should have run."

"Where to? Nunavut? The CORE has an office there."

"Anywhere."

I smiled. "To a place where the hot boys roam free, and the beer is always six percent."

"Where kids aren't getting killed by some sick mage with a vendetta."

"Where the only guy interested in me isn't a bitch-boy to the dark side."

"Where I'm not falling hard for a spatial profiler with an ass like Andy Roddick."

I grinned. "Are you? Falling hard?"

"Maybe."

"Well, that's good, right? At least we know we can still fall."

"But it hurts."

"Yeah." I leaned against him. "It hurts."

"So what do we do about that?"

I snapped my fingers and concentrated. A small tongue of flame, like the last cough from a dying Zippo, sprang to life in my hand.

"Luckily," I said, smiling, "we're kinda like superheroes."

He laughed. "Yeah. Maybe we are."

"And Thomas was an ass-face."

"He was."

"And you know what I'm thinking right now."

"That we should call a cab?"

"Yeah."

"Yeah." He pulled out his cell. "Already on it."

"If Mia's gone, can we watch *Big Business*?"

"Totally. There's bean dip in the fridge, too."
"And then can we organize the recyclables?"
"Boy, you know how to rip it up, Corday."
"I do. I do."

15

I never thought I'd end up back at the apartment where Jacob Kynan was found, but here I was, standing outside the entrance with my coffee and wishing that it were a mug of scotch rather than a Tim's double-double. Derrick and Miles shifted nervously on either side of me. We'd come back so that Miles could work his magic on room 208, where Jacob had spent the last moments of his life. The room's claustrophobic dimensions would actually make the spatial profiling easier, and Selena didn't especially feel like cordoning off a section of Stanley Park again.

So here we were. Back at the beginning.

"How does it work?" Derrick asked. "The profiling, I mean. Do you read the space around the crime scene like someone would read a book?"

Miles frowned. "It's more like—listening to music. If you're on the subway, listening to your iPod with those crappy little earbud headphones, you barely hear anything at all. But once you clear away the ambient noise, you can see how each song is actually put together, note by note." He grinned. "I have really good headphones."

"With me, it's more like reading a blurry book with one of those clip-on travel lights," Derrick said. "I can see part of the page, but not all of it. And whenever something comes into focus, the rest just gets blurrier."

Miles put a hand on his shoulder. "It'll get better with time. You're still learning. But you'll refine your powers with more practice."

I watched his hand linger for a moment. Then, like a kid stealing a lick of ice cream in secret, he reached up to brush the back of Derrick's neck with his fingertips. Just for a second. Derrick smiled. Miles dropped his hand.

I was going to kill someone if this went on for much longer.

"Okay," I said, "the building manager promised not to bother us. So let's go while the light in there is still good. Will the materia traces have faded too much by now?"

"I can still see them," Miles replied. "They make impressions, like bite-mark evidence or tire tracks. The outline stays even once the power itself has faded."

"Man—I'll bet we're not paying you enough."

He shrugged. "I like my job. And the city's nice. I could get used to it here."

Derrick's eyes brightened considerably at this, but he didn't say anything. I resisted the urge to sigh. People should get to be happy. People who aren't me.

We passed through the lobby and up the flight of concrete stairs that led to the second floor. I could hear the murmur of televisions from closed doors. The air was freezing, and I could smell the tang of vanilla. Maybe each floor had its own special designer scent.

The door to room 208 was still covered with caution tape, even though the cleaners had already come through here and whitewashed everything. We weren't looking for physical evidence this time. We were looking for a trace of something that even the most powerful microscope couldn't see.

Luckily, we had Miles.

I pushed aside the tape and opened the door. The bedroom had definitely been cleaned, but it still had a patina of darkness and blood to it that couldn't be washed away. Not that any of the hotel's occupants would notice. I had no doubt that the apartment would be rented as soon as we left. But I could feel the shadow of what had happened here. I wanted to get in and out as quickly as possible.

Quietly and efficiently, Miles unlaced his New Balance shoes and set them on the carpet. He had small feet, and his white socks made him look much younger and innocent, like a teenager about to lose his virginity.

"Getting comfortable?" Derrick asked, one eyebrow raised.

"It helps to have as much contact with the room as possible." Miles let his fingers trail against the fresh paint on the walls. "You don't get this opportunity with large, outdoor crime scenes. But this place is like a veal pen. Much easier to profile."

"You're like the room whisperer," I said, smiling.

He flashed me a quick sign: one hand in a closed C shape held to his mouth, thumb pressed against forefinger, then a dismissive downward sweep. *Shut up.* But he was smiling good-naturedly as he signed it. I felt, however oddly, that we were becoming friends. That was something I hadn't expected.

Miles walked in a slow circle around the room. He paused at the bed for a moment, and reached out with his hand, as if he was pressing against something invisible. He frowned. Then he stared at the wall by the bed—the arcs of blood had been washed away, but you'd still be able to see them with Luminol or some other chemical reagent. Blood was nearly impossible to get rid of, even with bleach. *All the perfumes of Arabia will not sweeten this little hand.* Lady Macbeth had been on to something, for sure.

Miles kept looking at the wall. It was white and clean, but I felt like he could see beneath it. Like he was a living infrared camera. He reached out, and I watched his fingers hover less than an inch away from the paint without touching it. Something in the room stirred. I felt a prickling in the back of my neck.

Red light bloomed beneath his fingers.

It pulsed for a moment, then spread out in veins and vesicles along the wall, remapping the direction of the bloodstain pattern. As I watched in fascination, a glowing tracery rose like ruby mist out of the bare white paint, coursing, flowing, slithering in all directions. Miles took his hand away, but the light kept branching out, forming new pathways, loops, and whorls, until I found myself staring at a luminous reproduction of the arterial spray that lay beneath the wall. It hung before us all—a macabre skein of bloody Christmas lights.

"Whoa" was all Derrick said.

"The space remembers," Miles clarified, looking at the wall instead of us. "Whenever blood is shed, it releases dormant materia flows that carve their pathways through space. It records the path of their energy, like vinyl records music."

"So you're just—playing the room?" I asked, once he'd turned to face us.

Miles nodded. "In a sense."

He walked over to the area of carpet where the cauldron had sat, pausing again. He frowned. "Something powerful was unleashed here. The space remembers it." His eyes looked dark. "It doesn't want to, but the memory's there all the same."

I tried to consider something so powerful that it scared . . . *space*. It baffled me. I suddenly wanted to go home and turn all the lights on.

He let his hand hover just above the carpet. Red light curled up from the ground, shimmering in the air like rose petals made of iron. It made a slow spiral pattern against the carpet, growing darker, until it had formed the outline of the cauldron. Unlike the pattern on the wall, this light was tinged with winking motes of black, like coal dust. They scuttled and made soft, papery whispering noises. Or maybe that was only my imagination. I willed myself not to look away.

"What are those dots?"

"Voids," he said slowly. "Bits of nothingness. They represent spots where the space was literally burned away. Destroyed."

"Is that even possible?"

He crouched on the carpet, staring at the matrix of red light with its curious specks of shadow. "With enough power—yes. Sometimes violent death creates a backlash, a kind of psychic scream. That sort of thing can actually peel away bits of spatial dermis, in the same way that a deep abrasion can peel away the top layer of skin. It's possible that Jacob's psyche did this before it collapsed."

Miles reached out and lightly touched one of the black specks. It hovered on the tip of his finger for a split second, like a beautiful onyx snowflake. Then it winked out of existence. Or back into *unexistence*, as it were.

"What about the ceiling?" I asked. "That's where Jacob died. There must be a lot of energy up there."

"It doesn't quite work that way." Miles stood up. "When we die, our energy scatters in all directions. It doesn't cluster. Materia tends to remain along the tracks it was summoned, maintaining its original directionality, but it can still wander off and get stuck behind corners. So we have to read the room as a whole."

"It's a gestalt thing," Derrick clarified.

I rolled my eyes at him. "Thanks, Professor."

Miles was already ignoring us again. He looked up at the ceiling, then back at the floor, as if following an invisible pathway. It made me think of a trot line: the nearly invisible lines of fishing wire that were often used to booby-trap meth labs. They were hung just above eye level with dangling fishhooks designed to catch you in all your most sensitive parts. And you could only really see them if you knew what you were looking for in advance. Miles, it seemed, knew what he was looking for.

He traced an arc with his hand from the floor to the ceiling. The air between his fingers rippled for a moment, and then fluoresced. Trails of greenish energy, like phosphorescent seaweed, burned to life at his touch, undulating in the fading light of the room. The materia flowed along the path of the arc, branching out into little spiderweb satellites that glimmered, like lone islands, or emerald shavings. He seemed to be painting with energy, or composing some kind of haunting, visual music. The materia ribboned and unscrolled itself across the space, until flared tendrils of light connected the floor of the room with the corner of the ceiling.

The majority of the energy was green, which surprised me. That was earth materia—my specialty. I was surprised I hadn't felt it before. But there were also traces of yellow and orange threaded through the matrix.

"Can you sort out the different flows?" I asked him.

"I can try." He followed the green crescent of light, probing it gently with his fingers. It wavered a little at his touch. Some of the threads actually drew back, like the leaves of a carnivorous plant, while others stretched toward him. I'd always known that materia was, in its own way, *alive*, but hadn't really thought about it until now.

"This weave of earth materia is strong," Miles said. "Like solid rock. It was used to anchor something higher up."

"The body?"

He followed the web of light, and his fingers hesitated around the spot where it flared orange. His eyes widened.

"This is gravimetric materia," he said softly.

"Well, that explains how he got Jacob's body up there."

"Jesus . . ." Derrick shook his head. "I thought it was just a trick of the air. But you're saying he actually reversed the flow of gravity?"

"Tweaked is more like it," Miles said. "These strands were woven quickly, and they weren't meant to last."

"You think he was in a hurry?" I asked. "Maybe he miscalculated somewhere. If he got sloppy, we might be able to find something probative left behind."

"I said it was done in a hurry," Miles clarified. "I didn't say it was sloppy. This is still expert work. You can't exactly play around with gravimetric flows, after all. The warp and the weft of thread into the spatial dermis have to be precise, like a surgeon's cut, or else you risk blowing yourself to bits."

"That would have saved us a lot of time."

Derrick chuckled. "Yeah. Killers are so inconsiderate that way."

Miles skirted the area around the orange materia, reaching up to investigate the glowing yellow strands above. His eyes narrowed. I watched him reach directly into the energy flow, and his hand rippled, like he was dipping his fingers in a swiftly running stream. Materia slid over his skin with a golden viscosity. I wanted to hold my breath. What if it . . . bit his hand off, like a hungry mouth? Wasn't he afraid? Did his insurance cover mystical amputations?

"I've never felt anything like this before." He turned to regard us, and I saw with unease that his pupils were scarily dilated. "It's not a flow that I'm familiar with. It's not elemental. It doesn't match up with any physical force that I know of."

Derrick frowned. "But—I mean, materia is basically a set of building blocks, right? You've got matter, liquid, heat, vapor, electromagnetism, gravity, and then both strong and weak nuclear force. That's it. There's nothing else."

"What about dendrite materia?" I gave him a knowing look. "Or necroid materia, for that matter? We don't understand them, we can't see them, but—we know they exist, right? Just like we know that both you and Lucian exist."

He made a face. "Well, sure. But whatever it is that Lucian and I 'do' with our powers—I mean, don't we just assume it's a kind of materia because we don't know what it really is? Dendrite materia sounds better than psychic voodoo."

"I don't know. I can't see your power, but I can feel it. And I *did* see Lucian's power—quite vividly. It was dark and alive, like the materia in front of us. So, even if we're not sure what it is, I think we can at least say that it's energy. Right?"

Miles reached deeper into the golden matrix. I saw his hand begin to tremble.

Shit.

"There's something *in* here," he muttered. "A trace of something. But I can't quite reach it. The pattern is so alien to me, I don't even know what I'm looking for."

"Maybe you should take a breather," Derrick said, catching my warning look. "We don't want to fool around with this stuff."

"This is what I do." His voice had a sudden edge to it. "I'm not playing around. I know there's something weird coded within these strands—I just have to untangle it. Like"—he grimaced—"unknotting a really snarled shoelace."

"Yes," Derrick continued, "but this shoelace could unravel the universe. I'm not sure it's worth taking a peek without—"

"Will you shut the fuck *up*? I'm fine!"

His voice was different. Lower, like a tape played on the wrong speed. I took a step toward him.

"Miles," I said, trying to keep the fear out of my voice. "I think the energy might be affecting you. Why don't you let us—"

"*Fuck.*" He stared at me. His eyes were all pupil now, and what little white remained was the color of blood. "Bitch, will you just leave me alone for two seconds? This is delicate work, and you wouldn't know a materia flow if it bit you in your fat fucking ass! So step *back*."

I looked at Derrick helplessly. This was not Miles Sedgwick. The Miles we knew had officially left the building.

Derrick narrowed his eyes, and I felt his power building. I couldn't see it, but I could hear it, like a sonorous bell tone in my head.

"*Miles.*" The sharp, atonal sound of what telepaths called *vox*—the control tone—echoed in the air between us. "*Come over here.*"

Miles just stared at him, uncomprehending. His fingers were still twined in the materia, and as I watched with a growing sense of dread, those golden threads began to wrap and snarl around his hand. The gentle, plantlike undulations of the materia became a distinct tugging motion. Miles lurched backward. I wondered if the energy itself could devour him. Judging from what I'd seen Mia's power do a year ago, I didn't doubt that it was possible.

Then Derrick did something unexpected.

I felt his power flex itself in concentration. Every muscle in his body seemed to tense for something. Then, slowly and deliberately, he traced a sign in the air. He held both hands in front of his closed eyes, thumb and index fingers pinched together, then opened up his palms in a dramatic gesture. As his fingers moved, his eyes snapped open. The movement seemed to occur in slow motion, and as I watched, a glowing outline followed Derrick's hands. It was faint at first, but when he opened his palms, it flared molten silver. It was like looking directly at an arc welder.

The outline of his hands burned in the air, a reverse shadow, silver-on-black. He seemed to be pressing the sign directly into what Miles had called the spatial dermis, just as a photographic image could be pressed into the silver emulsion of film. The sign hung before us, coursing with its own electric current, endlessly folding and unfolding itself into startling existence.

Wake up, it said.

Miles hesitated. Then he took a small step forward. The golden threads tore at his right hand, but Derrick's sign only burned brighter. I stared at the loops of liquid silver as they delicately unscrolled before me. Was this dendrite materia? The essence of every synaptic impulse? Or were my eyes playing tricks on me?

"Keep walking," Derrick said. His voice was steel.

Miles took another step forward. The luminous gold thorns made one last attempt to ensnare him. Then they fell away, and his hand abruptly lurched free. He stumbled. I thought he would fall, but Derrick was between us in the next moment. He wrapped an arm around Miles, steadying him.

The glowing sigil was gone. The air had returned to normal, but I could still see traces of power curling off Derrick. His whole body was steaming with it.

What the hell had just happened?

"Miles?" Derrick still had one hand wrapped around his waist, the other pressing firmly on his shoulder. "Are you okay? Let's see your hand."

I took a step closer and sucked in my breath.

Miles had claw marks on his hand.

The skin was ugly and red around the welts. They smelled of something familiar. Oil and ashes. That same trace of evil I'd been sensing for the last week.

"I . . ." His pupils were still wide, but this time I could

see the whites, at least. "I think I just need to sit down for a minute."

Derrick guided him to the bed. "We should get you to a clinic. There's no telling how serious these cuts are. I don't want to take any chances."

"They're fine. They don't hurt . . ." Miles flexed his hand and winced. "Much. They're like cat scratches."

"Miles"—Derrick glared at him—"the universe just *bit* you. I think some professional help is in order."

"Yeah." His voice was shaky. "You're probably right."

Derrick reached for my portable kit, pulling out a sterile antiseptic cloth and a coil of clean white gauze.

"This'll sting," he said, daubing a streak of iodine across Miles's hand with the cotton pad. Miles flinched a bit, but didn't say anything. Derrick tossed the packaging, then gently wound the gauze around three times, clipping the ends.

"Too tight?" he asked.

Miles flexed his hand experimentally. "Nope."

Derrick smiled. "Good. That'll do till we get to the clinic."

"Miles," I began, "what *was* that? When you touched the gold materia, your voice—everything about you—it changed."

"I don't know." He closed his eyes momentarily. "I just felt—empty. I don't remember." Concern flashed across his face. "What did I say to you?"

Oh, nothing. You just called me a dumb fat bitch. It's not like I'll be turning that little gem over in my paranoid brain for the next few weeks.

I smiled. "Nothing, really. You just sounded different."

Miles sighed. Then he turned to Derrick. "Can you reach into my bag and pull out the spare vacutainer? We need to get a sample of that—stuff. Whatever it is."

"You're not getting anywhere near it again," Derrick said. "I'll do it."

Before I could make a crack about chivalry, my cell rang. I didn't recognize the number. It wasn't a CORE extension.

"Hello?"

"You still want to deal?"

It was Patches.

I pushed down the butterflies in my stomach. "Of course. When and where?"

"I'll text the address to you. Come alone. Mister Corvid wants to meet you."

"Mister who—?"

He hung up.

Derrick gave me a look. "Trouble?"

"Maybe. Can you and . . ." I glanced at Miles, then sighed. "Who am I kidding? I'm sure you two can get yourselves to the clinic without my help."

Derrick smiled. "Should be able to manage it, yes."

"Good." My cell began to vibrate. "Because my night is about to get busy."

The address led me to a gleaming new high-rise on Hornby Street, where I assumed "Mister Corvid" would be waiting for me. Apparently, Hex dealers did quite well in this city, since the strata payments alone for a building like this would have bankrupted me. I buzzed suite 909, as instructed, and an unfamiliar voice answered.

"Yes?"

"I'm here to meet Mister Corvid," I said into the speaker.

A pause. "You were referred?" It wasn't really a question.

"By Patches. My appointment is for nine thirty."

Another pause. I suddenly envisioned a turret-mounted laser appearing from nowhere to vaporize me.

"Go to the west elevator," the voice said finally. "To the penthouse. Code 114. He'll meet you there."

The front door buzzed open. I walked through the foyer, which was floored in midnight black marble, past an empty concierge desk. A trendy shale fountain burbled innocently in one corner, surrounded by soft and pleasant lighting. There was something eerily Club Med about this place.

I stepped into the elevator and pressed the button marked PH. An LCD screen flickered to life, asking for the pass code. I typed in 114, and the doors closed smoothly with a soft chime as the elevator lurched to life. I noticed multiple cameras trained on me from the elevator's ceiling. Apparently, Mister Corvid valued his personal security.

The doors opened, and I found myself in a chic living room. It had all the right touches—cherry laminate flooring, generic art on the walls, even a few flowers nestled in expensive vases—but there was still something suspiciously nonhuman about it. Like the whole room had been programmed into a computer designed to approximate mortal behavior, and then spit out again, courtesy of Ikea and Pottery Barn. Everything looked sterile and untouched. The couch and ottoman were pristine. An afghan thrown over a chair in the corner was tilted just so, to look as if it had been tossed askew, when it had actually been arranged that way. Nobody had ever lived here.

"Come into the office," a voice called.

I walked down a short hallway and into a cozy parlor. Bookshelves lined the walls, and an enormous desk sat in the center. The desk was made entirely of frosted black glass, which gave the illusion of delicacy but reflected nothing save for chill, angular shadows. Mister Corvid sat behind the desk.

He was wearing a deep mauve dress shirt with a high collar—Ted Baker, I think—buttoned up to the top of his neck. He had pale skin the color of a washed-out shell, and startling green eyes. You didn't see that shade of green in human eyes. But I didn't need an occult manual to tell me that Mister Corvid wasn't human. His hair was almost silver and braided in dreadlocks, which had been swept up neatly over his left shoulder. A black pearl dangled from his right ear, winking. There was also a thin, vertical scar across his lip.

This gave me pause.

If I knew anything at all, I knew that Mister Corvid was *veritas*—a real pureblood demon, born and raised far away from the material plane. His genetic signature made me feel like I was being buried underneath a mountain of ancient earth, cold and wet and irredeemably dark, an enormity of shadowed presence. The thought of something equal to that, or even stronger—powerful enough to cleave into that perfect, bone-bleached skin—made my stomach cramp with fear.

His hands were folded in front of him on the desk. They were very long, and I could see night black veins crawling beneath them. Each finger ended in a tapered claw, but there was no visible separation between flesh and nail, so that the claws themselves appeared to be a bizarre fusion of skin, bone, and blood. A carnelian gleamed on his right index finger. I imagined those claws tearing through my neck. Good times.

"Have a seat." He smiled. His teeth were very white.

I sat down. "Thanks for meeting with me."

"It's my pleasure. Would you like a drink? I have pomegranate juice chilling in the fridge. Or wine. A Riesling, I think. Quite nice."

"I'm fine, thanks."

He sighed. "Are you sure? It's these little niceties that keep us from becoming entirely like animals, isn't it? Otherwise, we might as well be meeting in a dank basement somewhere."

"I'd be fine with that, too." I shrugged. "I'm adaptable."

"Well, that's good to hear." He picked up what looked like a brandy snifter and poured himself a drink. But the liquid wasn't brandy. I tried not to think too much about what it could be.

"Patches said that you don't often meet with people," I continued, keeping my best game face on. "May I ask why?"

"I have trust issues." He drained the glass, smiled, and looked at me. His eyes seemed to flicker through a number of different shades, but settled on the green of a glowing circuit board. "People often disappoint me."

"I get that."

"Patches mentioned that you were quite"—he blinked—"proactive in your dealings with him. Is that your usual style?"

"It seemed like something he'd understand."

"Ah. You've dealt with his ilk before, then."

I shrugged. "He's just a soldier. He understands the bottom line. I wanted to make sure that my message got through."

"I wouldn't worry about that." He was smiling with his

mouth, but none of the other muscles in his face seemed to move. I felt like an entirely different, ethereal part of him was casually wrapping its fingers around my neck. "I'm very interested in your proposition. Very interested."

"Then it sounds like we're ready to deal." I slid a suitcase across the desk. "We never hammered out an exact figure, but here's a down payment."

Mister Corvid's fingers danced across the leather of the briefcase for a moment, as if stroking it. Then he flipped open the lid, examined its contents without expression, and closed it again.

"Very nice. I have one question."

Uh-oh.

"What's that?" I asked coolly.

"How old do you think I am—Miss Corday?"

This was the part where I should have screamed *Hey, look over there*, and then run for the elevator. I'd never told Patches who I was. But Mister Corvid most likely had access to any database that the CORE could get its hands on. He wasn't only a professional—he was a pureblood.

"That—um—seems like an impolite question," I hedged.

"Oh indeed." His face was still as marble. "I'd like you to guess my age, though. Honestly. It would give me pleasure."

Demons suffered from reverse vanity. They all wanted to appear older than they really were, rather than younger, like humans. I could always play on that.

"Five hundred?" It sort of came out as a squeak.

His laugh was rich and rolling. I shivered. I could feel those spectral hands all over my face and neck, like spiderwebs.

"Miss Corday—have you ever seen a perfect, bloodred sunset, like a burning coin, sinking over a Mesopotamian village? Have you watched Egyptian women in yellow and blue silk dipping their bronze vessels into the filth of the Nile? Have you seen the *hetaera* with their beautiful, tanned limbs, resting against the sun-drenched walls of Thebes? Or the blue-skinned Celts with their hair soaked in lime, running naked through the forests of Carthage, their dogs trailing behind them?"

I cleared my throat. "Um—no."

He leaned forward. "I have. Does that explain things for you?"

I nodded slowly. "I'm beginning to get a picture."

"So we understand each other. That means, when I ask you what, precisely, you're doing here, I expect you to answer truthfully. I know you haven't come to buy Hextacy in bulk. Frankly, your department couldn't afford it."

I didn't doubt that.

"Why are you here, Miss Corday? It would be helpful if you could tell me in a few sentences or less. I appreciate brevity, and it will be a good exercise for you"—his expression didn't change—"should you survive to interview someone else like me."

I swallowed. Was it too late to update my life insurance policy? I'd heard you could do it online now. Maybe I could just sneak out for a moment to check my e-mail.

I remembered Lucian's advice when I'd first met with Duessa. *Always tell the truth.* Immortals valued honesty. It was one of the only things they valued, in fact. Thinking about Duessa gave me a brief spike of courage. It wasn't like I hadn't met with powerful immortals before. And what's the worst that could happen? Mister Corvid slices and dices me with those freak hands. Most likely, he transects my common carotid artery, or maybe my jugular, or even both. I experience a few moments of intense pain, then my body goes into shock and I exsanguinate. I bleed out on his lovely Berber carpet, and that's it. End of story. It actually sounded kind of peaceful.

"The CORE is conducting an investigation," I said finally. "Four youths have been killed in the past month—all the children of mages. Their murders all had ritual elements, and we found trace amounts of Hextacy, both at the scenes and in the blood and bone marrow of the victims. We believe that the killer is either a skilled mage or a nonnormate with access to significant mystical energy. He also has a vendetta against powerful mage families, although we're not sure why. He appears to be drugging or otherwise incapacitating them with large doses of Hex."

Mister Corvid nodded appreciably. "You really should have led with that. It's an intriguing angle."

"He's going to kill again." I tried to keep my nerves under control, but all I wanted to do was puke on his beautiful obsidian desk. "Soon. I've met with Duessa, and she suggested finding a midlevel dealer who sold Hex."

"Patches."

I nodded. "And he led me to you. So here I am."

"But what do you want from me exactly?"

"Mister Corvid . . ." The name sounded so odd on my tongue, like I was addressing my fourth-grade math teacher. "The killer is obviously buying Hex from a supplier, and you're the only supplier we know of who works in the city. There's a good chance that you've sold to him in the past. All we're looking for is a physical description, even a vague one. Anything that might help us track him down."

He tapped his finger claws together. It was disturbing. "Now that could be an issue. I do have client confidentiality to think of. If people learn that I've been discussing a client with the CORE, I could lose a lot of business."

Bargaining. Why was it always about bargaining with immortals?

"The CORE does have a vice division," I said slowly, watching his eyebrows—or what passed for them—rise at the mention of the word, "but they're not especially interested in tampering with the urban Hex trade. As long as you personally aren't selling to minors or normates, they can ensure total compliance."

"You mean they won't bend me over if they don't have to."

I smiled weakly. "I mean that, in addition to their existing cooperation, the CORE is prepared to guarantee you immunity in a variety of legal and paralegal venues. They're also prepared to refocus their policing efforts on your competition, which would effectively increase your sales base."

His eyes turned from green, to mauve, and back to green again. "How delicious. You'd cripple my competitors so that I could turn a profit—and all for a name?"

"Names are valuable in our line of work, Mister Corvid," I said, knowing that his real name was probably very different and unpronounceable. It would stick in my throat. "The CORE is prepared to cooperate with you, on the condition that you volunteer us probative information leading to the arrest of this killer."

"Will you try him in your mystical courts? Like some naughty warlock?"

"That's for the ADA to decide. Most likely, he'll be sentenced according to our legal precepts, yes."

"A fair trial for a monster." He shook his head. "How fascinating."

"Do you think you can deal with us, Mister Corvid?"

He leaned forward and stretched out his palm. The hem of his sleeve moved up an inch, and I saw a black tattoo on his pale wrist. It actually burned before my eyes: a salamander that danced and shuddered and flicked its tongue at me. I could almost hear it whispering.

I wasn't sure what he wanted me to do. Gingerly, I put my hand in his. It was surprisingly warm. His touch dissolved all of my mental barriers. I felt his breath on my heart, slipping through the pericardium, a dark vapor inside me. I shivered.

Satisfied, he withdrew his hand, and the finger claws went behind the desk again. The memory of his taint would stay with me.

"I can deal with you, and you alone, Miss Corday."

I nodded, trying to keep my shuddering in check. "That works for me."

"I know the creature of which you speak. I've dealt with it—transacted with it—on multiple occasions."

My stomach gave a lurch. "What can you tell me?"

"Have you ever taken Hextacy, Miss Corday?"

I frowned. "No. Of course not. That shit can kill you."

"A lot of things can kill you, if administered improperly." He reached into a desk drawer and withdrew a vial of green liquid. It was the color of his eyes. "Sometimes, in that delicate space between killing and learning, we can see what needs to be seen. Do you understand?"

"Not really."

He slid the vial toward me.

"What . . ." I blinked. "You want me to *use*?"

His nod was encouraging.

"No fucking way."

"This is a special batch. Its purity is really quite remarkable."

"I don't care. I'm not a Hex user."

"One time does not a user make, Miss Corday."

"Yes it does! That's how it starts!"

"Are you so afraid of it?" He smiled sadly. "Do you doubt yourself that much? If you're strong-willed, a little dose should be no problem for you."

"I'm sure you've said that to lots of crackheads before."

He tapped the vial with one claw. "The answers are inside here. More to the point—they're inside your own head. But this will unlock them."

With a little shock, I remembered what Duessa had said to me.

It's in there somewhere. Just keep digging.

Were they both right? Was it possible that I knew who the killer was already? That I'd seen it? Felt it?

Mister Corvid stared at me levelly. "On the street, a single dose of this would go for a cool eight grand. It's the closest you can come to seeing the future."

"This"—I shook my head—"this is against everything I believe in. I can't possibly drop a dose of Hex. I'll lose my job! I'll lose—everything."

"Or you'll gain the knowledge you need to find this killer." He shrugged. "Isn't that a fair trade? And besides"—his eyes gleamed—"haven't you always been a little curious? You're not entirely antidrug, are you? Tess?"

The way he said my first name made me want to throw up.

I stared at the vial.

"Well? What's it going to be?"

The green liquid shimmered, like something from Oz.

I walked out of the office with the vial. I didn't look back.

16

Derrick looked more than a little confused as he crossed the street, coming to stand next to me at the corner of Hastings and Columbia. It was getting chilly, and he shoved his hands into the pockets of his spring jacket, doing that impatient bouncing thing that people always do when they want to be somewhere else.

"I got your text," he said with a frown. "Cryptic much? I'm not sure why we couldn't meet at the house."

"It's a bit complicated." I glanced at the time on my cell.

"You waiting for something?"

"Sort of—um . . ." I flashed him an apologetic smile. "Okay, look. I've got this plan. But it might be crazy. I mean, it probably is crazy. But I need to make sure that you've got my back."

His frown deepened. "I've always got your back. What's this about?"

The 135 Hastings bus pulled up to the curb. As a stream of people got off, I recognized Wolfie and gave a short wave. He walked over to us and smiled. It was one of those corner-of-the-mouth smiles that usually precedes a bad decision.

"Hey." He cast a glance at Derrick. "So, did you explain shit to him?"

"Not yet. I was waiting for you."

"Whoa." Derrick was full-on glaring at me now. "What's going on? Have you two been working this case without me?"

"No! Nothing like that. But I did call Wolfie after I met with the supplier."

His eyes went flat. "You called him before you called me?"

Shit. This was not going well.

"Like I said, its complicated. Why don't we go—"

"I'm not going anywhere until you spill it. You've never had a problem confiding in me before. This shouldn't be any different, and the cloak and dagger shit is starting to piss me off, to tell you the truth."

"Wait until the punch line," Wolfie muttered.

Derrick seemed to retreat into himself. I could feel his muscles tensing. His expression went very dark. I hadn't seen him this angry in a long time. Not good. And we hadn't even gotten to the really insane part yet.

"What's going on?" he repeated. This time his voice was deadly quiet. It was that quietude that freaked me out the most.

I swallowed. "I called Wolfie because I needed some advice."

"What—I'm not good enough, all of a sudden?"

"Don't get your back up. Wolfie knew more about this—stuff—than either of us. That's why he's here."

He folded his arms. "Are you going to elaborate on what this 'stuff' is? Or should I prepare myself for a game of charades?"

"Maybe you should just show him," Wolfie said.

He scowled. "Yes. Why not? Show me this magic stuff, Tess. Whatever it is, it better explain why you're acting like such a head case all of a sudden."

I reached into my pocket and pulled out a cloth-wrapped bundle. Derrick took it from me and slowly unwrapped the contents. He stared at it for a moment, then handed it back to me, his eyes cold as glass.

"You're insane."

"Derrick . . ."

"No, you've seriously lost it this time. Do you have any idea how much trouble you could get in for carrying that shit around?"

"Well, Selena did originally plan for me to buy some. So I presume she knew that I'd have to actually touch it at some point, right?"

"Yeah, for the sake of the con. She didn't intend for you to be carrying it in your purse like some fucking Tic Tacs. *Jesus*."

I bundled the parcel back into my pocket. "Can we just talk and walk? It's a lot easier than standing on the corner. And people could be watching."

"Where are we going? Do I get to see your stash?"

"It's not like that, Derrick."

Wolfie started walking, and we followed him. I was glad that he was keeping out of this, although a part of me would have liked some support. Not that I expected it. Maybe Derrick was right. Maybe I really had lost it.

I told him about my conversation with Mister Corvid in fits and starts while we walked up Columbia. Dusk was settling like an iridescent haze on downtown Vancouver, making the buildings shine with a subtle purple afterglow. It was a certainly a beautiful evening for ruining my life.

"Wait." Derrick held up a hand. "You're telling me that this Corvid guy is *dealing* with the killer? Not only won't he give up the name, but now he wants to play both of you off each other and see who wins? That's fucked, Tess."

"He's *veritas*—a pureblood. They have a sick sense of humor. I'm not sure if he cares about either side winning, really. All he wants is to turn a profit."

"Sure, and if he gets to destroy the life of a CORE employee while he's at it, so much the better, right? Like a bonus gift with purchase."

"This isn't going to destroy my life."

I honestly didn't know that for sure.

"Tess—you need to listen to yourself very carefully. What

you're proposing is completely insane. This is the type of shit that we fight against every day. You want to become part of that nightmare? You want to invite it willingly into your life?"

"If it'll save more lives—why not? Isn't that worth it?"

"But you don't even know if this will work. You're taking it on faith from some pureblood demon whackjob. I mean, it could even be tainted. What if he gave you a hotshot? Maybe he wants to watch you fry your own brain."

"I don't think that's his game."

"You don't know his game!" He grabbed my shoulder. "Tess, we've got a life, okay? We've got a family. You can't make these split-second decisions anymore. We've got to think about Mia."

"Mia would want me to do the right thing. She'd want me to take the risk—I know her. I know what she'd say."

"So, because a fourteen-year-old kid says it's the right thing to do—what—that's all you need to know? If that were the case, we'd all be making out with the Jonas Brothers right now. *Listen* to yourself. You made up your mind before you even called me. I'm only here to clean up the fucking mess!"

I sighed. "You're here because I need you. I need an anchor. Wolfie can handle the assembly and delivery—he's here to make sure that everything's done right. But I need you to hold my hand and pull me back down—if I drift too far away."

"And you think you'll actually find answers this way? Are they even going to make sense when you're tweaking your head off?"

"I'm going to ground myself with earth materia. That should keep my body in a kind of stasis."

"Tess, haven't you read anything about this shit? It feeds on materia like candy! The more you use, the more powerful it gets. All you'll be doing is stoking the fire, and this may be a news flash to you, but the central nervous system doesn't particularly like being set on fire."

Actually, I did know a lot about it.

I knew, for instance, that Hextacy was twice as addictive as any alkaloid of morphine, including undiluted heroin. I knew that, in addition to binding at the brain's opiate receptors like any other narcotic, Hex could also triple and even quadruple the production of certain neurotransmitters, like norepinephrine and acetylcholine. Heroin had first been synthesized in 1874 from morphine, which in turn was gathered by scraping the milky white fluid from the unripe seedpods of *Papaver somniferum*, the poppy plant. The fluid had to be scraped by hand and then air-dried. In hospitals, they called it morphine; on the streets, they called it heroin.

But unlike the average bag of heroin, which might contain anywhere from thirty to fifty milligrams of the pure stuff—cut with starch or quinine—a dose, or "flash," of Hex came from purely processed organic materia. We didn't know what it was cut with. Maybe flesh and blood. Maybe the bones of warlocks. The processing occurred in the most clandestine of laboratories, and they were always abandoned when we finally got to them, leaving only the reek of chemical precursors and bad magic behind.

We had drugs that could mimic Hex, like Hydromorphone and Dilaudid, for the type of "breakaway" pain experienced by terminal cancer patients whose bodies no longer responded to other treatments. And we had Fentanyl—quite lucrative on the street—which could be delivered through a transdermal patch almost instantly. You could even suck on a citrate Q-tip and absorb it directly through the mucous membrane. But Hex could only be delivered intravenously. It needed blood to activate. And just as Derrick said, my own power would feed it.

My hope was that the earth materia, even if did strengthen the drug, would also tie me to the physical world and keep my vitals in check. It would act like an arterial line, connecting me to Derrick and Wolfie, so that all Derrick had to do was brush that line with his own power and I'd wake up.

Hopefully.

I knew that a dose of Hex this pure would tear through every nerve in my body like apocalypse on legs. I could be doing permanent damage to my central nervous system. It was possibly the stupidest idea I'd come up with since I'd decided to become a mage in the first place, when I was only twelve years old.

I also knew—in the same way I'd felt connected to Mia a year ago, knowing that I had to protect her at any cost—that this was the only solution. From the moment Duessa had suggested that I might have some knowledge about the killer locked inside my brain, I'd felt, deep down to the marrow, that she was right. When Mister Corvid said the same thing, I hadn't really been surprised.

This was something older than I'd first imagined. Something to do with me. And what I feared—what I still couldn't tell Selena—was that I understood only too intimately why this killer had been leaving magical artifacts at the crime scenes. Yes, it was a taunt, an insult. But the creature wasn't taunting mages in general.

It was taunting me.

I had a connection to this thing. I didn't understand how or why, but Duessa had seen it right away. There was demon in me, after all. I'd been conceived through an original act of demonic violence when my mother was raped by—something. That's where the magic came from. A place of shadow, blood, and smoldering power. For twelve years, I'd tried to bend it back into something good, tried to find the light and the warmth and the joy of having magic running through my veins. But the longer I stayed on this case, and the closer I got to this creature, the more hopeless I felt. There was a black hole inside me. This thing and I were connected by a strand of gleaming shadow, and instead of trying to break that strand, all I could do now was follow it back to its source. The memories before the power even stirred.

I needed to know what came first.

"Tess? Are you even listening to me?"

We'd stopped outside a run-down old walk-up apartment building, heavily shaded by rotting trees and a tattered green awning. It wasn't the sort of place where you composed a great piece of music or raised a loving family. It was, instead, the sort of place you went to forget everything about your life. A place for getting fucked up, fucked over, or simply fucked.

I turned to Derrick. "I don't know how to explain this to

you. This case—it's gotten inside of me somehow. It's gotten personal."

"That's exactly what I'm afraid of. You've lost all perspective, Tess. You're about to shoot your veins full of poison, and for what? The off chance that you might see some tantalizing vision of the killer? What if you just start drooling and pissing yourself like a goddamn crack addict—"

"You do *not* get to talk to me that way," I said. "Not you, Derrick. Not you. Okay? You have to believe me. You have to trust me, because . . ." I willed myself not to start crying like an idiot. "Because you're my partner, and my best friend, and I love you so much—and I can't do this unless you hold my hand."

His face was immobile. "I'm not going to watch you do this."

"You won't be watching. You'll be my spirit guide. My Virgil. You'll make sure I don't get lost in the inferno."

"I'm not even sure I can do that." I saw a crack in his resolve.

"You're stronger," I persisted. "Strong enough for this. And you're the only one who knows me well enough to be an anchor."

"What . . ." He stared at the ground. He was definitely wavering. "Fuck—I mean, what about coming down? How are you going to deal with the withdrawal?"

"That's where I come in," Wolfie said. "Duessa showed me how. It's called 'burnoff.' You can flush the body clean of drugs with, like, this huge-ass burst of materia. You almost have to raise the blood to boiling, but only for a second—"

"Excuse me?" I thought Derrick was going to smash him in the face for a moment, he looked so unhinged. "Did I hear you correctly? Did you actually just use the words 'blood' and 'boiling'?"

"Just for a second." Wolfie made a face. "It hurts. A lot. But Tess'll be drawing earth materia at the same time, which should protect her some. I'm not saying it'll be a picnic, but I don't think it'll do any long-term damage."

"Oh, no, of course not—except for nuking your insides and potentially cooking your vital organs." He stared at me. "You've totally stepped off from crazy. You're on some whole new lunatic plane now."

"It'll work, Derrick." I tried to sound patient. "I've seen them do it at the clinic with mages who are addicted, or people who get magically infected. Your body runs hot when you're on Ecstasy or GHB. This just makes it, you know—a bit toastier than normal. For a second or two. Not long enough to screw anything up permanently."

"Haven't you ever stuck your hand on a burner? That only takes a second, too, but the burn lasts. And you're talking about doing that to your insides. Tess—"

"It's not like that. I'm a miner—I deal with earth materia— and that gives me an affinity with heat as well. Wolfie"—I gestured to him—"is a spark. A very powerful spark. And he's done this before. He did it for Jacob."

Wolfie nodded. "Sometimes he was too fucked up for a date, but he needed the money, bad. So I'd burn the drugs out of his system."

"And he ended up dead."

I felt a flicker of heat course along Wolfie's body. His eyes narrowed on Derrick. "You saying I had something to do with that?"

"No, no . . ." I spread both my hands in a gesture of détente. "Derrick's just being who he is. My best friend. He's upset, and he doesn't want me to get hurt."

"I'm also pretty sure you've lost your mind."

"It's a good plan," Wolfie shot back. "It could work. And it's not like your people have come up with any other brilliant ideas. This motherfucker is still on the loose. If Tess thinks she can use the drug against it—why not? The Lady seems to think that she's on to something."

"The Lady's nuts, if you ask me."

Wolfie took a step forward. The temperature between us spiked. "What? I *know* you didn't just cast shade on Duessa—"

"Stop it! Both of you! I can't deal with any more pissing

contests." I exhaled. "This isn't even about me anymore. Wolfie, I appreciate your help, but I know you're only doing it because you want to get a crack at Jake's killer." I turned to Derrick. "And you can talk about Mia and our family all you want, but I know you better than you know yourself, Derrick *Bernard* Siegel."

He blanched at the use of his middle name.

"You think this plan has a shot. You're pretty sure it's brilliant, and that I can get away with it, too. What you don't want to deal with is what that means for me." I looked him in the eyes. "Because if I do have a connection to this thing, you know exactly where it's coming from."

"Your father," he said softly.

I nodded. "Bingo. Dear old dad. Maybe he brought this thing into the world. Maybe it brought *him* into the world. Maybe they're old poker buddies. I don't know the specifics, but I've felt this creature before. I remember it. And I know it has something to do with my past. You know—the part of my childhood we don't talk about anymore. The part where the photo albums are all blank. Or cursed."

"Our powers both come from the same source," Derrick said slowly. "I don't remember anything before I was adopted—my birth parents could have been from the ninth ring of hell. I've got no idea. And you've never known anything but Diane and Kevin Corday, the two most loving parents in the universe." He blinked. "It's been twenty-five years, Tess. This could unglue your whole life. You have no idea what you're going to see."

"I know I have to look. And if Diane and Kevin love me, that can't ever be destroyed, right? It's always going to be there. No matter what I see."

"The love will stay. Sure. But you could be letting something else in. Something dark and terrible and evil. And it'll stay there, too, like an oil slick in your heart."

"I don't want to interrupt this really intense moment," Wolfie said, "but this place isn't exactly the Hilton. There's an abandoned suite inside, and we jury-rigged the lock so that we can get in and out. But someone else could drop by anytime. If we're going to do this, we have to get a move on. I don't want company."

Derrick looked at me again. "Why here? We could have done it back at the house. We'd be safer."

"I'm not bringing this shit into our home. I never intended to. If this happens, it happens here, in this place. And then we'll never have to think about it again."

Derrick closed his eyes for a moment. Then he sighed. "Here." He reached into his messenger bag and pulled out a bundle of neatly folded clothes. It was my favorite pair of jeans, along with his oversized Food Not Bombs T-shirt. He'd even folded my socks and underwear atop the pile, like I was about to go on a camping trip.

"I brought these. Just in case you need to change—afterward."

I took the clothes from him. My mouth quivered.

"You knew."

He shrugged. "I suspected. And besides—one has to look one's best, even in the face of ancient evil."

I kissed him on the cheek. "You're amazing."

"I know. Let's do this before I lose my nerve."

Wolfie took us around the back of the building. We stopped outside a garden-level suite, and he knelt to push open the window, which was slightly ajar. It groaned, and I was afraid that the wood frame might snap for a moment, but Wolfie managed to slide it up so that we could fit inside. Feeling a bit undignified, I squatted and climbed through the dark opening. My left foot found purchase on a counter, and I lowered myself onto the hardwood floor.

The suite was a mess. Old needles, crack spoons, and discarded rubber tubing littered the floor and hallway. The sink was filled with broken dishes, and the air smelled like a mixture of urine, body funk, and mildew. A few scattered mats lay on the floor, along with some dirty pillows and cast-off furniture. Mostly just particleboard shelves balancing on milk crates and old, upturned boxes.

"Great," I said. "It's got a real Turkish prison feel to it."

"It's the space that's important," Wolfie replied. "Not the décor. And the bathroom is clean. I'll—ah . . ." He held out his hand. I gave him the vial of Hex, and he looked at it strangely for a second.

Was he jealous? Or just haunted by memories of doing this for Jacob Kynan? It couldn't have been easy watching your lover as he slowly killed himself.

"I'll go get the gear ready," he said at last, disappearing down the hallway.

I sat down awkwardly on one of the mats, and Derrick sat beside me.

"Reminds me of college," he said, a nervous little smile playing across his face. "Remember when we dropped acid for the first time?"

"You thought a giant rat from space was going to attack us. And I just kept eating Rice Krispies squares and hiding underneath the desk."

He looked at me. "You're really going to do this?"

"I really am."

"Then—I'm here." He touched my hand. "I'll be your Virgil."

"You are my Virgil, baby."

We kissed once, lightly, on the mouth. It didn't happen often. There was very little sexual about it, since Derrick and I had never been a hot item. It was more like an expression of absolute comfort. He was gay, I was straight—that would never change. At least I didn't think it would. But in those rare moments when we did kiss, I always had to think: *What if?* I wondered if he thought the same.

Wolfie came out of the bathroom holding a leather satchel with various pockets. He knelt down next to us, pulled up a broken-down table, and laid the satchel across it, like a doctor about to extract his set of surgical tools.

"How do we make it sterile?" Derrick asked.

Wolfie snapped on a pair of latex gloves. He withdrew a small jar from the satchel, along with a sheet of tinfoil, which he then spread across the table. Uncapping the jar, he spread some antiseptic gel onto the tinfoil. Then he withdrew two sealed packages, which he broke open, laying down a disposable needle and syringe.

"Well"—Derrick blinked—"I guess that answers my question."

"You don't fuck around," Wolfie said simply. "Not if you know how to do this. Not if it's your life."

"Was it . . ." I suddenly wanted to take the question back. "I mean, did you—"

"I used," Wolfie said, picking up an alcohol wipe. "Of course I used. But I've been clean for a while now. Intend on staying that way."

I rolled up the sleeve of my blouse.

I guess this was really happening.

I let Wolfie daub at the inside of my arm with an alcohol wipe. Then he fitted the needle to the syringe. Easy as snapping together a car part, or those Tinkertoy things you used to play with as a kid. Snap, snap. Build yourself a whole new world.

Wolfie took out a stainless steel spoon. "You can't use silver," he said absently, as if he were talking to himself. "Shit breaks down and gets in your veins. Just like you can't use a cigarette filter because it's toxic. That poison leaches into you."

He picked up the Hex. The green liquid seemed to flare and boil with light as Wolfie tipped the vial. An arc of emerald satin poured onto the spoon. He recapped it, and I noticed—a bit relieved—that it was still more than half-full. What would half a dose of Hex do to me? It had to be better than a full dose. Less fatal?

What the *fuck* was I doing?

He placed a hand underneath the spoon. I felt a flush of thermal materia, and curls of steam rose off the Hex as it boiled.

"Guess you don't need a lighter," Derrick said.

Wolfie tore open another package, then placed an antiseptic cotton swab onto the spoon, where it began to soak up the Hex. Gently, he inserted the tip of the needle and began to draw liquid through the swab. I watched the syringe fill.

Satisfied, Wolfie removed the syringe and placed the spoon to the side. He unfastened another pocket on the satchel and pulled out a piece of flexible rubber tubing, a dull yellow in color. "This shouldn't be too hard," he said. "You've got virgin veins."

"Well, at least some part of me is still a virgin." I held out my arm.

Wolfie looped the plastic tubing around my bicep. He tied the ends and pulled them tight. "This okay?"

I nodded.

"Good. Now flex."

Slightly embarrassed by my lack of upper-arm strength—although I was still pretty solidly built for my height—I flexed for him. The skin around my bicep was pale, almost translucent. Damn Irish complexion. He tapped the underside of my wrist gently. I watched, in a kind of horrible fascination, as my cephalic vein slowly flared to life, a current of blue across my skin. He'd better know what he was doing. If he stuck that thing in my brachial artery by accident, I was going to be mighty pissed off (in between spraying out arcs of blood all over Derrick's brand-new coat).

"Good veins," Wolfie said.

"Thanks. I think."

"All right. Deep breath."

I inhaled, then nodded.

No going back now.

I am the worst guardian ever. I am the worst parent in the whole fucking universe. Social Services is going to take Mia away. I'm a crack mom. I'm unfit—

There was no way to think about it. This was happening. I'd be different afterward. I'd still be Tess, but in a way, things would be different. That didn't mean I couldn't come back from it. That I couldn't still be—me.

Wolfie loosened the tourniquet, and then he injected the needle. I felt a heavy pinch, and a little spot of blood appeared as he pulled back the plunger, which meant that he'd found the vein cleanly. He pushed the needle in. I winced.

"Sorry. Has to be deep, or else you just skin-pop. I don't want to think about what injecting this shit into your muscle might do." He looked at me. "Ready?"

I closed my eyes and nodded. I didn't see him press the plunger down. I felt something cold shoot through me. Ice-water in my vein. Like Socrates in the *Crito*, feeling the low black pinch and flow of the hemlock.

The room took on a strange, silver cast. I was aware of Wolfie removing the needle, and I felt his thumb applying pressure to my arm. Derrick said something, but I couldn't quite make out the words. Everything seemed to be falling into static. I was a cipher: a warm beating heart surrounded by snowdrifts. I felt my breathing slow. *Narcotics depress your breathing,* I heard a medical textbook in my head say. But this wasn't in my head. It had nothing to do with acing forensic tests or being a good investigator. This was happening right now to my body. I was living my choice.

Invisible hands guided me to one of the mats. The sound of my own blood was incredibly loud, like the roaring of a train in my ears. The room seemed very dark, and everything was still frosted. I stared at the doorway. Silver smoke began to roil around its edges, like dragon's breath. It smelled sweet and somehow forbidden. Two eyes formed in the smoke. They dangled like rubies. Then the creature opened its mouth, spewing gemstones at me, each one exploding with a different bell tone. I wasn't afraid of the fire as it moved across my body. It was resplendent. Derrick and Wolfie flickered at the barest edges of my vision, like bruised clusters of light. I thought I felt Derrick's hand on my head, but it also felt like an insect's wings. A stuttering touch.

The smoke drifted toward me. I looked down, and I could actually see the tendril of earth materia that connected me to the ground, undulating in that sea plant way that the energy had when Miles was manipulating it. Did he see the power that way all the time? His life must have been a web of sparkling, multicolored lights, a prismatic shell that followed him around all the time. Was it maddening? Or were the colors a strange, paranormal sort of comfort, like a flickering diorama or night light? Proust's lantern flickering across the ceiling as he waited for a chaste kiss.

I let my fingers hover above the strand without touching it. I could feel the seismic energy that ensheathed the materia like copper wire, singing with power from the earth. The smoke curled around my outstretched finger. It wrapped itself around my wrist, following the pathway of my radial artery. A perplexity of things whispered inside the fog. I heard voices, grunts, half whispers, incarnadine laughs, and a hissing sound, like a feral cat might make. I saw flickers, heard chains clinking together, caught flashes of darkness and flame the color of lapidary. I wanted my body to dissolve into smoke. Already, I felt so much lighter.

The mat wasn't there anymore, or if it was, I felt no contact with the ground. The edges of the room had receded to lavender smears. Up and down seemed to peel away from each other, like one of those Band-Aid packages. Was I on the ceiling? Hey, kind of like Willow in that episode of *Buffy*. Maybe I'd turn into Dark Willow. I'd look damn good in that freaky leather bustier of hers.

As the smoke curled along the rest of my body, I tried to think if I'd ever felt like this before. When I was ten, I fractured my hip and got put on a morphine drip for three solid days. It felt like my body was paper thin, and I was floating in some Homeric wine dark sea with no thoughts of pain or discomfort. Just somewhere between sleeping and waking, the interval between life and death.

That had been black-and-white. This was in vivid Technicolor.

Tess.

Something buzzed around in my brain. I pushed it away.

Tess. Silence. Then: *Bitch, snap the fuck out of it!*

I looked up, startled. Derrick was standing in front of me. He looked wavery and a bit see-through, as if someone had made an overhead transparency of him and was fluttering it before my eyes. But he was there.

I can't normally open this channel, he continued, *but you and I are very close, and I think that boosts my abilities.*

So you're . . . actually in my head?

I felt him nod.

I wish I could tell you what this feels like.

I'd rather you didn't. Just concentrate on this hidden memory.

I can't see. Are you holding my hand?

Of course. I have been the whole time.

I smiled. *That's good.*

Don't get woozy. You have to concentrate.

I closed my eyes, imagining that we were in the Nerve, the CORE's sim-room. Freud said that the unconscious was like a movie screen, after all. I should be able to project my whole life back onto it. In theory.

So I reached for that dark little sliver. The strange feeling of cold recognition I got whenever I visited the crime scenes. The feel of Duessa's lips pressing softly on my cheek, like a moth's wings. The image of the *coire* and athame together, so familiar, like an act from a play I'd forgotten.

My mother appeared.

What?

She was standing in a doorway. She looked angry.

"Leave now," she said simply.

Someone was leaning against the doorframe. He seemed impossibly tall and thin, like a pillar of twined shadows. Was my subconscious distending him? Or did he really look like that? I could feel malice rising off him in whiskey fumes.

"She belongs to me, Diane."

"She's beyond your reach now."

"That category encompasses very little." He moved in closer. I thought I saw one of his eyes, winking in the darkness. It was the color of dirty ice.

"Get out. This place won't have you. It's protected."

"I can smell that. Learned some new tricks, have we?"

My mother drew something out. Something that gleamed. A bar of neon, or a slash of silver against the air.

She was holding an athame.

"I can think of somewhere I'd like to put that."

"I'm sure you can. Now go. I won't say it again." Her face was cold. I'd never seen it like that before. She was beautiful in her rage. "You won't see her. As long as I live, you won't ever know her."

"But I've got a much better health plan than you, Diane. I'll be alive when you're mulch in the ground. Then what happens?"

"You'll see." She flicked the edge of the blade. Green sparks licked the air. Green—the color of earth materia.

He shrugged. "Fine. If not today, then tomorrow. We're very patient." His mouth widened to a grin, and for the first time, I saw that his teeth were black and serrated. "It's in our blood."

His *we* echoed in my mind. I tried to peer past him. At first there was nothing, but then, gradually, a shape coalesced. It was man-shaped, but not a man. I saw a thin, angular form. Something that looked like a liquid black coat. Long fingers, like Mister Corvid's, clicking against each other. Skin so cold and blue it was cyanotic. Empty pits where eyes should have been. Holes leading into a void so black, it was forever. I wanted to scream. I think I did.

The dark shape closest to my mother turned. His features kept shifting, but those wasted, ice gray eyes locked on me. Something that might have been a mouth curved into a half smile.

"Tessa? Is that you?"

For a split second, I was two people. There was Tessa the adult, floating in a blissed-out Hex haze. And then there was the six-year-old version of myself, sneaking past my mother and peering out the door.

The thing without eyes turned toward me. Two small holes, like a maggot's air spiracles, clenched in the middle of its face, and I realized it was smelling me.

A name unscrolled in fire across my brain.

It hurt. The syllables grilled my flesh, each one a hot iron brand. I screamed. Then I heard Derrick say something. A shadow reached out to my left, and I felt him pluck the vibrating string of earth materia. His hand was in my guts. I screamed louder, and then the room came back into focus. The edges were still frosted with silver light, but I could see Wolfie and Derrick again.

"Tess?" Wolfie laid his hand on my arm. "You're coming out of it now. I'm going to flush your system, like we talked about. Are you ready?"

I nodded weakly. I think.

"It's going to hurt, baby." He tightened his group. "Okay. Now."

Someone touched an arc welder to my body. Flame blossomed through every vein and vesicle. I couldn't scream. I was a living scream. For a split second, I thought I was going to explode. The pain was a sheet of white light cutting me into a million different angles of flesh. I was on the butcher's block. Someone had harnessed a bit of starlight, and they were using it to shear through me. I was a loaf of bread caught in an electric slicer. My blood boiled.

Then it was gone. I fell forward, but arms caught me and lowered me to the floor. "Don't move yet," Derrick was saying. "Wolfie's getting you something."

My stomach heaved. I turned to the side, and Wolfie shoved a bucket under my head just as I started to puke. It came out in torrents. I sobbed and puked for what seemed like a good ten minutes. Then, weakly, I rolled over.

Derrick leaned in, placing his cool fingers on my brow. I felt him concentrate. His presence brushed my mind: a tickling feather.

"You're not broken," he pronounced. "That's good."

"Breathe in slow," Wolfie said. "And don't talk too much. You'll be sick for a while yet. Around midnight, you'll probably want to kill yourself. But it'll pass in a day or so, if you're lucky."

"Great," I said thickly. "Sounds like . . . one of my last relationships."

Derrick laughed softly. "How do you feel?"

My underwear was damp. I realized that I'd wet myself. I was also certain that I needed to throw up again.

"Been better," I told him.

"Can you remember anything you saw?"

I thought of the creature with no eyes, sniffing me.

"I remember—a name," I said.

"The killer's name?"

"No." I grabbed the bucket. "My father's."

I dimly heard my cell ringing as I puked again. It smelled like blood and ashes. The color was—indescribable. Like something radioactive. It was still happening in slow motion, so every turn of my gut felt like it would last forever. A symphony to reverse peristalsis. I closed my eyes.

Derrick answered my cell. There was some back and forth talk, and then silence. I felt him settle next to me.

Wolfie brought me a towel. I wiped off my face and looked up.

"That was Selena, wasn't it?"

He nodded slowly.

I knew why she was calling. I knew almost everything now.

17

I barely had time to wash my face and change into the fresh clothes that Derrick had brought me—thank God—before we were driving back down Hastings toward Nanaimo. I'd managed to keep myself from throwing up long enough to pop four extra-strength Motrin and a Gravol from my purse, draining a bottle of water in the process and still feeling like I could drink the Pacific Ocean. My insides were still hot from Wolfie's fire, and I could feel the residual Hextacy in my muscle, bone, and blood, like a parasite that wouldn't quite die. I lay curled up in the backseat, knees drawn to my chest, breathing hard—a wounded animal. Derrick concentrated on the road, but his eyes would flick to the rearview mirror every minute or so, checking on me. Wolfie leaned against the passenger window, silent, watching the dark street go by.

The car was either moving very fast or very slowly. I couldn't tell anymore. Gravity and distance didn't seem to make sense like they used to.

She's beyond your reach now. My mother's voice echoed through the smashed-in corridors of my brain. *You won't see her. As long as I live, you won't ever know her.*

My mother. Angry. Holding a ritual dagger.

Had she borrowed it from someone? No, I'd seen the sparks. I'd felt her power. She was like me.

Diane Corday was a mage.

I thought of what Derrick must have felt when he first realized that he was adopted. Like turning to a familiar photo album and finding that all the pictures had suddenly changed or gone fuzzy and blank. My life wasn't my life anymore. Everything I'd always known, everything I'd worked so hard to protect for twelve years—it was all twisted and mauled and broken apart now, as if someone had tossed a Molotov cocktail into my archive of memories.

The whole time. She'd always known. *The whole time.*

I had to tell Derrick, but I couldn't even articulate it. And there wasn't time. First we had to manage the latest crime scene, which I could already see in my mind. I should have seen it coming. It made a perverse kind of sense.

"Tess?" Derrick's voice still sounded a bit far away. "We're almost there—I'm going to look for parking now. If you can't manage this—"

"No, no." I swallowed. Each word tasted like bile. "As long as we don't have to walk very far. I can't possibly puke again. There's nothing left in my stomach, and the headache isn't as bad."

Earlier, it had been a sun going nova behind my eyes. Now it had settled down to a spreading, fiery ache. And beneath the pain haze, all I could think of was Mia, sitting in my mother's living room, laughing and chatting and having no idea that she was in the presence of a mage.

Had my mother known about Mia all along? She always called her different, "special." Did she know that the girl was VR-positive, that she carried the vampiric retrovirus? Maybe she even knew what had really happened with Marcus Tremblay.

I reached slowly for my phone. Gritting my teeth, I managed to text a short message for Mia and hit Send: *Coming to visit tonight.*

Damn right I was coming to visit tonight. I was coming with

every ounce of fury left in my body, and I was going to get some answers.

Derrick parked in the same space by the church on Penticton Street. Caution tape surrounded the yard of the old Victorian house. I wondered what the neighbors thought. At least the CORE didn't have sirens and flashing lights—only a lot of folks dressed in black who seemed to be in twelve different places at once. Eventually, I imagined, to cut costs, they'd employ one shape-shifter to cover the whole scene.

The occlusion field washed over me, bringing with it another spasm of nausea. I closed my eyes tight and counted to five. Cool air hit me in the face as Derrick opened the car door. I looked at him and smiled weakly.

"You don't have to do this, you know," he said.

Groaning, I untangled myself from the backseat. My legs were shaky, but they held as I leaned against the car.

"I really do," I said. "Selena and I have to talk. And we're bound to find something here. We tried so hard to get into this place before, and now it's like an open house. Feels weird."

"Like a violation, almost."

I nodded. "But it's our job, right? We invade people's lives—and deaths."

He took my hand. "Can you walk?"

"If I get to lean on you. Let's try to keep it inconspicuous, though. Selena doesn't need to know that I'm coming down from a flash of Hex."

"Your pupils are still the size of dinner plates. I think she's going to notice."

"Damn." I rubbed my forehead. "Oh well, I guess it's time for the truth anyways. What's the worst that could happen? If she demotes me back to OSI-1, at least I'll have less paperwork and I can work the swing shift."

"Or she'll eject us both from the CORE, and demonic assassins will make sure that we've been 'retired.'"

"You always look on the sunny side of the street, don't you?"

"It's a special gift."

Wolfie appeared next to us, looking nervous. "Should I be here?"

I nodded. "It's fine. You're kind of involved now."

"In a bad way?"

"There's really no good way left."

I took a long breath. Then, leaning on Derrick, I walked to the front door.

One of the photo techs recognized me, and looked on the verge of saying hello until she saw my face. Then she gave me a wide berth, stooping to get more reference shots of the front yard with her macro lens. I must have looked like the devil's ass. Funny how caked-on concealer still couldn't hide the fact that you'd been puking yourself inside out for a full half hour. Why did they even call it "concealer"? I needed something more powerful. Sephora must make some kind of demonic cover-up treatment, and I made a mental note to ask Cindeé about it.

The stairs were old and covered with an ugly plastic runner. I made my way up to the main floor, which was its own contained suite. There was a tray of latex gloves and shoe covers at the entrance, along with extra flashlights and a generator for the ALS and Cyalume filters. I turned to Wolfie.

"If you're going to come with us, you'll have to put on protective gear first. Otherwise, you can stay in the hallway, but don't touch anything."

"I can chill out here," he said, looking a little queasy. I'm sure he could detect the bitter, coppery smell coming from the next room, like rusting nails. Blood. Strange that he could stick a needle into my arm like an expert, but the smell of blood made him queasy. Everyone had different triggers.

"Don't talk to anyone," I told him, "unless a tall, scary-looking black lady with great hair asks you a question. Then tell her anything she needs to know."

"Scary lady. Great hair." He nodded. "Got it."

I slipped on a pair of gloves and shoe covers, quickly sweeping my hair back from my shoulders and tying it in a ponytail. It would be more efficient to get a shorter haircut, but what was the use of having red hair unless you were going to show it off? Besides, it always gave me an excuse to be late, since I had to wrap my head in a towel turban after every shower and wait an hour for it to dry. Sure, I could use my Conair to blow-dry it faster if I was on my way to work, but nobody had to know that. And with short hair I looked too much like a boy. My dating life was suffering already without adding gender confusion to the mix.

I ducked under the second line of caution tape—and stopped.

"Shit," I murmured. It was the only thing I could think to say.

I could imagine that this living room had once been comfortable and elegant, with classic furniture and beautifully refinished hardwood floors. Someone had put love and attention into making this the focal point of the suite. But it no longer resembled anything close to a home. It was completely destroyed from floor to ceiling. A dark green sofa lay in pieces in the middle of the room, shredded, as if a giant beast had savagely clawed it. Splintered wood and pieces of metal littered the floor around it, along with a fan of broken glass, like someone had waved a nightmarish wand to create random arcs of destruction. Shelves were overturned, spewing out shattered decorations, pictures, books, CDs, and other things that were now unrecognizable. An overturned chair had been snapped neatly in two. A plasma screen television was on its side, somehow still miraculously plugged in, cord stretched across the ground. The screen itself was cracked and showed nothing but a plane of shifting colors.

I glanced down and saw an eight-inch gouge in the wooden floor. It looked like a restless dinosaur had twitched its foot, shearing through wood and underlay as easily as a cat might crumple a foil ball. A yellow evidence placard next to the claw mark indicated that it had already been photographed. I stepped over it carefully.

"Tess." Derrick touched my shoulder, pointing to a broken frame lying amid the glass fragments. Reaching down, I used the base of my flashlight to flip it over. A familiar face smiled at me from the cracked glass.

Patrick. Caitlin Siobhan's official successor to the title of vampire magnate. He looked happy in the photo, at ease, more like the cute, messy-haired kid I'd seen hanging around Mia than the wasted boy I'd once seen lying in a hospital bed. A million-dollar question formed in my brain as I reached into my kit, pulling out brushes and black dusting powder for the gilt edge of the frame.

Where was Patrick?

I gently twirled the brush over the frame, letting the black powder fall like radioactive dust, or reverse snow. A few different prints rose to the surface. I doubted that any of them belonged to the killer—it didn't seem like the kind of creature that perspired or produced natural oils—but I tape-lifted them anyway, numbering and initialing each sample before I stowed it in my kit. The only real fingerprint we had so far in this case had been planted, and I still didn't know why.

I stood up too fast, and the room spun a bit. Derrick must have noticed my expression, because he gave me his arm to lean on.

"Thanks," I whispered. "My head still feels like a snare drum."

"Wolfie said it might be that way for a while."

"Guess it's my karmic punishment."

He gave me a long look. "I think you did the right thing. I didn't agree with it at first, and I sure don't feel good about it. But maybe it had to be done."

"We'll see," I said, picking my way through the rubble of the living room. "The night's still young. There's a whole pile of laws and regulations I could break before the sun comes up."

"I promise to bail you out."

"If you don't die from the paperwork first."

We made our way down a narrow hallway, keeping to the edge of the walls. I hadn't seen any blood yet, and I got the impression that—despite the carnage in the front room—things hadn't gotten really crazy until the struggle reached the master bedroom. It always ended in the bedrooms. They were liminal sites—places where blood, sex, and murder all converged.

The hallway had three doors. The first was small, presumably leading to a bathroom. It was shut. It didn't look like it had been disturbed, and there was no yellow tape to mark it as a point of interest. I walked past it. The second door was slightly ajar, and I caught sight of a neat room with midnight blue carpeting and white walls. Posters of bands and sports teams were tacked above a computer desk, and an unmade bed sat in the corner. Definitely Patrick's room. It looked virtually untouched as well. Either he ran into the master bedroom right away, or he hadn't actually been present when all hell broke loose. I was voting for the latter. Patrick was AWOL.

The door at the end of the hallway was open. As I got closer to it, I could feel the hair on the back of my neck stand up. A tremor passed through my gut, and for a moment, I was afraid I might spew bile and undigested bits of Motrin onto the floor. But the feeling subsided. I took a deep breath and stepped carefully into the room.

Even before my eyes registered the scene before me, I knew, sharply and with the sting of horror, that something cataclysmic had happened here.

Immortals didn't die easily, and they released a cascade of overwhelming power when their brains and bodies finally collapsed, like a circuit board exploding. Fragments of materia floated like ash in the air, dancing slowly in front of my eyes. Time operated differently past this doorway. The shockwaves of death had left a jagged impression at the temporal-spatial level, and everything seemed a few seconds too slow, as if the whole world had been ripped off its tracks and then redubbed out of sync. I moved my hand, and a faint afterimage trailed in its wake. This was going to wreak holy hell with our forensic tests.

Selena was standing by the window, examining the glass. A few other technicians were spraying the rug with Amido Black formula to make the blood stand out, stabilizing it so that it would photograph better. No one was standing by the bed, which gave me an unobscured view of what lay on it.

The other scenes had been so controlled and sanitary, arranged with surgical precision and laid out for us, like insane dioramas. Those edges and boundaries were nowhere to be seen this time. There was no elegant cut to the carotid artery, no blood pool collecting on the ground. This was pure savagery. It was lustful and apocalyptic. I almost couldn't look—but I didn't have a choice. Fuck if I ever had one.

The body was in pieces.

Someone had shuffled it like a deck of cards and then put it back out of order, with parts missing. A sheared-off arm ended at the elbow, and I could see strands of bloody tissue wrapped around the matrix of a shattered ulna, shockingly smooth and white against the avulsed skin and muscle. I didn't know where the rest of the arm was. I couldn't see it anywhere. The right leg was mauled with deep lacerations going down to the femur, which blossomed through holes in the flesh like a startling white shell, dotted with islands of bridging tissue and bloody detritus. The foot, weirdly enough, was untouched. It dangled off the side of the bed, perfect, with a pronounced arch that could only come from decades of wearing high heels. Such small toes. Almost like a child's. A single dot of blood lay stark on the pinkie toe, like a stray drop of nail polish. Otherwise, it could have been a catalog photo.

The other leg was twisted violently out from the body. Sharp edges of white peered obscenely through the skin of the distended ankle, revealing it to be an acute comminuted fracture— the closest you could come to having your foot twisted off without actually forcing the talus bone loose from the tibia. Deep bruising flowered across the shin and thigh—massive internal bleeding from the fracture, among other things.

A tattered dress just barely covered the torso, shredded in places and revealing the curve of the left breast. I wondered if the genitalia had been left unscathed, but I was afraid to look. This was a crime of unimaginable rage, a death rape, and I couldn't imagine that any part of the body had been left completely intact. A slim white arm lay draped across the abdomen, partially obscuring the space where the pubic arch ended and the stomach began. It looked artificial. Posed. Your limbs didn't fall gracefully like that while you were dying. They flailed and thrashed and clawed, spasmodic, as you voided your bladder and bowels. No control. Just the press of darkness, and then—I didn't know what. I'd never known.

Unlike the artisanal slash across the necks of the previous victims, this wound was messy and deep. The carotid artery hadn't just been transected—it was mauled. Bits of flesh and cricoid cartilage hung from the stellate gash, and even from a distance I could see the pulverized ribbons of what had once been the trachea. No doubt the hyoid bone would be in fragments somewhere beneath, although Tasha would have to search for it with a pair of forceps.

"What happened to her head?" Derrick whispered. His voice was dull, as if his mind had already checked out and left the room. It was a good question.

Her head—or what remained of it—looked like one of those anatomical models with the detachable plates that you find in a doctor's office. Whole segments were missing. Her jawbone was gone, the mandible completely ripped away from the coronoid process, and the surrounding musculature was ground hamburger. Part of her skull had disappeared, leaving the parietal bone only partially intact and looking like a startled comma, slick with blood. Her right eye was missing, and it had taken part of the ethmoid bone and orbital ridge with it, leaving a patchwork mess of macerated bone and muscle behind. The frayed edge of the optical nerve dangled from her eye socket like an abandoned speaker wire.

Her mouth was frozen in a scream, twisted by the avulsed bone, tissue, and decimated jawline so that it resembled a smirk. A sarcastic question mark lighting on her gloriously ruined face. Her hair—formerly orange—had become a feculent pillow of matted blood and gore. A few tawny strands still glittered in the mess, either shed naturally or torn from her scalp.

I turned away to look at the wall, which was a mistake. It glistened with arcs of cherry red arterial spray, only partially dried to reveal skeletonized swipes and fingers within the pattern. Vampire blood was almost pink, like human blood exposed to carbon monoxide. But that wasn't all. Something had played in her blood. Something had enjoyed itself immensely here.

If I hadn't already purged my stomach many times over, I would have been on my knees, retching, even after years on the job. Instead, all I could so was stand there, unable to speak, wavering but not falling as I leaned against Derrick's shoulder. He felt like the only human thing left in the room. Even if neither of us was completely human in the long run.

Selena finally turned from the window and stared at me. I wanted to shield my face, but with the floodlights set up in the room, there was nowhere to hide. I couldn't have looked good—even compared with what lay on the bed. Selena frowned for a moment, but then her expression shifted to professional resolve. She'd always been able to prioritize. *One fucked-up situation at a time,* she must have been thinking.

"Almost unrecognizable," she said simply, gesturing to the bed. "This feels like the finale to me. A real soaring note."

"It doesn't make sense, though. The other scenes were controlled—almost programmatic. The ritual element was clear. This is just . . ." I tried to take in the whole room, but found that I could only see bits at a time, as if my eyes had quit. "It's completely insane. Nothing like before."

"Someone flipped a switch," Selena replied. "This fucker's gone nuclear. It didn't care about the formula this time."

"This was a frenzy kill," Derrick breathed. "I mean, they knew each other, right? How else could her print have gotten on that cauldron?"

Selena glanced at her notebook. "The house is registered to a Katrina Glass, but we know that's not her real name."

"Caitlin Siobhan." I forced myself to stare at her. "That's who she is. Was. My God. A former vampire magnate, and this thing just . . . took her apart. Like she was a doll. How is that possible?"

"I know what you're asking yourself." Selena's gaze lingered on my pasty skin and blackened eyes for a moment, but she still wasn't ready to ask *that* question. "You've got to wonder—is this some fucked-up part of the ritual that we haven't seen till now? Or was it a mistake? A heat-of-the-moment kill?"

"I don't think it makes mistakes." I swallowed hard and walked carefully around the bed, examining Caitlin from a different angle. Her head dangled loosely on the crimped spinal cord, a smashed egg. The cord was still intact, though—if barely—which was why she hadn't desiccated like the vampires who attacked me in the subway. "But I don't think this was ritualistic either. It's the symptom of an all-out battle."

"Two immortals fighting." Selena shook her head. "Bound to get ugly. Looks like the fucking Thunderdome in here."

"It couldn't have gotten off easily. I mean, look at the living room. Caitlin must have left a mark on this thing."

"That might make it easier to find."

I met Selena's eyes. Truth time.

"I think it might be a pureblood," I said slowly. "Something native to the shores of hell. The form that it has in our world could be—erratic. It might be hard to see at all, which would explain why there's no trace left at any of the scenes."

Selena looked sideways at me. "And does this inspiration have anything to do with the truck that apparently hit you in the face tonight?"

"Maybe." I smiled, but it hurt. "I do think I'm finally starting to put some of the pieces together. But there are still a lot of gaps. Which is why I need to ask you—"

She raised a hand to preempt me. "Corday, I swear to sweet baby Jesus, if you ask me for a favor, I will smack you into yesterday. Understand? I'm in no mood to deal with anything *close* to the shit you pulled last year. And I can smell it coming already."

"It's not like that." I struggled to negotiate a thin line of truth without spilling my entire hand. It was like skating through a minefield. "I've done it right this time, Selena. By the book, like you told me to. I've signed all the proper forms, I've reported everything to you—all the conversations with Lucian, my interviews with Duessa and Wolfie, even when the vampires attacked me in the subway—you know all of it."

Except for the part where I injected myself with Hextacy, saw an image of my pureblood demon father, and discovered that my mother's a witch.

Selena's eyes were flat. "*All* of it? Every last speck?"

I made a motion with my head—not quite an affirmative nod. More like a sideways turn whose interpretation was ambiguous at best.

"And the supplier?" Her tone was particularly cold.

I looked at Derrick. Wolfie had dumped out the rest of the Hex, so there was no physical evidence of my brush with hard drugs, but a simple blood test would confirm what I'd done. Selena could order that at her discretion. Or not.

"He wouldn't give up the buyer's name," I said. Derrick's eyes flickered, but he didn't interrupt. "But he's going to give the money back."

Once I beat the living shit out of Patches and retrieved it myself.

"What did he say to you about the buyer?"

It would have been too risky to wear a wire, so there was no official transcript or recording of my interview with Mister Corvid. I could have told Selena just about anything. But I'd already been a big enough asshole tonight. I owed her some truth.

"First he showed me the Hex. He said it was more concentrated than the stuff on the street that he was distributing. Then he said that he'd sold multiple times to a buyer who fit our description. He wouldn't tell me who it was, but he said that . . ." I swallowed around a lump in my throat. "He said that the killer had . . . a connection to me. Something hard to define. Like I'd encountered it before."

Anger danced in her eyes. "What sort of connection exactly?"

"I'm honestly not sure. I mean, I never knew my father. He could have all sorts of connections. But Duessa said something along the same lines."

"*Did* she?" Selena folded her arms. "You left that out of your incident report."

"I—didn't really understand it at the time." That was almost true. "I don't know what else I can tell you right now. I've got partial answers and half-truths from two demons, neither of whom I really trust. But they also don't have a reason to lie."

Selena digested this slowly. I could see the muscles in her jaw working. "You think this has something to do with your family?"

"I don't know yet. That's why I need to see my intake file—the whole thing, from the time I started with the CORE until now."

"Those records are sealed."

"I know."

She stared at me for a long while. "Something's kinky about this tale of yours. Something you're leaving out."

I looked at the floor. It didn't seem right to lie in this room, where Caitlin Siobhan's soul—or whatever passed for a vampire's soul—hung around us like a pale, whispering filigree of light twined with shadow. Her presence here was still overwhelming, and would be for a good long while. I doubted that anyone would be able to live in this house for the next few decades. The feeling of dread would linger until it forced them out, and anyone with even the most nascent telepathy would go crazy from the psychic weight pressing down on them.

Some part of me also felt like I owed Caitlin something. She'd done her best to protect Patrick, and judging from how happy he looked in his picture, she'd succeeded until tonight. She gave him a home when she could have just abandoned him. And she'd most likely spent the last few moments of her unlife protecting him. She deserved better than listening to me shovel my own shit.

"I did something stupid."

Derrick went pale, but he still kept quiet.

Selena merely blinked. "Go on."

"When I met with Mister Corvid, he suggested a very . . . *unorthodox* method for gleaning information about the killer.

So I followed his suggestion. The—ah—*experience*—helped me clarify a few ideas. About the murders, and their possible connection to me. Nothing concrete. But there were hints." I could barely meet her eyes. "You could even call them visions. If I'm going to make sense of what I've been seeing and feeling lately, I'll need to look at that intake file."

Selena seemed to be looking right through me. "Visions" was all she said.

"Daimonic inspiration?" I tried to appear naive rather than duplicitous.

She ground her teeth. "Exactly how unorthodox was this exercise that you tried—at the suggestion of an immortal drug supplier?"

"It was a radical expansion of consciousness." That sounded about right. "Selena, have you ever read anything by Carlos Castaneda?"

She exhaled and looked at Derrick. "Siegel. You've always been"—her eyes swept back to me—"not insane. Unlike this one. So tell me—what did she do? And what agency do I need to call?"

Derrick seemed to consider this. He was about to answer when the door to the bedroom opened, and Miles walked in.

"Sorry I'm late. I had to take the—" His face drained of color as he saw what was lying on the bed. "Oh—holy *shit* . . ." Then he gagged and turned away. Derrick took his arm lightly.

"Breathe through your nose. And try not to look too hard. I promise, this is as bad as it ever gets."

He sounded like a seasoned OSI. My heart gave a little tug. He really was changing—growing in power and experience. I didn't know how to deal with it. The fear that he might somehow outgrow me was almost paralyzing.

"Well, this is . . . certainly more interesting than pay-per-view," Miles said quietly, between short, sharp breaths. "Usually, the body's gone by the time I get here."

"Just pretend you're in an episode of *Dexter*." Derrick smiled at him. "There's a way to stare at this invisible spot, above and to the right of the body, so you don't actually see it all at once. It's a trick that Tess showed me."

Miles tried to follow his directions. "It's hard for me. Usually, I'm looking everywhere at once."

Derrick signed something, his motions uncharacteristically slow. Nerves? Or was he trying to inject emphasis? He waved both hands across each other, palms downward; then he gestured to his own eyes with his middle and index fingers, following this with a sign that I was chillingly familiar with: both hands drifting parallel, palms upward, then reversing themselves smoothly. *Dead.* He placed a palm over his chest, and then his stomach, as if delineating pieces of his own body. Then he pointed to his eyes again, crooking the index finger of his right hand and circling it with his left, as if describing a target. Finally, he touched his chest, smiling. I managed to piece the movements together, mostly because they were slow.

Don't look at the dead body. Just look at me.

Miles blushed slightly. "Sure. I can do that."

"Look, this is all very cinematic . . ." Selena's voice had a definite edge. "Very *CSI: Miami*, I'm sure, but we've got work to do. Tess . . ."

"I can explain everything." I held up my hands. "I promise. Everything and the kitchen sink. Just give me the rest of the night to work on a hunch."

"Will this hunch lead us to Patrick, the magnate successor? Because right now he's like an atomic bomb loose in the city. With Caitlin dead, his powers will be rising to the surface, and not in a sweet, coming-of-age way."

"More like a homicidal, living-weapon kind of way," Derrick clarified. "Like Henry Fitzroy on crack. Not the Showtime version."

"I can find him." I held her gaze. "Eight hours. Give me that much."

She nodded after a moment. "Eight hours. After that, you report in full. I want every minute of those eight hours accounted for. If I like what I hear, I'll make a call to Esther in Records, and she'll deliver your intake file."

"The word 'awesome' isn't big enough to describe you."

"Fuck you, Tess." She smiled wryly as she said it. "Now get

out of here before I make you start analyzing blood spatter. You used to be good at stringing."

"That's because my life's always one thread away from falling apart." I took one last glance at Caitlin's body and headed for the door.

"I suppose I'm driving?" Derrick asked.

"Unless you want us to end up in a ditch, yeah." I turned to Miles. Everything was so fucked up already—might as well push both our lives over the edge. "Why don't you call us when you're done here, and we'll pick you up. We can swing by the hotel and get Baron, too—as long as I don't have to walk him in the morning."

His eyes widened as I said "morning."

"You mean—ah . . ."

"I mean we could use the company. We've got a big house with lots of rooms, and your hotel sucks. None of us are getting much sleep tonight, so we might as well pool our resources and stick it out together."

Derrick grinned stupidly. "That's a good idea, Tess. Strategically speaking."

"Of course it is. So—we'll pick you up in a few hours?"

Selena was ready to jump out a window.

"Sure." Miles looked as happy as a person standing next to a disarticulated body *could* look, all things considered. "Sure. Baron will appreciate the extra space."

"Baron's a smart dog," I said. "Okay, let's do this. I need a coffee in the worst way, and we've got a long drive ahead of us."

"Where are you even going?" Selena called after me.

I strode down the hallway without looking back. "Family reunion."

.18.

We got as far as Surrey—just past the Port Mann Bridge with its rust-colored web of struts and girders, and its insanely narrow four-lane traffic—before my body found a new way to betray me.

"Gas station," I hissed at Derrick, "*now.*"

Wordlessly, he pulled off at the 114th Street exit and drove to the nearest Shell, which had one of those depressing attached convenience stores with inappropriate lighting and employees who always looked vaguely comatose. The car had barely stopped running before I leapt out, snatching the key to the restroom from the attendant before he had a chance to say anything. I ran past the fossilized muffins, the energy drinks, and the walls stacked with Fritos and chocolate-covered pretzels. Mecca was at the end of a long, erratically lit hallway strewn with empty milk crates and busted aluminum shelving.

The restroom door swung inward to reveal a grimy concrete cell with an empty paper towel dispenser, but I didn't care. I would have settled for an outhouse at this point. I slammed the door shut behind me and locked it.

I spent the next twenty minutes hanging on to the wheel-chair rail for dear life as my bowels played the tune of apocalypse. I thought I'd already puked everything up, but apparently, there was a secret cache of—something—just waiting to go nuclear. Wolfie had warned me that, as I came down from the Hex, I'd probably feel like I wanted to kill myself. "There's really no words for how it feels to be *junk-sick*," he told me. "Just try to take care of yourself, and it'll pass. But it'll seem like forever."

I realized now what he meant.

There were knives in my gut, and ringing in my ears, and now a molten flurry exploding out of me in spasms that made me dig my fingernails into my knees, wishing I could yell but afraid that someone outside might hear me and call the police.

If this was what it felt like to come down from heroin, I knew that I'd never be addicted to hard drugs. I couldn't possibly do this more than once.

Every one of my joints hurt and itched like mad. Fingers, toes, kneecaps—everything was on fire and crawling with bugs and aching so bad. I felt hot and cold, soaring between fiery highs and frigid lows—Derrick's shirt was already stuck to my body from sweat—and I kept swallowing around this awful tickle in my throat that wouldn't go away. It was like some demon had reached down my esophagus and was casually, madly tickling me with a feather, laughing the whole time.

I wanted to knock over the enormous display of Gatorade bottles outside and start ripping into them, chugging down those sweet, generic flavors with dumbass names like "grape snowstorm" and "winter rain." I wanted my throat to unhinge like a Vailoid demon's Carcharodon jaws—the blueprint for great white sharks—growing to hideous proportions so that I could drink everything in sight.

Finally the last spasm seemed to pass. I was shaking, but the roiling in my stomach and bowels had subsided a bit. It was a miracle that no one had broken down the restroom door by now. Maybe Derrick was guarding it. That would be sweet of him. Most likely, though, he was still in the car, tapping his fingers on the steering wheel and wondering if I'd fallen into another dimension.

Shakily, I pulled my up my pants and wobbled over to the sink. The mirror reflected back a pale, sweating mess with pasty lips and deep circles under her eyes. I looked like a hardened addict. Wolfie hadn't been kidding about how powerful Hex was. Of course, you were generally supposed to come down from it over the course of twelve hours, as opposed to my accelerated detoxification. My body was royally pissed, and it wasn't going to let me off easy, not once. I could hardly blame it.

I closed my eyes and placed both hands on the rim of the porcelain sink, trying to feel the earth materia coursing just below me. It was faint, but present. I tugged on a strand gently, and something sluggish, hot, and sweet flowed up the length of my arm. I couldn't draw too much too fast—it was like trying to slurp a burning-hot bowl of soup when you were practically dying of hunger. But I managed to take little sips. The power soothed my insides, unknotting some of my muscles and making it easier to breathe.

I splashed some water on my face. My hair was a lost cause, but the ponytail hid most of the tangles and snarls. Concealer wouldn't do shit for the circles under my eyes, but it didn't really matter now. My mother wouldn't get the chance to ask too many questions. I'd be the one conducting the interrogation tonight.

I dropped the key back on the counter and kept walking. The attendant gave me a suspicious look but didn't say anything. I eased myself back into the passenger seat, only to discover that Derrick had been shopping while I was in the ninth ring of hell.

"Here." He passed a plastic bag over to me. "I got you some essentials."

I pawed through it. "Pepto, ginger ale, soda crackers—*ooh*, cherry lozenges . . ." I smiled weakly at him. "It's the best gift bag in the world right now. Thanks."

"I tried to plan for every type of organic breakdown. How are you feeling?"

"Like I just shit out a cruise missile. I think it's starting to let up, though."

"Thanks for painting me that watercolor." He started up the car. "Have some of the ginger ale. That's what my mom always gave me when I had an upset stomach."

"That's what moms all across North America have been prescribing for upset stomachs since the nineteenth century." I made a face. "It actually doesn't cure anything. There's almost no ginger in it, and the high sugar content is a diuretic."

"Fine. I'm sorry I didn't consult a pharmacology manual before buying your soda. I'll be more diligent next time."

"I *like* it, though." I uncapped the bottle and took a cautious sip. "The bubbles always make me feel better."

"If I were a more powerful telepath, I'd be able to trigger a cascade of serotonin in your brain," he said, "which would make you feel a lot better."

"I've had enough chemicals running rampant through my body. I don't need any more whacked-out neurotransmitters." I looked at him. "And besides—you *are* a powerful telepath. I'm still not sure what you did back at the hotel, but you saved Miles from getting chewed up by raw energy. You've gotten a lot stronger."

"Aw, shucks." He looked away.

I smiled to myself.

We made it to Elder Heights without further incident. I found that if I stayed very still and kept my eyes half-closed, the vibrations of the Festiva—which was surely as immortal as a vampire in its own right—were actually soothing. I ate little bits of soda cracker like a bird, washing them down with ginger ale. By the time we took Exit 119 and slipped away from Highway-1, I was starting to feel almost human again. Not especially ready to confront my mother about being a duplicitous magic user, but still much better than I'd felt an hour ago.

We turned from Vedder Road onto Hocking Street, and the familiar landmarks began to appear—my old college, the pizza joint where my cousin still worked, the fried chicken place that was always one health code violation away from being shut down (it would just rise phoenixlike and reappear on the other side of town anyway). Before I knew it, Derrick was parking adjacent to my parents' town house. The living room was bathed in a warm glow. Dad's car was gone—he must have been working late. He'd become convinced over a decade ago that not even a small army of young sales staff could possibly run his electronics store without constant supervision. He still printed out every label himself, down to the smallest transistor. It was a miracle that my mother hadn't set fire to the place years ago.

Derrick shut off the engine. I was about to reach for the car door when he put a hand on my shoulder.

"Not so fast. I just drove an hour and a half on the freeway so that you could have a nightcap with your mom. Not that I don't love Diane and all, but we're in the middle of a murder investigation, and you ran out of Caitlin's house like the devil was chasing you." He sat back in the driver's seat. "I'm not going in there until you tell me why we're in Elder and what your mother has to do with all this."

"If you wait five minutes, I promise it'll make sense. You're about to see a performance that'll bring down the house."

"No. You're going to tell me right now."

I suppose I could have argued. But really, how often did he demand anything of me? Usually, Derrick was the giving one, the one who put up with my whole spectrum of bullshit without complaint. All he wanted now was the truth.

"I saw something when I was in that Hex dream," I said.

"Of course you did. I saw it, too."

My jaw literally dropped. "You . . ." I stared at him. "I mean—you saw the whole thing, with my mother?"

"Yeah." He smirked. "She had a sweet-looking athame. Nicer than yours. Was that hilt mother-of-pearl?"

I resisted the urge to punch him. "You *saw* it, all of it, and you didn't say anything? Oh, for . . ." I shook my head. "Why the hell didn't you say anything? I've spent the last two hours trying to figure out the best way to explain it all, and I felt so bloody guilty, and the *whole time* . . ."

I trailed off. He just looked at me.

"Why didn't you say something?" I repeated.

"Why didn't *you* say something?"

"Don't get cute." I exhaled. "First Wolfie was there, and I wasn't sure how much I should say in front of him. Then Selena was there, and I *really* didn't feel like a complete debriefing was the way to go, especially since she's already on the verge of firing me. Again."

"You told her more than I expected you to, though." He nodded in approval. "Almost the whole truth. That must be a milestone."

"Please don't play good cop with me tonight. This isn't exactly the easiest thing to process. I mean, my mom's a witch. She lied to me. And now I've got to go in there and confront her, inside the house where I grew up, and that's about the shittiest thing I can possibly think of." My voice almost broke. I could barely look at him. "And I can't help thinking—every time I see that *thing's* face, I just—"

"No, no, no, a thousand times no." He cupped my chin. "This is not your fault. You didn't force that creature to go on a killing spree. It may have some connection to you, or to your father the pureblood, but it chose to murder those people."

"But it knows me, Derrick. Fuck, it's taunting me. Making me squirm. If I hadn't taken this case . . ."

"You can what-if yourself to death, but it won't do any good. This thing is a force of nature. If all it wanted to do was get to you, there'd be no need to go around killing innocent people. It could have just grabbed you ages ago."

"That's really comforting."

"It's not about you, Tess. This fucker is crazy. It's from another world, and it wants to cause naked destruction in ours. Your feeling like shit is only a symptom."

"It doesn't feel like a symptom," I said brokenly. "It feels like my fault."

"I say this with love," he replied, "but, honey, you're not that important. This thing is ancient and pure evil. Its whole existence couldn't possibly revolve around some detective from the CORE. It's not a personal vendetta. This thing is killing because it needs to. Understand?"

I nodded slowly. I wasn't sure I believed him, but on some level it made sense.

"Okay. Now let's go piss off your mother."

"That should be easy." I opened the car door. "I've been doing it for the last twenty-five years."

I opened the door with my old key, since I couldn't face hearing the sound of my father's novelty doorbell, which played the *1812 Overture* at earsplitting levels. It didn't really matter, since my mother had a way of knowing exactly who was at the door; she claimed that my father and I had different footsteps. Now I wondered if it wasn't a more occult sense that she was relying on.

Derrick politely took off his shoes, but I didn't bother. I walked up the newly refinished steps, into the living room with the big-screen TV that my dad had insisted was a perfectly sensible tax write-off. My mother was sitting on the couch with Mia, fiddling with the remote. "God, I don't know how he programs this thing. It makes about as much sense as an abacus to me . . ."

She saw me, and just for a second I saw a curious expression pass over her face. Surprise? Guilt? I felt ice in the pit of my stomach. Then she smiled widely.

"Tess! You're early. We were going to watch *Pride and Prejudice*. The new version has a very fit Scottish actor playing Mister Darcy, and if you can ignore that girl with the overbite playing Lizzy, it's not all that bad."

"It was so cool, like, in Regency times, when guys wore those short pants," Mia said to her. "Like bloomers, but for guys."

"You mean knee britches."

"Oh my God, yes. That's *hilarious*. Knee britches." Mia was eating what looked like a handful of M&M'S. God, did this house have a never-ending supply of candy? Ever since I was a little kid, my mom could just whip out fun-sized Snickers and Winegums from these secret caches, like she was stockpiling for a nuclear winter. I blamed her entirely for my acne in middle school.

"Mom—I have to talk to you." The words came out barely

audible, but she heard them. Her resolve cracked, just a bit. I could see it.

"Well, in that case, we'd better put some more tea on. Sweetheart . . ." She called into the kitchen. "Tess and Derrick are here. Bring out some extra mugs."

I blinked in confusion. "I thought Dad was . . ."

Lucian Agrado emerged from my mother's kitchen.

He was carrying a tray with four steaming mugs of tea, and he smiled at me as if this were an everyday occurrence. It made about as much sense as seeing Tasha Lieu, our CME, emerging from our rec room after playing a bracing game of air hockey with my dad. Some worlds just weren't supposed to mix.

What the hell was he doing here?

"You're here." I looked at him pointedly. "In my mother's house."

"He showed up earlier tonight, shortly after Mia and I got home from shopping." My mother gave me a look that conveyed volumes. "Apparently, he was worried about us both, given the fact that there's a serial killer on the loose."

"Mom, you've never met Lucian before. He could *be* a serial killer."

Lucian didn't even look phased by this. "She knows I'm not."

"Mia knew him," she said, as if that cleared everything up. "And he has an honest face. I couldn't very well leave him out on the front porch waiting for you."

I stared at him. "You were waiting for me?"

"We need to talk."

"Yeah." I turned back to my mother. "It's a busy night for that."

"Lucian says you two work together," she continued, and I realized with horror that she was essentially trying to pimp me out. "Aside from Derrick, I think he's the first person from your office who's ever come to visit."

"You met Selena once, Mom. Remember?"

"The tall, angry woman?" She frowned. "Yes, I remember."

"Tea?" Lucian offered me a mug. "It's Raspberry Zinger."

"What are you *doing* here?" I asked him again.

"I told you—"

"Oh, what, you decided to drive to Elder because I might be there? That is all kinds of creepy, Lucian."

"I took the bus, actually."

Mia gave me a look. "Dude got on a *bus*. Just to check up on you. Seems like he really cares, *Tessa*."

"Don't you have a car?"

"I live in Yaletown—there's really no point."

"Yeah, I guess you sank a lot of money into that warehouse, too."

"Actually, that's paid for."

"Really?" Derrick finally chimed in. "Must be expensive."

"More reasonable than you'd think, especially with no strata costs."

I wanted to rip my own head off. This was not going according to plan. My mother was now entertaining a necromancer, and all I'd managed to do so far was ask him the same question twice. As life-changing nights went, it was more of an Atom Egoyan film than an emotional rollercoaster.

"Mom, we need to talk," I began again.

"Yes." She leaned forward. "You mentioned that before. Mia, why don't you and Lucian go downstairs and search through the DVD collection—"

"No way." Mia crossed her legs on the couch. "This sounds way too good to miss. I can tell when Tess is freaking out, because her left eye starts to twitch . . ." She smiled at me. "And there is it, twitching away."

"I need to speak to my mother in private." I folded my arms. "Now."

Derrick rose with a sigh. "Come on. There's Playstation downstairs."

Lucian brightened. "Do they have that zombie game?"

"Probably."

Mia hesitated. I almost said something sharp to her, but then I saw the curious expression on her face. She wasn't deliberately being willful. She was worried about me. She didn't want to leave.

"It's okay," I told her. "It's not a big deal."

I'd never told a worse lie in my life.

Mia shrugged. "Fine. Afterwards, I want a dipped cone from Dairy Queen. They're open for another hour."

"Sounds like heaven." I tried to smile.

She followed Derrick and Lucian downstairs. I suddenly felt tiny and powerless. Without them acting as buffers, it was only me and—well, the most important woman in my life. The one who'd been there from the very beginning.

And she'd been lying to me for years. Just like I'd been lying to her. Maybe it was an inherited trait.

"Well." My mother fiddled with the cuffs of her shirt. I realized that she was nervous, too. Somehow, that made me feel better.

"Well," I replied.

She met my gaze. "Ask me. All you have to do is ask me."

I sat down next to her. I couldn't get the words out. My hands started trembling, and she touched my arm, stroking it lightly.

"You are everything to me," she whispered. "Don't you know that, Tessa Isobel? Everything. You always have been."

I stared at her. "You're a witch," I said finally. "Like me."

"Yes."

"Why didn't you tell me?"

She looked sad. "I wanted to protect you. We led very different lives, you and I. The CORE . . ." Hearing my mom say that word was almost obscene, like she'd said a much different C-word. Never in my whole life did I expect her to say it.

"So you know about them."

"Of course. I used to work for them."

My head was spinning. "Were you like me? An OSI?"

"Yes. I had a partner, like you have Derrick."

"Who?"

"Meredith Silver."

A wave of nausea washed over me. She'd been friends with my old teacher. They'd been as close as Derrick and I.

"Did you . . ." I swallowed. "I mean, did you convince her . . ."

"I asked her to train you. She was the obvious choice." My mother's eyes went dark and liquid, obsidian. "It was a terrible loss, her death. It tore my heart out. I wanted so badly to be at the funeral."

"But I was there. I might have seen you."

"I could have remained hidden, if I'd really wanted to. But the CORE hadn't been my life in such a long time. It felt wrong."

I shook my head. "I don't understand any of this."

She smiled, and it was that familiar smile I'd seen all my life, but also different. Weary and hardened, like she'd been through a war.

"Everything I did was to protect you. I left the CORE because I thought you could have a normal life. On some level, I knew that was impossible. You had so much power in you. Even when you were only a baby, I could feel it, pouring out of you like silver light. You were so beautiful, Tessa. And I knew, the moment you were born, that I'd kill anyone who tried to hurt you. I'd snap their necks with my bare hands." She looked away. "A mother's love isn't all teddies and balloons, you know."

I saw her holding the athame again. I could believe it.

"But why did you leave the CORE? You must have known I'd end up there. Didn't it make more sense to stay?"

"It's complicated."

I gave her an exasperated look. "Yeah, well, there's a necromancer playing *Grand Theft Auto* in your basement right now. That's pretty fucking complicated, too. I think we've gone past the need for qualifiers."

"Lucian has a heart. That makes him different from most of his kind. You must be able to see that just by looking at him." She gave me a look. "Even then, it won't be easy for the two of you. The CORE has ironclad rules. You two will have to be extremely careful—discreet . . ."

"We're talking about *you*, Mom." I stared at her. "Why did you leave the CORE? And why did you lie to me?"

Her eyes fell. "I made an arrangement. I can't explain all of it."

"You can try. Who was this arrangement with?"

"The senior committee members. The ones whose names you won't ever know unless you've done something remarkable. Or something very, very bad."

"So you made a deal with the higher-ups. Why?"

"After you were born, I needed to live differently. *We* needed to live differently. Unmonitored, unfettered—I didn't want to keep looking over my shoulder, only to see the flash of a camera, or a sleek black car pulling away. I was tired of hearing a *click* whenever I picked up my phone."

"It sounds like you were under surveillance."

"We're all under surveillance, darling. All the time. The CORE has records of everything you've ever done. They're like Emerson's disembodied eye, invisible and floating, staring at you from above. They know absolutely everything—even things you don't know yourself."

Slowly, I felt myself beginning to understand. "But you wanted off the grid. That's why. You didn't want them watching you."

"Exactly."

"Because of something you had planned. Something you didn't want them to see." Her expression wavered. "Am I right?"

"More like—something I might have to do." I saw her eyes harden. "Something I was prepared to do, if necessary."

"So you bought your anonymity. But how? Nobody leaves the CORE without being tracked for the rest of their lives. How did you do it?"

"I can't tell you that." She sighed. "But I paid a high price."

"What about Dad? Does he know?"

She raised an eyebrow. "He may have gotten an inkling over the years that my past was—unorthodox. Frightening, even. But he's never said anything. He certainly doesn't know what I am." She looked at me. "What *we* are."

"Demons," I breathed. "Or half-demons anyhow."

"I always assumed you'd learn about your biological father—in time. I only wish I could have shielded you from the knowledge."

"But that's the problem!" I stood up. "We've spent so many years 'shielding' each other from crap that now, when the truth counts for so much, we're totally in the dark! I'm tired of lying. You must be tired, too."

"Exhausted," she agreed.

"So tell me the truth. What do you know about this killer?"

She paled slightly. "Don't go after it, Tessa."

"But it *knows* me. It knew my father, right? I saw the two of them together, in a dream. And you were there."

She nodded. She was so calm, it made me want to scream. "Yes. I felt those memories come to the surface tonight."

If she knew about the Hextacy, she didn't say anything. Maybe it was a mother's selective sight. Or maybe she would have done the same thing herself.

A possibility unnerved me. "You didn't . . . block them, did you?"

"I would never do that. You blocked them yourself. You were only a child, after all, barely six. You couldn't have understood the enormity of what you were seeing. You couldn't possibly have known."

"He looked at me," I whispered, "that thing with the eyes like dirty ice. He looked at me, and I was more frightened of him than the creature standing behind him, the one without any eyes at all."

"Because he knew you."

I started to shake again. "I felt like—he *owned* me."

"That's not true." Her grip on me tightened. "He has no real power over you. Always remember that. You're linked to him, yes, by virtue of genetics, but you're not his daughter. You're *my* daughter."

"But I'm a product of you both." I felt a darkness creeping into me. "I can't deny it. That monster will always be my father."

"He can't hurt you—not directly."

"That's what you said in the dream."

She nodded. "It was another favor. Bought with an even higher price."

"Maybe he can't hurt me, but this other thing can."

"Yes. It's very powerful."

"But what is it?"

She smoothed her long, graying hair. She'd colored it a few weeks ago, and the gray was just starting to show through again. In my dream, her hair had been like fire, like a Valkyrie. She'd been so full of love and rage.

"An Iblis," she said finally. "A guardian."

"Of what?"

"The spirit world. There are doors that lead there—places a living person can get through, if they know where to look—but each one is guarded by an Iblis. Your father made a deal of sorts with this one."

"I knew it." I felt like I might throw up again. "Mom, this is my fault, isn't it? Derrick's wrong. This is about me."

She shook her head. "Oh no, Tessa, it's not. The Iblis knows you, certainly, because of who and what your father is. But these killings have nothing to do with you. It's a kind of horrifying coincidence."

"I don't understand."

"I'm not sure I fully understand it either. All I can say is that, years ago, your father made a deal with the Iblis to grant him access to this world—our world. The Iblis took something from him in return. Now, it's gotten a taste for our world, and it wants to stay. But beings of that sort can't exist here for long. They . . . start to fray. They break up into shards and fragments, and eventually they dissolve."

I felt that familiar stab of cold. "Is that part of it? The ritual, the symbols—are you saying that this thing is trying to use magic to change the rules?"

"That would be my best guess. It must have learned things from your father—powers and procedures that are forbidden. Things far worse than necromancy."

"But why would it want to stay here?"

She sighed. "Maybe it's running from something. Maybe it

wants a world full of mortals to feed on. Either way, judging from the last kill, it's very close to completing the ritual that will fully corporealize it."

"Caitlin." I shook my head. "You felt that, too?"

"Just because I'm not in the CORE doesn't mean my powers are any less active. I'm not as strong as you—I never was—but I'm no pushover."

"I believe that. I saw your athame."

She nodded. "I haven't held that in over a decade."

"Where is it?"

"In a safe place."

I briefly imagined my father stumbling upon a blood-forged magical dagger by mistake while looking for a letter opener. The thought made me smile despite myself. It was all so absurd. Having magic didn't make us any better at communicating or being part of a family. It just made things even more unpredictable.

"You must know about Mia," I said finally.

"I know that she's precious."

"She has a lot of power, Mom. Raw and unfocused. It scares me."

"I can help with her. I know what to look for, and what to stay away from. You don't have to raise her alone, Tessa."

I started to cry. It was stupid and unavoidable. My face wouldn't cooperate with my mind at all, and I felt the hot tears come streaming down my cheeks.

"Oh, little duck . . ." She hadn't called me that since I was six. "It's okay." She took me in her arms. I laid my head on her breast, and she smoothed my hair. "It's all going to work out."

"I'm actually"—I sniffed, looking up at her—"*happy.*"

"You are?"

"God, yes! I've been so confused this whole time, felt like such a fuckup trying to protect Mia, even with Derrick's help. But I don't have to lie to you anymore. I can actually *ask* you things. Like, not just about parenting. About—other stuff."

"Like demons."

"Yeah." I let her keep stroking my hair. "Like demons."

"Don't go after it," she repeated. "It's cunning, and very

strong. If you have to, come at it with a group. Use different powers, different kinds of materia. Try to disorient it. But don't face it by yourself."

"I won't. I promise."

It was a lie that we could both agree on.

.19.

I slept for most of the drive home, so if there was any tension, I wasn't consciously aware of it. I lay nestled in the backseat with Mia, and the last thing I remembered before falling into darkness was Lucian saying something to Derrick about waterfront property values. The idea of them sharing the front seat was like matter and antimatter colliding, but the universe hadn't been destroyed yet, so we seemed to be doing fine. Mia was pensive, staring out the window, but as I started to slip away, I felt her arm brushing mine. It was a nice feeling.

I awoke briefly when we picked up Miles from the hotel, and things got very interesting for a bit. There was some bickering over who should sit where, since the Festiva wasn't exactly a luxury sedan, and quarters were cramped already. Derrick proclaimed that, as driver, he got to call shotgun and choose his "wingman," which was a clear ploy to get Miles in the front seat, but nobody protested. I guess he deserved a little hand-holding over the stick shift, especially since he'd driven both ways. He'd also been awfully understanding about my foray into hard drugs, and he was keeping his mouth shut about a whole spectrum of craziness. Some paradise by the dashboard light was definitely in order.

So I didn't complain about getting squeezed between Lucian and Mia, while Baron lay on top of my feet, looking genuinely excited about the car ride. His belly was warm and soft, and it made me want to join him, curled up on the floor mat.

I put my head on Lucian's shoulder. It meant whatever it meant. He didn't say anything, but I felt his hand on the small of my back. He smelled good. I closed my eyes, and when I opened them again, we were home.

We all struggled out of the tiny car, and I couldn't help but laugh. It was like an urban fantasy novel standing on my front lawn. There was the cynical telepath with a heart of gold, the brooding necromancer whose past was catching up to him, the spatial profiler who'd wandered into our nightmare almost by accident, and the fourteen-year-old nascent vampire who could blow us all up if she lost control of her powers. And then there was me—plucky, bitchy, tactless, exhausted, unlucky in love, and still reeling from the world's worst narcotic hangover.

If we were a TV pilot, I doubt we'd make it to series. But there'd sure be one hell of a cult following.

"Um—Tess?" Derrick was giving me a weird look. I couldn't take any more looks, questions, or demands. I wanted a hot shower and a device that could erase the last few hours of my life. It made me think of something I'd read in one of my favorite mystery novels: *God is a bullet, straight to the head. Just when you start to feel better—you're dead.* That's what I wanted. A God-shaped bullet that could make me forget about everything. Too bad the solution was a tad permanent.

"What is it? Is it a demon on our doorstep? Because I left my Glock inside the house, and I don't feel like fighting. Can we just run it over with the Festiva?"

"It is, in fact, a demon," Derrick said. "But this one has a name. And I think you've met him before."

I didn't want to look. I really, really didn't. But I opened my eyes, which had been clenched tightly shut.

A dirty, scared-looking teenage boy was sitting on our front porch.

"Patrick?"

He looked at me sharply. "Are you Tess Corday?"

I nodded. "How did you find me?"

"Caitlin gave me your address. She said if there was ever an emergency and I couldn't find her, I should come here and wait for you. So here I am." His eyes were very wide, as if he was running on pure adrenaline. "I haven't heard from her in hours, and I was afraid to go back to the apartment. She said it wasn't safe there. I didn't have anywhere else to go."

His eyes fell on Mia, and he looked even more startled. It was weird enough to see one of your classmates outside of school for the first time. Weirder still when they turned up surrounded by mages.

"Aren't you Mia Polanski?"

She raised an eyebrow. "That's my name, yes. And this is my house. So far, you seem to have a fairly good grasp of the concrete, Patrick."

He took us all in, looking a bit overwhelmed. "Do all of you live here?"

Mia rolled her eyes. "No. Tonight we're having a sleepover. I live here with Tess and Derrick." She gestured to us. "They're my legal guardians. Although I don't think they're entirely on the level *all the time*, if you get my drift."

"Mia . . ." I warned.

"This is Miles Sedgwick." She pointed to him. Miles gave a small wave. "And his dog, Baron. Miles is going to get lucky tonight."

"*Mia!*" I wished fervently for a remote control that could turn her off. Miles had the grace to blush. Derrick glowered at her, but secretly, I could tell he was pretty psyched about the prospect of fooling around with Miles.

"And lastly, we have Lucian Agrado." She made a comely gesture, as if this were an infomercial and Lucian was a food dehydrator. "He's pretty much the bee's knees as far as Tess is concerned, but don't spread that around. We like to encourage a real *Port Charles* atmosphere around here. Lies, secrets, misty cutaways. Sometimes you can almost hear the voice-over."

I turned to Patrick. "Mia's the funny one. Can you tell?"

"I gathered that." Despite the façade of calm, I was pretty sure that Patrick was about to collapse. I could see his hands shaking.

"Come inside," I told him. "We have to talk. But first, I'll get you some food. And some clothes. It looks like you got dragged behind a bus."

"I was hiding in some dirty places," he said, falling into step behind me as I opened the door. "It was kind of exciting at first, but that wore off."

"It always does." The warm, familiar smells of the house greeted me: the old hardwood floors, the echo of whatever had been baking in the oven yesterday, and the crisp odor of detergent and fabric softener. It was the exact opposite of what I'd been smelling for most of the night: blood, iron, and death.

I couldn't tell Patrick about Caitlin right away. I had to ease him into it. He may have been the magnate's successor, with untold vampiric powers at his disposal, but I'd seen the rock posters and the dirty laundry in his bedroom. He was still just a kid. When you spent too long in a job like mine, you started to become immune to basic human compassion and contact. Guns, powders, bloodstains, and autopsies became more routine than sharing coffee, making dinner, watching a play. I always had to remind myself that other people didn't understand that world. You couldn't just say "disarticulated body" to them and hope for a coherent response. They needed to process.

"I'll grab some clothes," Derrick said, heading for his room upstairs. Miles looked at me for a moment, then shrugged and followed him. Great. Leave the vampire kitten to me while you smooch upstairs. I rubbed my eyes. The monster migraine was still there, and all I wanted to do was pop some Motrin and sink into a bath full of Epsom salts.

"I'll—ah—see if I can whip up something to eat in the kitchen," Lucian said. "I'll bet we could all do with a late-night snack."

I stared at him. Sometimes, the stuff that came out of his mouth was so undeniably wholesome, I forgot that he could raise the dead. Maybe. I still wasn't sure what the limits of his necromantic abilities were. I didn't particularly want to find out—not after what I'd seen last time.

Baron curled up on the couch next to Mia. She crooked her finger at Patrick and smiled wryly. "You. Doorstep boy. Sit down."

Patrick blinked at her for a moment, confused. Then he took a seat next to her, settling awkwardly on the couch, arms ramrod straight at his sides.

"This is weird," he said simply.

"There you go with grasping the concrete again." She sighed. "Let's talk about something normal. Tell me about AP chem."

He stared at her. "You want to hear about my chemistry class?"

"I have to take it next year, so I need the dirt. How are you with molar numbers? Pretty solid?"

God bless her.

I made my way into the kitchen, where I found Lucian chopping vegetables on the cat-shaped cutting board that my mom had given me last Christmas. She gave me something cat-shaped every year. His long fingers were a blur as he sliced through a shiny red pepper. He was almost a little too deft with the knife.

"We have vegetables?"

He grinned sideways at me. "You've got a lot of random stuff in the fridge, but I managed to assemble a fry-up of sorts. Patrick won't complain. At that age, I would have eaten anything put in front of me."

"He's shell-shocked. I have to tell him about Caitlin, but I don't know how."

"Tell him the truth. He may hate you for it now, but in the end, he'll respect you for being honest."

"He's a kid, Lucian, not a Klingon. He's not honor-bound to respect me. He's scared and lost, and now I have to tell him that his only friend in the world is dead." I blinked. "Permanently dead. Not just undead."

"I assume that Caitlin was . . ." He trailed off. I stared at the diced pepper on the cutting board. It made me think of her decimated body.

"She was obliterated," I told him. "She's not coming back. That thing took her apart, piece by piece. It was one of the most fucked-up things I've ever seen."

Lucian's eyes went soft with pain. "She was so beautiful. Caitlin. And so powerful. She always tried to do the right thing. It's a terrible loss."

That was exactly what my mother had said about Meredith Silver. How odd to think that Lucian had shared a kind of relationship with the vampire magnate. He'd respected her. Maybe even—

"Were you two ever involved?" It came out before I could stop it.

The blade paused, midway through the red pepper. "Involved?"

"You know what I mean."

He didn't look up. "We never slept together, if that's what you're asking. And I wouldn't exactly call her a friend. But she taught me a lot. I looked up to her."

Hearing someone say that they "looked up to" an immortal killing machine was no less unnerving than it sounded.

"I didn't mean to be weird about it." I leaned against the counter. "I'm still just trying to put the pieces together."

"Am I part of the puzzle?"

I gave him a long look. "You always have been."

He looked over his shoulder at me, and I could barely see the white lily tattoo peeking over his collarbone. There was another mystery. Who or what had marked Lucian Agrado? And what, exactly, was he hiding from in his Yaletown fortress? Knowing my luck, he was simply hiding from me.

There didn't seem to be much else to say. We fell into an oddly steady rhythm, chopping and cooking and making little jokes about how small the kitchen was, like this was a perfectly ordinary night. It took about twenty minutes to produce a meal on autopilot, and to our credit, it actually looked good. I came into the living room with a steaming bowl for Patrick, only to discover him wearing Derrick's Veda Hille T-shirt and a pair of old, baggy jeans. Derrick and Miles were notably absent. Horny bastards. Still, I couldn't fault them. I'd most likely be doing the same thing, if it were on the menu.

I handed him the bowl. "Eat."

Patrick didn't need to be told twice. He fell to like a starving man, devouring the rice, veggies, and peanut satay with incredible gusto. Mia raised an eyebrow, but said nothing. I picked at my bowl, still feeling like solid food was a bit beyond me.

He was done in about two minutes. The food gave him back some color, but not much. I wondered how long it would take for the vampiric changes to begin asserting themselves. Lucian had said that he was unlike other vampires. He could obviously still function in the daylight, and he was craving peanut sauce instead of human blood, so that was a plus. Maybe, if we handled him with kid gloves, we'd actually be able to ease him into the change. He could even become an ally.

Or he could just murder us all in our sleep. It was fifty-fifty at the moment.

"Thanks," he said, wiping his mouth with the back of his hand. "I feel a bit better. I guess I haven't eaten since this morning."

"Remind us to keep you out of the pantry." Mia slid the bowl away. "You're like a hoover with an appetite."

He managed to look embarrassed. Then his expression changed. His eyes met mine, and they were bleak. "Tess—do you know where Caitlin is?"

I exhaled. "There's no easy answer to that question."

"Don't coddle me. Just tell me the truth."

Bless him—trying to look so fierce and grown up. He wasn't ready for this. He was barely three years older than Mia. Just a kidlet. I never thought I'd feel this old at twenty-five, but I couldn't deny it.

I looked at Mia. Her eyes seemed to say: *Might as well give it to him.* She'd heard more than her fair share of atrocities, after all. Probably it was better to strike hard and fast. Then we could all pick up the pieces later. The thought was strange. Maybe that's what I'd become in the last year. Someone who put everyone else back together. Like a soul doctor. I worried that Mia might sue me for malpractice when she got older and realized how messed up I really was.

"She's dead, Patrick," I said. My voice was flat. "She was murdered by a serial killer—a demon who's also killed four other people. Kids, actually. The children of powerful mage families."

He frowned, like I'd just spoken in another language or asked him to assemble my dining room table from Ikea. "She's dead."

It wasn't a question. More of an echo.

"Yes. She was killed tonight."

"You said"—he swallowed thickly—"a demon? That's who killed her?"

I nodded. "A very powerful demon. We're tracking him. Did . . ." I wasn't quite sure how to phrase this without breaking open his life even further. "Did Caitlin explain to you—about demons?"

"She's a demon," he replied. Still using the present tense. If there'd been any doubt in my mind that Patrick was involved in Caitlin's murder, it was gone now. He was simply another victim.

"Yes. Caitlin was a vampire." If not for the word "vampire," it might have sounded like I was lecturing a small child. "And so are you, Patrick."

His eyes were glassy. "Yeah. I know."

Mia paled at this. She shifted next to him, but didn't move away. We'd had the same talk with her a year ago, but back then, there'd been a lot more yelling. Patrick's reaction was the opposite. He was almost serene.

"How much did Caitlin tell you—about being a vampire?"

His voice had grown hoarse. "She said that I was different."

"What did she say, specifically?"

He frowned, as if trying to remember. "She said—that I would change more slowly. That I could do different things, but not right away. It would take time. She said that it wasn't a bad thing. That it was a blessing." He looked me in the eyes. "That's what she called me. Her special blessing. When I woke up in the hospital room, I was alone. But then she appeared. I had a fever and I thought I was going crazy, but then I could hear her voice in my mind, and it was like putting my hands in cool water."

"You're a part of her." Lucian spoke for the first time. "Her power, her legacy, is in your blood. Some things will take a long time to surface, but other things might happen quickly. So quickly, you'll be confused and frightened. But Caitlin also left a set of instructions in your mind, like a blueprint."

This was news to me. "She did?"

Lucian nodded. "It's part of the succession process. Caitlin left a mark on Patrick, and that mark affects every cell, every atom, in his body. He'll have guidance, but it won't come right away. That's what I meant about being scared."

"So she's—like—inside me?" He turned to Lucian. "How do you know about it? Were you friends with her?"

Boy, wasn't that the million-dollar question tonight?

"We knew each other, yes," he replied. There was a low, surprising confidence in his voice. Maybe Lucian was exactly what Patrick needed right now. "I can explain some things to you. But not all of it. Eventually, you'll have to talk to others in your community. They'll know a lot more."

"Other vampires?"

He nodded. "Caitlin had many allies. She was loved and respected, and most people in the community will defer to you. Some won't. The issue of loyalty is complicated, but we can deal with that later."

Patrick turned back to me. "Why did another demon kill her? I don't understand. I mean—she was really powerful, right? People were afraid of her."

"We're not entirely sure." Now was not the time for an infodump, especially since Patrick looked dizzy again, like he might throw up on my couch. "The killer probably knew Caitlin, and she may have a connection with the other victims.

Aside from that, we're still working on it. Our job right now is to keep you safe."

"Am I next?"

It was a fair question. "Possibly," I said. "But then again, we're all at risk. This thing is dangerous and very smart. The best thing we can do now is stick together. Which is why you'll be crashing with us tonight."

He nodded slowly. "That's good, since—I guess I'm homeless."

A look of sympathy passed over Mia's face. She remembered exactly what it felt like to have her family destroyed, her home taken away from her.

"This is a hella big house," she said, standing up. "Come on. I'll show you the spare room, and we can steal some blankets from Derrick. He's a total queen about his sheets and has, like, five matching sets."

"Okay," he said shyly.

"Follow me." She led him down the hallway. My heart gave a lurch as I realized how quickly she was growing up. It wasn't fair. She should be hanging out at the Metrotown mall and texting her friends about boys and homework and Miley Cyrus, or whatever fourteen-year-olds talked about. Instead, she was planning for her SATs and fetching clean sheets for the next vampire magnate.

"They'd better not get too friendly," I muttered to myself. "The last thing we need around here is a Jamie Lynn Spears crisis."

"Vampires can't reproduce," Lucian clarified.

"Oh. Why not?"

"They don't have a functioning reproductive system. All of their organs harden and atrophy after the change."

"So, they can't—" I waved my hand uselessly in the air.

"Cum?" He shook his head. "No."

"But he's a magnate. What if he has, like . . ."

He looked at me expectantly.

"Don't make me say it. He's seventeen, Lucian. He should be a white-hot sex machine at that age. And Mia's young, true, but she can also be—curious. I don't want her curiosity to lead her into that spare bedroom."

"Trust me. Vampires can't reproduce. They also can't spread STIs, because they don't have living tissue. Their blood is noncirculating. They can only get hard if they have fresh blood inside them."

"Huh. I never thought of that before." I frowned. "But if they can't . . ."

"Cum?"

"Stop *saying* that! She might hear you!"

He smiled wryly. "Are we in a church? I'm sure Mia's old enough to figure out those particular mechanics."

I sighed. "Chances are, she has a better grasp of it than I do. It's not like I've been terrorizing the dating scene lately."

"Me neither. It's been a quiet year."

I hadn't expected him to say that. "Really?"

He nodded. "I've been distracted. Mostly kept to myself."

"Even with that executive fuck chamber you call a warehouse?"

"You'd be surprised how much of a turnoff it can be. In case you haven't noticed, it's a little rough around the edges."

"I like the edges just as they are."

He smiled. "Really."

This was quickly getting into dangerous territory. "I need to have a shower," I said, getting up. "It's only a matter of time until there's a line for the bathroom, so I'm going now. I'll only be a few minutes."

"Can I fix you a drink in the meantime?"

The question disarmed me. I wasn't sure what I thought about Lucian pawing through my liquor collection, which mostly consisted of Maker's Mark and some dessert wine that had lain untouched since my mother brought it over.

The CORE has ironclad rules. I heard my mother's voice. Not that I wasn't a world-class expert at breaking the rules by now. But Lucian and I were so different, magically speaking, that it was almost a cross-species relationship. The CORE would rather have us both locked in padded cells.

"Maybe—um—something really light," I said. "I've had enough weird substances floating through my body lately."

He seemed to take that in stride. "Just something to help you sleep."

"I don't need any help in that department," I said, heading for the bathroom. "I'm dead on my feet already."

I eased myself into the yellow-tiled shower. The hot water was like a blessing raining down on my entire body. I let myself go unfocused for a while, and I could feel the aqueous materia curling around my limbs in little blue sparks, adumbrating my body and mixing with the steam. I closed my eyes. In this world, everything was perfect. I didn't have to leave. I could stay here forever, and maybe Lucian would even join me, if I asked nicely—

The thought sent up a red flag in my mind. No shower time with Lucian Agrado! That was the last complication I needed tonight.

I emerged wearing my plaid UBC pajamas and an oversized T-shirt, without a bra. I wanted to send the right message: No sexy. Not tonight. Lucian smiled when he saw my ensemble. He was pouring red wine into two mismatched cups.

"Is that my *Get Fuzzy* mug?"

"You didn't have any wineglasses."

"Yeah, we're not exactly the Hyatt." I glanced at the bottle. "Bordeaux? Where did you find that?"

"It was hiding on the top shelf."

"Must have been a housewarming gift. I didn't even know it was there." I sat down on the couch—near enough to be sociable, but far enough to stay platonic. "At least I look a bit more human now." I'd scrubbed away the caked-on concealer and untangled my hair as best I could. It was damp and curled against my shoulders.

"You looked good before." He handed me the mug. "You always look good."

Great. The pajamas obviously weren't working.

"I checked on Mia," he said absently. "She and Patrick are fooling around."

My eyes widened.

"On the computer," he finished, smiling.

"Right. They're probably looking up how to assemble a bomb."

"They were just on the Internet Movie Database. Mia was educating him about French-Canadian cinema."

I shook my head. "That kid's never predictable. Not in the least."

I sipped the wine. It tasted like raspberries and something infused with smoke. I felt it warm my stomach. "It's good."

Lucian shifted position, and I saw that one of his feet was absently scratching Baron's belly. The dog was stretched out before him like a disciple. Lucian's socks, I noted, were black and faded. I spied a hole in one of them. The pink of his heel showed through. It was suddenly the sexiest bit of flesh I'd ever seen. I concentrated on my wine, telling myself to take it easy. Otherwise it would go straight to my head.

Twenty minutes later, it had gone straight to my head.

"Really?" Lucian laughed, his cheeks slightly flushed. It was nice to realize that even necromancers could get lit. "You really made out underneath a Boyz II Men poster? On a pink-ruffled bedspread?"

I nodded. "Scout's honor. And Derrick's tongue kept, like, *darting* between my teeth, like this crazy little minnow . . ."

Lucian cracked up. "Maybe that was his technique."

"I *know*, right?" The mug balanced precariously in my hand. "Like, what if that was his very best move?"

"Watch out, boys. Here comes *the minnow*."

"The tongue!" I giggled. "The scary tongue!"

"What if he's doing it to Miles right now?"

"He probably is."

"And Miles is just, like, dodging the minnow tongue . . ."

I made a weaving and bobbing motion, and Lucian laughed. "He's like, why does this dude keep trying to lick my teeth?"

"I'm sure his kissing has improved since then."

"Maybe. I hope so."

"I'll bet Miles has game, even if Derrick doesn't. He

seemed to have a rockin' little body underneath that cute Windbreaker."

Curiosity got the better of me. I took another drink, swallowed, and felt the warmth burn down my throat. "Have you been with boys, Lucian?"

He wiggled an eyebrow at me. "Have you been with girls, Tessa?"

"Ugh! That's what my mom calls me."

"It's a beautiful name."

I looked down to hide my burning cheeks. "I was with a girl once in college," I said diffidently. "It wasn't earth-shattering. Mostly, I was surprised how *wet* some girls could get down there. It was like I needed hip waders or something."

"Did you like it?"

I shrugged. "It was different. I didn't *not* like it. And I actually came pretty hard when she went down on me. She really knew what to do with her thumb and pinkie finger. *Skill*, I think it's called. Not like most guys, who sort of, just"—I made a clawlike motion with my right hand—"you know? Like they're scratching a lottery ticket. It's not really that complicated. We don't have manual transmissions."

He grinned. "Some guys like to complicate things. Usually, if you follow your instincts, it all works out fine."

"So what about you?"

"What about me?" He took another sip.

"Boys! Have you ever been with any boys?"

He shrugged. "I'm nothing if not adventurous."

"So, are you . . ." I spread my hands.

"I'm basically hetero," he said. "But I'd say I'm open to possibilities."

The "basically hetero" part relaxed me a bit.

"What's this . . ." Lucian made a face and reached behind him. "I think I'm sitting on something." He pulled out the stereo remote.

"Sorry. It gets stuck between the pillows."

He flicked the power button. There was a soft click, and then a familiar song filled the living room.

"Greg MacPherson," he said. "I approve."

"Well, you know me—always dying for your approval."

Lucian stood up, setting his mug down.

"What are you doing?"

He smiled and extended his hand. "Dance with me."

I snorted. "You're not serious."

"I'm dead serious."

The pun made me smirk. "As a necromancer, wouldn't you have to be undead serious? Or 'mostly dead' serious?"

"Just dance with me, Tess."

I put down my wine. "This is dumbass romantic."

"That's me. A dumbass romantic." He wiggled his fingers. "Come on."

Warily, I took his hand. It slid over mine, warm and certain. I wrapped my arms around his neck, and the palm of his hand pressed against my back. I started to laugh. I couldn't help it.

"I feel like we're at the prom."

"We are. Can't you see the streamers?" He smiled. "Blue and gold and red, draped across the ceiling and the couch. And all the balloons."

"Purple and silver," I said, moving closer to him. "Like on my sixth birthday. There was a cake with butter cream icing. And games. And I got to eat all the pizza I wanted. I ate so much that I puked."

He laughed softly. "That sounds like you."

I tucked my head into the crook of his neck. Beneath the clean-smelling deodorant and the hint of sweat, I could smell *him*. The real him. Coppery, dark, like bitter herbs and licorice and smoke. I closed my eyes. The music washed over us, and I felt so light. My bones were transparent and made of fire. If Lucian let go, I'd float upward, just like one of those purple and silver balloons. I'd be lost forever.

Your voice is nothing against the noise
Of the engine grinding out that summer line,
Coast in slow over Reno; the Diablos
I can almost see the waves break on the dial.

"I've never been to Reno," I sighed.

He kissed me then. It wasn't an angry, immediate kiss, like we'd had in the bedroom of my old apartment. This was a slow, patient, timeworn kiss. His lips just seemed to settle on mine. I let him in. His breath tasted like peanut sauce. I ran fingers through his baby-fine hair, soft as corn silk.

I pulled away. "Lucian . . ."

"What?"

I looked down. "I don't exactly feel sexy right now. I'm wearing my rattiest old pajamas. No makeup. My hair looks like a bird's nest, and my breath probably smells . . . really gross. I don't even want to talk about why. Every muscle in my body hurts, and now I'm kind of buzzed—but not *drunk*—so I realize that this is probably a really bad move. And the worst possible timing ever."

"You're beautiful." He rubbed his thumb across my cheek. "You can't help it. There's no way you couldn't be lovely and sexy and amazing."

I narrowed my eyes at him. "Did you take lessons or something?"

"I always tell the truth. It's kind of my thing." He smiled. "And you, Tess. You're kind of my thing. Or kind of mine. At least, I want you to be."

"Yours?"

He nodded.

I closed my eyes. "This isn't allowed. I promised . . ."

"Whom?" His lips were close to my ear. His voice was scarcely above a whisper. "Whom did you promise?"

"Selena."

"And . . ."

"And . . ." I frowned. "Other people . . ."

"*And* . . ." He raised an eyebrow.

"I'm not even supposed to be touching you."

His hand was around my waist. "You're not touching me. *I'm* touching *you*. So, really, I'm the one who's breaking the rules, not you."

I chuckled softly. "Well, that's a switch."

His mouth hovered over mine. "I don't care about traditions

and regulations. I just care about you—us—in *this* moment. That's all."

His breath smelled sweet.

I groaned.

"We can't be too loud. I don't want Mia to feel like she's living in a bordello."

"Quiet as little mice." He nibbled on my neck. "Promise."

I practically yanked him down the hall and into the bedroom, checking to make sure that we weren't being watched. The bed was a disaster. Stray panties were lying on the quilt, along with dirty, balled-up shirts. It smelled like hairspray, and a wet towel lay on the floor, next to the en suite bathroom. I'm sure there was an open box of Tampax in there as well, since Mia kept stealing them.

"Oh God," I whispered. "This is terrible. I'm a pig. There's nothing romantic about this at all . . ."

He kissed me again. "I don't need romance. It's overrated."

I sat down on the bed, trying to brush away the stray clothes. "I'm sorry . . ." I said, in between kissing him. "I was going to clean, I really was . . ."

"Don't let a serial murder investigation get in the way of your housecleaning," he murmured, licking my neck.

I closed my eyes. Lucian settled on top of me. His hands were doing a lot of very skillful, interesting things. I twisted the edge of the quilt. Kneeling half on the bed, he slipped off his shirt. His tattoos were almost iridescent in the dim light of the room. There was a swirl of thorns, a Mayan snake, a raven's feather, and other small lines of runic text that I couldn't recognize. I kissed his chest, then his throat, feeling it throb underneath my tongue.

"Condoms?" he murmured.

"Bedside table."

I pulled my huge, ugly T-shirt off. I suddenly felt very pale and small, my breasts hanging there, my hands on his shoulders. It seemed ridiculous to be almost naked but still wearing flannel pajamas. He kissed my breasts slowly, then his hand slid down my pajama bottoms. I breathed in sharply as his fingers curled around me, then inside me, one at a time. His movements were calm, almost lazy, as if we had hours and hours to kill doing nothing but this.

I no longer cared that I hadn't shaved down there, or that my legs were rough and stubbly, or that my hair looked like shit. Lucian Agrado was happily, competently fingering me, and that was pretty much all I could concentrate on at this point.

I squirmed and lay back. He smiled. I fumbled with his belt. The buckle snapped against my knuckles. It stung, but I flung it on the ground. Lucian chuckled softly, unbuttoning his jeans. I slid them down. He wasn't wearing sexy black underwear like last time. These were straight-up plaid boxers.

"Nice," I whispered, stroking the fabric.

"I got them in a two-pack." He kissed me. "At Costco."

"A man who loves a deal," I murmured, reaching into the narrow gap until I felt his dick. It was semihard. I pulled it out, tugging on the skin gently. He made a small sound and closed his eyes momentarily. Then he slid the boxers down and straddled me, jeans still around his ankles, black socks pushing against the bed. I yanked my underwear down, reaching for his dick again. It was warm in my hand.

I giggled.

"What?" His tongue was in my ear.

"I'm holding your cock."

"You are indeed. And it's very happy about that." He rolled a condom on.

I kissed him long and deep. Then I guided him in, breathing sharply as he slid forward, his mouth still pressed to mine.

"Unh—fuck," I whispered. It was the most articulate thing I could say.

His fingers were wrapped in my hair. The rhythm was slow at first, then faster, then slow again. I shifted position, trying to get more leverage with the pillows, until my back was pressed against the headboard. He reached down, his fingers going to work again, and I gave a little start as fire traced itself along my thighs. Two of his fingers seemed to linger outside, gently prodding, but the other two were on a highly site-specific mission. I wrapped one leg around him. I flicked my tongue across his nipple, and when he groaned, I used my teeth.

He sped up, his breathing getting more ragged. I reached beneath him, pressing gently with my thumb. He ground his ass against my hand. Taking this as a fairly clear invitation, I found something more direct to do with my own fingers. It was clearly the right decision. He bucked against me, his mouth open, and I kissed him, biting a little, my mouth full of his taste and his scent.

I came hard and fast. My head struck the wall, and I felt my legs turn to jelly as the fire washed up every inch of me. Lucian made a crazy, unexpected noise—something between a grunt and a low, throaty whimper—and then I felt him come. He collapsed on top of me, still on his knees, panting into my neck.

The whole thing had taken six, maybe seven minutes. But all seven of those minutes counted, and I sure as hell didn't need anything else.

I sank into the pillow. It smelled like cold cream. I laughed.

He was still breathing heavily. "What?"

"We forgot to close the door."

We both stared at the open doorway in disbelief. I started giggling.

Lucian kissed my throat. "You think anyone saw?"

"I don't know. I wasn't exactly watching."

"Oh? I thought your OSI training would take hold. Aren't you supposed to be watchful and ever-vigilant?"

"That's the Marines."

He curled onto his side, one leg draped warmly across me. "Sleepy now."

I sighed. "Thank *God*. You have no idea how tired I am. I was scared that you might want to cuddle or watch TV."

"All I want to do is pass out."

I settled in next to him. "We have to wake up early. Should I set the alarm?"

"I'll wake up. I've got an internal clock."

"Of course you do."

He kissed the nape of my neck. "Good night, Tess."

I murmured something in reply. His arm slipped around my waist, and then the darkness came down, like a summer storm, drenching everything and raising licks of steam from the imaginary pavement. I smelled rain.

Then I was gone.

.20.

I woke up in a neat little cocoon of bedsheets and, for a moment, wondered if I hadn't traveled back in time to when my mother used to tuck me in tightly, grinning as she pronounced: "Snug as a bug in a rug." My lingering hard-drug hangover, along with my sex hair, confirmed that I was not, in fact, six years old again. I was alone in bed, and early morning light was streaming through the blinds. I glanced at the clock: 7 a.m. Consciousness was a bitch.

And what had happened to the necromancer?

I briefly imagined Lucian waking up next to me, taking one horrified look at his surroundings, and then bolting out of the house. My room still looked like a nuclear testing site, and the panties balled up on the floor weren't getting any more glamorous in the searing light of day.

I threw on a purple terrycloth robe—Derrick called it my Dorothy Zbornak robe, from *The Golden Girls*—and padded on bare feet into the hallway. I could hear the shower running. Maybe he really was still here. It seemed almost too good to be true.

I noticed that the door to the spare bedroom was closed. Feeling a bit like a lunatic mom, I pressed my ear to the door. I could hear snoring. It was far too low and symphonic to be Mia, so I guessed that Patrick had slept alone. Still not entirely convinced, I mounted the first three stairs, listening carefully. Mia's room was closest to the stairway, and usually I could hear the explosive sounds of her banging around in there as she did . . . whatever teenagers did in their rooms.

I was rewarded with faint strains of music coming from her room. A moment later, she cranked up the volume, and Defiance, Ohio floated down the stairs and into the living room on a wave of cymbals. I'll bet she heard me on the stairs. Damn, that girl had ears like a trained peregrine falcon.

> And I miss that place behind my house
> Where I hiked and climbed and played,
> Where I ditched this noisy century
> Or just hid out from the decade.

I thought how strange it was that a kid like Mia and a guy like Lucian Agrado—who knew how old he was?—would like the same band. So many of their songs were about anxiety and loss, but they were also just kids themselves. Too young, it seemed, to really know how mourning worked. Yet, a clear vein of sadness hummed to life, somewhere in the center of my body, as I listened to their voices.

I thought about how I used to hate Elder, how I dreamed of turning eighteen and getting the hell out. It didn't matter where. But I'd never really escaped. Like a powerful gravity, it pulled me back, with strands of guilt, fire, and love.

The familiar streets where I'd grown up, the cars parked on wooden blocks, the boarded-up corner stores, the grassy field of my old middle school, where I got trashed on Smirnoff Ice and tried to piss standing up against the wall of the gymnasium, only to fall down, laughing and snorting as my boots kicked up the soaking turf. I thought of the powers and the demons and all the immortal strands that slept beneath those ancient intersections, the traffic lights changing from red, to yellow, to green, as vast giants turned beneath the earth. And I thought of my parents and all my childhood friends, animated by their own fierce lives, having no idea that the awkward, tawny-haired girl with the braces was fighting monsters and harboring vampires in her spare bedroom.

It wasn't so bad, Elder. It was a place, like any other. And the ties that bound me to home weren't entirely constricting. They were like those veins and arteries in my body, pumping blood forward and back: a dark latticework of flesh, bone, and miracles that made me think—if only I listened hard enough—that even 100 kilometers away I could hear the dense rumble of my hometown breathing, quietly, next to me in the dark.

I walked through the living room, pausing at the kitchen entrance as I heard laughter and smelled something cooking. My spirits rose. I peeked around the corner and saw Derrick standing in front of the stove, tending to something in a cast-iron pan. (He'd insisted on getting cast-iron pans because he claimed they had a "food memory" that made everything you cooked in them taste good. I think he was just being fussy.) Breakfast smelled like heaven.

I leaned in a bit farther, and my suspicions were confirmed as I saw Miles standing just off to the side. He was pulling on his shirt—I guess he'd gotten out of the shower immediately before Lucian hopped in—and I was momentarily distracted by his lithe, muscular body. He had a swimmer's build, and his chest was dusted with blond, almost golden, hair, which I hadn't expected.

He also had a tattoo on his left shoulder. It was *le petit prince*, standing with his rapier in all his blue and red finery, and below him, in flowing script: *Vous êtes responsable, pour toujours, de ce que vous avez apprivoisé.* They were the words of the wise fox to the little prince: "You are responsible, forever, for what you have tamed."

Derrick and Miles were signing rapidly to each other. I saw

what looked like the handshape for "bad," but it was hard to tell, especially with Miles, whose long, graceful fingers moved with uncanny speed.

Derrick motioned to himself, then brushed the palm of his right hand down his cheek twice. He reversed his palm, touching his chin, and then flicked it sharply downward, as if indicating something negative. Then he made a quick C shape next to his forehead, lowered his arm, and made a similar gesture beneath his right shoulder; it looked like he was outlining a badge, or making the sign for the RCMP.

Oh.

I rolled my eyes as I got it: "I've been a bad boy, Officer."

Miles grinned, touching Derrick's chest with one hand while he signed with the other. I caught the sign for "power"—one hand outlining a bulging, invisible muscle—and then what may have been "search" and "seizure." Boy. I'd never realized until now how dirty ASL could be.

Derrick laughed softly. Then he leaned in, eyes closed. They kissed. It was like my kiss with Lucian—slow, almost lazy, but still charged. Miles put his hand gently on the back of Derrick's neck. Derrick was a bit taller, so Miles had to reach up to do it, which was kind of endearing. Derrick half turned, trying to keep his eyes on the frying pan, but Miles pulled him back, saying something inaudible. Derrick giggled, then wrapped an arm around the other man's waist, tugging him closer. Miles still had his shirt half on, and Derrick's fingers stroked his back.

"Gay porn!"

Mia exploded past me into the kitchen. Miles went red and pulled away, feverishly tugging his shirt back on. Derrick's hand lingered on his back.

"You wrecked a moment," I told her.

She rolled her eyes. "Yeah, that's me, the moment wrecker." Then she wiggled her eyebrows at them suggestively. "Don't let me stop you, boys. I've watched *Queer as Folk*. Nothing surprises me."

"The real-life version is still a bit different," Miles mumbled. "And I don't exactly look like Gale Harold."

"Naw, you're prettier, Sedge." Derrick kissed him on the neck. He looked embarrassed, but also slightly pleased. Miles was obviously shy. I hadn't seen Derrick with a man in a long time, but he seemed to have gotten a lot more confident over the years. Maybe he was just in a better place now.

I smiled crookedly. "Sedge?"

"I told you that nickname in confidence," Miles growled at Derrick. His soft, nasal voice couldn't really sound all that threatening, but his eyes flashed.

Derrick shrugged. "No secrets in this house. Besides, I like it."

At least I wasn't the only one who'd gotten lucky. Mia glanced from me to Derrick and then back to me again. She sighed explosively.

"I'm going back to my room. You all have impulse-control problems."

She swept out of the kitchen, running into Lucian on her way out.

"Morning." He smiled at her. Derrick must have lent him some clothes as well, because he was wearing an old shirt with a Joe Average print that looked stretched around his arms and shoulders. His biceps were distracting.

Mia scowled at him. "You all suck." Then she clomped upstairs.

Lucian blinked in her wake. "Did I say something wrong?"

"No. She's just a teenager." I beckoned him in. "Derrick and Miles made breakfast. In between smooching."

"Well, well." He grinned at them, pulling up a seat. "It's about time. Why did you two wait so long? We thought you might never get your groove on."

Derrick narrowed his eyes. "Were you two placing bets?"

Lucian leaned back in his chair. "Only about who was pitching. I figured you were both switch-hitters, but Tess insisted you'd be in the dugout."

Derrick turned three shades of red.

"That was an *inside thought*, Lucian," I said, glaring at him. "You weren't supposed to repeat it."

He shrugged. "No position is better than any other. Sometimes it's nice to catch a few fastballs, if you're in the mood for it."

"Right." Miles smoothed his hair, which was useless. It looked perfect. "Can we end this sports analogy now and have some breakfast?"

"Coffee's in the pot." Derrick pointed. "The good stuff from JJ Bean."

I practically lunged across the kitchen, pouring two cups and handing one to Lucian. "We don't have any sugar. Or cream. I think we have some orange juice and an old carton of molasses, though, if you want to get really adventurous."

"Black is fine." He sipped it affably. "I tend to live on diner coffee."

"So . . ." Derrick handed me a plate of fried potatoes with chorizo sausage and green peppers mixed in. "What did you two get up to last night?"

"Tess and I had intercourse."

I almost spit out my coffee and dropped the plate at the same time.

"Really." Derrick's left eye seemed to twitch. "And how was that?"

"Just splendid." He took another sip of coffee. "Tess, would you agree?"

I stared fiercely into my mug. "Mm-*hmm*. Yes."

He leaned over and kissed my forehead. "I'm glad."

"So what's the plan today?" Derrick handed Miles a plate.

"I'm going to the lab. I have to talk to Selena. After that, I think we should meet downtown and figure out our next move. Patrick can't be left alone."

"We'll stay on him," Lucian said. "I have to meet with Duessa."

I blinked. "You do?"

He nodded. His look was placid. Obviously, he wasn't going to tell me more.

"Grab Wolfie, then," I said, "while you're there. I think we might need him."

"Will do."

"Miles"—I turned to him—"I might need some information from the CORE's Ontario offices. Is that cool?"

"Of course. I'll do everything I can. The bureaucracy there can be tricky, but I've got friends in Data and Records."

"Perfect." I drained my coffee and stood up. "Let's all meet across the street from the lab at noon. Public restaurants and cafés are best, I think. I don't know what this thing's range is, but it seems to prefer the dark corners and alleys."

"Is Selena going to release your file?" Derrick asked.

I ran a hand through my hair. "I hope so. Either that, or she's going to lock me in a padded cell and throw away the key."

"At least you could bounce in there," Miles said.

"Bouncing's what Tiggers do best," Lucian added solemnly.

I stared at him. "You're really kind of a freak, aren't you?"

He smiled. "Does that bother you?"

"Surprisingly, no. But I've never had good judgment."

I ran for the shower.

Selena was nice enough to hand me a coffee when I got to the lab, which convinced me that she wasn't about to confiscate my athame or set me on fire. Still, she was a hard one to read. Even though it was shit coffee from the break room in a paper cup, and I'd already had the good stuff at home, I smiled and took it. If ever there was a time to be twitchy and preternaturally aware, it was now.

I sat down in the chair across from her desk. She'd finally managed to clear most of Marcus's old paperwork away, but there was still the odd file or two with MT stamped on it in red. I wondered how long it would take to expunge all lingering traces of him. I could still feel the weight of his deeds in this room, like a thick, unpleasant odor. Maybe Selena would finally take my advice and move to the empty corner office that overlooked the street.

"Okay." She sipped her coffee, grimaced, then set it aside.

"Technically, it's been eight hours. Where's our missing teenage boy?"

"Asleep. In my spare bedroom."

I tried to keep the smirk off my face, but I don't think I succeeded.

Selena shook her head. "You must have some badass connections that I don't know about, Tess. How do you manage to score this shit?"

I shrugged. "It's a gift. I'm a good detective."

She gave me a long look.

"Fine. He showed up on my doorstep. Almost gift wrapped."

"That sounds more plausible."

I rolled my eyes. "Caitlin told him that he could trust me—that if there was ever an emergency, he should look for me. I guess she trusted my ability to protect him."

"She may have thought there was safety in numbers. How many people do you have staying at that crazy house of yours, as of last night?"

"Just Miles," I hedged.

"I call bullshit." She drained her coffee cup. It was like watching a lifelong alcoholic drop a shot of whiskey. "Try again."

I sighed. "Lucian's staying with us, too."

"Ah—so we like him now, do we?"

"He has a certain . . . *skill set* . . . that I think complements our case."

"I'm sure he does." She stretched, trying to loosen a cramp in her shoulder. "Just keep in mind that his *skill set* is incompatible with yours. He may be a tall glass of water in a black T-shirt, but he's also a necromancer. He's off-limits."

I nodded. "Of course."

"No, not 'of course.' I want to hear you say it. *Yes, I understand that he's off-limits,* Selena, *who is my boss.*"

She stared at me levelly.

I'm a bad person. I'm a fuckwit.

"Yes, I understand," I repeated slowly. "He's off-limits."

"Good." She gave a long sigh. "You know what I need,

Tess? I need a nice long sleep in a real bed. One of those feather mattresses with the eiderdown duvets, and those really soft sheets."

"You don't like your bed at home?"

Selena gave me a flat look. "My husband's in it."

"Oh . . ."

"Anyways"—she waved a hand—"that's not important. When are you bringing the boy in so we can process him?"

"I told him to come by around noon. He was sleeping when I left."

"He could have slept just as well in CORE custody, if you'd dropped him off last night instead of playing house."

"He's currently being watched by a necromancer, a telepath, and a dude who can see the invisible. I don't think he'd get very far if he tried to run, Selena."

She shrugged. "Fair enough. As long as he shows up, as promised."

"So, then . . ." I let the question hang.

She raised a hand. "I've spoken with Esther in Records. She'll unseal your intake file and let you see it. But first things first." She leaned forward. "What made you drive all the way to Elder last night to visit your mom? I know it wasn't because you love her spareribs, even though Siegel's always raving about them."

Give a little, get a lot, I thought.

"I'll need to see my intake file to confirm it," I said, "but I found out last night that my mother used to work for the CORE. She was an OSI, like me."

Selena frowned. "And she kept it from you all this time?"

"She thought she was protecting me. She also did it with the blessing of my old supervisor, Meredith Silver."

"Ah—Meredith was crafty. If she didn't want you to know something, you'd never pry it out of her." She sighed. "With both of them working against you, there's no way you could have known. That's tough, Tess."

As far as I knew, Selena came from a normate family. Obviously, her husband knew nothing about what really went on at the lab. But lately, I'd been getting the sense that she had a pretty spacious closet full of skeletons. It wouldn't have surprised me to learn that she'd been through something similar.

"Thanks," I said. "It feels pretty—fucked up. But I'm working through it. For now, there's something more important. I need to know everyone that was present and accounted for when I registered with the CORE."

Her eyes narrowed. She was on to me already. "You think your mom has some connection to this thing? That maybe your link to it comes from her side of the family, not just your father's?"

"I can't be certain. But she thinks that it's trying to enact some kind of ritual—a complex spell that will guarantee it a real, corporeal form in this world."

She frowned. "You're not just talking about a pureblood, then."

"No. An Iblis. That's what she called it."

Selena paled. "A gatekeeper. One of those half-there, half-not things that guards the liminal spaces between life and death—between our world and all the strange shores beyond, where true demons and who knows what else make their home."

"There's still something that's driving me crazy, though." I tapped my fingers on the table. "We haven't figured out where this thing got its tools from. It obviously has an athame, and it left us that cauldron. If it's only semicorporeal, it can't just carry that shit around all the time. It must have a place to put them. Even if it doesn't 'live' there, all things considered, we must be able to track it. Like tracking a wolf to its den."

Respect flashed in her eyes. She smiled. "That's a good theory. Still, it's not like you can buy an athame from a pawnshop. They're specifically calibrated to their user's body. And they have to be forged. Your athame would probably burn it, or at least cause it physical pain to hold."

"And that's the thing . . ." I put both hands on the table. "I think it would need a human accomplice to pull this off. Someone who has access to a house, a car, an archive of magical tools. In essence, a mage with a vendetta. It needs all the trappings of a mortal life in order to lure its victims. Think about that poor kid, Henry. He was savagely raped, multiple times. Do you think some half-corporeal spirit could do that, or would even *want* to? Seems more likely that it was a real sick puppy. A flesh-and-blood mortal with an axe to grind."

"Like a warlock?"

I shrugged. "Maybe. Or even someone who works here. A lab tech, maybe. Someone with access to the evidence locker. Chances are, it's someone who retired a long time ago. But I'll bet they were here when I first arrived. And I can't explain it, Selena, but I have this *feeling* . . ." My eyes were wide. "I just know that there's something in my file. Originally, I thought this creature was targeting me, that it was actually killing these people to fuck with *me*. But now I think it might be a bizarre coincidence. Like this thing, my mother, my father, and I are all spokes on some insane wheel. And the only record going far enough back to confirm it—"

"I've got you." She rose. "You don't have to push me over to convince me. Stranger things have happened around here. I want to make sure you're prepared, in case this doesn't all fall into place."

I frowned. "Prepared how?"

"If you're wrong—if this thing really has nothing to do with you—then we're still left chasing a ghost. And there's a good chance that it'll swoop right under your radar and attack that kid, Patrick, if it really wants to."

"I never said I could protect them all," I murmured. "I understand that."

"You understand, sure—but there's a difference between understanding and actually keeping yourself from working a dead angle. If this goes cold, I don't want to see you tearing through the lab like a maniac looking for some invisible scrap of evidence." Her eyes were warm, but steely. "I want to see you at home, with a CORE surveillance guard, protecting yourself and your family. Got it?"

I nodded. "I promise. This is my last crack. After this, no more late-night car rides or cryptic excuses."

"I don't believe you for a second." She smiled. "But then, if I were in your shoes, I'd probably lie, too. So I won't take it personally."

She stood up and walked out of the room before I could respond. I followed her down a long hallway, three flights of stairs, and through a security door. Then we stepped into a freight elevator. Selena smoothed her hair and pressed the red button, which made the tired gears scream to life. The Office of Records was almost as subterranean as Tasha's morgue. Some employees suspected that it might bleed into another dimension.

The elevator doors opened onto a long brick hallway. This was a much older part of the building—or one of the buildings that the CORE had purchased at the turn of the century anyhow—and the black-and-white-tiled floor had a charming, sanitarium-style verve to it. I felt like Dorothy in *Return to Oz*. There were cracks running in all directions, since the maintenance folk were usually too scared to come down here.

There were no doors—only a long, interrupted expanse of brick wall. If you knew where to look, though, and how to knock just right, you could find entrances to secret storage chambers and other oubliettes—places where you put things to forget about. Rumor had it that a few of those doors acted as wrinkles in space and time, but none of us were qualified to find or use them properly. That was probably a good thing.

The hallway ended in a sliding glass door, which hummed silently open for us as we approached. We'd already passed through a dozen invisible security checks, so they knew precisely who we were and what we were allowed to access. Nothing surprised the Office of Records. Or rather, nothing surprised Esther, the caretaker, who for all intents and purposes *was* the Office.

She sat in a swivel chair behind a stainless steel desk. The only word you could really use to describe Esther was "nondescript." Her height and weight were perfectly average. She had a sensible haircut, her brown hair ending in a completely even line just before it reached her shoulders. She wore a black turtleneck sweater that came practically up to her chin, and a long, black leather skirt. I almost thought I could see a pair of New Balance sneakers peeking out from the hem, but I wasn't sure.

Her eyes were framed by a pair of light, silver-rimmed glasses. She smiled as we approached the desk, and I saw a dozen images flicker rapidly across the surface of those glasses, like a disjointed film. I caught my face in the image stream, but when I tried to peer closer, it was replaced by a blue-tinged shadow. No one had ever seen Esther's eyes—only the ghost images that flickered across her otherworldly lenses. She was a living data medium. As far as we could tell, she was linked in to every computer system, every monitor, every fiber-optic cable in the CORE complex. Even Becka hadn't been able to explain the symbiotic connection to me, but she'd used words like "biomechanoid" and "wet works," which made me squirm.

"Selena." She inclined her head. "Tess. How can I help you?"

I always wanted to whisper, "Showtime, Synergy," like the holographic computer from *Jem*, when I was in Esther's presence, but that didn't seem like a good idea. I'd never been entirely sure if there was a sense of humor coded into the deep structures of her cybernetic personhood.

"I called down earlier," Selena replied, a note of testiness in her voice that seemed to be disguising a broader discomfort. It was nice to know that even she got the creeps whenever she had to spend time in places like this. The CORE, despite its technological savvy, had an eldritch set of foundations—like ancient bones—beneath its glassy surface, and the magic suffusing this room was part of that older power. It could be a bit overwhelming at times. No one was quite certain how many long brick hallways like the one we'd just crossed were hidden away in vacant, inaccessible buildings, or how many strange caretakers—like Esther—waited patiently underground, communicating with people like us only when it was absolutely necessary.

"Of course." Esther slid something across the counter—a small microphone with a flexible base and wireless receiver.

"I'll need your security code." She glanced at me, and I saw something flicker across her lenses. It looked almost like a wash of purple flame, then the sheen of a pistol, then a locked room—empty—then blue and black shadows again. Like the feed had temporarily shut off. "Don't worry. It will be updated as soon as you leave. It doesn't matter if you say it aloud."

It's not like I could do anything with her access code, since it was voice-keyed. I guess Esther was just being careful. Who knew what odd supervisors she had to answer to. Maybe her boss was a big computer. Maybe the building itself was her master.

Selena cleared her throat, then spoke a string of numbers and letters into the microphone. "I heart kitties" wasn't really an option for access codes around here. The CORE tended to prefer algorithms and protein sequences.

Esther slid the mic back under the desk. "Very good. Give me a moment while I retrieve the storage medium."

The wall behind her desk was a pane of smoky quartz, at least twelve feet high from floor to ceiling and perfectly opaque. Esther touched something beneath the desk, and the wall vanished. Behind it were row upon row of translucent shelves, each filled with wafer-thin objects that looked like memory sticks. Each wafer fit into a steel port, and different-colored lights flickered next to them—red, gold, green, orange, and blue. I wondered what a red light meant. It couldn't be good.

Esther scanned the wall of information, and images flickered across her lenses too quickly to discern. Then she reached up and withdrew one of the memory sticks from its port. The light next to it had been orange a second ago, but when she disconnected the wafer, it went black.

"What does an orange light mean?" I whispered to Selena.

She shrugged. "Probably better not to dwell on it too much."

Esther placed the storage medium on the desk in front of me, and I saw that it was completely transparent. It wasn't made of glass, though. It looked like some sort of lightweight plastic, or maybe a variant of silicone. Different-colored sparks played within the guts of the memory stick, like fireflies caught inside. I picked it up. It was warm, and almost weightless.

"You can view the contents in that room," Esther said.

I was about to ask, "What room?" but then I looked up and saw that a door had opened in the brick wall to my right.

"Please don't try to remove your flash drive," Esther told me. "It has to remain in Records at all times. When you're finished, bring it back to the desk."

I smiled shyly. "Thank you."

Her weird, polychromatic lenses fixed on me. I thought I saw Lucian's face in them for a second, then what looked like a basement or a bunker of some kind, then Mia holding something in her hands, then Derrick—it was like scanning a DVD at 10X speed. I wasn't sure if she was looking into my mind, or if she somehow had a hard line into my memories. If they were memories at all.

"You're welcome, Tess." She returned my smile. It was an odd gesture when I couldn't actually see her eyes.

Selena followed me into the viewing room, which was an empty bank of LCD screens with no keyboards attached, just touch pads.

"I'm looking over your shoulder," she said firmly.

I nodded. "It's only fair."

I plugged my flash drive into the nearest port and sat down. The screen was dark for a few seconds, and then I heard a chime, and the words CORDAY, TESSA ISOBEL, COMPLETE RECORD appeared in plain white letters. It was almost like one of those MS-DOS interfaces from years ago, before Windows XP and Mac OSX and all the pretty graphical operating systems that sprang from the nineties. I assumed that the interface was basic to keep it secure and encrypted.

I also wondered how *complete* it really was.

This is the CORE, Ben Foster had said. *I'd be surprised if their records didn't go back to well before the Flood.*

I scrolled through the first few screens. Whenever I paged down, I'd see a block of impenetrable ASCII characters rather than text. Then the screen would refresh, and the symbols would transform into standard English characters. Heavy encryption. The first few pages were concerned with vital stats: height, weight, ABO type, allergies, materia proficiencies and affiliations, and hard-coded files of my epithelial and mitochondrial DNA.

Just in case they need to clone me.

I paged down to the intake form, which had to be filled out whenever a potential mage joined the CORE. It was both a legally and mystically binding document, signed and sealed with a drop of my own blood.

"I know you're hiding in here somewhere," I murmured.

There was a list of names under COMPLIANCE PRESENT. My own name, of course. Meredith Silver. Diane Troy.

"Diane *Troy*?" Selena asked.

"My mother's maiden name." I sighed. "So she was there. Just like she said. She and Meredith arranged everything."

"Wait." Selena frowned. "Scroll down."

Beneath my mother's name was Nicholas Tamsin, the acting field chief, who would have had more or less the same job as Selena (we preferred "unit supervisor" instead of "field chief" now). Below his name was Alec Reynolds, who'd been the head of DNA and Toxicology over thirteen years ago, when it was still one department. Lab supervisors had to sign as witnesses.

Beneath Alec's name—

"Oh flying *fuck*," I whispered. "I knew it!"

Selena took a step back from the monitor, as if the name alone might burn itself out of the screen.

Marcus Tremblay.

I hadn't met Marcus until I'd already been here six, maybe seven years. He'd transferred into the unit supervisor position from some other department. There was absolutely no reason for him to appear on my intake file, seven years before we'd even been officially introduced. But I also wasn't surprised to see it.

"He's listed as 'AP Research,'" I breathed. "What does that mean? Why would a researcher be present at an intake?"

"Advanced Projects Research," Selena clarified slowly. "That division got absorbed into the Development branch—almost ten years ago, I think. APR was dissolved when I was barely an OSI-2."

"Why was it dissolved?"

She frowned. "There were some—concerns—over what was coming out of that division. Procedural infractions. Funds that went missing, or that got channeled into bizarre side projects. The whole thing was a major shit show."

"But Marcus was the head of this Advanced Projects division?"

She nodded. "I guess so. I never knew. It would make sense for someone high up in Development to be present during an intake, especially for the materia competency tests and physical exams. Marcus would have been roughly the equivalent at the time, so he signed as head of APR. After that division got torched, he must have taken a lateral transfer to some other admin job, and then he just kept spidering his way up until he made unit supervisor."

"That means"—I closed my eyes—"Marcus and my mother did meet. Their signatures are practically right next to each other on the intake form. He could have easily found out about my father, and if he was head of research, he would have had a fuckload of resources at his disposal. You said money was flying all over the place, right? Getting channeled along all sorts of weird pathways?" I looked at her. "What if one of those pathways led to the Iblis?"

"You think Marcus summoned it before he died?"

I felt flushed. I was still exhausted, but energy was pouring through me. I knew I was close. So close I could feel the heat of the flames on my neck.

I turned to her. "Selena, you were complaining earlier about having to deal with all of Marcus's old paperwork."

She nodded. "I've still got a stack of it."

"Do you know who handled his estate?"

Selena looked momentarily confused. "You mean a family member?"

"I doubt it. The CORE takes care of its own, remember.

I wouldn't be surprised if a third party dealt with everything."

"The lab was in chaos back then. I hadn't even been made acting unit supervisor yet, so I wasn't part of the process." She looked angry at herself. "I honestly don't even know where the fucker is buried."

"I get the impression that you weren't supposed to," I said. "None of us were. But I know someone who can find out."

I ejected the flash drive, my hands shaking a little from excitement. Trying to appear level, I returned to the desk. Esther smiled at me. I handed her the memory stick, and she replaced it in the wall. The light next to it blinked orange. Then the opaque black wall reappeared, as if it had always been there. I had no idea how the spell—if it was a spell—worked. I wasn't sure I wanted to know.

"Is there anything else?" Esther asked. From her skeptical look, it was clear that she knew we had another question.

"We need to see another employee's flash drive," I said.

Her lenses went dark. "I'm afraid that's impossible. These data mediums are protected under the Privacy Act."

"This employee is deceased."

Something like a comma of green light flickered across her lenses. Maybe she was establishing an uplink. She inclined her head.

"Usually," she said, "when an employee dies—depending upon the circumstances—his or her data medium is wiped clean and destroyed."

"You said *usually*."

She nodded slowly. "If a deceased employee has high clearance, their records may be preserved in the system. But they're on a different network. Whose profile are you looking for?"

"Marcus Tremblay."

She seemed to consider this for a moment. "He was your old supervisor?"

"I was directly involved in his final case. He almost killed me. If anyone should have access to his file, it's me."

Esther drummed her fingers on the desk. Her lenses were

nothing but a plane of shadow with a single, infinite blue line bisecting them.

"I have to make a call," she said at last.

I looked at Selena. She shrugged, but her eyes betrayed surprise. Neither of us had any idea who—or what—Esther might be calling.

She punched a number into her cell. "Yes, it's Esther, from Records." A pause. "Yes. Both of them. Agent Corday would like to view Marcus Tremblay's record." Another pause. "Right. That's what I thought. Thank you."

She clicked the phone shut. The call had lasted only ten seconds at most, but I'd felt the tug of materia, the sharp tang of magic in the air. That was no basic long distance plan she was using. She may very well have been calling another dimension. Or maybe the call got routed to another hidden room in another dark corner of the building, someplace I was glad I'd never see.

"Well?" Selena leaned against the counter.

The wall behind her vanished again. Esther reached up to withdraw another flash drive, and I noticed that it had a blue light next to it.

"You'll have to view this on my console," she said, plugging the memory stick directly into the port of her computer. "You've been granted tertiary access, which means that you can only read certain parts of the file. You can ask me what you're looking for, and if it's not restricted, I'll bring it up here on the monitor."

What monitor—

But it had already slid soundlessly out of the desk. TREMBLAY, MARCUS HOWARD, PARTIAL RECORD glowed across the screen in white text.

"Who handled his funeral and estate?" Selena asked.

Esther's fingers danced across a hidden keyboard. The screen refreshed, displaying a long page of data. There were gaps in the paragraphs, and some lines were blacked out. But most of it was legible.

"The record indicates that his estate was processed by a

company called Delacroix Holdings," Esther read. "They dealt with the funeral costs. It also appears that Marcus was cremated, and his ashes were disposed of."

"Disposed where?" Selena asked.

Esther frowned. "That information isn't available." I guess that meant it was classified. "But nobody signed for the cremains. They were never processed."

"Where is this Delacroix Holdings company based?" I asked.

Esther tapped. The screen refreshed again, and I saw an address.

"London, Ontario." Selena's hand was on my shoulder. "Only a few streets away from where Tamara Davies was killed. Jesus, Tess." She looked at me. "Sometimes your intuition scares me. You've really found something here."

I tried to smile, even though my "intuition" scared me as well.

"What do they do," I asked, "this Delacroix Holdings?"

"That's not in the file," Esther said.

I gave her a long look. "Aren't they a publicly traded company? There must be a record somewhere of the majority shareholders."

"I suppose—"

"I mean, we could hunt for it, right? But you'd be able to find it a lot faster with all of this specialized equipment."

Her expression seemed to waver for a moment.

"It would save us a trip to the White Pages," Selena said finally.

She knew damn well that the record Esther could pull up would be far more detailed than some PDF file we could track down on a corporate database. We were all shimmying around the truth.

Esther started tapping. I noticed that she was looking at an entirely different screen, though. She planned to control our access even further.

"They're a real estate company," Esther said finally. "They deal in condos, waterfront property, conversions, and *very* expensive renovations." She peered at the screen. "The CEO is listed as Guillaume Delacroix. The majority shareholders are all from the same family. Thierry, Patrice, Sabine—"

"Bingo," Selena said.

"Sabine *Delacroix*." I turned to her. "It can't be a coincidence. Especially after those two vamps attacked me in the subway. Sabine and Marcus had a lot of different entanglements, and this must have been some kind of failsafe on his part. If he died, Sabine's 'people' would take care of everything."

"The whole Delacroix family." Selena shook her head. "They've probably been running that company in one form or another for centuries."

"What about his personal effects?" I asked, turning back to Esther. "His condo, his car, everything—who has it now?"

She turned back to the screen. "I doubt I can give all of that information to you. But some of it might be available." She tapped for a while. "It says here that most of his possessions were auctioned off, since no family member was named as a beneficiary in his will. Delacroix Holdings actually owned his condo."

"I knew he shouldn't have been able to afford that place," Selena muttered. "It had a view of False Creek. The strata alone would have bankrupted him."

"Was *everything* placed on auction?" I pressed. "What about the things he may have left at the lab?"

"It might help if I knew what I was looking for," Esther said mildly.

"I want to know what happened to his athame."

Selena looked at me. "I know what you're thinking . . ."

"Really? I barely know myself." I shook my head.

Esther frowned at the screen. "Sensitive items like that are impossible to ship through regular channels. It would have to go through a courier affiliated with us." She tapped some more. "Okay. There's no listing for the athame itself, but there was a shipment of 'personal items' sent from his former office." She scratched her head. I'd never seen Esther do that before. "Odd."

"What?"

"The parcel was shipped a day before he died."

I slammed my hand on the desk. "That fucker! He *knew*. He knew ahead of time—or at least he suspected—what was going to go down that night, in Sebastian's old apartment with Mia and me. So he got rid of anything that might be tainted."

"So he has ties to the Iblis—if that's what this is." Selena tried to peer at the screen behind the desk, but it was out of view. "If Delacroix Holdings dealt with his estate, they probably dealt with the courier, too. One big happy vampire family."

"You think . . ." Esther gave us a long, curious look. "You're suggesting that someone, or something, is using a dead person's athame?"

We both nodded.

She steepled her fingers on the desk. When she spoke, her voice was very quiet, almost a whisper. "That is possible. When a mage dies, his or her athame becomes an empty vessel, like a battery drained of its charge. But an echo of the soul remains. If someone was powerful—and patient—enough, they might be able to resurrect that echo and rekindle the blade."

"But it would be—different," Selena clarified.

"Twisted." Her lenses flashed red. "Malformed. The athame could only be used for unlawful rituals."

I exhaled. This was it. This was the missing piece. Marcus *fucking* Tremblay was haunting me from beyond the grave.

"Where were his personal effects shipped to?"

"That isn't available."

I scowled. "You mean it's classified."

"It isn't available," she repeated, her voice flat.

"Yeah, well—luckily, I've got another source." I pulled out my cell and turned to Selena. "Miles has a Sidekick, right? That's got a pager with two-way text messaging capabilities. What's his number?"

She looked it up in her phone. "Here."

I sent him a feverish text message:

Find out everything you can about Delacroix Holdings in

Ontario. Use every contact. It's vampire-owned, and I need their shipping manifest.

Testimony to Miles's lightning fingers, a reply appeared a few seconds later: *On it, Kojak. Meet us across the street at 12. If I get fired, you're buying me lunch.*

It seemed like a fair deal.

Esther was frowning at me. I had to remind myself that she'd jumped the chain of command in order to let me view Marcus's file.

"Thanks, Esther. We really appreciate your help," I said.

"Don't thank me." She adjusted her glasses, and I saw—of all things—a slowly expanding pool of blood reflected in the lenses. "At least not yet."

21

"Are you sure you're ready for this?"

I stood outside the entrance to the morgue with Patrick, who was so pale and still that he barely appeared to be breathing. Maybe his vampire instincts were finally starting to kick in. I watched his fingers, almost a shade of white gold, as they clutched the fabric of his rumpled painter jeans. A curl of dark hair fell across his face.

"You don't have to go in there," I told him again. "Tasha just requires a positive ID from someone who isn't an employee with the CORE, but Lucian can always do that. There's no need for you to see the . . ." For some reason, I didn't want to say "body." "I mean, it's not really her anymore, right? It's only what's left behind."

His mouth was clenched. "No. I have to."

"You don't."

He stared at the steel doors. "You don't understand. This—it's a part of who I am. I have to see her. I'm not sure why. I just know that I do."

I nodded slowly. "Okay. I'll be standing right next to you,

then. It'll only take a second, and then we can leave right away."

He didn't answer.

Lucian came walking down the hallway. We'd left Mia in the break room with Derrick and Miles, since a trip to the morgue seemed like it might stretch the definition of responsible parenting, even for us. It felt strange to be having these conversations about demons and serial murders in front of Mia, but I also understood that she was part of this world now. She had a right to know what was going on around her, and that knowledge could act as a safeguard, preparing her for what was to come. I didn't want her traipsing down dark alleys, whistling to Mariah Carey on her iPod, totally unaware of what could be watching her. But I didn't want her scared stiff either, afraid to move or even breathe. It was a tough line to walk. Generally, she surprised me with her maturity and her willingness to listen.

"How are the three musketeers?" I asked him.

"I think Miles is teaching Mia how to swear in ASL. Derrick's checking out that Ontario contact that Miles gave him."

"You think it's on the level?"

"Could be. You'll have to let Selena figure out the next step, though. I doubt she'll let you run another solo mission. Not after what happened last time."

"I do have the tendency to get myself humped."

"Not always." He raised an eyebrow. "You can be pretty capable."

I started to say something facile in return, but then I looked at Patrick again. This had to be done. If he was strong enough to come this far, it was the least I could do to lead him over the threshold.

I put a hand lightly on his shoulder. "Ready?"

He nodded, exhaling, which made me feel better. At least he still breathed.

Patrick glanced quickly at Lucian. The embarrassment was clear in his face, as if he were asking us to keep a night light on. "Are you—um . . ."

Lucian stood next to him. "I'll be in there with you."

"That's good." He looked away. Lucian might actually be the best influence for Patrick, which made a twisted kind of sense. It takes a village to raise a vampire.

The temperature dropped to a chill two degrees Celsius as we stepped into the morgue. I could see Tasha leaning over the stainless-steel autopsy table, speaking quietly into her digital recorder. I'd called down earlier, asking if she could do anything possible to make Caitlin's obliterated body suitable for viewing. She promised to try.

She looked up, waving with a bloody glove. "Hey, Tess." Her expression curdled slightly as she saw Lucian. "And Mr. Agrado. Hello."

"Dr. Lieu." He inclined his head. "It's an honor to meet you."

She seemed taken aback by his politeness. Then her eyes fell to Patrick, and I saw her whole face soften. "You must be Patrick."

He nodded.

"I'm very sorry for your loss, sweetheart." Her fingers hovered over the body, which was covered by a white sheet. "Normally, we'd do this over closed-circuit television. But this case is a little different. So I'm just going to pull this sheet down—only a little bit—so that you can see her face. If you recognize her, all you have to do is nod. Then it'll be over. Okay?"

"I understand," he said dully.

"Good. I'm going to lower the sheet, then. Remember, you only have to nod."

Tasha pulled the white sheet down to Caitlin's chin. I was amazed. She'd almost completely reconstructed the woman's face. Caitlin's hair was smooth, as if it had just been brushed. Tasha had sewn her scalp back on, and I assumed that she'd filled in the missing parts of her skull with mortuary-grade epoxy. Her eyes were closed, and I saw that the CME had done her best to clean up the surface around her right eye socket, which had been savagely mauled. The sutures were almost invisible. I looked again at Tasha, noticing for the first time the dark circles under her eyes, as well as the two empty coffee cups on the desk behind her. Obviously, she'd worked all day on this. I didn't know quite how to thank her.

"That's her," Patrick said softly.

Tasha started to pull the sheet back up, but Patrick reached out swiftly, grabbing it from her. Tasha's eyes widened as she touched Patrick's hand momentarily, and then she jerked away, as if he'd burned her.

"I need to see the rest of her."

She frowned. "I don't think that's a good idea . . ."

"I need to." His eyes were black beneath the fluorescent lights.

Tasha looked at me helplessly. All I could do was nod.

Slowly, Patrick tugged the sheet down. It was clear that Tasha hadn't had the chance to repair the rest of Caitlin's body so thoroughly. Her right arm was still missing at the elbow, and her left leg was criss-crossed with horrible gouges. She was naked, of course, and I saw for the first time that her genitals were untouched—smooth, unblemished skin and a triangle of pale red hair. That discounted any theories about her murder being psychosexual, which still left us with questions about why Henry alone had been so viciously raped.

I wanted to cover up her lower half, but Patrick didn't seem to be dwelling on it. Gently, he reached out and touched the white pit of her neck, above her right clavicle. The same spot where Lucian's tattoo flared. What was it about that spot?

Smoothly, as if it were the most natural thing in the word, Patrick reached down and pressed his lips to Caitlin's neck. I felt something unravel in the air—a current of power suddenly swirling to life around us, dark and resinous, as if someone had locked the entire room in amber. When Patrick stood up, his eyes were a shade of yellow that I'd seen only once. The eyes of an arctic wolf.

An impossible shudder passed through Caitlin's body. The spot where Patrick's lips had touched her began to smoke, glowing red. Then she simply . . . dissolved. It was like every bone and muscle in her body gave a great, heaving sigh, and then fell apart. Her flesh crumbled, her bones shivered and desiccated, right on the table. Within seconds, there was only a dark stain left.

Patrick blinked. His eyes had returned to their usual shade of brown.

"We can go now," he said simply.

Tasha looked horrified and speechless.

"Okay, Patrick." My hand hovered just above his shoulder. "Let's go."

Lucian stared at the empty table for a second. I couldn't tell what he was thinking, but his face was hard.

Then we filed out of the morgue—two adults on either side of a tall, pale boy, each of us keeping our distance, suddenly afraid to touch him.

A page from Selena forced us to change direction, and we found ourselves heading toward the ballistics lab instead of the break room. I was surprised to find a crowd standing outside the entrance to the lab. Derrick leaned against the glass partition with Miles standing next to him. Mia stood a bit off to the side, talking to an indistinct figure in a gray hooded sweatshirt. The figure turned, and I saw that it was Wolfie. Lucian had come through. He smirked at me, and I nodded.

And now we were seven. It was a good number. Seven deadly sins, seven samurai, 7-Eleven. It seemed to fit.

"She paged you, too?" Derrick asked.

I nodded. "Do you know what it's about?"

"Nope."

Selena emerged from the ballistics lab. She crooked her finger. "Come in. All of you. And don't touch anything unless Linus says it's okay first."

"I get to see the weapons?" Mia looked awed.

"From a distance," Selena said firmly. "Although we do have some protective gear for you. Linus picked it out special."

"Awesome," she whispered.

Great. Selena had just become her new favorite person.

We all crowded into the ballistics lab, standing dutifully next to the steel counters and GSR-testing equipment. A water tank stood in the middle of the room, which was used for test-firing ammunition, as well as a block of yellow ballistics gel for measuring impact velocity. It wiggled like Jell-O. Mia reached out to touch it, but Selena shook her head. Silently, she put her hand down, looking at the floor.

Linus looked up from a comparison microscope and grinned at us. He'd put on a little weight, but it looked good on him. His cheeks were fuller, and he'd started to grow a beard, which made him look bearish but also kind of jovial. Santa Claus with a Sig Sauer. I briefly thought of that scene from *Scrooged*, where Santa has to defend his workshop with a semiautomatic. It was hard to keep a straight face.

"Hi, everyone!" I don't think I'd ever seen Linus this excited before. He was normally so bland and wry-humored, but now his eyes glowed almost feverishly. He didn't usually interact with this many people.

"Is there a party that I didn't know about?" I asked Selena blankly.

She smiled. "Of sorts. Linus and I have been talking, and we think it's in all your best interests to give you some tactical equipment."

"Freakin' *sweet*," Mia exclaimed, although her voice was still soft.

Selena raised a hand. "Understand that this is a direct reflection of the *CORE's* interest in your case. The higher-ups have okayed the insurance cost of dispensing some of our more expensive tactical pieces. The trade-off is that you don't get to run into any abandoned warehouses with guns blazing. This is an official operation, and we're going to do it according to policy. That mean's you'll be monitored at all times."

"You're the boss of us," I confirmed.

Her eyes grazed me. "That's right, Tess. We'll be in constant contact with wireless headsets. We'll be watching your team from every angle. If things get too hot and I say the word, you *disengage*. No questions. Got it?"

I nodded solemnly. I'd never had the CORE fully backing

me on an operation before. It was exhilarating, but also scary. Dozens of eyes would be watching me, waiting for me to shoot myself in the foot. Literally.

"We're a team?" Patrick asked. There was a note of cold humor in his voice. Even though his eyes had returned to their normal color, I still thought I could see flecks of gold inside them.

"Two teams, actually," Selena clarified. "Alpha team will be our offensive group. That's Tess, Lucian, and Wolfie."

Wolfie looked up in surprise as she said his name. "For real?"

"Duessa called me this morning to vouch for you. So you're in. Just follow my orders and don't do anything stupid."

That must have been why Lucian was meeting with Duessa. I gave him a surprised look. He merely winked at me.

"Okay." Wolfie braced himself against the steel counter. He was nervous, but I could see the flush of excitement on his face. "I'll do my best."

"Beta team," Selena continued, "is Derrick, Miles, and Patrick. Derrick will run as much interference as possible with his abilities, and Miles will act as our point man, reading the space for us. Patrick, you'll stay with them at all times and act as a communiqué. Your job will be to watch their blind spots, see what they can't. And if something doesn't look right, you tell me right away. Got it?"

Patrick nodded. "Sure." His voice cracked a little. "I can do that."

I knew that Selena was making his responsibility sound far more active than it really was. In essence, she was putting him between Miles and Derrick so that the two could keep an eye on him. She knew that he was much more likely to get into trouble on the sidelines, especially if he got restless and decided to go hunting. This way, he was in the action, but still protected.

"I've got faith in you." She held his gaze. "You've had a real tough couple of days, but I know that you're strong. And the worst will be over soon."

He simply nodded. But I could see the flash of pride in his

eyes. I'd never known Selena to be this gentle before. She had a way with teenagers. Maybe I should ask her to start hanging out with Mia.

As if on cue, Mia stepped forward. "Selena? What about me?"

"Are you kidding?" Selena grinned. "You're the linchpin, kid. You'll be in the mobile HQ, monitoring all the cameras and radios. That's six video screens with nonstop action, and you'll see all of it, like nobody else can. Your eyes are probably sharper than mine, so I'll be relying on you to catch what I miss."

Before Mia could reply, Selena reached into her pocket and withdrew something that looked like a tiny flashlight. It was a black cylinder with a blinking red button.

"This is the kill switch," she said. "It's connected to every headset and every pager. If you see something that looks wrong, all you have to do is press this button, and everyone will get the signal to abort." She placed it in Mia's hand. "You've got control over the entire operation."

For a second, I thought Mia might see through the ruse. The "kill switch" was probably just a laser pen that Linus had rigged with a flashing LED light.

But Mia's expression was undeniably solemn as her fingers closed around the black cylinder. She held it close. "Thanks, Selena," she whispered.

Selena nodded. "You've dealt with a lot of crazy stuff in the last year, and you've proven that you're solid. I trust you, Mia."

She blushed slightly. "Thank you. This *rocks*."

Man. Selena was much better than I gave her credit for sometimes.

She turned to Linus. "Are we ready for the tour?"

He was already smiling. "Step right up, folks." He walked over to the reinforced steel door of the weapons vault, set in the far corner of the lab. "Few people ever get a chance to see this place. I think you'll like it."

He withdrew a keycard and swiped it through a reader on the door. Selena did the same with her own keycard. The computer processed their biometrics, humming for a moment. I heard the loud bang of the steel tumblers moving, and then the door to the vault swung open. Cold, stale air rushed out of the entranceway.

We all followed Linus down a flight of steel steps that led to the subterranean weapons and tactical equipment locker. He stepped confidently through the dim blue light provided by overhead panels, while the rest of us gripped the cold handrails, trying not to stumble. After we'd gone about three stories underground, we came to a Plexiglas door. Blue light shimmered in lines around it. Electrical materia flows. Not the kind of security system you wanted to tamper with.

Linus waved his hand over an invisible sensor, and the door slid open. Lights flickered silently on past the entrance, revealing a vast room—walled entirely in steel—that was roughly the size of a hotel lobby. There were no shelves or pedestals. Every piece of equipment was magnetically affixed to the walls, and locked sliding drawers lined the sides, no doubt filled with more dangerous and fascinating things.

"Impressive," Lucian murmured.

Linus inclined his head. "Thanks."

Mia peered at a cluster of subcompact, semiautomatic pistols. Several of them had modified triggers, light sights, and other extras.

"Guess I don't get one of these," she said.

I couldn't tell if there was relief or disappointment in her voice.

"We're not in the business of arming kids," Selena said. "Besides, some of those triggers require almost twenty pounds of force to pull them. The kickback would only end up hurting you. And then you couldn't be our eyes and ears."

"Yeah." She looked away from the gleaming sidearms. "That's true."

I breathed a colossal sigh of relief. Mia would never touch a loaded gun—not on my watch. I cringed whenever she picked up a knife to chop fruit.

"What about me?" Patrick asked. He didn't sound eager. Just curious, as if Linus were handing out free suckers.

"No guns for you either," Selena said firmly. "But you'll be well protected, don't worry. Linus has some more useful equipment for you."

As if on cue, Linus pulled out one of the drawers. He withdrew a leather and nylon harness with green, flexible plates of armor affixed to it.

"This is a STRIKE Cutaway Ballistic Vest," he said, holding it up so that Patrick could get a closer look. Linus adopted a hushed, almost sacred tone, and I realized that this was what he loved more than anything: explaining tactical equipment. "It's light—barely three and a half pounds—and has removable soft plating with overlapping side coverage. The armor's made from woven aramid, which is a rigid composite of polyester and titanium filaments with a polyamide resin matrix." He stroked the surface of the plates. "The strands of aramid elongate when they're exposed to heat, and they can withstand the shock of heavy-duty fragmentation rounds. It offers the best blunt trauma protection for its weight and size, which includes materia decompression and sonic blasts."

Patrick looked a little speechless.

"It's even got a five-year warranty," Linus said, grinning. "I'll show you how easy it is to put on in a minute. For now, I've also got this for you . . ." He scanned a wall of knives, and I imagined his brain classifying and weighing each blade. Then he snatched a fixed blade that was slightly curved. He handed it gently, hilt first, to Patrick, who took it with an expression bordering on wonderment.

"This is a Nightwing fixed blade," Linus explained. "It's very sharp, so keep it in the holster at all times. You're only to use it for emergencies. Got it?"

Patrick nodded slowly.

"The Nightwing is awesome," he gushed, the responsible tone vanishing from his voice as plain excitement took hold. "It's ground from S30-V stainless steel, and has an ergonomic handle that's easy to grip, even if you've never held a knife before. The blade is five point nine inches long, and has adjustable spines with a black tungsten coating. If you're going to use it . . ." He carefully wrapped Patrick's fingers around the hilt. "Keep your whole hand under the metal tang, for protection. Slash with it downward, and keep your grip firm. Don't just swing it around wildly."

"I'll try to remember," Patrick murmured. I caught a definite note of fear in his voice. The seventeen-year-old kid had replaced the vampire, which relieved me a bit. Hopefully, that hesitation would keep him alive. Or as "alive" as he'd ever be.

"As for the rest of you . . ." Linus's enthusiasm was infectious. "All I can say is, I am *sooo* jealous."

"Let's hurry this along," Selena warned. "There isn't time for show and tell."

Linus reached for a pistol and handed it to me. "This is for you, Tess."

"I already have a gun."

"But not *this* gun."

I rolled my eyes. "Don't get too hard describing it to me, Linus. Selena's right. We're kind of pressed for time here."

He had the decency to blush, but was undeterred in his exposition. "This is a Glock forty-five subcompact, tactical issue. It weighs barely twenty-five ounces, even when loaded, and the trigger needs less than five pounds of pressure. The magazine—"

"Is expanded to hold ten rounds instead of the standard six," I interrupted him smoothly, grabbing the pistol. "It's front-sighted, and six point three inches long with a one point eighteen inch barrel width. It's also got a tactical light and speed-loader cartridge." I flicked the ejector port, and the ammo pack dropped into my left hand. "Hey, are these hollow points? I was expecting Glazer rounds."

Linus looked on the verge of sulking—I'd ruined his description. "They're filled with a liquid materia polymer," he said, "under high pressure. The copper jacket is designed to shred when it hits anything semisolid, including the sort of magnetic aura that a noncorporeal creature might exude. When the round separates, it releases a burst of thermal materia that will instantly combust."

"Magic napalm," I said. "Very cool."

He let go of the gun, a little unwillingly. "It's got a night sight, too," he mumbled, "and the grip is specially designed so that you can hold it with your athame. It's also been retrofit with a biometric sensor, which prevents anyone but you from firing it."

I holstered the Glock. "I still prefer my athame. But this'll be handy if I find myself in a real FUBAR situation."

"What about me?" Derrick asked. "What do I get?"

Linus grinned. "Oh, man. You're gonna *lose* it when you see this." He reached into another drawer and pulled out a second pistol. This one was made entirely of carbon blue steel, and Derrick whistled when he saw it.

"This is a Glock, too," Linus explained, "but it's the G34 model, which has a slightly longer barrel for improved accuracy." This was a nice way of saying that Derrick couldn't hit the broad side of a barn. "That's not what's really special about this baby, though. Here. Hold it." He gave the pistol to Derrick. "Tell me how it feels."

Derrick slid his hand around the grip. I felt a flicker of something—very subtle, but still present, like a whisper of power—and his eyes widened.

"Does this have dendrite materia in it?" he whispered.

"Dendrite materia is too unstable to isolate. But it *does* have a transdermal sensor on the grip. The sensor emits radio waves at an extremely high frequency—over four hundred GHz, at the far end of the microwave spectrum and well above the audible human range—but telepaths like yourself can pick them up, as long as you're within ten millimeters of the pistol itself."

"So I have—what—a psychic uplink with this gun?"

Linus nodded. "It'll calibrate itself to your synaptic patterns. If you concentrate, you'll be able to aim it with your thoughts. Do it right, and every shot will be ninety-nine point nine percent accurate, give or take a brainwave."

Derrick cradled the gun. *"Sweet,"* he whispered.

I rolled my eyes.

"Now for you, Detective Sedgwick." Linus turned to him.

Miles gave the lab tech a cool stare. "Just because I'm deaf doesn't mean that I need some sophisticated gadget to compensate. If you pull a Bluetooth hearing aid out of one of those drawers, I'll beat your ass down."

"I'd believe him," Derrick added, holstering his new gun. "He's got surprising upper-body strength. And great triceps."

Miles grinned at him. "Thanks."

Linus raised his hands in surrender. "No worries, I wasn't going to suggest anything like that. I do have something I think you'll like, though." He slid open a panel in the wall—how did he know where everything was?—and withdrew a small metal box. He flipped open the lid and took out a pair of slim wrap-around sunglasses. The frames looked like they were made of carbon steel, and the lenses were blue crystal and opaque with a dark sheen.

"What are these?" Miles asked suspiciously. He looked so wary that, for a moment, I thought he might sniff them.

"Selena told me about your sensitivity to materia flows," Linus said, "and I remembered that we'd ordered a pair of these but never gotten the chance to use them. Why don't you try them on?"

Gingerly, Miles took the shades and slipped them on. His mouth became a small, startled *O*. "Whoa. This is like— *Technicolor*. How does it work?"

"The lenses are made of crystallized materia that amplifies your own sight. Even with a perceptive wearer, the traces would normally only show up as different-colored smudges. But your vision is a lot clearer."

He nodded. "I barely have to concentrate at all. I can see traces that would usually be almost invisible."

"They might give you a headache after a while. So use them sparingly."

Miles turned to Derrick. "How do they look?"

Derrick smiled. "Like I want to rip all your clothes off."

Miles cocked his head. "Excellent."

"So . . ." Lucian stepped forward. "What do you have in mind for me?"

"Oh. Um . . ." Linus looked a tad embarrassed. "Selena said that you didn't really need weapons." He blinked. "She said you were dangerous enough. And we don't have anything capable of manipulating necroid materia, since we're not even sure how it works in the first place."

Lucian gave him a predatorial smile. "Fair enough."

"Same goes for you," Selena said to Wolfie, who was looking expectant. "You're already a spark at the height of your powers. You don't need any—enhancements."

Wolfie shrugged. "I kinda figured."

Selena turned to me. "Okay, Tess. Now that you're all geared up—what's the status with that intel from Ontario?"

"Miles can answer that," I said smugly. He'd come through in a big way.

Miles removed the sunglasses, shaking his head slightly as if to clear it. "Tess had me call in some favors. I managed to get ahold of the shipping manifest for Delacroix Holdings, which is based in Hamilton."

"Do I want to know exactly how that happened?" Selena asked.

Miles smiled wanly. "I don't think so. At any rate, the manifest indicated that a private courier—licensed by Delacroix—picked up some of Marcus Tremblay's personal effects from the lab. All the proper signatures are there, but I think some of them were forged. Otherwise, you would have realized what was going on."

"Where was the package shipped to?"

"I tracked it to some property that Delacroix leases. A house, I think, although there's nearly an acre of land around it. The property's in South Delta."

"Far enough away that we'd never look for it," I said. "Practically farmland. Does anyone live there now?"

"It's listed as being condemned and slated for demolition. There's probably all sorts of caution tape and fences around it to keep people away."

"It'll get demolished, all right." My hand closed around the pistol grip. "We're going to burn it to the ground."

"Easy, Tess." Selena gave me a look. "We're going to be smart about this. Who knows what traps this thing has laid? We'll have to surround it first and secure the perimeter. After that, we'll send both teams in."

"Great," Derrick said. "Then we can attack a pureblood demon that has no corporeal form. Easy as *Ghost Hunters*."

"I'll be able to see it . . ." Miles reached for the glasses again. "Especially with these. And Tess can hurt it with those bullets. Materia-based attacks should work. At the very least, we've got a shot."

I slammed the ammo pack into my gun, chambering a bullet. "A shot in hell." I squinted, aiming at an invisible target. "But that's all we ever really get."

22

It was less of a house and more of a crumbling mansion—the sort of place where you could picture Miss Havisham dancing around in widening circles of madness while the living room heaved and collapsed all around her.

The front porch was quietly rotting, and several of the steps leading to the front door had long become dust. The property was surrounded by a fence topped with barbed wire, and CONDEMNED signs had been slapped up in various places, along with messages about an obscure zoning conflict that only the most pedantic observer might try to puzzle out. There was an acre of devastated land around the house, ringed by clumps of dead brown grass and anemic trees whose gnarled roots looked uncomfortably like half-buried limbs, their white bark festering with moss and deep rot. There may have been arable farmland nearby at one point, but a circle of decay seemed to emanate from the very foundations of the place, leaving everything around it desiccated and withered. The air smelled of mold and rotting fruit, and beneath that—like a velvety patina that had been collecting for decades—was the unmistakable reek of iron and blood.

It was perfect. Nothing but a pureblood demon could survive here.

I stood in the yard, flanked by Derrick and Lucian, who both had their eyes trained on the porch as if something evil might explode out the front door the moment they looked away. Probably a fair assumption, although from what we knew so far about the Iblis, sudden attacks didn't seem to be its style. More like psychological warfare. Miles was examining one of the crippled trees. Wolfie, who was standing a few feet away, glanced at him warily, obviously trying to suss out how his powers worked.

Miles frowned. "They're not dead exactly. I can still pick up trace amounts of materia in the deep root structures. It's more like they're being *drained* by something. It's keeping them alive, but barely."

Wolfie kicked one of the trees with his boot. "Undead is more like it."

"This whole place is a graveyard," I muttered.

"It'll be difficult for you to draw power here," Lucian said. "Everything's being leeched away. The Iblis has probably been feeding off this area for some time."

"There's always life somewhere," I replied, touching the hilt of my athame. It was faintly warm. I had to believe in something deep down, beneath the layers of decay, something bright and unkillable. If I couldn't—what was the point?

Patrick was very still next to me. His skin looked almost translucent in the light, and his eyes were flecked with gold. He was becoming less human with each passing hour. Something had changed when he'd touched Caitlin's body. He'd absorbed her power somehow, and maybe her memories with it. He seemed constantly lost in thought and distracted, as if his mind was turning over endless possibilities. I only hoped that he'd be able to focus when the time came for action. As loath as I was to use him like this, we needed the strength and speed of a vampire—even a newborn.

Selena emerged from the line of trees, where she'd parked the mobile HQ van. A dozen CORE agents were already deployed around the property. I saw her adjusting a Bluetooth headset, mumbling something beneath her breath. Selena hated technology. I think she would have been happier carrying a double-edged spear.

We'd all been decked out in matching ballistic vests, which could absorb enough penetrating force to stop a vampire's teeth (although I figured they'd probably aim higher than our chests). Even Mia had a smaller version that resembled a life preserver, and it made me think that she was six years old and about to visit the waterslides for the first time. Thinking that was better than dwelling on the reality of the situation. At least she'd be safe in the armored van with Selena.

"Everything's ready." My boss gave me a look. "What about you, Corday? Any last-minute nerves?"

"Nothing I can't handle."

"Remember what we talked about. You stay in formation, and you stay in contact. Don't switch your radio off—not even for a second. Keep together and sweep the house one floor at a time. When you find that thing, *do not* engage it. Keep back and give us the signal. Reinforcements will come in through every door, window, and ventilation shaft that they can find."

"Don't engage," I repeated numbly.

"Hey." She snapped her fingers in front of my face. The gesture startled me, and I really looked at her, as if for the first time. "That's a fucking order. This thing will take you apart if you try to come at it. We've got a whole team of combat-trained mages circling the house, and they know exactly what to do. Understand?"

I nodded.

"Good. Be careful. Do what your training tells you." She smiled. "You'll be fine, Tess. I'll buy you breakfast tomorrow morning."

"Can we get hash browns?"

"Yes. We can get hash browns."

I returned her smile. "That's good."

Selena tapped a button on her headset. "Mia, are you there?"

The small speaker in my ear crackled. Then I heard Mia's voice, which made me relax a bit. Only a bit.

"I'm here, Selena. Over."

"How's the perimeter look?"

"You have to say 'over' each time. Over."

I chuckled beneath my breath.

Selena rolled her eyes. "How's the perimeter look? *Over.*"

"The teams are all deployed. And please call me M-Command. Over."

"I'm not calling you M-Command. Over."

"M-Command did not copy. Please repeat. Over."

"Why did we give her control of the radio again?" Selena asked me quietly.

"To keep her out of trouble."

"Well, it's not going to work if I kill her first."

I heard Mia's voice again. "Tess, are you going in? Over."

I smiled. "We are, Mia. Wish us luck. Over."

There was silence. And then: "Good luck and I love you. Over."

I closed my eyes. "I love you, too. Over."

Lucian touched my shoulder. "Time to move?"

I nodded, gesturing for everyone to follow me. "Let's go."

We moved carefully up the stairs, avoiding the gaps. The door was unlocked, and I imagined that anyone who ignored the barbed wire, condemned signs, and general air of danger pretty much deserved what they got if they decided to walk in.

The foyer reminded me of a large-scale version of my dad's garden shed: old pieces of machinery were scattered at the foot of a long flight of stairs, and spiders crawled over everything, ignoring us. Patches of light showed dusty footprints on the floor. There'd obviously been some traffic in this room, and recently.

"No splitting up," I told Lucian. "We stay together, no matter what. Let's take the living room first."

He nodded.

We walked down a short hallway and into what, years ago,

might have been called the parlor, but now resembled a landfill.
A gutted couch lay on its side in the corner, hemorrhaging gray
clumps of stuffing. The floor was thick with debris, mostly
wood and glass, but I noticed scraps of cloth and other things
that shone dully. I knelt down and picked up something, dusting it off.

"Is that a badge?" Lucian asked.

"Looks like it." I could just see the letters RCMP stamped
into the metal. There were dark brown spots on the corner.
Blood. "Looks like they had visitors."

"Can I see it?" Patrick whispered.

His voice startled me. I'd forgotten that he was even here.

Shrugging, I handed the badge over to him. Patrick squinted
at it for a moment. Then, as if it were perfectly commonplace,
he licked the spot of dried blood. His tongue was shockingly
pink in the dim light of the room.

I shuddered.

"Old blood," he confirmed. "Months."

"Wonder where the body is?" Derrick asked. "Maybe the
Iblis ate him?"

"I don't think it eats people."

"We don't know that for sure."

I continued through the living room, scanning the walls and
floor. Places like this were always full of sliding panels, hidden
closets, and trapdoors that led to underground cellars—all
cozy spots where a demon might choose to sleep.

If it slept at all.

A door to the right was slightly ajar. I held the Glock level,
placing my left hand on the butt of the gun while my right
tensed on the trigger. I turned to Lucian.

He nodded.

I kicked the door open.

There was nothing but a grimy bathroom inside. A colony
of spiders had made themselves at home in the dirty toilet
bowl, and the porcelain sink was cracked down the middle.
Filthy water ran down the walls from a leaking pipe. There
were spots of skeletonized blood on the white tiles. Whatever

started in the living room had obviously continued in here. The end couldn't have been pleasant.

"It's fine—"

As I turned, I just caught a glimpse of something blurry, like a shadow crossing the floor. My eyes widened.

"What is it?" Lucian asked.

The shadow flickered again to my right. It had eyes.

"Fuck," I whispered.

Something slammed into Lucian. He went down with a cry, and I heard growling, like a dog had gotten loose in the house somewhere. But it wasn't a dog. I saw eyes, teeth, and long fingernails, all blurring into a sheen of cold fury.

Then Patrick was in front of me.

He moved so fast that he seemed to just materialize, not bothering with the intervening space. His form blurred for a second, and then he was between Lucian and the thing on top of him. I realized with a start that the growl had been coming from Patrick's throat. His eyes were the color of dark pyrite.

The shadow coalesced into a wiry black form with close-cropped hair. Lucian had one arm locked around the vampire's neck, trying for a choke hold, but the creature's full weight was on top of him and he couldn't get the proper leverage. Hot saliva dribbled from the vampire's mouth, and his eyes were red-rimmed, the pupils astonishingly black, like eclipsed suns. Deep in bloodlust. There'd be no reasoning with him, no chance for parlay.

But Patrick, it seemed, had no desire to talk.

Still growling low in his throat, Patrick reached out, his hands locking around the vampire's waist. The muscles in his shoulders tensed, and then he lifted the vampire clear off the ground, snarling. Lucian rolled away, scrambling to one knee. The vampire howled and thrashed in Patrick's grip.

He locked both his arms at the elbow. Then he squeezed.

His captive screamed. I heard his ribs cracking. Patrick kept squeezing, tighter and tighter, until I heard a soft *plsshh* of air escaping. He'd punctured the vamp's lung. Blood spattered from the vampire's mouth in three short bursts, like a sprinkler. Then his struggling ceased. Patrick gave his torso a sharp, wrenching twist, like he was uncorking a bottle of champagne, and more blood sprayed from the vamp's mouth and nose. His eyes went dark. He'd severed the spine.

Patrick dropped the body to the floor.

He stood there for a few seconds, panting. His eyes flickered. Slowly, the golden gleam in them subsided.

"Patrick? Are you . . ." It seemed ludicrous to ask if he was all right.

"I'll be fine," he whispered. "Let's keep going."

Miles and Derrick both stared at him with expressions of veiled horror.

My headset crackled. "Tess?" It was Selena's voice. "We heard a scuffle. What's your status?"

"We're okay," I said. "Patrick dealt with it."

"Good. We'll be standing by, then."

"Guess we know for sure now that it's employing vampires," Derrick said. "That must be how it manages those elaborate crime scenes."

"Sabine." Her name curdled my stomach.

"Who's Sabine?" Wolfie asked.

"An undead princess with a real hate-on for Tess," Derrick replied.

I sighed. "I'll explain later."

"First things first," Wolfie said grimly.

He placed his hands on the vampire's still-twitching body, and I felt him concentrate. The fire was almost bloodred in the shadows. I turned away from the stench, but it was over in seconds. Wolfie's fire burned hotter than the usual kind. There was nothing left but a crumbling, calcined skeleton.

A few tongues of flame licked hungrily at the floorboards, but Wolfie simply glared at them, and they winked out of existence. I wondered what it would be like to have such control over my own powers.

"Now we can go," he said, adjusting his I ♥ SASKATOON cap. I noticed that he was the only one who didn't seem uncomfortable around Patrick.

"You all right?" I asked Lucian.

He nodded, wincing. "I'll be a walking bruise tomorrow. But I'm good."

We doubled back slowly, past the flight of stairs and along the opposite hallway, which led to a kitchen and attached pantry. Broken crockery littered the floor like porcelain bone fragments, and the sink was overflowing with debris. The linoleum had peeled away in long strips, and I could see the rotted framework beneath. It felt like we were walking through a decomposing body.

I stepped over the splintered table, peering through the dim entranceway that led to the pantry. A few bottles of preserves were still intact on the shelves, their contents floating in pectin like amniotic fluid. The majority of the jars had been shattered, and lumps of grayish syrup and vegetable matter covered the floor. I scanned the walls, but the room seemed to be a stand-alone, perfectly enclosed.

"Nothing here," I murmured.

"Should we try the stairs?" Derrick asked.

I frowned. "I don't think we should be going up. If the Iblis is here, it's going to be as close to the earth as possible. There must be an underground cellar. We'll have to search under things for a trapdoor." I turned to Miles. "Can you look for traces of materia residue on the floor? There might be some heat differentials if this thing has an underground entrance to its lair."

Miles nodded and put on the blue glasses. "If it's there, I'll find it."

We combed the living room again, kicking over furniture, shifting debris around, looking underneath the moth-eaten rug. Finally, Miles snapped his fingers and pointed to a spot in the far corner of the room.

"Thermal materia," he said. "It's gathering here."

Patrick leaned forward, his eyes narrowing.

"Ah," he said. "I can see the door now."

"I'm sure glad we brought you," I said, giving him a wan smile. I didn't want him to feel like a freak.

He returned my smile shyly. "Thanks."

"Since you're the only one who can see it . . ." I gestured to the spot on the floor. "Think you can open it?"

Patrick nodded. He got down on one knee, his slim fingers probing the surface of the wood. I saw his hands grasp— *something*. It was invisible, but clearly solid. Then he tugged at it with a grunt, and I heard the creak of grinding wood. The air seemed to flicker, growing indistinct for a moment. Then I saw a trapdoor attached to an iron rung and, beneath it, a square of utter blackness.

"Tricky," Lucian murmured.

I touched my earpiece. "Selena, we've found an entrance. We're going in."

"Copy. Be careful, and stay on this channel. We'll try to boost the frequency in case there's interference underground."

I reached into my jacket and drew out a Cyalume stick, motioning for the others to do the same. Except for Patrick. I was sure that he could already see in the dark. I snapped the stick down the middle with my thumb and forefinger, and it began to give off a weak, neon green glow.

"Everyone ready?"

They all nodded.

I shifted the Glock to my left hand, keeping my right braced against the grimy wall as I descended a narrow flight of stone steps. I could feel packed earth, spiderwebs, and other, nameless things against my fingertips, but I didn't think too closely about what they might be. I concentrated on the faint green aura of the Cyalume stick, which just barely revealed patches of the earthen walls, flecked with stone and glistening roots. It felt like we were journeying into the black core of the world itself.

I counted almost thirty steps before my boots touched soft, packed earth. The air was cool and smelled like decaying leaves. I could hear water dripping somewhere and, farther in the distance, something that sounded like a low rumbling. A generator maybe? It seemed like the most comforting possibility.

We continued down a narrow, low-ceilinged passageway, holding out our green glow sticks like eerie fireworks.

After about five minutes of walking, I felt Lucian come up behind me.

"We're almost past the property line now," he murmured. "I wonder how far this corridor goes? We must be under the neighbor's yard."

"No neighbors," I said, suppressing the urge to shiver. "Not for a mile. We may as well be in another country."

The corridor widened a bit, and we found ourselves standing in something like an antechamber. Two tunnels branched off in opposite directions, forming a junction with the passage we'd just come down.

"Great." I tried to peer farther ahead, but the blackness was thick as tar.

Miles put the blue glasses on. Then he frowned. "I'm barely sensing anything from either direction. Very faint traces of energy, but nothing conclusive."

"Patrick?" I turned to him. "Are you—ah—*getting* anything?" I didn't want to say "smelling" for some reason. It just seemed too bestial.

His eyes narrowed. He seemed to be testing the air.

"They both smell bad," he concluded. "But the tunnel to the right smells the worst." He made a face. "Like rotting fruit."

"Rotting fruit it is, then."

I led the way down the tunnel that Patrick had chosen. I could detect faint whiffs of what he'd smelled so clearly, like a subtle, disgusting bouquet of dead flowers and decomposing fruit. Maybe the Iblis kept body parts down here. Maybe its corporeal form was a bloody mess of sewn-together hides, like Buffalo Bill.

Patrick made a hissing noise. We all stopped short. I saw him straining forward, every one of his senses working. His eyes reflected back the Cyalume glow, flaring momentarily like gemstones.

"There's something here," he whispered. "It's getting closer."

"More vampires?" Derrick asked.

"I'm not sure." He frowned. "I'm still getting the hang of

this. It's difficult to sort out all the competing smells. But there's definitely *something*—" He turned around sharply. "Wait. There's two of them."

I swallowed. "Two?"

"They're coming from opposite directions."

"Cornering us," Derrick said grimly. He held out his Glock, and light flickered against the carbonized blue steel of the barrel. I hoped Linus was right about that sensor. I didn't want to be the only one who could shoot straight.

"They're about fifty feet away," Patrick whispered.

Lucian took up a defensive stance. I felt my stomach flip as he began to channel power, and strands of wine red light curled between his fingers. Necroid materia. Wolfie stood next to him, flicking his thumb and forefinger together, and tongues of flame leapt to life at the point of contact.

Miles drew his Sig Sauer, which I'd forgotten about.

"What ammo is that loaded with?" I whispered. I held the Cyalume close to my face so that he could read my lips.

"Black Talon. Not combustible rounds, like yours. Linus said he didn't have time to modify the barrel and firing pin."

"You'd better get behind me, then." I gestured to the wall. "Aim for the head and the heart, and don't stop shooting until you've used the entire clip. You might be able to slow them down if you hit the same spot enough times."

I heard him swallow. "Got it."

Patrick suddenly growled, like a dog whose territory was being encroached on.

Two shapes burst into the light. They were blurs, but the slimmer one with long hair whipping around might have been a woman. Their eyes bounced the light back, just like a cat's. I sighted along the length of the barrel. I didn't want to waste too much ammo, since these rounds had been specifically designed for the Iblis.

The vampire on the left went for Lucian. He was a walking target for them. Maybe they could smell the necroid energies on him, like a cloying perfume. The vampire slashed at his throat, but before his long nails could make contact, Patrick had already grabbed him from behind.

This one was stronger. He shook off Patrick's grip, then backhanded him sharply across the face. Patrick staggered, spitting out blood, and the second vampire moved in. They were hunting like a pack.

I steeled my shoulder, aimed at her neck, and fired.

The flash was dazzling, and I almost had to turn away. Fire blossomed like a deadly orchid in the vampire's throat, and she shook her head, spraying blood in all directions. Her screams filled the corridor. The fire crawled up her hair, licking at her cheeks and eyes.

Wolfie stepped forward. The first vampire leapt at him, but Patrick barreled forward, knocking the attacker's legs out from under him. They both hit the ground, rolling and snarling, two rabid pit bulls. Wolfie reached out, and fire exploded from his upturned palms. The vampire shrieked and fell to her knees, clawing at her face as the incendiary bullet continued to burn her from the inside. Wolfie clenched his teeth and kept the flames on her. Within twenty seconds, she was curled in a smoldering heap, charred knees drawn to her chest in the "pugilist pose" that dead bodies assume once the muscles and tendons have melted. I gagged from the smell.

The remaining vampire flipped atop Patrick's chest, pummeling him. Patrick jabbed his fingers into the vamp's throat, snarling and spitting. The vampire raked claws across his face, and Patrick thrashed beneath him.

A bullet tore through the vampire's eye socket, vaporizing the eyeball in a spray of blood and clear fluid. Another round exploded through his neck. He cocked his head, as if silently questioning something, as a third and then a fourth bullet cracked into the plate of his skull. Finally, his grip on Patrick weakened, and he began to sway. A fifth shot took his right hand clean off, and I put a hand over my face to shield myself from the bone fragments as they went flying.

The vampire's body gave a great shudder, and then he collapsed against Patrick, blood pooling around him. The shudder became a grand convulsion, and as I watched, his form liquefied and turned to greasy ash on the floor. One of the rounds must have severed his spinal cord. Patrick rolled away, looking like he might be sick, as the remains of the vampire's body curled into black detritus, calcined bone, and foul-smelling liquid waste. Steam rose from the ground.

I turned, thinking that Miles had fired the rounds. But it was Derrick who stood just to my left, feet spaced evenly apart, right shoulder cocked back as he held the smoking Glock level in front of him.

"I guess that sensor works," he said mildly.

23

After Selena had placed teams on the opposite
side of the entrance, we continued on, farther into the gloom.
The radio was starting to get patchy. I didn't want to think what
would happen if we lost contact entirely with the world above.
I was already getting more claustrophobic by the second, and
the Cyalume glow was barely enough to see a few feet in front
of my face. The only ones who seemed relaxed were Patrick and
Lucian. I guess they were used to the dark.

Derrick was at my right. "I've got a feeling," he said.

"I don't like your feelings. They never bode well."

"No, those are *your* feelings. Mine are usually okay."

I sighed. "What is it?"

"Aren't you getting the sense that this has been too easy so
far? I mean, it was tricky enough to find this place, sure. But
then there's—what—a single vampire guarding the whole
first floor? Then Patrick finds the entrance, easy as pie?" He
frowned. "A creepy, hypersensitive, undead pie, sure, but
still—you get my drift. Even the sentries in the corridor were
easy to take out."

"Too easy, you think?"

He shrugged. "I want to see the silver lining here, I really do. But I have to wonder what's on the other end of this tunnel, and why it doesn't need much heavier protection. Maybe because it's not really scared of anything."

"It's an Iblis. A pureblood demon that lives in some kind of *bardo*-world between the living and the dead. I don't think it has to scrap with anything too often."

"You said it might not be fully corporeal."

"I'm only guessing. But my mom seemed to think that it was killing in order to enact a ritual that will make it flesh and bone."

"But if it's already this strong, why would it even *want* to be corporeal? Wouldn't that be a downgrade?"

I shrugged. "I don't know how its mind works. But it's obviously friendly with Sabine, if these vampires are willing to act as its bodyguards. And she's at the top of the food chain. So this thing's definitely got pull."

"*Pull?* Is that what we're calling it when something disarticulates a vampire magnate with its bare hands? Because I can think of some other words."

"I'm not sure that was all the Iblis. Maybe the other vamps lent a hand. I mean, that bedroom was like a war zone. Even the lab wouldn't be able to figure out where each wound came from."

"Wait." Lucian came up next to me. "Do you feel that?"

Curls of force licked across my bare shoulders, like warm breath. I let myself go unfocused for a moment, and the power hit me full in the chest. I closed my eyes, beginning to sweat. I could feel it bearing down on me, so fucking heavy, layers of silt, rock, and gem-studded earth. Shadows, striae, and networks of blackened bone, like some unholy perversion of a cathedral's ceiling, pressing down on my neck. It was all I could do not to sink to one knee.

"Tess?" Lucian's hand was on my shoulder.

I pushed the presence away, erecting a wall of earth materia in front of me. The air seemed to ripple. I counted to three, and then took a deep breath.

"I'm fine. It just caught me by surprise, that's all."

"I'm afraid to put the glasses back on," Miles admitted. "I'm not sure what I'll see. But it won't be good."

Patrick's eyes had gone very wide. "It smells like . . ." He turned around in a slow circle, inhaling deeply. "I don't even know. I can't place it." He stared at me. "There's nothing in this world that smells like that."

"It's not from this world," I said slowly, strengthening the barricade of materia that coursed in front of me. "That's why we're sending it back."

"I think I should be in front," Lucian said. "This power feels—familiar to me. I might stand a better chance against it."

I nodded. "Do you want my gun?"

"The minute I need that, I'll be dead."

I knew the feeling.

I tapped my earpiece. "Selena? We're almost there."

Her voice was barely audible. "Proceed."

We continued down the corridor with Lucian in front. I could see what looked like a pale glow emanating farther down, and the walls were getting wider, the ceiling higher, as we moved forward. Gradually, the earth beneath our feet became cement, and the glow up ahead grew brighter. It was coming from behind a door set into the end of the passageway. The door hung open, just slightly. I could hear a strange pounding on the other side of it.

"I'm going in," Lucian whispered.

Slowly, he opened the door.

The room beyond was surprisingly large, with high ceilings that had been carved directly from the rock above us. The walls and floor were made of concrete. They were bare, save for the odd ripple or scar where the liquid concrete had settled over an uneven spot or a protruding stone. A single lightbulb hung on a cord from the ceiling. It swayed slightly, although there was no breeze. The air was solid, almost syrupy, and had a tang to it that only came from being deep underground.

Wooden shelves lined the far wall, but I couldn't make out all the objects that lay on them. Most of them gleamed, like they were made of metal. A long wooden table stood a few feet away from the shelves. Its surface was pockmarked and heavily stained. I wasn't sure if the stains were blood or not.

A figure stood in front of the table, its back to us.

It wore dark pants with steel rivets going down the side of them, and a black hooded sweatshirt. Remembering Wolfie's description of Henry's former dealer, I looked down at the boots that the figure was wearing.

HEAVEN, said the right boot, in gleaming silver stencil. HELL, said the left boot, in bloodred garnets that caught the light of the naked bulb swinging overhead.

The Iblis.

We all stood in the entranceway, afraid to move. Power made the creature's form shimmer indistinctly. I flashed back to fighting Marcus Tremblay. Even borrowing strength from Mia, he'd been difficult to beat. And this thing was in an entirely different league. Derrick was right. It didn't employ much protection because it didn't give a shit about anyone or anything finding it.

I gripped the hilt of my athame. It was hot.

"Tessa." A voice sang my name out. *"Tessa Isobel. Why did you keep me waiting so long, my flower?"*

The sound of its voice was like a nail in my heart.

The Iblis turned to face us. All I could see beneath the hood were its eyes. They were the color of a manic purple sunset, and they burned in the darkness, seething, throwing off sparks.

"I knew your father, Tessa Isobel." I could feel it smiling as it stepped forward. Its heavy boots made no sound against the floor. "He had a special name for you. His *little bloody flower.*"

I aimed the Glock. "Don't like flowers. I'm more of a candy girl."

"You don't like guns either." I could feel its oily presence, a hot smear of tar across my mind. I shuddered. "But we both have a fondness for knives. I like all sharp things, really. All things angular and hungry."

I kept the gun trained on him. It made me feel better, even if it was useless.

Those ancient eyes flicked to Lucian. He frowned, and I realized that the Iblis was reading his thoughts.

"Child of the dark." There was laughter in its voice. "Sweet little *perrito*. Little *Lucian Eskame Agrado*. 'Eskame' means merciful, you know." It took another step toward us. "Are you merciful, Lucian? Hmm?"

Lucian stiffened.

"I was there," it continued softly, "when that beautiful nurse brought you to the precincts of the silent city. I shooed the spider demons away from you. I held you as a squalling infant, Lucian Agrado. And I put my mark on you."

I stared at the lily above his collarbone. So that was it. The necromancer had been marked by an Iblis. But why?

"I remember you," Lucian whispered.

"Of course you do."

The Iblis lowered its hood.

Its face was very white. One side was covered by a writhing web of purple veins. Lights seemed to flicker inside them. The other side was smooth, untouched. Its glittering eyes were sunk into sharp, hollow cheeks.

And there was a hole in the top of its head.

The hole was cruciform, extending in four perfect segments across the occipital and temporal plates of its skull. The cuts were perfect—like the delicate fontanelles of a baby's skull that simply hadn't jointed together yet. Or a jack-o'-lantern that had been carved with unerring precision.

Glowing purple vapors drifted from the gap in its skull. They curled and sparked around the Iblis, flickering silently. I thought of a steaming cauldron. The vapors seemed to pool behind its eyes, transforming them into chilling stained glass, before rising up to vent into the air. Were its insides on fire? I didn't want to know. That same energy coursed along the tangle of veins on the left side of its face.

"I knew someday," the Iblis said, "you could be useful. Like your brother, Lorenzo, was useful to me."

His brother? The one who died?

"Don't you fucking say his name!"

The tattoo on Lucian's neck began to glow. He cried out, grabbing at the flesh as if it burned him.

"That day has come." The Iblis smiled. "And now you are mine."

Lucian turned to me. His eyes had gone pale and blank. He opened his right hand, and I felt him drawing power.

"Tess . . ."

Petals of green fire swirled between his fingers.

"Lucian, he's controlling you . . ."

"*Tess.*" Something flickered behind his eyes. The light in his hand grew brighter, and I saw black flecks swirling inside it. The same flecks of dark nothingness that Miles had seen in the hotel room. Void. The power of decreation.

I took a step backward, raising my athame. It burned my fingers.

The Iblis laughed. "Dance with her, Lucian!"

"Tess—I . . ." Pain gripped his face. Then a strange calm. "You have to shoot me. Right now."

I stared at him. "What?"

"It's using all of my power, all at once." Blood trickled down his nose. "This fire will unmake anything it touches. Cell by cell, it will tear you apart."

"Not if you fight it!"

He couldn't even shake his head. Green flame poured like rich, alien wine down both of his arms, pooling in the air before him, swirling and crackling. I could feel a pressure building in the back of my head, a pinprick of agony.

"Shoot me," he whispered. "Aim for my heart."

There was spittle on the corners of his mouth. It was taking every fiber of will left in his body just to talk to me.

"Lucian . . ."

"If I'm lucky, I'll come back," he said. His eyes had gone black.

My hand trembled on the Glock. Fumbling, I switched out the ammo pack, removing one of the incendiary rounds and replacing it with a jacketed bullet. I was crying. "Fuck. Oh *fuck*—"

"Do it now!" He raised both hands.

Even in agony, he was beautiful. So fucking beautiful. That face.

My lips on his caramel skin.

His scent. Burnt herbs, cinnamon, sweat.

His mouth on mine. His tongue caving me in.

The dark silken embroidery of ink on his back and shoulders. The newest tattoo on his right thigh, the one I'd wondered about before, and then finally seen.

It was script. *Eskame.* Merciful. Just like the Iblis had said.

The feel of him hard in my hands, moving, a lone bright hunger.

You looked good before, he'd said to me. *You always look good.*

And so did he.

I squeezed the trigger.

The recoil slammed into my shoulder, and I stumbled. Lucian took four rapid steps backward. His mouth opened. Then he sat down heavily, his arms going limp. Blood spread rapidly across his shirt. He looked up at me. His eyes were soft and brown again, and his head lolled to one side.

"Good," he slurred. "Good . . . shot. Tess . . ."

His head fell forward. Blood pumped steadily from the wound. His body gave a long shudder, and a thin trail of black spit leaked from his mouth.

Then he was still.

"Shit," I heard Derrick whisper.

"Wasn't that unexpected?" The Iblis grinned. "I'm—"

I squeezed the trigger again, this time aiming at its head. The incendiary round hit with a flash of cherry red light, and fire bloomed. The Iblis staggered.

"Wolfie!" I screamed.

He stepped forward, raising his hands. An arc of flame lit up the air, bathing the Iblis in red and white-gold. I smelled burning cloth and flesh.

"Derrick!" I leveled my gun. "Aim for its legs . . ."

I didn't have the chance to fire a third time.

The Iblis stepped forward, raising both of its arms. Two circles of light, almost coin-shaped, glowed in its palms. Wolfie's flame guttered and died. He tried to summon another burst of thermal materia, but the Iblis closed its right hand into a fist. Wolfie screamed, sinking to the ground, as if something was strangling him.

Derrick fired, aiming for its hand. The bullet ricocheted with an unexpected *clang* as it struck metal. Grinning, the Iblis flexed its hand, and I realized that iron bolts had been driven through its palms. The surface of the metal was etched with bizarre engravings, uncannily glowing the same red-purple color as deep tissue.

I couldn't look at Lucian. He'd ceased to exist for me.
He's gone. You have to focus.
If I'm lucky, I'll come back.

His last words haunted me. What did luck have to do with it? Why would the Iblis go to the trouble of marking him—possibly even *nurturing* him—if it only planned to let him die? Had the Iblis killed his brother? Nothing made sense.

Wolfie was still choking.

That was something I could deal with.

I concentrated, staring at the space between Wolfie and the Iblis. I could see the tendril of materia flickering in the dim light, wrapped around Wolfie's throat. Drawing my athame, I leapt forward and slashed with the blade. It gleamed as it cut through the strand of power, and I heard ringing in my ears. Touching its power—even just a stray thread—was like hitting a rock wall. I blinked to clear the spots from my eyes. Wolfie rolled back, gasping, curled on his side.

"That's lovely blade work, Tessa." The Iblis reached behind it, drawing something that shone darkly. "I have one, too, you know. I borrowed it."

"You stole it from Marcus, you mean."

It shrugged. Marcus Tremblay's athame looked like a coal black sliver in its right hand. Nothing about it was sacred anymore. Flows of materia warped and shredded around it, gleaming like deadly abalone. It was a mote in the eye of the universe now, a weapon of avulsion and unmaking.

"Is that what you used to kill them?" I asked. As long as I could stall it, we might be able to think of another plan. I touched the earpiece.

The radio was dead.

Oh hell.

"Of course." It twirled the corrupt blade between its fingers, like a circus performer doing tricks. "I used it to cut their throats. All but Caitlin." Its look went distant. Its form seemed to shimmer, the skin going translucent, and for a heartbeat I saw the curled gray smoke creature, tall and thin like a spearhead, that had sniffed the air in my dream. Without the meat suit, it was like a pillar of smoke with two winking eyes, pits that led into the white-hot flame of another world.

"You tore her apart."

It nodded, smiling. "She smelled so good when her flesh came unbraided, when her bones snapped. When she screamed. Her blood was . . . *intoxicating.* The power and the weight of all those years, and it gushed out of her, into my hands, my mouth. Oh, I could kill her again and again, and never tire of it."

"But why? She wasn't like the others." I tried to signal Derrick with my eyes. If that sensor on his gun was really emitting radio waves, it might be able to boost the signal on my earpiece. I could get a message out to Selena.

And what would I say? *We're seriously humped.*

Realistically, there was only one solution. Only one message to send.

Burn the house to the ground.

We'd all die. But hopefully we'd take the Iblis with us.

"Why did you kill her?" I was startled to hear Patrick's voice. He'd been so still in the background, I'd once again forgotten that he was here. But he was standing next to me now. I couldn't see what color his eyes were. I wasn't even sure it made a difference. The Iblis had made short work of his tutor, a far more experienced vampire with centuries of training. It could probably eat the boy whole.

But it entertained him with a look. "That's an interesting question, night child. Why do *you* think I killed your dam?

She who gave you rich, dark blood, and all the power and the fury of a new unlife?"

Patrick drew a step closer. "I think it was part of your ritual." Obviously, he'd been following our conversations more than I gave him credit for. "It was messy and violent—not like the others—but it was still part of the design."

"And what design is that?"

"You're trying to become flesh." Patrick flexed his own hand for emphasis. "That way, you won't have to live on those other shores. The darkling plains. You want to live here, on this world, where the mortals are plentiful, and the power is hot and bloody and alive all around you. Whatever they call it. The *materia*."

The Iblis inclined its head. "I did develop a taste for it the last time I visited this world." It looked at me. "Your father had told me how lovely it was, the power that you mages could feel beneath your skin, in your veins, but I didn't believe him until I felt it for myself." It closed its eyes. "Like honey and blood. Like the screams of all the dead in all the worlds. It tasted so good."

"And that's why you killed them?" I asked incredulously. "You killed the children of mages to *become* a mage? To be like us?"

"Not like you, Tessa." It smiled. "Much, much better than you."

I shook my head. "You can't do that by murdering people."

"Ah—but I'm not just murdering them. I'm freeing them. Making them so much better." It ran fingers along the charred surface of Marcus Tremblay's athame. Cords of green light slithered across it, hissing, crackling. "Your *Hextacy* is what does it. The drug is made from materia, ground from the bones and the blood of the world. When they die, it opens a glowing doorway in their flesh. An ingress that leads along the shadowed paths, into the secret chambers that drive the universe itself. That last flare of power—the agony of their death—is like God's fingernail splitting the skin of an orange, fraying the fabric of the real. And then the universe bleeds. For me."

I shook my head in disgust. "You're using their souls to rewrite your own existence. To give yourself corporeality so that you can channel more power, and still more, until—"

"Until nothing in this world moves, or twitches, or breathes unless I make it so," the Iblis said. "And trust me, Tessa. It's far more than the power I enjoyed in that realm between the worlds. Even the flesh, the encumbrance of it, the sickening feel of blood simmering in my veins, knowing that my cells are rotting, one by one, even as they come into being—it's all very much worth it. There, I was a guardian." It spread its arms wide, as if it would rise into the air. "Here, I can be God."

"But why *them*?" I stared at it. "Those innocent kids? Their power wasn't even in full bloom yet. They were practically normates."

"They were the only ones that let me get close," it said, eyeing me with cool interest, as a crocodile might eye a water bug. "My form was incomplete. But they didn't care. They just wanted the drug." It smiled. "And their power wasn't unfinished—it was *ripe*. They crunched like hard strawberries in my mouth. Their hearts were snap peas. Fresh green beans, cold and hard and delicious, ripped from the pod. Leaving only a husk behind."

I closed my eyes against the image. "They were estranged from their families. Jacob was a runaway, and Henry was an orphan."

"Yes. After I orphaned him." It grinned at my outrage. "There was nothing else to be done. I needed another, and he was cute as a march hare, that little one. Sweet little bobbin." It breathed in, as if inhaling some phantom scent. "His father already beat him, while his mother looked on. Killing them was doing the world a favor, really."

I tried to imagine the Iblis feeling compassion. It seemed impossible.

"You started in Ontario," I said finally. "With—"

"With the one that Sabine gave me." He smiled. "Beautiful Sabine. So treacherous. She was the one who gave me the dagger . . ." He flicked the athame, and multicolored sparks hissed along the tang of the blade. "And then the girl. So perfect in her terror. Stolen from her safe, middle-class home. And it began."

Sabine must have gone through Marcus's notes. Somehow, she'd known about the Iblis. She'd known how to call it. Which meant that only she knew how to destroy it.

"Did you rape them all, too?" I was startled to hear Wolfie's voice. "Was that fun for you? What you did to Henry?"

"What *I* did to him?" It frowned. "You mistake me for my minions. The vampires that you dispatched outside." It shook its head. "They did get much too excitable, especially with poor Henry, who could knit his own flesh and bones back together. What a marvelous power *that* was." It blinked. "But I didn't touch them, at least not *that* way. I needed cold, hard flesh for that. The vampires provided it. That was my agreement with Sabine."

"I'm sure it wasn't the only one," I countered.

His eyes came back to me. "I followed an old myth," the Iblis said. "Something I heard long ago. Do you know it, Tessa? In the twilight of the world, there existed a race of giants. The children of the sun, the moon, and the earth."

It was the old story of Aristophanes. I cursed inwardly.

"The hermaphrodites," I said.

"Yes! Vast beings, joined eye to eye, face to face. Two boys, two girls, and a boy and a girl fused together. The gods feared their power. And so they were riven, cut in twain with lightning. And they became the sexes."

I thought of the mural on Duessa's wall, realizing, then, that she must have copied it from somewhere long ago. Someplace that both she and the Iblis had visited.

"You saw a mural of it," I said quietly.

"Yes." Its eyes danced with sparks. "When I met Caitlin for the first time. She ran a venal house, you know, a long time ago. And she had that mural painted on the wall, right near the entrance, so all could see. To her, it represented all the infinite forms and possibilities of desire."

The Iblis smiled. "I can remember her leaning against that wall. The hot stone beneath her long, splayed fingertips. Her jade bracelet. Hmm. She was one of the most beautiful things I've ever seen. I knew then. I knew that she'd be useful. And when she wasn't looking, I found the spot on the wall, the spot where she'd been leaning." It licked its lips with a forked tongue, black, like a dried piece of leather. "I stole her essence. What you call her *print*."

"That was tricky," I said, trying to signal Patrick, who seemed to hover just on the edges of my vision. "Saving that for over a century. You planned ahead."

"I planned this for longer than you could ever conceive of." The Iblis kept me in its gaze. "To me, that mural hinted at something much better. The key to something vast and shattering. And I remembered—it was very far back, but I'd heard of it, whispered somewhere. I remembered a curse. A curse that could only emerge from desire. From drug-fueled ecstasy."

"You killed them in a pattern." My voice fell.

"Two girls," it said with a lilt to its voice. "And two boys. And then, finally, boy and girl together. Caitlin and her pup."

Its eyes fell to Patrick.

He was the missing piece. The final aspect to the ritual.

"And then," the Iblis said, "there was *one*."

It raised its arm. Patrick's body spasmed. He rose jerkily into the air, his sneakers trailing a foot off the ground. The Iblis twitched its finger, and Patrick floated toward it, clutching at invisible threads around his neck.

"Caitlin was no longer the magnate," it growled. "But you *are*. And your blood will be the sweetest of all, boy. I'll be licking you off my lips for days, like a smear of warm chocolate, decadent and fine."

I reached deep, as deep as I could, and felt the earth materia slumbering feathery and dark beneath my feet. Drawing as much of it as I could hold, I marched forward, holding the athame before me.

I heard Derrick's voice in my mind, clear as a struck bell. The connection between us was still there.

I got through to Selena. Reinforcements are coming.

We don't have time for reinforcements. There's only one move left.

A pause. Then I felt an overriding wave of sadness as he understood. I couldn't look at him. I couldn't look at Lucian's body. I could only stare straight ahead.

Aim for the gap in its skull, Derrick thought fiercely. *That's the link between the worlds, the spot where it isn't quite real yet. Miles can see the nexus where all the materia is swirling. It's like a pinhole-sized universe. If you strike it there, the chain reaction might destroy it.*

And us with it.

But I was past worrying about that.

I raised my blade. The Iblis turned to me. Before it could move, I fired the Glock with my left hand. I held on to the trigger, firing again and again, the sound deafening me as I aimed for what I hoped was its face.

I saw a flash of blazing purple light. I stabbed with the athame, channeling all of my rage, grief, and boiling heartache into the blow.

Something exploded in front of me. I felt myself turning over and over in empty space. I was airborne. Then I struck the wall. Sparks burst white in front of my eyes, and I felt instantly sick. The athame dropped from my nerveless fingers.

The Iblis was kneeling in front of me. Light dripped from its eyes.

"Really, Tessa? Shooting drunkenly—*that* was the plan?"

I couldn't speak. There was a pinching coldness in the back of my neck. I was too stunned to be horrified by it. I couldn't feel my legs. Only something hard and surprisingly sharp digging into my left arm.

The Iblis picked up my athame. It examined the blade coolly, then tossed it, out of reach. "These things will get you into trouble," it said.

I strained to look past the creature, but I couldn't move my head. Patrick was facedown on the cement, unconscious. Derrick and Wolfie were approaching from behind, but I had no idea what they planned to do. Whatever it was, it wouldn't be quick enough. The Iblis already had what it wanted. And that had never been me. Patrick was its missing prize, not me. I'd simply been the bait, the shiny toy that it dangled in order to force the boy out of hiding.

All this time, it had simply been using me.

I tried to concentrate on the ache in my arm. It was the only part of my body that I could feel, aside from my head, which was spinning.

The Iblis drew closer. It touched the edge of the black dagger to my right cheek, and I didn't cry out, even as I felt my skin burning.

"You're beautiful," it whispered. "Like your mother."

"Fuck—you . . ." I managed to slur.

It shook its head. "No, Tess. Fuck *you.*" Its smile was terrifying. "I was prepared to show you things. So much. With my power, you could walk between the worlds. You could walk right up to your father, in the twilight realm. And before he had a chance to say anything, you could bury *this* . . ." He pressed harder with the knife. I could see the smoke twining from it. "Right in his heart. Isn't that what you've always wanted to do? Isn't it what you were born to do?"

He lowered the knife, placing it against my throat. I tried to move my left arm. I could wiggle my fingers, but barely. No time left. Never enough time. Oh God.

Derrick. Mia. I love you. Oh, I love you so much, and I'm sorry, I'm so sorry, I couldn't win this time. Even after my mother—

My mother.

You're beautiful. Like your mother.

A spark flared somewhere inside my dying brain. Was I dying? I flexed the muscles of my left hand. The sharpness was cutting into me. I felt for it—

"Too late." The Iblis started to draw the blade against my neck. I felt warm blood on my throat. I tried to scream, but couldn't. The pain was real.

Then it stopped.

I tried to focus my eyes. As I stared at the Iblis, I saw that something was different. Vines of earth dark light were drawn across its arms and legs, pulsing with flickers of blood and ebony. It had dropped the dagger, and its unholy eyes were narrowed, more in frustration than pain. I looked over its shoulder.

Lucian stood behind it. Both of his hands were raised, and black vines trembled as they hissed and curled from his fingertips. His shirt was covered in blood.

"I got lucky," he said.

I reached down with my left hand, searching for that flash of pain, that unexpected sharpness. The sleeve of my coat had torn halfway off when I fell against the wall, and the inside pocket was shredded.

My fingers closed around a handle. It was hot.

I stared in wonder as I lifted a blade into the air. The hilt was carved of pearl, and it shone like an alicorn, like the bones of a seraph, like the perfect white of the snowdrifts I'd played in as a little girl. The blade was tapered, and the cruciform hilt gleamed with bloodstone, amethyst, and beryl.

It was my mother's athame.

Jesus. She must have slipped it into the deepest pocket when I wasn't looking. Maybe she'd even sewn it in. I could just picture my mother, humming quietly in the middle of the night as she worked my jacket through her sewing machine.

I'd never seen her athame before, but I could feel her in it, every inch of her. I remembered her holding me, smoothing my hair gently. *Don't face it alone,* she'd said.

But I wasn't alone. She was with me.

Don't you know you're everything to me. Don't you know?

"You're right." The Iblis turned to regard me, its eyes suddenly small, like winking, murderous stars. "I'm just like her."

I drove the knife into its skull. It slid between those smooth, glowing plates, so perfectly, as if it had been forged for this purpose alone. To close the bloody, unnatural wound of this demon's wretched consciousness.

I pushed it in deep. All the way down to the hilt.

It staggered backward. The knife burned white-hot, like a diamond shard, flaring so hot and so bright that I had to look away.

The Iblis screamed.

And screamed.

And screamed.

Light boiled and seethed over its body, stripping away the flesh, layer by layer. First the dermis melted away, then the yellow fat—bubbling like polenta in the pan—then the red and blue muscle underneath. The tendons liquefied, the bones dissolved, until all that remained was a burning outline, a nuclear shadow with a gaping mouth.

Then the scream turned inward, sucking in all the light with it. A powerful wind rushed through the chamber. I saw two eyes floating in a cloud of poisonous smoke. I heard my name rising from the heart of all that evil.

My mother's athame clattered to the floor. It winked at my foot. A glass slipper. I looked at it and laughed. Had she sewn it into my jacket? How did she sneak it in there? It didn't matter anymore.

The Iblis was gone.

Derrick, Wolfie, and Miles were all rushing toward me. But a small, blurry shape outran them all. It was Mia. She tore through the entranceway and ran to my side, collapsing to her knees. That girl always could move fast when she wanted to.

"Tess?" She was crying. "Tess, can you move? Can you feel my hand?"

I smiled weakly at her. "M-Command? Is that you?" It was hard to speak.

She laughed through her tears. "Yes. It's me. I'm squeezing your hand. Can you feel it? Can you feel my fingers?"

"Yes," I said softly.

"You can?" She put her arms around me. I realized that we'd reversed positions since the last catastrophe. Before, I'd held her, telling her that everything was going to be all right. Now, she was holding me.

"I love you," I whispered into her hair. "Over."

She laughed. "I love you, too. Over."

I stared at my mother's athame. It had come to rest next to mine. The blades were almost touching.

I closed my eyes.

Epilogue

I woke up in a CORE clinic, my arms covered in tubes and wires, my body aching, aching, aching.

I woke up, and I saw the most amazing thing.

Derrick and Miles were sitting on a small couch. Derrick was half-asleep, his head drifting onto Miles's shoulder. Miles was writing in a book. I thought it was a book of crosswords at first, but it was just sudoku. Patrick was leaning against the doorway of the room. He didn't seem to be looking at anything in particular.

Lucian and Mia were sitting next to each other in two broken-down chairs, and it looked as if Mia was teaching him how to play a handheld video game. "No," she was saying, "you can't attack the Swamp Lord until you level up your cleric."

"But I've got the Staff of Neutrality."

"You've got a *piece* of the staff. It's useless without the Gem of Primordial Knowledge. You might as well attack him with a badminton racquet."

"I don't see why I can't just use one of my three wishes."

Mia rolled her eyes. "Have you learned *nothing* in the past hour?"

"Evidently not."

Everyone was here.

But that wasn't the *most* amazing thing.

The most amazing thing, really, was Wolfie standing at one end of the window, staring at the city beyond, and Devorah Kynan standing at the other end. It seemed impossible for them to occupy the same room. But here they were. Wolfie had his I ♥ SASKATOON hat turned backward. Devorah was wearing a sleek charcoal jacket with a flared collar. She played with one of her buttons absently.

"She really defeated it single-handedly?" Devorah asked.

Wolfie nodded. I realized with a start that they were talking about me. "Stabbed it right in the fucking head. Craziest thing I've ever seen. She was amazing."

Devorah shook her head. "I can hardly believe it." She stared out the window. "I was in Rome. Looking for allies. Calling in favors. Doing research on the families. I seemed to have the whole world under a microscope. I was doing everything in my power to track down this creature, and it was here the whole time, living in some condemned rat hole. Invisible."

"Officer Sedgwick found the house."

She glanced at Derrick and Miles. Pain flashed across her eyes for a moment. Then she spoke, not looking at Wolfie.

"Jacob loved you. Did you know that?"

"I did." Wolfie spoke in the barest whisper.

"He talked about you. I think you must be a good person."

Wolfie stared at her. Obviously, he didn't know what to say.

"I knew how dangerous his life was," she continued. "I knew that. But he always seemed on the verge of quitting. *Soon, Mom. I promise.* That's what he said. And I pretended to believe him."

"It's hard to get out," Wolfie said.

"I know that he was taken care of. Duessa's a lot of things, but she's not negligent. I know she watched out for him. And

I was jealous, in a way. She got to see him all the time. I had to settle for visiting hours."

Wolfie looked at the ground.

"There are things I can't stop thinking about." Devorah laughed softly. "Ridiculous things. Like a picture book that I used to read to Jacob when he was little. He forced me to read it nearly every night. *Laila Tov Yareah*."

"Goodnight Moon," Wolfie said.

She looked at him, startled. "You speak Hebrew?"

"I went to Hebrew school when I was a kid."

"Jacob, too." She shook her head.

They were silent for a minute more. Then Devorah pressed her fingers against the window. She lowered her head.

"Bachedar hashinah yesh kairot irkim," she murmured. *"A'ch'lo t'zom y'lo."*

"In the great green room," Wolfie translated, staring in the opposite direction as Devorah, "there was a telephone."

"V'lo adom porecha, t'zol ha'kir tami'onih . . ."

"And a red balloon, and a picture of . . ."

"Shel pirih t'zom yareah."

"A cow jumping over the moon."

I remembered the book by Margaret Wise Brown. I could see the green room now, and the cow jumping over the moon, and the three little bears sitting on chairs.

Devorah stared out the window. "Goodnight, Jacob."

Wolfie hesitated. Then he wrapped his arm around her. They stood perfectly still like that, the spark and the sorceress, not speaking. There was nothing left to say.

"Hey!" Derrick looked up. "She's awake!"

Lucian and Mia walked over to my bed, flanking me.

"How was your nap?" Lucian asked.

"Oh, lovely. How long was I out for?"

"Almost two days."

"Jesus." I groaned. "I hurt."

"You got banged up pretty good. There was some swelling around the base of your spine, and they had to keep you out for a while."

"I can feel my legs again." I winced. "Almost wish I couldn't."

"You'll heal."

"Yeah." I smiled. "We all will." Then my eyes burned a bit. "Hey—you died, remember?" My voice was barely a whisper.

"I know. I was there."

"Don't do *that* again, okay?"

He kissed my forehead. "Okay."

"They said you might be able to go home tomorrow," Mia said. "But only if you're really good, and you don't try anything funny or yell at anyone."

"I'll be good."

"We have, like, *no* food in the house," she admitted, "and Derrick's been eating Top Ramen and drinking hospital coffee, and he wouldn't listen to me when I told him how bad that was. But he'll listen to you."

"He'll listen when I bury my foot in his ass, you mean."

Derrick winked at me. "Yes, ma'am."

I heard a cell phone vibrating. Miles glanced down at his Sidekick, then groaned and rolled his eyes. "Sorry. I have to take this. I've still got some arrangements left to make." He smiled warmly at me. "Good to have you back, Tess."

"Thanks, Sedge."

He chuckled at the sound of his nickname. Then he ducked outside.

"Arrangements?" I asked.

"Miles is moving to Vancouver." Mia grinned at me. "Derrick hasn't been this happy since *Battlestar* was renewed for a final season."

"Selena scored him a position here," Derrick said.

"And I'll bet you've been smiling like an idiot since you heard."

He nodded. "Yep."

I looked up at Lucian. "What about you? What are your plans?"

He winked. "I'm staying right here."

"Good answer."

Patrick was looking at me from across the room. His eyes

had lost that frightening gold color, but there was still something inhuman about them.

"Hey, Patrick."

He blinked. "What? Sorry, Tess—I was drifting." He grinned sheepishly. "I'm glad you're awake."

"What were you thinking about?"

He shrugged. "Figuring out what I might do next. I'm old enough to be legally emancipated. But I'll have to find a job, I guess."

"Wouldn't it be easier to just live with us?"

Mia stared at me, open-mouthed. "How hard did you get hit?"

Patrick smiled shyly. "Are you being serious?"

"Absolutely. You can keep an eye on Mia."

She rolled her eyes. "Thanks."

In the back of my mind, I knew that I was asking him for a lot more. His senses must have picked up on Mia's VR+ blood by now. He knew that she carried the virus. And what happened if the medications stopped working? What happened if she drifted toward some dark place, where we couldn't follow? Only another vampire could pull her back. Only Patrick would be able to recognize the signs for sure.

And we'd be watching him, too. He had no family. No friends. No sire to show him how to be the next vampire magnate. He just had us.

Lucky I wasn't the kind of girl who believed in odds.

"Besides," I said, "you're tall enough to clean the gutters. Everybody wins."

He flushed slightly. It was nice to see color in his face.

"Is it . . ." He blinked. "I mean, yes, *yes*, I'd love to. It sounds perfect. But, I mean . . . is it really that simple?"

I looked around the room. I scanned the expectant faces.

God is a bullet, I thought, *straight to the heart. Just when you think you're finished, there's a second start.*

"It can be," I said.

Afterward

There are various queer-friendly advocacy groups in Vancouver, including the Downtown Eastside Women's Centre, the LGBT Centre, Vancouver Status of Women, PACE, Out on Campus, and Pride UBC. Anyone in the United States can also call the Trevor Project at 866-488-7386.

Part of the proceeds from the sale of this book go to the LGBT Centre in the West End. They are located on Davie and Bute, and can be contacted at 604-684-6869.

**Explore the outer reaches
of imagination—don't miss these authors
of dark fantasy and urban noir that take you
to the edge and beyond.**

Patricia Briggs	Karen Chance	Anne Bishop
Simon R. Green	Caitlin R. Kiernan	Janine Cross
Jim Butcher	Rachel Caine	Sarah Monette
Kat Richardson	Glen Cook	Douglas Clegg

penguin.com

M15G0907